THE POSSESSIONS

THE POSSESSIONS

A Novel

SARA FLANNERY MURPHY

HARPER

An Imprint of HarperCollins*Publishers*

THE POSSESSIONS. Copyright © 2017 by Sara Flannery Murphy. All rights
reserved. Printed in the United States of America. No part of this book may
be used or reproduced in any manner whatsoever without written permission except in the case of brief quotations embodied in critical articles and
reviews. For information, address HarperCollins Publishers, 195 Broadway,
New York, NY 10007.

HarperCollins books may be purchased for educational, business, or sales
promotional use. For information, please email the Special Markets Depart-
ment at SPsales@harpercollins.com.

FIRST EDITION

Designed by William Ruoto

Library of Congress Cataloging-in-Publication Data has been applied for.

ISBN 978-0-06245832-2

17 18 19 20 21   RRD   10 9 8 7 6 5 4 3 2 1

To Ryan, who sees me

Certainly they are my lips that are being kissed . . . Yet how can it be? It is a horrible feeling, thus losing hold of one's identity. I long to put out one of these hands that are lying so helplessly, and touch someone just to know if I am myself or only a dream.

—Elizabeth d'Espérance, *Shadow Land*

THE POSSESSIONS

The first time I meet Patrick Braddock, I'm wearing his wife's lipstick. The color is exactly wrong for me. Deep, ripe plum, nearly purple, the type of harsh shade that beautiful women wear to prove they can get away with anything. Against my ordinary features, the lipstick is as severe as a bloodstain. I feel like a misbehaving child trying on her mother's makeup.

In the photo of Sylvia Braddock that lies on my bedroom floor, the lipstick looks perfect.

Most of my clients send only a handful of images: yearbook head shots, studio portraits against amorphous fabric backdrops. I prefer the candids slipped in as afterthoughts. Ordinary, tender images with tilted frames, red pupils, murky lighting. Unstaged photos offer less space to hide. I make note of the strata of clutter on a living room floor, the prickling distance between a husband and a wife when they don't realize anyone is watching, and I know everything I need to know about these strangers' lives.

Mr. Braddock has sent dozens of photos, enough to retrace the full six years of his marriage to Sylvia. Their wedding day, sunwashed beaches, landmarks scattered across the continents; work events with careful smiles, parties with blurred laughs. Nobody is more present in the chronology of Sylvia's life than her husband. At my job, I order the world into patterns with the incurious efficiency of a machine, and the Braddocks' pattern is a simple one.

They're in love. A showy love, drawing attention to itself without necessarily meaning to.

Sylvia only wears this exact shade of lipstick in a single image. I've checked and checked again, struck by its absence. In the photo, she's naked. She lies on a bed, unsmiling, propping herself on her elbows. Against the deep plum of the bedspread, her body is so pale it seems lit from within. Details stand out with startling clarity. Her areolas, precisely delineated as the cheeks painted on a doll. The winged origami of her hip bones. The lipstick.

I arrive early at work before our encounter, the tube clutched warm in my palm. Mr. Braddock is my first client of the day. He's scheduled his encounter on a Thursday. It's the middle of March, a time when the Elysian Society traditionally experiences a slow period. No sentimental holidays, no blooming flowers or first snows to breed guilt and nostalgia. Just the unbroken lull of late winter.

Opening the door, I assess Room 12 with a practiced gaze. The suites at the Elysian Society hint at familiarity without fully resembling anyone's home. Dark hardwood floors; a framed painting of water lilies floating on gem-bright water. Two low-slung, armless chairs face each other in the center of the room.

Anything that could disturb this impression lies hidden in plain view. For instance: the small white pill in its crimped paper cup and the larger paper cup of room-temperature water, both arranged on the end table. These designate the chair I'll take.

Outside, the latest snow of the season clings to the curbs in an exhaust-glittered crust. The air inside the Elysian Society hovers at sixty-five degrees. I'm barefoot. My work uniform is a white dress, so fine my flesh scarcely registers its touch. I hold myself steady, suppressing the urge to shiver.

The door swings open before I can respond. I turn, thinking that Mr. Braddock is already arriving. After memorizing his face in the photographs, I'm curious to see him in person.

Jane stops in the doorway. "Everything's all right, Eurydice?"

"Of course," I say. "Come in."

As an attendant, Jane has the luxury of dressing more warmly than the bodies. She's jarringly mundane in her lint-speckled cardigan, like somebody intruding on a dream. "The lipstick," she says, sketching a quick line around her own mouth. "It's a little uneven."

"I didn't realize." I hesitate, then hold out the tube. "Do you mind?"

The lipstick on my mouth is a soft, intimate pressure. Its tip is blunted from use. There's a subtle taste lingering beneath the medicinal sweetness. Sour and human. I think of the saliva and skin particles that must linger on the lipstick's surface.

Nausea clenches at my jaw.

"You've worked with this client before?" Jane asks.

"First time," I manage. The nausea dissipates as quickly as it came. "He sent the lipstick ahead of time."

Jane is silent. We both know this goes against routine. Most clients bring their loved ones' possessions in person, lending me the effects for the duration of our time together. The fact that Mr. Braddock has given his wife's lipstick to a perfect stranger creates an impression of either unusual trust or unusual carelessness.

"It's really some color." Jane caps the lipstick. "Girlfriend? Mistress?"

"Wife," I say.

"Second or third?"

"First," I say. "They were married six years."

"There you have it, then," Jane says, mildly disapproving, as if she suspects that I'm lying. "I never would have guessed first wife. That's midlife crisis lipstick if I ever saw it."

I don't answer.

"That looks much better, at any rate," Jane says. "I'll send him in."

The moment she shuts the door, I'm blank. Since I joined the Elysian Society, my emotions have evolved. They've gone from unwieldy to finely attuned. Ready to snap into nothingness. What used to be a struggle is now a simple reflex.

The knock is timid at first, nearly too low to catch. By the time I cross the room, the second knock is steady and assured. I open the door.

Most of my clients are different in photographs than in person, a disappointment in one direction or the other. In the back of my mind, I suspected that Mr. Braddock would change in the flesh. In photos, his good looks have the quality of a movie star or a young politician. A charisma too polished to exist outside a static image.

But he's exactly the same. I'd know him anywhere. The only difference is that Mr. Braddock appears strangely smaller as he stands in front of me. Maybe because of the tiredness that shows beneath his eyes in lavender shadows, or the poor job he's done of shaving. A red nick blooms like a kiss mark on his jaw. Or maybe it's the absence of Sylvia by his side that shrinks him, cutting him neatly in half.

"Do I have the right place?" he asks. "Room 12. She said you'd be waiting."

"You're at the right place, Mr. Braddock," I say.

After I close the door behind him, I turn to see that he's moved to the center of the room. He stands in front of the painting with his hands clasped behind his back, his posture holding the studied attentiveness of a man visiting a museum.

I hang back, allowing my client this last ordinary moment before his world changes. The first encounter is always delicate, a tricky dance that must conceal its very trickiness. It's my job to feel out the clients' moods without them realizing I'm doing so. Some pretend it's all a joke; some are suspicious, hostile, waiting for the figure to emerge from behind the curtain; some are painfully earnest, willing it all to go smoothly. But at first, all of them, all of them, are terrified.

Mr. Braddock points at the painting. "Monet?"

"An anonymous artist, I believe." I gesture toward the chair. "Please."

When we've arranged ourselves, Mr. Braddock's eyes go to my mouth, darkened with his wife's lipstick.

"Can you tell me whom you're hoping to contact today, Mr. Braddock?"

The clock is already ticking. He's booked the standard time. Half an hour, doled out precisely and sparingly as medication.

"My wife," he says, and leans back. "My wife," he repeats, half wonderingly. He stares straight ahead, as if the words hang suspended between us.

"Do you have a special message for your wife?"

"I'm not sure." He shifts closer to the edge of the chair. "Should I?"

"Some clients find they have a better experience if they're prepared with a message," I say. "But it's entirely at your discretion, Mr. Braddock."

"I want to talk to her again," he says. "The way we'd talk before she—"

I let the silent part of his sentence unspool before I continue. "I'm going to ask you to share a memory with me. A memory of Sylvia." He winces instinctively at her name, as if I've cursed. "It's best if you share a memory that's as recent as possible. I know it might be painful," I add, because Mr. Braddock has dipped his face into his hands.

But when he looks up, his eyes are dry and clear as shards of glass.

"We were at the lake," he says. "Lake Madeleine, outside the city. It was our first time visiting. Sylvia suggested the place. The cabins had these huge windows in the living room. It made me feel like a fish in a bowl, looking out at everything. Or maybe everyone was looking in at me. At us." He pauses. "Is this too much?"

"Not at all, Mr. Braddock," I say. "Details are helpful."

I listen without interrupting as he talks. Most of my clients are rushed and halting, recounting memories with the clumsy bluntness of children recalling dreams. But Mr. Braddock shares the last weekend he spent with his wife as if it's playing on a screen in front of him.

When he stops speaking, the silence dissolves like a fog. I tip the pill into my palm. Among ourselves, we bodies refer to the pills as lotuses, a nickname established before I arrived. There's no official name for the capsules, no imprint or marking on their powdery surfaces, so *lotus* works as well as anything else.

With my free hand, I reach for the cup of water. "Shall we begin, Mr. Braddock?"

"Wait."

I don't move. I'm aware of the waxy coolness of the paper cup against my lips.

"What we're about to do—it won't hurt you, will it?"

None of my clients has ever asked this question before.

"The process is entirely safe, Mr. Braddock."

"All right." He holds out a palm toward me. "I wanted to check. Please. Go ahead."

I slip the lotus between my lips and swallow. The sensation is as unsurprising now as drawing a breath or falling asleep. A numbness spreads across the body, the blood growing sluggish. The eyelids turn weighted. The body is rearranging itself to make room, my consciousness rising and scattering like wary birds sensing an unknown presence.

Mr. Braddock moves closer, his knee pressed hard against my own. He must realize his mistake; he moves away almost as soon as I register the touch. But when his clothed knee meets my bare one, I feel the hard bubble of his kneecap through the fabric, and a brief, thrilling warmth. I'm pulled back into my body, all the work I've done to become somebody else unraveling.

He recedes from my vision, moving backward so fast I can't reach him. I open my mouth to warn him, but it's too late.

I'm already gone.

I open my eyes. For an unsteady moment, my limbs aren't in the right place. Then I settle back around my body like dust resettling on a surface after being disturbed. My palms and soles sting. I stare around Room 12 as if I've never seen it before: the shimmering water in the painting, the empty shells of the paper cups.

Gripped with urgency, I look at the chair across from me. Patrick leans forward as if I've caught him on the cusp of rising. He clasps his hands between his knees, his jaw tight, his whole frame strung with tension. When our eyes snag, his face lights up with a hopefulness that begins to fade again immediately.

"Mr. Braddock," I say.

Patrick exhales abruptly and leans back in his chair, his posture loosening. He nods once. As if we've settled something. When he stands, I tilt my head to take him in: his height, the glitter of his downturned eyes visible beneath his lashes.

"Thank you," Patrick says. He's cool. Courteous.

There are questions I should be asking him. I have a script to follow this first time, easing the transition between one identity and the other, reassuring him that I'm once again a stranger. But something stops me. I stand without speaking and go to open the door, stepping aside to let Patrick pass. His gaze brushes against mine as he moves into the corridor. His eyes are unreadable, purposefully closed off to me. I ignore the instinct to follow him.

TWO

Sylvia Braddock has been dead for nearly eighteen months.
    She drew her last breath sometime between the last day
of August and the first day of September. The Braddocks' trip
to the lake was her idea, a small retreat before the summer came
to an end. Lake Madeleine lies an hour from the city: a body of
water spilling across nine hundred acres, fringed by frothy, overgrown forest. Along the lake's winding perimeter, enterprising
spirits have carved out pockets of civilization over the decades.
The resort is self-consciously rustic, conjuring up images of nos-
talgic summer camps, creaky family cabins passed down from
generation to generation, but filtered through a lens of luxury.

    The end result is too stuffy to attract much upscale clientele,
too expensive for sunscreen-blotted tourists. Sylvia had heard that
the cabins offered city dwellers a chance to escape without going
too far. To breathe in a dutiful dose of fresh air, examine the sensation of wilderness and solitude, and then return to normal life.

    Soon after the Braddocks arrived at Lake Madeleine that
August, they recognized the couple staying in the next cabin.
Patrick's colleague, married to a friend of the Braddocks. One of
Sylvia's many small matchmaking successes among her circle of
acquaintances. She immediately suggested the four of them spend
time together, folding the other couple into the Braddocks' plans
as easily as if she'd expected to find them there. Patrick couldn't
find a polite way to protest this, even as he knew that Sylvia

would slip into her role as hostess. Expansive, dazzling, unable to reenter the more intimate world of being his wife.

By Saturday evening, Patrick was depleted: exhausted by the small talk, the bright beat of the sun, the previous night spent drinking, surrounded by the acidic veil of citronella lanterns. He made his excuses as Sylvia escaped into the nearest town with their friends.

She arrived home from dinner later than Patrick expected, the tint of wine on her breath. He tried to convince her to come to bed; Sylvia was edgy from drinking. The last time Patrick saw his wife, she was sitting at the edge of the bed to remove her shoes. Head bent. Dark hair falling over her face to reveal the graceful slope of her neck.

She was gone the next morning. Patrick waited. Her shoes stood outside the bedroom door. Sandals with needle-thin heels, perfectly lined up, as if she was just about to step into them. A towel lay in a moist, crumpled blossom from last evening's shower, fragrant with shampoo. When Patrick called his wife's phone, it vibrated violently on the windowsill.

It was past noon before the thin threads of Patrick's worry and impatience solidified into fear. Sylvia had woken before sunrise the previous morning to take a quick swim in the shallow water nearest the beach. She'd been back in time for breakfast.

That afternoon, Patrick walked the perimeter of the lake. When he returned three hours later, exposed skin blooming with mosquito bites and long, raw scratches, his friends were waiting. They seemed reluctant to meet Patrick's eyes as they discussed what to do next. Stranded in the absence of their gazes, Patrick began to understand all of this as pointless. A temporary buffer between not-knowing and knowing.

Half a day passed before they retrieved Sylvia's body. Within this time, Patrick turned into someone to be protected and distracted, shuffled off with the local sheriff's deputy. The deputy and his wife kept up with a soap opera, and so the deputy patiently explained to Patrick a labyrinthine plotline in the latest episode. A woman who coerced her identical twin into taking on the life she didn't want, only to envy her sister's unexpected happiness.

"Grass is always greener," the deputy said. Patrick nodded and nodded in agreement, imagining his wife pulled from the depths of the lake like a flag of surrender.

Later, he'd learn that Sylvia's body was caught in the weeds near the middle of the lake. It was ruled an accidental drowning, an unskilled swimmer going out too far. Most likely, they told Patrick, she'd been lost in her thoughts, unsure of her own abilities, until it was too late.

'm yanked awake like a fish with a hook lodged in its mouth. Immediately, I recognize the signs of a long and dreamless sleep. My throat aches; my hair is tacky with sweat.

Lying in bed, I let the previous day come back to me piece by piece. The string of clients I saw after Patrick, their tics and mannerisms. Ms. Sawyer dabbing a tissue delicately beneath each eye. Mr. Kent's hands held together, palm to palm, in his lap. A strangely prayerful pose.

I left the Elysian Society late in the day. As usual, I was the last to depart. The sunset was a hot, melted layer at the bottom of the sky. I ticked past the predictable landmarks between the Elysian Society and my apartment. A corner grocery, always shining with humid fluorescence, like a greenhouse. A billboard, the newest ad peeling off in lacy strips to reveal a denture-bright smile. During the drive, a radio talk show host spoke with a calibrated mix of excitement and somberness about a body discovered near a subdivision across town. I let the details anchor me, comforting in their unremarkable ugliness. *No sign of a struggle. Blunt force trauma. Anyone with information, please come forward—*

When I try to recall what happened after I arrived home, my memories turn dimmer. I remember retreating to my bed earlier than usual. Eight in the evening, or earlier. I must have fallen asleep. Now, the clock tells me I've been gone for twelve solid and implacable hours.

Rising reluctantly, I make my way to the bathroom. My body feels stiff and disjointed. Every inch of my skin is as sensitive as the skin revealed beneath a bandage. Somewhere down the hall, a neighbor plays music. The bass echoes thickly, the beating of an enormous heart. I'm surrounded by other people's vices in this apartment. Theatrical sex moans, cigarette smoke, bitter arguments, energetic thumps of TV; it seeps in at all hours.

In the bathroom, I reach for the faucet. The showerhead shudders once before spitting out a patchy spray. At the edges of my mouth, a taste swells. Lake water. Stale and silty, like the air on a hot day just before the rain.

I step back from the lip of the bathtub. In the mirror above the sink, my reflection is all wrong against the backdrop of my bathroom. It takes me a moment to understand why. Sylvia's lipstick clings to my mouth, turning my lips smaller and more prominent at the same time.

I rub my mouth with the back of my hand. The lipstick stays. I try again, more roughly. As the shower water hisses behind me, I take a square of toilet paper and scrub it across my lips, harshly, until the skin stings like a fresh scrape. There's a slick, shocking streak of color on the paper.

I drop the blotted tissue into the toilet. It flowers open in slow motion before I flush.

The Braddocks are in my bedroom, Sylvia's face fanned across the floorboards. I stoop to collect the photos. I sit on the edge of the bed to sift through the images. Slowly, this time, with a methodical patience. I want to see and understand each separate image. Perversely, I hope the Braddocks have changed. I hope they're ordinary now, glossiness scratched off to reveal people no more remarkable than any of my clients.

But the pattern reemerges, frustrating in its unyieldingness. They're in love. Charmed by their own lives. I stop at their wedding portrait. Sylvia gazes directly into the camera, her veil blown back in a gauzy plume, a slight widow's peak emphasizing her heart-shaped face. Patrick looks sidelong at his bride. The formality of their pose only emphasizes the tenderness of his straying gaze, as if he can't resist the pull of Sylvia's beauty. As if he can't believe she's there without seeing tangible proof.

I hesitate before I turn to the last photo in the stack. The one with the bed. While the other photographs are precisely matched, rectangular and uniform in size, this one has a distinct weight to it. A square silhouette. The Polaroid's white border gives it the quality of a relic: ephemeral and formal at the same time.

The difference extends to the image itself. The discrepancy between the dewy-bright bride and this naked woman is striking. Sylvia scarcely seems to age throughout the course of the photographs. Her black hair always worn just below her shoulder blades, her sophisticated style unchanging. But the woman in the dark lipstick is peeled back and exposed in a way that has nothing to do with her body. It's all in her expression: a directness. A fierceness.

My mind fills with something out of an old medical illustration. Sylvia's skin folded back like curtains to reveal her interior, plump pink organs and coiled muscles. Above this, she smiles, unconcerned and daring me to look.

Nudity is forbidden at the Elysian Society. I've come across a scattering of these photos throughout the years, and I consider the images mostly harmless. Vein-marbled thighs and fleshy breasts, commonplace as household objects. Always before, though, I've reported the photos, declining to work with the clients. People can be quick to test boundaries at the Elysian Society, feeling out soft spots and loopholes. Any infringement at an early stage is a risk. I know this.

I remember the press of Patrick's knee against mine. The shocking immediacy of his body. Heat darts down my spine.

I rise from the bed. The photos shed back onto the floor in a slippery rush, and my heel tamps down on Sylvia's wedding-day smile as I walk across the room to prepare for work.

The Elysian Society stands in a limbo of a neighborhood. The area has a reputation for benign danger, hinted at rather than seen. The streets are populated with abandoned homes and condemned buildings. Boarded-up windows are painted the same shade as the brickwork, giving the impression of featureless faces. The neighborhood offers the Elysian Society an automatic privacy. Here, our clients are less likely to run into anybody they know.

Many decades ago, the building that houses the Elysian Society must have belonged to an affluent family. From the outside, the cool white brick and tightly shuttered windows produce the exact impression that clients want when they come to a place like this. Elegant, but not funereal; old and established, but unconnected to scandal or witchcraft. At a squinting angle, it could be a church. A museum.

Appointment times are carefully staggered, with clients dispatched to their designated rooms soon after arriving. Each client should feel as if he's entering a private landscape. The Elysian Society's waiting room isn't for visitors; it's the space where bodies congregate between encounters. Unlike the encounter suites, the waiting room bears the layered marks of aging. Sepia water stains embellished on the ceiling, carpet loose over aging floorboards and pocked with sunken patches. Couches share space in front of a TV set that displays grainy videos, random landscapes with soothing instrumental music rolling behind the images. A pleasant, wordless distraction.

This Friday morning, I arrive early enough that the waiting room is mostly empty. A redheaded body watches the TV without interest. A boy with stark cheekbones yawns into his fist, eyes glassy as a doll's from the lingering effects of a lotus. I spot an older body, salt-and-pepper hair and a gently creased face, as if her skin has been folded up and then smoothed out again.

"Edie."

I turn. Leander approaches, smiling. Some bodies wear the pale, plain Elysian Society uniforms with a stiffness or hunched apology that highlights the strangeness of the outfit until that's all that stands out. Bodies like Lee complement the simplicity of the uniform: his wide-set green eyes, clean-shaven jawline. The white pants and airy shirt, even his milky-pale bare feet, all seem an extension of his youthful handsomeness.

"I hear you're wanted," Lee says.

I shake my head slightly. Lee's been a body for two years now, a record closing in on mine by steady increments. The friendliness we've developed is mostly due to his patience. The first time I instinctively smiled back at Lee, the first time I was grateful to see a familiar face in the waiting room, I almost felt like he'd tricked me.

"Mrs. Renard needs to speak with you," he clarifies. "Whenever you have time."

"Do you know what it's about?" I ask.

"I'm only the messenger." But Lee's distracted. His eyes shift over my face. "There's something different about you today," he says. "Did you cut your hair?"

I reach a hand to my hair. Blond, coarse, and prone to dryness. Gathered into a simple knot at the nape of my neck. I cut it myself, chopping it bluntly to my shoulders once a year. It's nearly at its longest point right now.

My mind slips to Sylvia's hair in the photographs. Blue-black as a raven's wing, the iridescence of oil on asphalt. I imagine its texture. Sleek and smooth. Silkiness pressed under my fingertips.

"I might look tired." I bring my hand down quickly. "I've had trouble sleeping."

"No, no, you look fine," Lee says. "I'm imagining things. I'm sorry."

"Just a trick of the light," I suggest.

Lee smiles. "Whatever it is, it's not a bad change."

His voice holds a coaxing note under the surface. I mirror his smile. "I should really go see what she wants," I say.

Moving into the low hall that connects to the offices, I shake off the regret I feel whenever I can't match Lee's warmth. He always makes it so easy. A small detail offered about his life, trailed by a blank slot of silence. I'm grateful, in these moments, for the excuse the Elysian Society provides. Turning my reticence into a virtue.

Mrs. Renard's office door stands ajar, a sliver of light cracking the edge of the paneled oak. I tap. "Come in," Mrs. Renard calls.

She sits behind her desk, elbows spread wide and hands clasped together. At the edge of the desk, she's arranged several tissue holders. Tissues extend upward like static smoke. The whole room is lined with books, some so old they're unmarked and shedding like snakes. These books, and a lampshade with shimmering beadwork, are placed there for the benefit of our more superstitious clientele. A pewter cross on one wall comforts clients who are here straight from church services, confessional booths. Otherwise, the office could belong to a pricey therapist.

"Eurydice," Mrs. Renard says. "Thank you for coming to see me."

I hover near the door, aware of a third presence in the room.

At first I think she's a client, but she wears a white dress identical to my own.

"This is Pandora," Mrs. Renard supplies, following my gaze. "She just joined us. I was telling Pandora that she has a client interested in working with her. You'll like Mr. Womack," she continues, speaking to Pandora now. "He lost his wife five years ago. They'd been married several years before that. She was only in her thirties. A terrible loss. So unexpected."

"Suicide?" Pandora asks.

"A stroke," Mrs. Renard says. "We don't work with suicides at the Elysian Society."

"You needed to talk with me, Mrs. Renard?" I ask.

"Of course," she says. "Pandora, I'm afraid we'll need our privacy."

When Pandora passes me, she brushes her gaze against mine and smiles. I smile back a second too late, a reflex that startles me.

When we're alone, Mrs. Renard sighs. "Well. Eurydice. It's been some time since we've sat down for a good chat, hasn't it?" Her voice is colored with surprise. "You look quite well."

"So do you." I can't help noticing that she's changed. Her dyed burgundy hair shows gray at the roots, like dust gathering on a bright tablecloth, and the wrinkles seeping out from the corners of her eyes have deepened. She reminds me of someone recovering from a long illness.

"I'll cut to the chase, Eurydice," she says. I lift my chin in a show of attentiveness. "You've reached an important milestone. I wanted to acknowledge that." An indulgent smile.

The window behind Mrs. Renard's desk is one of the few in the building that hasn't been cloaked over with heavy layers of curtains. The sunlight in here always seems more rarified than the sky outside. The light through the bare panes is raw and brilliant, bubbled with dust motes.

Mrs. Renard leans back. "It's been five years, Eurydice. Five years today since you stood across from me and told me you wanted to become a body."

As she says it, I remember. The awareness of this anniversary has been restlessly circling my mind for months now. I've kept it at bay so far.

"I still recall that day quite clearly," Mrs. Renard continues. "You were a much different woman back then. A girl, really."

I clasp my hands in front of me. A light tremble runs through my muscles, and I squeeze my fingers tighter, then tighter, as if I can remove this response by force.

"This past week alone, I've interviewed half a dozen girls who fit that same mold," Mrs. Renard says. "New to the city. Craving a fresh start. What's remarkable about you is that you didn't merely find a fresh start inside these walls. You found a whole life."

My past self hanging back in the corner of the room, watching me and summing me up. Gauging which parts of me have grown. Which have stayed the same.

If Mrs. Renard notices my discomfort, she ignores it. "How many of your coworkers can say that?" she asks. "You see the true potential of being a body. You understand what some of the others never will: that it's a talent. A skill."

My muscles uncoil. The memory dissolves and scatters. When I smile this time, I can actually mean it. "Thank you, Mrs. Renard."

"Of course, I would like to see you spend more time with the others," Mrs. Renard says. "The other bodies could stand to learn a thing or two from you."

Guilt worms through me, leaving a dark trail. Patrick's face flashes across my mind, then Sylvia's; the lipstick, his knee against mine. "I'm honored that you have faith in me," I say.

She rises, moving to where I stand by the door. I'm so accustomed to seeing Mrs. Renard behind her desk that I'm surprised at how small she is, a head shorter than me. Her fingers shimmer with stacks of rings; she wears an elaborate caftan, overlapping layers of fabric. I notice a bruise half hidden by her neckline, a mottled darkness against her sun-coarsened skin. Then she's pulling me into an embrace.

I try not to stiffen, overwhelmed by her solidity, her fleshy, sweet smell. No one has touched me in so long. Her grasp is strong and assured, and when she lets go and steps back, I'm un-anchored for a moment. As if I'll float away.

"I'm proud of you, Eurydice," Mrs. Renard says. She plucks at her neckline. The tip of the bruise vanishes. "Please know that you can always come to me. With anything."

The halls are too dark after the dazzling sunlight in the office. I blink hard to clear my vision, moving rapidly toward Room 12, arms crossed over my chest.

I'm an outlier at the Elysian Society. Most of the bodies barely survive a year. The majority leave after a month. Some vanish after a week or even a single day. Always without warning. My first few weeks, I barely spoke to the others. I passed unnoticed, learning the inner workings of the place like someone thrown into the water and forced to learn to swim.

After a month, I had a full roster of clients. I became adept at setting them at ease, asking the right questions. Back then, my success wasn't due to a robust work ethic or a newly uncovered talent. I was simply caught up in the relief of the work. The ability to escape myself.

Another body cornered me in the waiting room one morning, demanding an explanation. She was middle-aged, her cheeks dimpled with acne scars. I'd noticed her. She was loud, always talking. Her breath sometimes held a pungent mix of cigarettes and peppermint gum, both forbidden.

"What's your secret?" That's how she phrased it, and my heart-beat pulled tight as a wire until I realized there was no way she could know. She pushed on: "You just have the right look. One of those faces that could belong to anybody. People are always mistaking you for someone they know, right?"

"Not really," I'd lied.

A week later, the woman was gone. It struck me as vaguely ominous at the time. But I began to understand how often new workers joined and how casually they vanished. After one year at the Elysian Society, a mere third of my original coworkers remained.

Mrs. Renard's point about spending time with the other bodies stings. She's missed or maybe ignored an essential part of who I am here. My success relies on keeping a distance, biding my time quietly, no distractions. I watch the others. The way they talk and gossip and flirt, drawing their discrete identities fully to the surface, and how much harder this makes it when they swallow the lotus and allow a stranger inside their flesh.

It's simpler my way. When I'm inside the Elysian Society walls, I ignore myself. I become lost in the repetitiveness, the monotony. For years, the rules have anchored me, giving me something sturdy to grasp when what I'm doing yawns dark and bottomless at my feet.

And now I've slipped, just the slimmest fraction, into that darkness.

THREE

When I passed my four-year milestone, Mrs. Renard made one small concession. I spent years shuffled around like the rest of the bodies, sometimes in Room 3, sometimes in Room 15. After I'd been working for four years, all my encounters shifted to Room 12. Mrs. Renard never directly mentioned it to me, and I never thanked her, but I feel a sense of belonging whenever I enter Room 12 now. A small, neat space that's all my own.

Today, though, something's different. I can't shake the sensation of a criminal slinking back to the scene of the crime. Everything looks the same, but a fine, dark skein of memories clings to every surface, altering the air.

It tugs at my gaze after a second: Sylvia's lipstick. The bullet-shaped case stands on the end table. I forgot to return it to Patrick after our encounter.

I pick up the lipstick, cradling the delicate weight in my palm. Bodies are required to use loved ones' belongings during encounters. Sweaters rubbed thin from frequent wear, necklaces shadowed with tarnish. The idea, Mrs. Renard explains, is that the dead are drawn to and comforted by the items they cherished during life. Like dogs trailing familiar scents back home.

Privately, I'm always reminded of a story I read as a child. The greedy woman who steals a bone from a graveyard and takes it to her kitchen, haunted that night by a moaning ghost. *Give me my bone.* Even as a child, I found the story as much sad as frightening.

This idea of the dead still caught up in the material world of the living.

I close my fingers around the lipstick.

For a crooked second, Sylvia is in the room with me. A drowned specter, white skin peeling away like fruit rind, eyelids eaten into filigree by the fish.

And then the impression slips sideways and I become the drowned woman. My skin waterlogged and dripping, hanging in tatters around me.

When the knock comes, I drop the lipstick as if I've been burned. It rolls beneath the end table, sucked into the shadows.

"Ms. Mendoza," I say, answering the door. I'm relieved that my voice is strong and cool. "Please, have a seat."

This client has worked with me for three years. Today, she wears pearls around her throat, her gray-streaked hair braided neatly. Most clients dress up for encounters. They don't want their loved ones seeing them looking shabby or uncared for.

Accepting the perfume bottle that Ms. Mendoza passes to me, I rub the fragrance on my wrists, quick and businesslike. The incense of roses fills the room.

Ms. Mendoza inhales. "Oh, I've been so looking forward to this visit."

"It's been a while since we've seen you," I say. Ms. Mendoza is the type of client who craves socializing before encounters, and I let myself enjoy her plain warmth.

"I've had a hard time making it out here to see Veronica lately," Ms. Mendoza says. "Personal matters. Hopefully she understands."

"I'm sure she does."

Ms. Mendoza goes silent then, hands folded on her lap, watching me expectantly. I tip the capsule into my palm and pause, suddenly confused. My heart swells with a misplaced panic. "Could I have a moment, please?" I ask.

"Of course, dear," Ms. Mendoza says, but not before I see her flinch of impatience.

I shut my eyes, take a deep breath. Will my stubborn brain into blankness. It takes a second, but then it comes: the slowed heartbeat, the weightiness of the body around me. The fear swirls out of my mind, the last dregs of water spinning and sliding down a drain.

I open my eyes and reach for the cup, swallow the lotus. It barely takes any time before I'm gone.

I open my eyes. Rough scrapes of sound and light move through my head. A woman talking low in my ear. The cold panels of light flashing by one by one as I'm pushed down a corridor, prone on my back.

Ms. Mendoza busies herself in her purse. Her eyes have the vulnerable, rabbity look of recent tears. "That was lovely," she says. "So good to reconnect."

Ms. Mendoza's twin sister died three years ago. It was a slow death. Leukemia. At first, hope was interrupted by bad news, a lumbar puncture suggesting the cancer had metastasized. Near the end, according to Ms. Mendoza, it was the reverse: the progress of death stalled by pockets of hope. Experimental treatments became cruel in their suspension of the inevitable. A torturer's techniques. Even so, Ms. Mendoza had barely let a week pass before she came to the Elysian Society.

This isn't unusual. I've seen people waste so little time that they've arrived at Room 12 with eyelids still swollen from the funeral. For some clients, working with me is like returning to a conversation after a brief interruption, scarcely noticing that anything has changed. A sentence started in one woman's mouth and ended in mine.

But I've also known people to wait for decades, letting everyone believe that they'd moved on. Completing the dutiful stages of mourning, crafting new lives in the space left behind. And then waking up with the simple, unignorable urge to talk to their wives, best friends, daughters. When this happens, the Elysian Society is waiting for them. Offering bodies aged in a perfect time lapse, the girl who died at eighteen finally granted the mercy of wrinkles and gray-dusted hair, or else bodies as young and untouched as beloved memories.

I study Ms. Mendoza now. The fussy movements as she dabs beneath her nose, the way she folds the tissue into a bulging square. I don't feel anything toward her. No curiosity, no familiarity. She's just a woman. A paying customer.

Before I leave the Elysian Society, I check the schedule Jane has prepared for me. The lineup of familiar names (*Park, Brown, Loudermilk*). There it is: *Braddock, Patrick*. He meets with me next Tuesday.

It's early for a second encounter. Most clients need a few weeks before the ragged ache of longing takes hold again. I press my finger down on his name. Deep inside, a stirring. Light and swift.

It's dusk when I leave. The air holds a chill that razes the evening sky into clarity. I nearly stumble over someone sitting at the bottom of the steps. She turns and looks at me, startled, as if I'm the one out of place.

"Pandora," I say, remembering her name with an effort. "What are you doing here?"

Her cheeks are glazed from the cold, her posture tightly coiled. Her knee jitters up and down. "Hey," she says. "You again."

"The bus stop is a few blocks from here," I say.

She wears a flimsy faux-leather jacket over her white dress, a pair of puffy boots that turn her legs weedy in comparison. "I was hoping someone would give me a ride," she says.

"I'm afraid I'm the last one leaving."

Pandora just nods at this, pulling her arms tighter around her body.

"Do you need me to drop you off somewhere?" I ask, reluctant, and she's rising to her feet before I've even finished speaking.

I pull onto the main road. "Where are we headed?" My car is tidy but shabby, an older model. The gust from the heater is blazing hot against my hands and knees, leaving the rest of my body too cold.

"Sycamore," Pandora says. "I'll tell you when we're closer."

"Sycamore?" My fingers tighten automatically on the steering wheel; I keep gazing ahead at the soft discs of headlights from oncoming traffic. "Not 801 Sycamore?"

She twists her upper body to get a better look at me.

"I lived there myself once," I explain. "Years ago."

I can almost hear her deciding whether or not to pursue this further, the sharp crackle of her curiosity. "Renard helped you out too?" she asks at last.

"She did." We pass the shell of a restaurant that burned down last month, stately black peaks and jagged crests. At night, the silhouette reminds me of treetops in a forest. "Years ago."

"How many years ago?"

"A few," I say, brusque. "I was new to the city."

"Well, I'm new here too," Pandora says, as if we've stumbled across an amazing coincidence. "Where are you from?"

My chest tightens. "You wouldn't have heard of it," I say.

She doesn't pick up on the sudden coolness in my voice. "Oh, like a small town, you mean?" she asks. "Because—"

"I'd really rather not discuss it," I interrupt. "It was a long time ago."

"Hey, sorry," she says. "I was just going to say that I come from a small town too."

We don't talk again for a few minutes. I'm preparing myself

to see Sycamore again. Even the drive here, trailing my old bus route, holds an uncanny layer of déjà vu. After a moment, Pandora reaches over and turns on the radio. The newscaster's voice enters the car, fuzzed with static, stray words cracking down the middle.

. . . suspected foul play has left local homeowners concerned for their safety. Authorities are still trying to identify the victim. Dubbed Hopeful Doe, the young woman is estimated at between seventeen and twenty years old, and . . .

I reach to turn the radio off again, leaving a ringing silence.

"Hopeful Doe," Pandora repeats. "Seriously? Where'd they come up with that?"

"Like Jane Doe," I say. "It's a way to humanize her, I suppose."

She huffs. "There must be a less corny way to do that."

We're getting closer. I recognize the church at the intersection, the boarded-up liquor store across the street, decorated with graffiti in an ornate floral pattern.

"While we're on the topic," Pandora says, "do you have a nickname? Everyone seems to have nicknames there. I'm using Dora."

"Most people call me Edie," I concede.

"That's cute. Cuter than Eurydice." She falls silent again, but I sense her watching me. Every time she talks, Dora's a shade too eager, as if she's been storing up words and has to pace herself. A clear symptom of loneliness—it took me a long time to outgrow it.

"That's real sad," Dora ventures. "That girl they found." She pauses. "Can you explain something to me?"

The apartment complex is just ahead. A squat brick structure fringed with metal stairwells that remind me of barbed wire coils.

In one window, the blue of a television screen lights up the blinds, flashing in a cryptic Morse code. "I'll try," I say.

"Why can't we contact suicides?" Dora asks. The bluntness of the question, its childlike lack of apology, startles me. "Back in the office," she continues. "Remember, I asked if someone had committed suicide, and Mrs. Renard—"

"I remember." As if I'm moving obediently through a recurring dream, I pull into the parking lot and shut off the engine. "It's not what we offer at the Elysian Society," I say. "It never has been."

"Right, but people go there to get answers," she says. "After a suicide, that's when people need answers the most, you know?" The stiff and shiny folds of her jacket, hunched around her shoulders, remind me of the wet, crumpled wings of a hatching bird.

"Possibly," I say. "But it's a risk. It's too dangerous."

Dora frowns like a child trying to understand an obscure parable or a boring sermon. "I thought this place was different from the others," she says. "Safer."

There's a testing press of challenge in her voice. I know she's referring to the small, homegrown operations that spring up like toadstools in suburban basements, grandmotherly living rooms, the back rooms of struggling storefronts. Amateur channelings: inexperienced bodies swallowing down concoctions as limp as baby aspirin, or else pills so potent that they leave bodies froth-lipped, bug-eyed. The Elysian Society has purged these smaller attempts from the city and the surrounding suburbs, but they still thrive in certain pockets around the country.

"The Elysian Society *is* safer," I say. "But it's safer because of the rules. Because of what we won't do. The risks are still there, and the consequences are just as dangerous."

"Dangerous how?"

With the heater off, the car is filling up with chill, rapidly as rushing water through a crack. I almost tell her. Tell her about what happened in Room 7; explain why we use paper cups for water, never glass. But I only learned these details through rumors, whispers gradually stitched together to create an ominous whole. The stories have always felt most powerful glimpsed in the shadows.

"Listen, I have an early day tomorrow," I say instead.

At this, Dora springs into motion, opening the car door, slipping out into the night. "Thanks for the ride," she calls, her voice trailing in before the door shuts behind her.

With Dora gone, the memories squeeze in tighter and closer. When I started at the Elysian Society, I'd been living in a motel room. Mrs. Renard offered to let me stay in the furnished apartment she owned. Close to the Elysian Society and perfect for a temporary home. She skimmed a modest amount from my earnings each month. More than fair in exchange for a place where I didn't have to sign my real name, where I didn't have to worry about the barest essentials. It was a simple sketch of a life, sitting there waiting for me.

But even as I recognized Mrs. Renard's generosity, I grew to hate the space. Everything I held back during my workday, everything that vanished when I swallowed the lotus, collected in the cracks of my mind like condensation. It was only when I was back on Sycamore that I'd remember. I spent most of my time in bed. Desperate to distract myself, I'd look out the window at the road, the headlights of the cars going past, and imagine myself in each car. Each one taking me to a separate destination, alive with its own possibilities. I'd become one person in that sleekly feline luxury sedan, an entirely different person in a rust-streaked pickup.

As I'm pulling back onto the street now, I glance back at the building just once. My eyes automatically land on the third window from the left, the top story. My bedroom window. It's dark now. No glimmer of life.

At home, waiting for sleep, I search for more details about the dead girl. Because nobody has claimed her, there are no photographs of Hopeful Doe during her lifetime. No school photos or birthday-party shots with friends' faces blurred away. Instead, the sites and channels use a wistful police sketch. Rendered in pencil lines, Hopeful Doe's face is easy to visualize hanging in a fluorescent-lit school hallway. It has an intimate quality, like an earnest self-portrait drawn by a future valedictorian.

They found Hopeful Doe on the edges of an aspiring gated subdivision. Only a few families had settled there, carrying out their lives surrounded by grandly empty houses in various stages of completion. Haughty skeletons. The house that held Hopeful Doe was vestigial, built decades ago. Unoccupied for years, dowdily outdated and scheduled for teardown.

The night before the demolition, a teenage girl from the subdivision went exploring. The corpse that would become Hopeful Doe was in a closet in the back room of the condemned house. She wore a blue sundress. A single diamond earring. According to the reports, when the teenager first saw Hopeful Doe's legs tucked together, she thought they belonged to a discarded store mannequin. Whoever left the body must have hoped it would be overlooked entirely, the girl's identity swept aside with the rubble and the wreckage.

Clicking back to the police sketch, I lean in closer to the screen. The dead girl looks familiar. It's a quick, intuitive connection, a recognition that makes sense for just a moment before the sensation fades again. Every time I attempt to place her, Hopeful Doe slips a little further, disintegrating under my gaze, until her face is a complete stranger's again.

can feel it. Little flashes of strangeness, stepping outside myself. It happens when I'm waking or falling into sleep, when I'm performing a mindless task that doesn't require my attention. A disorientation that renders all my surroundings suddenly too vivid, as if I'm looking around at a new landscape. All the soft, well-worn familiarity has been stripped off to reveal a place that's unnervingly foreign, every angle bristling and razor sharp.

Each time, right after I come back, I think her name: *Sylvia*. *Sylvia*. I remember in Room 12 when her husband's knee touched mine, and how that moment tugged at the center of the neat knot of my life. Unraveling something.

Sylvia.

When I was a new body, there was one topic that always caught my attention as I sat alone in the waiting room. It was the only thing that sharpened my dreamlike listening into actual eavesdropping. Possession was a rare topic, always hushed: one person laughing, one chiding, another dismissive. The stories were less specific anecdotes than hints and suggestions. But it was enough to grip my imagination. These bodies who opened themselves up to loved ones and then never came back. Their homes stolen out from under them by sly houseguests.

I'd lie in bed at night and picture it. My body no longer mine. My hands not mine, my mouth closing around another woman's words. I'd wonder: Did it happen all at once? Would I close my eyes as the lotus slipped down my throat and then never open them again? Or was it a slow process, a wearing away? The gradual invasion of impulses and dreams and instincts, of preferences and thoughts?

Five years ago, the idea of this happening didn't inspire any particular fear. Just a numb curiosity. As the years passed and I stayed myself, I forgot to worry about it; no matter how many lotuses I swallowed, I'd blink awake each morning in my own bed, firmly tied to my own flesh. I let go of that fear, relegating it to the same place as all the other things I ignored and overlooked.

On Tuesday, I'm sick. It strikes without warning. My jaw closes in on itself. I'm light-headed, my body rolling out from under me. I rush from Room 12, barely making it to the restroom before I'm gagging.

Afterward, I reapply Sylvia's lipstick in the mirror. My face is so pale and damp that it has a strange newness to it, like the skin that grows back over a wound. In contrast, Sylvia's lipstick is darker than ever. Draining me to sustain its color.

The restroom door clatters open. A body with short black hair enters, stopping short when she catches sight of me. Her face reflects my surprise.

"Ana," I say. "I didn't know you were working again."

"Good morning to you too, Edie," Ana says. Other than Lee, she's one of the few bodies I talk with regularly. We're friendly in an accidental way. Ana comes and goes, working for a few months and then disappearing, her patterns secretive and erratic.

"No offense," Ana says now, "but I don't think that's your color."

It takes me a moment to catch on. "It's for a client," I say. "His wife's."

She laughs. "His wife had shit taste." Ana hovers behind me

in the mirror for a moment. Her fingers flash over her inky hair. "Oh, come on. Don't give me that look. The color is a little much for someone as pasty as you, that's all."

"It's not about me."

"No, of course not," Ana says. "Of course not." She plucks a hairpin from near her temple and sticks it between her lips. The pin juts like a snake tongue. "You know how they say blush makes you look like you just orgasmed?" Ana says, muffled. She plucks the pin from her mouth. "I was reading in a magazine that women wear lipstick to remind men of their labia." She emphasizes the last word, popping her lips around it like she's working over a lollipop.

My lips are suddenly leering and obscene. I drop my eyes. Beneath the embarrassment, there's a rush of excitement. "That's not appropriate," I say.

"I don't see why not."

"You know why not." Clutching Sylvia's lipstick, I feel foolish and uncovered. As if a stranger just slid an exploring hand up my skirt.

Ana angles her face from side to side, sucking in her cheeks, then smooths down her hair. Floating next to her in the mirror, my own reflection feels extraneous. Ghostly. "By the way," Ana says, "I was wondering if you've seen Thisbe around lately."

"Thisbe," I repeat.

She sighs. "Please tell me you know her." When I don't respond, she prompts: "Tiny thing. Blond? Your color, maybe. She joined at the start of the year."

"I know who she is," I say.

"So you've seen her around? She owes me some money."

"She left," I say. "Not long after you did."

In the mirror, Ana's gaze meets my own. She seems on the verge of speaking. Then she turns, moving away as quickly as she came.

"Good luck with your client," she says.

M r. Braddock. Welcome back."

I find myself watching closely as Patrick moves to sit. His movements carry an automatic assuredness, the muscle memory of better days. It makes him vulnerable and powerful at the same time. I imagine the women in his life bringing him home-baked pies in low-cut dresses, making dewy promises that they'll do *whatever they can to help him through this difficult time.*

I angle my knees away from Patrick's. "A small piece of business, Mr. Braddock," I say. "You left your wife's lipstick here at the Elysian Society last week."

He blinks. "I left it for you," he says. "I want you to have it."

"I see." My face betrays nothing. "Do you have a special message for your wife today?"

He runs his thumb quickly over his chin. "Not really. I want to talk to her again, same as last time." He smiles. "Does it help you, knowing what I'll say to my wife?"

"This is about you and Sylvia. Don't think about me."

Patrick's smile deepens. "Hard to do when you're sitting right there."

"Think of me as a means to an end."

"That seems a little harsh," he says. "How many people do you work with in a day, anyhow?"

"It depends," I say after a second of hesitation. "Some days five or six. Other days fewer."

"And it doesn't get hard on you, doing this with so many people?"

I consider Patrick, stalling. With a few male clients, I detect flashes of a proprietary attitude in the way they stare at me. But I recall Patrick's abashed smile in his photos and something shifts: I see in him the traces of a man who's humbled by his own life, a man who tries conscientiously to balance the scales.

And here I am, a woman sitting in front of him in a dress as thin as tissue paper.

"It's not difficult at all," I say. "I enjoy my work. And now, Mr. Braddock, we should begin."

Surprise passes over his face. "Of course. I apologize."

After I swallow the lotus, I watch Patrick for as long as I can. As the eyelids lower, as my mind lifts away from the body, cloud light and drifting. He doesn't move this time. He keeps to himself, maintaining a safe distance.

open my eyes and look directly into Patrick's. I'm smiling. The surface of my skin is warm and sparkling, my head heavy with a blissful drowsiness.

"I've missed you," Patrick says, low. "You can't know how much I've missed you."

but I've been right here

A sharp splinter of confusion breaks through my happiness.

I've been right here all along

He leans forward. I know that he's about to reach for me. He's going to take my hand in his, run his thumb along my skin. Something else gives. My smile turns heavy on my face. A limb that's fallen asleep. He becomes a client again, and I'm a body, untouchable and temporary.

"Mr. Braddock," I say, with an effort.

Patrick sits back. He doesn't hide the movement of his gaze over my mouth, my hands in my lap, my bare feet planted on the floor. I sit, barely breathing as I allow him to piece me back together.

"Aren't you cold?" he asks. "I'm cold looking at you. It's freezing in here."

"Not at all," I say. "I'm quite comfortable."

He stares at my bare arms. "I feel like I should offer you my coat."

"That won't be necessary." I catch an unexpected note in my words. Close to flirtatiousness; a bright spill against my voice.

Patrick smiles, but he's distracted, seriousness already moving in behind the smile. "Tell me something," he says, near a whisper now. "Do you remember?"

I shake my head.

"After you take that," he says, flicking a hand toward the lotus, "do you remember what you say? What she says," he corrects.

"Mr. Braddock, bodies don't have access to these exchanges," I say. "It's a private process. Don't worry."

"I know, but—"

There's a staccato series of taps on the door. Jane opens the door to Room 12 and leans in, expression bland. "Mr. Braddock," she says, "I'd be happy to direct you toward the exit if you've forgotten the way."

"No," he says at once, and his voice has turned formal. "Thank you. I remember."

As Patrick leaves Room 12, he hesitates for the briefest moment on the threshold, as if he wants to turn and look at me. But then he walks into the corridor, and the part of my brain that follows him as if magnetized, sensitive to his every move, strains after him.

"Quite the chatterbox," Jane says, once he's out of earshot. "Isn't he?"

I straighten my shoulders. "No more than some of the others," I say, daring myself to look at her coolly and evenly.

"Hmm." She gazes at my mouth. "He's the one with the wife and the lipstick?"

"Mr. Braddock is a good client," I say. "He's reliable and polite. I'll be glad if he stays with me."

"Oh, he will," Jane says, dismissive now. Patrick left the chair skewed when he left. She takes the back of the chair with both hands and straightens it in one neat, aggressive movement. "That type always stays with the same body."

At home, I'm edgy. I walk through my routine: dinner, washing dishes, watching TV, folding laundry. I try to focus, but I find myself staring off into space, clutching a half-folded blouse like it's a prop that someone forced into my hand.

Patrick's question in Room 12 has echoed through the rest of my day. Usually, I experience my client's loved ones as abstract and raw-edged presences. Vivid, quickly fading scraps of other lives.

I was evasive with Patrick in Room 12 today. The truth is that Sylvia's memories have lingered. One image in particular, clear and deep. I remember Patrick's hand against me, at my waist. The golden hairs at his wrist, his long fingers holding the ghost of a summer tan. One or two fingernails endearingly frayed, as if he bites them when nobody is watching. I could reach right into the memory, interlace my fingers with his. Feel the light calluses of his fingertips.

In the bathroom, I lie in the bathtub, the rush of water surrounding me. My proportions distort slightly beneath the surface. I reach my hand between my legs. Although I haven't touched myself like this in months, my muscles begin the movement automatically.

When everything in me turns tight and frantic with desire, I slip my upper body under the surface. The water laps warm against my lips. Against my ears, all I can hear is a pulsating and distant roar. My hips lift of their own accord, greedy for more.

I submerge my entire head. My nose stings. I open my eyes, stare through the water at the creeping stains on the ceiling, until my lungs burn. At the moment when I think my entire body will pop like a balloon, I come up gasping.

In the silvery surface of the faucet, my face is so warped it could belong to anybody. My wet hair, my wild eyes, my mouth a dark, open smear as I suck in breath after breath after breath.

FIVE

The bedroom floor. I come back to myself so quietly and easily that I don't realize anything is unusual at first. Then the wrongness of the situation descends on me.

Through the open wedge of curtains, the sky is just lightening. I kneel on the floor. A reverential pose, like a praying child. My hands lie clenched against my thighs. I look around at the landmarks of my bedroom, anchoring myself. My bureau, right in front of me. The bed across the room. The end table, holding the Braddocks' photos. Sylvia's face shines out of the shadows.

try to remember

try

In my own bed again, waiting for sleep, I scan my memory. I don't know if I've ever sleepwalked before. What I do in my sleep, my unconscious tics and habits, how I appear to other people: these are parts of myself I can't decode alone. I'd need a partner, an observer.

I turn to face the wall, not letting myself start the calculation: how many years it's been since I've had someone like that in my life.

Unlike many of my clients, with their formal, vaguely funereal outfits, the client I meet on Thursday morning wears black leggings tight as snakeskin and a velour track jacket. A heart-shaped zipper pull dangles beneath the pouchy dip of her throat.

"Welcome to the Elysian Society." I smooth my skirt over my thighs. "This is your first time working with us, Ms. Fowler?"

"Mrs. Fowler," she corrects, swinging her ankle. "Candace Fowler."

I nod a brisk apology. "And whom do you wish to contact today, Mrs. Fowler?"

Her voice drops into a conspiratorial hush. "First, I need to know I can trust you."

"We have a strict confidentiality policy at the—"

But Mrs. Fowler holds out her hand. "Nuh-uh, nuh-uh, I know all that crap. I'm asking if I can I trust *you*, personally. Not the whole place, but you."

I'm briefly transfixed by her eyelashes. Sticky with mascara, wavering insect limbs.

She seems to take my silence as cooperation. "I want to contact Hopeful Doe. I lied," she adds, proud. "On the forms, I said I wanted to contact my cousin. But I'm here to bring that sweet girl's killer to justice. Get some answers."

"I'm afraid you can't contact the deceased unless you knew her personally during life."

She's sucking hard on her lips. "This murder affects me personally, young lady," she says. "It affects my family. She showed up near my home. It was my daughter who found her. My girl, forced to see something like that." Mrs. Fowler leans toward me as if she can transmit the horror through physical proximity. "I know how these things work. The police will lose interest. Meanwhile, I'll be going to bed every night wondering who's out there."

"Mrs. Fowler," I say, "I understand your concern. But if you'd read our policy—"

"Oh, all right." Her voice grows honeyed; we're just a couple of girls exchanging gossip over coffee. "I always come prepared." She winks, a quick snap of her eyelid, like a baby doll tilted back. "I'm not sure how much of a cut they give you, sweetie, but I'm sure it's not enough. The pay is never enough for this work, is it? I can only imagine what it's like for you girls." I stiffen. "Whatever they pay you, I'll double it. Triple it, I don't care."

"You don't seem to understand," I say, frustration turning me blunt. "I can guarantee that you won't find the answers you're looking for, Mrs. Fowler. Have you brought an object that belonged to Hopeful Doe during her lifetime?" I rush ahead, knowing that she hasn't. "Besides, victims who died violently aren't known for being compliant. They're confused. Their memories can be scrambled, unpredictable."

Mrs. Fowler cocks her head, pert as a lapdog. "Isn't there some way around that?"

"I'm afraid not."

At this, Mrs. Fowler smiles as if she's caught me in an obvious lie. "It just so happens that I did my research, young lady," she says. "I know you can just take more of those." She gestures at the lotus in its paper cup. "Two or three."

I open my mouth and then shut it, biting off my words on an inhale. There are stray pieces of information floating around. Shared by amateurs, small-time entrepreneurs, former bodies spiteful or cavalier enough to share whatever they knew. Some of the information is accurate. Most of it isn't. Still, Mrs. Fowler shifts in my eyes, turning from housewife-gone-vigilante to somebody more thorough. A woman accustomed to getting her own way.

"The Elysian Society simply doesn't work that way," I say. "If you're interested in taking that kind of risk, I'm sure you could locate a willing participant elsewhere."

"Find some quack online, you mean? Show up to an abandoned building and get murdered myself in the process?" Mrs. Fowler sniffs deeply, like she's trying to find the source of an odor. "Nah.

This place might not look like much, but I've heard it's the best you can get."

"I'm not sure that you fully understand what's at stake," I say. "Taking more than one lotus isn't safe. It could hurt the body."

She sweeps her eyes up and down my body. "You strike me as a hearty-enough specimen."

The hairs at the back of my neck rise. "Surely you don't expect me to endanger myself."

"You chose this line of work," Mrs. Fowler says. "You chose to treat your body this way. Why not at least do some good?"

I stand too quickly, helium light. "I'm afraid I'm going to have to ask you to leave."

For a moment, it seems she won't budge. Then Mrs. Fowler is a flurry of motion, rising and heading for the door. She keeps talking: "What you do here, people might call it freaky, but you could help people. The fact that you don't? It's shameful." She looks right at me. "That baby's blood is on your hands now."

When Jane comes into Room 12 a few minutes later, she stops short, looking between me and the empty chair. "She wanted to contact Hopeful Doe," I say, weary. "I've sent her away."

Jane's expression is blank for a moment, then takes on a grim focus. "You did the right thing, sending her away. I'll be sure that Mrs. Renard hears about this."

"Thank you," I say.

"You've been following that case?" Jane asks.

"A little," I say. "It's so sad."

"Very sad." Jane glances at the empty chair, as if some version of Mrs. Fowler lingers there. "You did the right thing," she repeats.

Coming into the waiting room after Mrs. Fowler, I catch a low murmur of voices. One voice rises up from the tangle of words, followed by muffled laughter.

Curious, I move to the farthest end of the room. They're clustered on the floor, cross-legged. I realize that they chose this spot because they're partially hidden by a couch; Jane won't walk by and spot them. Ana sits against the wall, head tilted to show the long lines of her throat. A trace of a bitter scent surrounds her, overwhelming in the bland air of the waiting room.

"Can we help you?" Ana asks.

The other three bodies have stopped talking. They examine me with a bemused hostility, like kids on a playground approached by a younger child. When I make eye contact with the girl sitting directly in front of me, she smiles. I recognize her: Dora.

"Jesus, sit down already," Ana says. "It's making me nervous just looking at you." She pats the floor with one hand, the way she'd call a dog.

Automatically, I sit at the edge of the group, folding my knees beneath me.

"What were you saying?" an older woman asks Dora.

"Oh, yeah." Dora scratches at her neck. "The guy who lost his wife. His wife was thirty-something when she died, so I don't understand why he'd choose me. I just turned twenty. I thought I'd be channeling granddaughters or daughters or high school friends."

"Twenty, thirties," the woman says. "What's the difference? Wait till you're my age. You only get grannies. Half the men who walk through those doors are my age or older, but you wouldn't think it to look at my client list."

"You're talking about Womack?" Ana asks Dora. When Dora nods, she goes on: "Womack is a rite of passage around here. If you're halfway pretty, you're going to get him at some point. He watches for the new bodies. He tries them all." She winks. "A real connoisseur."

"You figure his wife was a swinger?" the older woman asks. "Maybe this is what she wanted. Get a cuter body each time. Doesn't sound so bad to me."

The others laugh.

"Yeah, or maybe she didn't want this at all," Ana says. I can't tell whether her sternness is mocking or sincere. Ana can be like this, disguising her emotions as exaggerated versions of themselves, like caricatured masks. "Maybe she was a good little wifey, and Womack never cheated. Now he gets to have his cake and eat it too. Feel all virtuous, visiting his dead wife. See a pretty girl in her slip at the same time."

Dora wraps her arms around her upper body. I remember how hard it was to grow accustomed to the thinness of the dress, a sensation like being naked in a room full of strangers. "He can just do that?" she asks.

"Of course," the other girl says. Tiny pockmarks dot her nose and the skin above her lips; scars left behind by piercings. "If he pays for it."

"I thought clients would want to work with just one body," Dora says.

"Most can't," says Ana. "We don't have a stellar employee retention rate."

"If you last for a year or two, you'll have regulars," the older woman adds. "But until then, you're stuck with whatever you can get."

"I'd like to have regulars," Dora says.

"Careful what you wish for." Ana lifts her hand to her mouth. She holds a cigarette delicately between her fingers. She makes eye contact with me briefly, daring me to react. "The way I see it," she says, once she lowers the cigarette, "the clients who don't care are the true romantics. They can look at any random face and find the person they love. It's sweet, if you stop and think about it."

"Regulars must care more," Dora persists. "You're not just a body to them."

"But you are just a body to them," I say. "You always are. You have to be."

The others turn to me in a little flurry of movement, as if they'd forgotten I was here.

"I have more regulars than anyone," I continue, though their attention is a prickly, uncomfortable weight. "Being a body is all about your receptiveness to the clients. To their loved ones." I hesitate, seeing Sylvia's imperious beauty superimposed over my ordinary face. "If you start believing that your client needs you, specifically, then you're failing at your job."

Dora's eyes on me are tentative and considering. Her hand moves to her hair, as if she's disconnecting her curls from her identity.

"Thanks for that cheerful PSA," Ana says.

The older woman smirks, gazing at the floor. The girl with the scars reaches over to pluck the cigarette from Ana's hand.

"I'm only trying to help," I say.

"How long have you been here now?" Ana asks. "Ten years? A hundred?" She laughs. "You've memorized every last idiotic rule. So if anyone needs a refresher course on that, we'll be sure to come to you."

The girl leans across the space between us to pass the cigarette to Dora. I notice that her fingernails hold a trim of old nail polish, scabbed red at the edges. With one quick guilty glance at me, Dora accepts the cigarette.

"The rules are for our protection," I say.

"Ooh, my protection," Ana repeats in an exaggerated voice, words rounded like puffy balloons. "Sounds serious."

"Look what happened to Thisbe."

I'm not sure why I say it. Maybe as an experimental nudge, maybe as a way to hurt her. Ana's eyes blaze wider for a fleeting second; then her expression snaps back into its usual carelessness.

"Who's Thisbe?" Dora asks, looking between us.

"Forget it," Ana says. "Edie doesn't know what she's talking about." But her mouth has a sour twist to it.

After a silence, Dora hands the cigarette to Ana. It's a stub now, glowing hazy orange at the tip. Ana lifts up a flap of carpet near the baseboards, revealing a floor vent screwed firmly into place. She dips the cigarette beneath one of the slats.

"You think you're so much better than the rest of us," Ana says abruptly. "Perfect role model. Never a toe out of line."

The nicotine turns me dizzy.

"Maybe you're looking at this all wrong," Ana says. "I used to date a guy who thought he was smart for asking these pseudophilosophical questions." She deepens her voice, low and dopey. "*Can ugly women be faithful? Is it really being faithful if nobody else wants you?*" She snaps back to her normal voice. "Real asshole, right? But he had a point. The same principle applies to you, Edie. Are you better than us for avoiding temptation, or is it just that you've never been tempted?"

I can feel the others' eyes on me. "It hasn't always been easy for me to follow the rules," I say quietly.

Ana shrugs one shoulder. "If you say so." Light and mocking.

"Just today," I say, "there was a client who came to me wanting to contact a murder victim. The body they found in that subdivision. Hopeful Doe."

They're all silent for a minute, the words settling into their brains. I notice the piercing-scarred girl looking at each of us in turn, trying to piece together what her reaction should be.

"Seriously?" Ana asks. "One got past Renard. It's been a few months since the last attempt."

"Candace Fowler," I say. "I nearly couldn't convince her to leave."

"What did she want?" the older woman asks. "Jane told me about a man who thought the Black Dahlia was his soul mate. Was she one of them? Gets all weird about a murdered kid on the news, comes here hoping to be a surrogate mommy?"

"No, no," I say. "More straightforward than that. She wanted to solve the case."

"Ah, detective fantasies," the woman says sagely. "Should have guessed."

"It's too bad," Dora says. "That poor girl." When she catches my eyes on her, she goes on: "I know it's against the rules, but you could have helped her."

"It would have been much too dangerous," I say.

"Where's your sense of adventure, Edie?" Ana asks, a needle glinting in her voice.

"So what would you have done?" I ask her.

"If she came to me?" Ana crushes the cigarette, grinding it against the vent's metal rim. Then she flicks the butt down into the darkness. I see the tiny contrail of the dying embers for a second. "Who knows. You're right. It'd probably be too risky to work with her here."

When she rises, the others follow her lead; the older woman drifts away. I stay seated, my skirt twisted around my thighs. I'd nearly forgotten how Ana can make me into the odd one out. How easily she can tease my awkwardness and stiffness to the surface.

I'll see him again in five days. The thought is suddenly and deeply comforting.

"One word of warning," Ana says. I look up to find that her eyes have softened. "Everything in moderation. You pour too much time and energy into a job like this, and you may as well be a ghost yourself."

SIX

The sensation of Sylvia's presence is there and gone, like catching a shadowy movement from the corner of my eye. I'm brushing my teeth. I blink, and my reflection is a stranger's; blink again and I'm myself. I'm washing a dish and my hands suddenly are not my own. They're too large, chapped and pink. I soothe myself by identifying the freckle near the base of my thumb.

Small moments. Easy to justify and ignore.

Still, I think of Thisbe. Ana's mention of her, that day, has excavated a whole string of details from the depths of my memory, detritus snagged in a trawling net.

Thisbe wasn't remarkable. A body with mouse-blond hair. Pretty in an accommodating way, features transforming with a shift of the light. I saw her with Ana sometimes, the two of them in the waiting room, heads bent together. I knew Thisbe wouldn't last long. There was a neediness to her that marred her otherwise smooth surface. Once I came across her crying in the restroom. She'd looked up without seeing me, her eyes glossy and raw-rimmed.

At the time, I'd wanted to tell her that she should leave her personal problems at home. Instead, I'd walked out, allowing her the space to collect herself. And when she quit the Elysian Society days later, I remembered that moment and I wasn't surprised by her departure.

The rumors started after she'd been gone for several weeks.

Gossip at the Elysian Society comes in sudden bursts, every few months. Curiosity and boredom attaching randomly to whichever body had left most recently. Thisbe's story was fairly tame. Someone had seen her standing in front of the restroom mirror, tugging at her cheeks and her forehead as if they weren't her own. As if she could remove a mask.

The rumor lost momentum quickly. Now, though, I think of Thisbe plucking at her skin. This could be how it started for her. Not with a cold finger against her spine or a clawed shadow along the wall, but with something as warm and inviting as what I feel when I think of Patrick.

We have to stop meeting like this."

It's the third time we've sat together in Room 12. Today, I allow myself the luxury of taking time to notice the details. The automatic pose Patrick assumes. Knees open, arms crossed. Guarded at the heart. The clothes he favors: button-ups, scuffed loafers, the expensiveness suggested through simple lines.

"It's a joke," Patrick says when I don't respond. "It's OK to laugh."

I smile a second too late. "Do you have a message for your wife, Mr. Braddock?"

"I thought we could talk about you."

A spike of dread. "If there's an issue with my performance, the Elysian Society would be happy to help you find a replacement—"

"God, no," he says. My heart swims with gratitude. "It's unfair, you knowing about me when I don't know anything about you. So." Patrick stretches a hand toward me. "Tell me about yourself."

I cross my legs and uncross them.

"It doesn't have to be about you," Patrick says, voice gentler now. "That's against protocol here, isn't it? It can be about anything."

Still, my mind slips across a bare expanse. I don't know how to have a normal conversation anymore. All the small similarities, the details and experiences, that other people use to build connections: these don't exist in the life I've created.

Then my mind lands on a topic, and I'm so thankful I speak without thinking. "What do you think of Hopeful Doe?"

"Think of her?"

I've said the wrong thing. Patrick's brows are drawn together, his lips still holding a smile, as if he can't tell whether to go along with a joke or take offense.

"Well," he says at last, measured. "It's terrible to lose a life so young."

I want to pluck my words out of the air, slide them back between my lips. It must haunt him to see Hopeful Doe's face splayed across the news. I've committed the unforgivable sin at the Elysian Society. Bringing grief into the room when I'm supposed to banish it.

"When Sylvia passed, it ended up in the news," Patrick says. "Maybe you noticed."

"I don't really recall," I say carefully. Now it seems like a betrayal that I ever could have dismissed Sylvia Braddock as a stranger, changed the channel to a more interesting death.

"I was lucky," he says. "It was kept pretty quiet. But any death that attracts attention—it's hell, when you're on the inside. Dealing with your pain while everyone has their face pressed against the glass."

"You must be grateful you had friends with you that weekend," I say.

"Friends?" he repeats.

"The couple at the lake."

"The Damsons, you mean?" he asks after a second. "They weren't much help. They tried, but they were caught in the middle of it. Viv was seeing a grief counselor before I was."

I put the name together in my head: Viv Damson. It's glanc-ingly familiar, like the name of a childhood classmate or a neigh-bor I scarcely knew.

"Every time there's something like this," Patrick says, "I re-member what it was like. It took away my appetite for these things."

"But Hopeful Doe's loss is nothing like your wife's."

Again, I've said exactly the wrong thing. His eyes shut off to me. Room 12 seems to expand, growing airier and colder. An impersonal space, edging us further apart.

"Mr. Braddock, I'm sorry," I say impulsively. "Can we start over?"

It takes a moment. Then Patrick's posture relaxes. He looks up at me again, face cautiously brighter. "Well, you don't get that chance often," he says. "You should take it when you can."

"I was hoping for one more snow," I say, "before the warm weather arrives." It's a bland observation, insignificant. But the words feel right, warming the room like a flame.

Patrick smiles. "I'm with you."

I take a deep breath, radiant with relief.

"Winter is a tough sell," Patrick says. "Nobody wants to see fall end, or spring. Summer gets its share of mourners. But winter, it's just—" A shrug. "Gone. No backward glances."

"I've always loved winter," I say.

"It's the most private time of year," he says. "Everyone stays indoors, focuses on their own pursuits. Maybe that's why we like it." He gestures between us. "Winter makes it easier to pass un-noticed as an introvert."

The way he says *we*, that easy bringing together, swells inside me. He's recognized me, gathered me onto his side. I feel the di-vision split across my understanding of my place in the world: the two of us and then everyone else. A swift, perfect fracture.

"Shall we begin?" I ask.

make a conscious effort to perform well with my other clients. Sylvia's dark lipstick stands in my own medicine cabinet, a contrast to my utilitarian lineup of painkillers, eye drops. Spurred by guilt over how much space she occupies in my mind, I review the files and photos of my clients' loved ones.

Bethany, who died in an accident, drunk behind the wheel. Her older sister, Mary, agreed to buy alcohol for Bethany's Sweet Sixteen. Bethany stayed in a coma for a year between the accident and her death. Since then, her sister has slowly withdrawn from the family. As far as I can tell, Bethany is the only relative Mary talks to anymore.

Elinor, whose grown son found any excuse to avoid visiting his mother in her nursing home. He sees Elinor once a month, like clockwork, now that she's tucked safely in the family plot.

Tracey, who died pedaling her bike along an overpass on her way to visit her best friend. Her black T-shirt blended with the dusk, so the teenage driver of a 1983 Camaro didn't see her when Tracey swerved to make a left turn. The driver of the Camaro and Tracey's best friend eventually married, their shared guilt merging into something close enough to love.

I'm grateful for the chance to lose myself in the weight of the routine. Downing the lotus over and over, surfacing like a swimmer for a bracing breath of my own body before I submerge again.

At home, that's when I'm unguarded. That's when it happens with increasing frequency. It's more than physical. Not recognizing my own face in the mirror is a discrepancy I could grow used to, over time. I haven't belonged to myself for years; working at the Elysian Society, I see my body as an object on permanent loan. A door without a lock.

But it's more than that. One evening, I catch sight of a plum on the counter, big as a child's fist and grayish-red. I want to laugh. It's an instinctive catch in my brain, the lingering memory of a long-ago inside joke. But I don't have a punch line. Every time I see the plum, I have to fight back someone else's laughter. Finally, I throw it away.

Kneading my hair during a shower one night, I become aware that I'm touching a stranger's body. As limp and heavy as an animal's stripped pelt. A corpse's hair.

Unlike the other impressions, this one doesn't fade quickly. I leave the shower and lie, soaking, beneath the covers, keeping my body distinct and separate. No part touching any other. I want to reach for a zipper and pull at the nape of my neck to step out cleanly.

it's not yours

nothing here is yours

Hours pass before I feel secure inside my flesh again. I've left the shower running and the water bites at my hand when I turn off the faucet, cold enough to yank my breath from my lungs.

Following a long winter, the weather hurries to catch up. It's April, the heat of each day an exploring touch. Flowers burst frantically in spots where I'd forgotten flowers ever grew. Buds appear along branches one evening and expand into blossoms the next. Everything smells like dark, loamy soil.

The whole city seems energized. A memorial sprouts at an intersection not far from the Elysian Society. A floral arrangement shaped like a heart, propped next to a plywood cross. Painted across the cross's center beam: WE PRAY FOR YOU HOPEFULL DOE. "It's as if nobody ever died in this city before," Ana says, coming into the waiting room, full of pleased disgust.

I've just returned from meeting with a client. The nickel plating of his wife's pendant leaves a nagging itch on my skin.

Ana hesitates before she moves toward me. "What are your plans for this weekend?"

I'm silent, trying to figure out her angle.

"I'm sure you'll be up to something amazing," she says. "Sky-diving. Meeting strangers for weird sex. It's always the quiet ones who are trouble."

"Do you need something, Ana?" I ask.

She plucks at a stray hangnail. "On the off chance that you're free this weekend, you could come out with us." Ana speaks carelessly, but I catch a shift in her expression: a faint rise of color that turns her vulnerable.

"Why would I do that?" I say it before I can stop myself.

"It's my birthday."

This takes me aback; I can't remember the last time I acknowledged my birthday. It's become a string of numbers. Rote identification, no more meaningful than my thumbprints.

"Your boyfriend's going to be there," Ana goes on.

My heart stutters. "I don't know what you're talking about."

"Oh, sure you do." Ana lowers her voice. "Leander?"

"Nothing's happening between us."

"Yeah, yeah, you'd never stoop to a workplace affair. But he never shuts up about you." She prods the inside of her cheek with her tongue. "You two would be a good match."

"Who else will be there?" I ask, not taking the bait.

"Your little protégée. Dora. I invited her along so you'd have someone to talk to. See what I'm willing to do for you?"

I'm scarcely listening. A body has just entered the waiting room, carrying an aura of some musky cologne. A pungent, leathery smell. As the scent seeps into my nostrils, I'm tense with lust. I'm engulfed in the warmth of breath against my neck, the sweat on Patrick's skin.

"When are you meeting?" I ask Ana.

"I figured about nine, Friday," she says. "Nice and early."

"Maybe I'll be there," I say.

She grins. "Well, well," she says. "I'm glad you've had a change of heart."

want to tell her that I'm still in love with her."

The man across from me, Kenneth O'Brien, is a new client. He's handsome in a tentative way that could go to seed at any moment.

"There might be a miscommunication, Mr. O'Brien," I say. "You're here to contact Margaret Ross?"

Pinkish bull's-eyes stand out on his cheeks, but his eye contact is so fixed, it's reckless. "That's correct," he says.

"The forms suggest you're still married. To a Lindsey O'Brien."

He's been married for four years. In half the photos that show him and Margaret together, Mr. O'Brien's wife is also present, a cheerful, sturdy blonde to Margaret's sharp-boned frame. Four months ago, Margaret Ross died in her sleep from an undiagnosed heart problem. Though Mr. O'Brien's report doesn't corroborate anything, slipping past the question with eyes averted, I study Margaret's bird-wing elbows and the visible bones in her chest. And I wonder.

"I never told her how I felt," Mr. O'Brien says. "There was never a good time. She was with somebody, I was with somebody. I married Lindsey while Margaret was in a relationship that seemed to be going somewhere. Why put my life on hold? And I love Lindsey. She's a wonderful woman." He looks at me accusingly.

"Of course," I say.

"She thinks I'm at therapy. Lindsey's been so understanding since Margaret died." Mr. O'Brien fidgets, twists his watch around his wrist, and then falls into stillness. "I used to think: What will I do if something happens and I've never told her?

I tortured myself, imagining if I never got up the nerve to say anything." Mr. O'Brien clasps his hands together. "But I couldn't hurt Lindsey like that."

Pain slices at the edges of my careful blankness. Shockingly sharp yet small, like a wasp sting or a paper cut.

"That's all I could think, when I got the call," he says. "I thought, I have to tell her. I better tell her, before it's too late."

"Mr. O'Brien," I say. He looks up at me, eyes blunt and clouded. "The Elysian Society exists so that you'll always have time to say these things."

He considers this. "You think I'm a terrible person, don't you?"

"I can promise you that I don't." I reach for the lotus. "Shall we begin?"

SEVEN

A familiar voice rises from a sea of strangers' bodies and turbu-lent music. Calling my name.

I move through the gloom. Cigarette smoke and colognes create a cloud in the orange lighting. Women in clinging tops, variations on the same style, line up at the bar, slouching backs jutting in waves. A few people turn, their gazes slipping off me.

"You made it," Lee says when I arrive at the table.

For a second, I think I've taken a seat among strangers. Ev-eryone looks so different out of the Elysian Society uniforms, bareness replaced with markers of individuality that seem embar-rassingly intimate. Ana's halter top is low-cut, her eyes doubled in size with shaded layers of makeup. Dora, across the table from me, has her hair down in a soft mass of curls.

Ana has been talking to a body I know only vaguely, a younger man with close-cropped hair, but she cranes around at the scrape of my chair. Her face is feverishly rosy. "Oh my God," she says. "You have to be fucking kidding me. Are you still wearing your uniform?"

"I couldn't. . . ." I start, but I don't have anything to say, and I'm sinking with panic.

She laughs. "I would have told you not to wear it, but I thought you'd *know*. Jesus, Edie. Don't you own any other clothes?"

"All right, all right," Lee says. "It's an honest mistake."

Ana turns away, biting back a smile.

I clutch uselessly at the front of the white dress.

"You look fine, you always do," Lee says. "Look, can I get you anything? A beer?"

"Thank you," I say. When he rises to make his way to the bar, his knee presses against mine. I pull back quickly; Lee murmurs an apology.

Patrick's knee against mine. I glance around the bar, as if he might be sitting at a corner table, waiting to approach. I hold my breath until I'm satisfied that he isn't. Of course not. But in my mind Patrick's everywhere, the whole world suffused with the thrilling prospect of him.

Dora leans toward me. Without meaning to, I stare at the sweat-shiny hollow between her breasts. "Would you like my shrug?" She doesn't wait for an answer, already wriggling her arms loose. I take the sweater, touched at the ease of her offer. It's wrong for me, sheer and crimson, sparkling threads woven throughout.

"Red looks great on you," Dora says. She's using that magnanimous tone that pretty women use with plainer ones. I don't mind. "You should wear bright colors more often."

"Well, I don't have many chances to dress up," I demur.

"Yeah, I didn't bring much along," Dora says. "I'm sick of wearing the same stuff every day. Maybe we could go shopping?"

"Maybe," I say after a surprised second. I can't tell whether this suggestion is an overture of friendship or an attempt to draw a favor from me.

"I don't know the city yet," Dora says. "I thought I'd have time to explore, get out and meet people. But this is the first time I've done anything outside of work. Pretty sad, huh?"

Lee returns. The glass he places in front of me brims with a deep, clear yellow. I take several long drinks, the beer settling in my belly.

"How are you finding the work so far?" I ask Dora.

She pulls her mouth to one side, glances up at the ceiling. "Oh. Fine. I guess. My roommate left. She'd only been there a week and then I wake up today and all her stuff is gone." She closes her fingers and then opens them, like a magician revealing a dramatic absence. "She's just vanished."

"That's typical," Lee says. "Plenty of people find that the work isn't for them. It helps to have certain personality traits."

Ana's been shooting glances at us. Now she leans over the table to address Dora. "What you want is to be like her"—and Ana stabs a finger at me—"and have no attachment to anything. Or anyone. Be a recluse. A nun."

The beer lodges in my throat like a burble of laughter.

"That's what Lee really meant," Ana continues. "He's too nice to say it."

"I didn't mean that," Lee says.

Ana stands, touching the tabletop with her fingers for support. "I'll be back. Don't talk about anything interesting while I'm gone." In motion, she's lithe and sparkling. Men's eyes track her openly.

"Renard said something," Dora says. I turn back to her. "At the end of my interview, she said she could tell when people had something special. And she thought I had it." With her hair down, Dora is achingly young. "But she probably says that to everyone." She's trying for a joking tone; I catch a twinge of wistfulness.

"Not to me," Lee says, good-natured.

I hesitate for a long moment. A memory of the first time I stood in Mrs. Renard's office works its way through my brain. "I can't remember."

"I'd take it as a compliment," Lee says to her.

Dora grins at him. Her drink is neon, fading into the surrounding ice. When she lowers her glass, she licks her lips, unselfconscious. "Most of my clients aren't so bad," she says. "I thought they might be weirdos. Spooky? But a lot of them are sweet. They just want to talk to their daughters again."

"I can see you being a daughter," Lee says.

Ana leans against the bar, arranged so that her breasts and hips are pointed at the room. She talks over her shoulder at the bartender, and she and I notice at the same time when a man detaches from his table and comes to stand in front of her.

"Are you a mother?" Dora asks.

I realize she's talking to me. I'm overtaken by a dense chill that rises, separating me from everyone else here. Muting the lights like a finger pinched over a flame, pressing down the voices and music so that they turn meaningless.

gone, all gone

Then I force myself to focus; the world pops back into clarity. "Only sometimes," I say. "I'm a wife. Not always, but usually." I wonder if I'm blushing. Absurdly, I want to talk about him. "One of my best clients right now is contacting his wife of six years. She drowned at Lake Madeleine."

Dora makes a murmur of dutiful sympathy, but it's Lee who looks at me. "Wait," he says. "Lake Madeleine? I know who you're talking about."

"I don't think so," I say.

Lee points at me, squints. "She was named, um, Celia? Or no, don't tell me." He holds up a palm. "Sylvia? Sylvia sounds right." My scalp prickles. "I remember when that happened. I followed it for a while."

"It was on the news?" Dora asks.

"Briefly," Lee says. "As I recall, the question was whether he'd sue the resort where it happened. For negligence. There was some issue about whether the wife drowned because of fault on their part. Not marking the dangerous areas of the lake. But then the whole thing vanished. I assume they settled out of court."

Patrick never mentioned this. A sense of betrayal plummets

through me, stone heavy, as I realize that he's kept aspects of his wife's death cloaked from me.

A noise grabs at my attention. A sharp lift of voices. When I glance over, Ana stands with her arms wound across her chest. The stranger leans over her, his hand gripping the bar. He's taller than her by a foot. Through his unseasonable winter coat, his frame suggests a restless energy.

"The husband is an attorney," Lee is saying. "I wonder how he's holding up." His eyes twitch toward me. "Not too well, I'm guessing."

I've been drinking steadily. Everything is starting to feel tilted, flat, like a picture held up at the wrong angle. "Do you know who that is?" I ask Lee, gesturing at the bar. "One of Ana's clients?"

Reluctant, he follows my gaze. "I doubt it," he says. "We choose this bar because we won't run into clients."

Ana's moving back to the table now, the stranger following in her wake. He reaches out to touch the small of her back. Her expression is hectic, brilliant and tense as a live wire.

"Edie." I turn to Lee. His eyes are serious, his face close to mine. His breath is warm against my neck; the finest curl of steam from a cup. "If I'm right about who your client is, he shouldn't be coming to the Elysian Society," he says, low in my ear.

"Why's that?" I ask.

But Lee leans back, his expression growing formal again. Ana has reached the table. Behind her, the stranger doesn't try to hide his stare. His eyes linger on Dora. He's middle-aged, roughly handsome. There's an arrogance in his face: he's smiling like someone who's figured out a secret.

"All of them—?" he asks Ana, nearly too low to catch.

Ana ignores him. "So, something's come up," she says. "I know, I'm a flake. The rest of you should stay. Have fun. God knows we all could use a drink."

I'm fixated on the stranger's hand on her elbow. The easy possessiveness of the gesture.

"Your friends can come with us," the man says. "I don't mind." His gaze has shifted to me. His eyes are watery, threaded with pinkish veins. "Don't I know you?" he asks me.

Ana laughs. "Her? No. Rob, nobody knows her. She never leaves her house."

"No," he says. "I'm serious. You look so goddamn familiar."

I don't panic. Keeping my expression blank, I slide through the faces in my memory. The ones I've allowed to grow dust-blurred and indistinct. Even after I erase five years from the stranger's face, he stays opaque. I don't know him. My stomach unclenches with relief.

"Don't tease her," Ana says. She tugs at his sleeve. "Let's get out of here."

When they're gone, the rest of us sit in an uncertain silence. I can tell that Lee is waiting for an opportunity to return to our conversation, his patience like a soft itch. Suddenly, I can't breathe. The room is overwhelming, the throb of music, the overlapping scents of a dozen bodies. Through the window, I still see Ana's black smudge of hair.

"I should be going too." I ignore Lee's open disappointment, not letting myself meet his eyes as I say good-bye.

Tipsy, I see the bar as an obstacle course. Bodies perched on stools, bodies swaying next to tables, bodies peering into their phone screens. All I can think is how strange they are. So solitary, occupied by one heart. One mind, eating itself like a snake devouring its tail. These other people seem so lonely that I can't bear it, and then a man pushes against my elbow, roughly enough that I'm not sure he sees me, and I'm less than one. A sliver of a person.

Outside on the sidewalk, the damp night air brings me back. Ana lights a cigarette, her hand curled protectively around the flame. When she turns to me, her expression is both defiant and sheepish. A child expecting a scolding.

"He's just pulling the car around," she says, breathing out a tendril of smoke.

"You work with him?" I ask.

"Not exactly." Ana stares across the street, as if she's addressing somebody else and I happen to be nearby. "It doesn't have any-thing to do with the Elysian Society, OK? It's my own shit." She waves the smoke away with a graceful gesture. "I know it must be hard for you to imagine having a life outside of that place, but some of us do."

Ana has held other work over the years. I assume that's why she vanishes periodically, returning like a cat wandering home after accepting food on strange porches. It's always made me uneasy to know that the Elysian Society is just a job to her, no better or worse than any other. Looking at the exposed curve of her breasts, think-ing of the stranger's hand on her elbow, I wonder what her other work entails.

It must show on my face. "It's not what you think, Edie," Ana says.

"I know." I speak too fast.

Ana taps her cigarette. The tip falls to the sidewalk and fades into the asphalt. "Well, I'm glad you came tonight," she says. "I'm sorry if it wasn't as exciting as you thought it would be. Or if it was too exciting." She smiles, wry. "What were you talking about while I was gone? Anything interesting?"

"No," I say, and mirror her smile. "Not really."

A car pulls up along the curb. Expensive and silvery, all low angles, windows so shadowed that I can't see the driver. Without looking at me again, Ana slips inside the car. I catch a flash of her tight smile, the particular mix of blankness and brilliance, like the filament at the heart of a bulb.

EIGHT

At home, I can't relax. I'm oversaturated: the alcohol, the conversations, the other eyes on me. Without the pattern of the Elysian Society, the outside world is unmoored. Anybody could say anything, do anything. It's a constant undercurrent of chaos, one that everyone else is strangely capable of ignoring.

Even before I became a body, I could feel it where other people couldn't. The unpredictability that lapped at the edges of our lives, threatening to suck us under. The Elysian Society has given this fear a structure. Funneled it into a framework of routine, allowing me to step outside myself and become a silent bystander to other people's grief.

I was twenty-five years old when I began work as a body. Now I feel as if I haven't aged, as if the world has continued on without me. I understand what people mean when they talk about spinsters or old maids. Women whose hearts are suspended in time, locked safely behind glass like museum artifacts.

Five years ago, this is exactly what I wanted.

I gaze around my apartment with the dismissive eyes of a stranger. All my furniture is cheap and hastily constructed, like displays in a store. It gives off the impression of sturdiness, but looking too closely reveals the peeling veneers. One half of my living room houses boxes and a small filing cabinet. All the files and photos I've collected from clients. Their memories crowd out my own.

This was originally an improvement. It was only after a year of work that I rented my own apartment. All the upgrades I've made to my life since then have been in a similar vein. A used car instead of a bus pass, a plain winter coat to replace one coming apart at the seams. My life is neat, self-contained. A serviceable life. A placeholder.

Tonight, the silence feels like a force that could smother me. A pillow held over my face.

I sit in my car, twenty minutes from my apartment. I'm parked on a shadowy corner.

Across the street, a small café is still open. A young woman with dark hair bends attentively over her phone. Next to the café, a bookstore is already closed for the night, silhouettes of the shelves visible beyond the darkness. And there's the doorway I'm watching, tucked into a row of townhomes. Long staircase, looping wrought iron railing. A plaque gleams on the wall outside the entrance, a glint in the shadows. CASTLE & CLARK LLP.

The neighborhood sits within an unpredictable system of locked gates, homes surrounded by elaborate gardens and deep-set porches, like guests at a party who wish to be admired but not approached. I've passed through this area occasionally. Maybe that's why this location came to me so quickly after Lee mentioned it at the bar.

I shut my eyes. She waits inside my eyelids. Sylvia, nimble and immaculate as she greets her husband after work. Her black hair is pulled back, revealing a ballerina's neck.

he doesn't love me anymore

I open my eyes. As if conjured by dark magic, Patrick stands across the street, his back to me as he locks the door. His hair is a shade too long at the nape of his neck, a cowlick that's absurdly vulnerable. A child without a mother to tend to him.

Somewhere behind me, a shattering of glass breaks the silence. I turn my head. A green-aproned waiter from a restaurant across the street is emptying a cascade of bottles into the trash.

When I turn back, Patrick has stopped. He's looking at me. In the diffused light of the street lamps, his face is as indistinct as if I'm viewing him on a grainy screen. I must glow through the darkness. My white dress, my colorless hair. I can't move. His eyes on me shove me backward, hold me in place like a physical restraint. Hands on my shoulders.

look at me

Then Patrick moves on, head ducked, until he turns a corner and is lost.

When I start toward home, my mind is so razed that I can barely find my way. I can't stop imagining what would have happened if I'd stepped out of the car, if I'd called out. Part of me thrills at the idea.

Still. Still. Outside Room 12, a man like Patrick Braddock would never notice a woman like me.

was instructed to wear a simple outfit when I interviewed at the Elysian Society. Nothing formal. Nothing flashy, no distracting accessories. In the motel mirror, I scrubbed my face pink and pulled my hair into a damp ponytail.

My outfit was the best I could do with what I'd salvaged from my life. White T-shirt, tea-colored skirt. Approaching the Elysian Society building for the first time with my naked face, I was embarrassed. Back then, it was rare for me to leave the house without makeup.

Mrs. Renard didn't ask me to sit down. I stood in the middle of the office, clasping my hands in front of me. Without any distractions, I was strangely conscious of my body. The submerged thump of my heart. My soles pressed to the floor.

"You're not from around here?" Mrs. Renard had asked finally.

"No," I said.

"But you have family or friends in this area?"

"I only moved here a week ago."

"You moved alone? Are you married, in a relationship?" She paused. "Children?"

I hesitated. "I'm single at the moment."

"At the moment," she repeated. "But you'd like to meet someone." Her tone shifted into a gossipy lightness, with an edge to it. A piece of shiny foil with a sharp tip.

"I prefer to be on my own," I said.

A lift of her eyebrows. "That's a rare trait in a girl your age. Refreshing."

Not sure how to acknowledge this, I'd merely nodded.

"You might find these questions invasive for a job interview," Mrs. Renard had said.

The truth was that I hadn't noticed. In my raw state, I felt it was only natural for someone to rummage through my past.

"You'll forgive me for the question I'm about to ask," Mrs. Renard said. "Have you experienced much loss?"

I'd looked at the floor: the frantic pattern on the rug. The embellishments rising like vines, wrapping around my ankles and legs, pulling me down beneath the surface of the floor.

"Young lady." When I lifted my gaze, I found that Mrs. Renard's demeanor had softened. Her eyes on me were forgiving; I could abandon my secrets to her, toss my sins into her like coins into a well. "This room is private," she'd said. "Nothing leaves these walls."

And so I told her everything. I felt each admission rise off my tongue and leave me lighter, cleaner. The melancholy slant of the afternoon light through the window burned on my skin. When I finished, I was scraped hollow.

"You know what we do here?" Mrs. Renard had asked.

"Yes," I said. "I know."

"It doesn't frighten you, the idea of other people speaking through your mouth? The idea of your hands moving when you're not there?"

I glanced down at my hands, imagining them jerked into motion without my consent. After the past few months, my skin was parched and blanched, like something tucked away from the sunlight for decades. The bones at my wrist jutted painfully.

"No," I'd said. "Not at all."

"Perhaps it should frighten you. It frightens most people." She'd flicked her eyes up and down the length of me. "Why doesn't it worry you?"

Pulled along by the momentum of my confession, I told her. I told her that I sometimes forgot my body was even there. That there were other, harder days when I wanted nothing more than to ignore it and yet felt trapped inside it. If my body could become a useful thing to people who needed it, then I wouldn't refuse.

"Selfless," Mrs. Renard had said. Not with admiration or approval, but as if she was applying a label. "I think you'll do well here."

Passing through the parking lot afterward, I saw an older couple, their eyes pink and tight from crying. The man helped the woman into the passenger's side. They turned their heads at the sound of my footsteps. Their gazes slipped right across me. Already, I felt invincible. My naked face a perfect mask.

brought this for you." Patrick smiles like a date with a box of heart-shaped chocolates.

The box is surprisingly heavy as I settle it on my lap. I can't remember the last time I opened a gift. Lifting the lid, I stare down at the bright jumble of objects. The hard twinkle of earrings against a lacy and translucent scrap of silk. A box filled to the brim with romantic gifts. More than romantic: intimate.

"I thought you could wear some of them," Patrick says. "During our encounters."

I'm gazing at a perfume bottle shaped like a faceted heart. The bottle is nearly empty, just a centimeter of liquid resting at the bottom of the frosted glass. All the signs of use spring into focus. Long, dark hairs caught in the teeth of a tortoiseshell comb, the fingerprints milky on the surface of a powder compact mirror.

My stomach lurches. I shut the lid too fast.

Patrick reaches out his hand and places it on top of the box. His fingers are next to mine. The space separating our bare flesh is only the length of a discarded eyelash. Heat hangs shimmering between us.

I move my finger. I have enough time to register the warmth of his skin, the pinch of his wedding band, before I take a firmer grip on the box and shift it over to the table.

Patrick withdraws, settling in his chair. "Will you still wear the lipstick, though?"

"If you want me to, Mr. Braddock," I say.

"It looks good on you."

This close, Patrick's eyes are green, run through with streaks of a brown pale enough to be gold. I'm flooded with a sense of belonging as deep as a physical embrace.

It's the way he's looking at me. Even my kindest clients have a certain manner of meeting my eyes, before or after encounters. It still stands out to me sometimes. The sensation of being looked at so searchingly, vacillating between familiarity and disappointment. Just waiting for me to become somebody else. And for years, I've accepted it. Wanted it.

Patrick, though. Today, Patrick looks at me as if I'm right here in front of him. As if he sees a person who is already whole and complete.

Every inch of my body alive with warmth, I reach for the lotus. "Shall we begin, Mr. Braddock?"

t's not until late at night that I examine the contents of the box more closely, swirling my fingers through the salvaged remnants of Sylvia's life.

Earrings. Princess-cut emeralds dangling from slim posts. The bottom of the box is lined with a sharp clutter of loose bobby pins, dark ones that would stand out in my blond hair like surgical scars.

The most confusing item is a small piece of clear plastic, curved like a crescent moon. It takes me a moment to realize that it's an orthodontic retainer. A perfect mold of Sylvia's top row of teeth. I hold the retainer on my flat palm, studying the whitish crust that collects along the ridge of the inverted molars. A musty smell floats up, like sour milk. Proof that Sylvia once possessed a living, breathing, imperfect body, complete with parts that secreted and leaked.

I imagine Patrick walking through the silent rooms of his house, collecting Sylvia from the corners of their life. Some clients have a hard time entrusting their loved ones' belongings to me, even for half an hour. Other clients can't seem to give away enough. They ply me with mothball-scented sweaters, sneakers with dirt still caught in the cleats. They give me items that I can't use during encounters. Old toothbrushes and combs, favorite stuffed animals. It's possible that Patrick has donated Sylvia's dresses to charity and distributed her favorite books among grieving family members. Maybe I'm another way of clearing space.

Or maybe I'm his way of returning his wife's belongings, the fussy things he never quite understood, to their rightful owner. That relentless ghost in the story, grasping for the material ruins of her body.

Give me my bone.

I can't remember how that story ends, I think, falling into sleep. I can't remember whether it was the woman or the ghost who won in the end.

On Tuesday evening, I'm drained completely. My last client of the day was Abilene Osgood, a woman who lost her fifteen-year-old daughter. Most of my clients compose themselves by the time I return. After encounters, they're calmer than when they arrived. With Mrs. Osgood, I wake to find her face still twisted with such raw and private grief that I'm ashamed to witness it. She looks at me as if I'm the invading spirit in her child's body.

When I enter my apartment tonight, there's a buzzing. By the time I locate my phone on the kitchen table, the screen shows that I've missed five calls. I don't recognize the number.

As if sensing my presence, the phone vibrates to life in my hand.

I answer immediately. "Hello?"

"Jesus. I was getting desperate."

"Ana?"

"I need a favor."

A hard plummet into disappointment that it's her voice and not his. But I listen. "You have every right to say no." Her words are tight and clipped. "Could you come get me? I don't have money for a cab."

I follow the hasty directions Ana gives me, looking for Apple Blossom Inn. The name is discordantly quaint for the part of town I'm driving through. An area near the freeways. The overpass in the distance holds a glittering procession of headlights. I pass squat, windowless buildings with sagging fences.

The sign for the Apple Blossom Inn is partially lit against the dusk, fluorescent strips visible through the plastic shell. SSOM INN. I pull into the parking lot. The hotel is a row of rooms angled like an L around the lot.

A door across from me bursts open and Ana comes out. She moves quickly, head down, as if shouldering through a crowd of people.

Through the door that Ana left hanging open, there's a visible wedge of rumpled bedspread. A shadow fills the doorway. The stranger from the bar. He follows her at a more leisurely pace. There's a stark contrast between their bodies, urgency versus calmness. It creates the impression that they've been pasted into the wrong frame together, spliced from different scenes.

I reach across to open the passenger-side door. Ana slides in, muggy with perfume and sweat. I'm so used to her subdued scent at the Elysian Society that I'm startled more by her smell than by the bandage-tight dress that winds around her body.

"Let's go," she says.

But the stranger has come to the driver-side window. With the glass between us, I'm like a caged animal. His presence seems oddly amplified by the thin layer between us.

"She your replacement?" he asks Ana. "Not bad."

"Ignore him," Ana says.

"Hey, it came to me, Blondie," he says, voice muffled. "I know who you remind me of. That girl. The one on the news all the damn time."

My heart drops, but I keep looking at him. He holds my gaze through the shell of the window. Then he laughs and turns away, shaking his head.

"Just go," Ana hisses.

I pull away, glancing in the mirror to look behind. He stands in the parking lot, stock-still and unperturbed.

"He was at the bar that night," I say, losing sight of the inn's sign.

"Oh, very good," Ana says. "Gold star for you."

She's so diminished that her sarcasm has lost its bite. "Where do you live?" I ask.

"Poplar." She sighs. "This will sound crazy, but . . . can I stay with you?" She worries at a fingernail. "I don't want to be alone."

"You're welcome to stay," I say, hiding my surprise.

"Look, I'm sorry I called," Ana says after a few moments. We're passing one of the city's hulking industrial buildings, its sides embroidered with ivy. "You're the only person I could think of who'd come. Everyone else has their own shit to deal with."

"How did you get my number?" I ask.

"I have my ways." She sighs, shifts. She's starting to look more relaxed; she sinks back in her seat. "God, what a creep, saying that to you. I'm sorry, Edie."

When I unlock the door to my apartment, Ana pushes past me. I hang back, as nervous as if I'm the visitor. In the twilight, the apartment is pitiful, but Ana doesn't seem to care. She sits on the couch. Grabbing the remote, she lands on a local talk show where the host leans forward to address the audience, face contorted with sympathy.

"I'll get blankets," I say.

I return a few minutes later to find the TV muted. When I pause in the doorway, Ana turns her palm toward me. "Friend of yours?"

It's a photo of Sylvia, her arm around Patrick, staring directly, too directly, into the camera. Daring me to speak the truth.

"No." I drop the blankets on the end table, reach out my hand. "Just a client's wife."

Ana ignores me. "She was pretty. A little thin for my taste."

"Please, Ana," I say, and she surrenders the photo to me. I clutch it to my chest protectively, as if I can defend Sylvia from Ana's glib appraisal.

"You know, I should apologize," Ana says, watching me. "I was wrong about you."

"How so?"

"You care about your clients."

Not sure what to say, I nod tersely.

"And I care too." Her voice takes on a cautiousness that reminds me of an adult bargaining with a child. "That's why you and I are more alike than you realize. I just go a little further." She brings one knee up to her chest, revealing a comma of underwear. "Rob was a client at the Elysian Society. He stopped coming maybe six months ago. I got in touch with him. We started working together on our own time."

On the TV screen, a man with a loopy grin sits between two women with identical teased hairstyles. *WOULD YOU GIVE A CHEATER A SECOND CHANCE?*

"God, Edie," Ana says. "Are you playing dumb to make me spell it out for you? You must know. You've been with the Elysian Society forever." She sighs. "I do what we do at the Elysian Society, except that my clients get something more. They get what they really want when they come to see their wives and girlfriends."

"You sleep with them." I want to say it out loud.

"Don't use that tone," Ana says, though my voice was flat. "It's not much different than what everyone does. You ever fantasize about somebody else while you're in bed? Imagine you're with some hot stranger, your cute neighbor. Turn the body you're with into a placeholder. Well—" She smiles dryly. "I'm sure *you'd* never do that. But we mortals do it all the time."

I don't rise to Ana's swift jab. Her argument has the feeling of a justification she's repeated in her own head.

"Really, I wonder why all the bodies don't do it," Ana goes on. "You sit across the room from some poor schmuck who just wants to be with his girlfriend again. After a while, you feel like an asshole for standing in his way." A quick, strange laugh. "I do, anyway."

I sit next to Ana, making sure my body doesn't touch hers. A flash of heaving hips, sweaty skin, glazed eyes. On screen, the talk show host's lips move and move.

"This is what Mrs. Renard protects against," I say. "It's what she doesn't want for the Elysian Society, the whole reason she started a place like this—"

"Please," Ana says, biting my words off, crisply scornful. "You don't have to give me the whole spiel. I know the mission statement. But come on. Renard looks around, notices people making money by channeling on their own terms. Calling the shots, working out of their homes. A community thing. And she turns it into a factory. Now we all have to play by Renard's rules. If she won't give them what they want, I will."

"You don't have to drag the Elysian Society into it," I say. "Do it on your own terms."

"No way," Ana says. "You want me to die of an overdose, chugging downers? The lotuses are clean, at least. Safe. I do have some standards. When you add the lotuses, subtract Renard's rules—" She waves her palms in a game-show-hostess gesture. "Well. That's when the magic happens."

Through murky rumors among the bodies, tossed-off scraps of her own ramblings, I understand that Mrs. Renard has a monopoly on the lotuses, working out an arrangement with the pharmaceutical distributor. It's a twenty-hour drive to reach the next city with an organization similar to the Elysian Society. Between here and there, the smaller chances for channeling have been driven to the edges, starved out. Anyone who's interested in being a body, or using a body, comes to the Elysian Society eventually.

"How do you get the lotuses?" I ask.

"From Jane."

"Be serious," I say.

Ana laughs. "Don't underestimate her. Jane's like me, an old-fashioned entrepreneur. Do you think she'd stay at that crummy job if she wasn't making extra?"

I'm not sure what I want from Ana. Half of me wants her to break down, but another part thrills at her lack of apology. "You must be afraid," I say. "Alone with those men."

A strange shadow skids over her features. "Don't judge by what happened tonight." Ana picks at a fleck of dry skin on her ankle. A bead of blood pops up, tripling in size until it slips down her ankle. "Robert isn't a bad guy," she says. "It's hard for him, being so close to her and still having that distance."

I don't answer.

"It was a stupid fight," she says. "He wants things from me I can't give him."

I'm about to ask what more Ana could give, but she's transforming into her usual self, glossy and impenetrable. "Look, I'll be out of here first thing. I owe you." She reaches for the pillows and blankets.

As I rise, a question presses at my lips. "Are you the only one who does this?"

"No, Edie," she says. "I'm not the only one. People have been doing this for years. Funny, right?" A wry twist of her mouth. "Renard zaps all the weeds on the front lawn, sits around admiring her perfect yard. She doesn't even realize that the weeds have come back, growing right under the floorboards. Right under her nose."

"You could get in trouble," I say, imagining bodies in hotel rooms across the city—a hairline fracture that proves itself, on further inspection, to be a network of spreading cracks. Damage so deep and widespread that there's no way to contain it.

"Is that the way you see me? The one who's spoiling it for everyone else?" She leans over to remove her shoe, fumbling hard. "If anybody is the odd one out at that place, it's you."

On the screen, one of the women is crying. Without sound, the exaggerated rise and fall of her shoulders makes it look as if she's laughing into her hands where the audience can't see.

"Good night, Ana," I say finally.

In my own bedroom, I can't resist anymore. My mind clouds with images: Patrick's fingers inside me, Patrick's lips on mine. The desire is painful, like being cracked open slowly. I know what the inside of his mouth tastes like, the exact pressure of his body inside and against mine.

I slide my hand beneath the blanket. Sleep pulls at my edges. My rational mind clicks off, replaced with the voluptuousness of long-buried memories.

As I shift against the mattress, Patrick's face changes. He's Ana's Rob, eyes clear and assessing. I want to stop, but I can't. Then I don't want to anymore. Rob's face wavers, changes. Now the man pressing me open beneath his weight is Mr. Morris, with the freckled lips and shiny forehead; now Mr. Deehan with his perpetual sunburn; now Mr. O'Brien's vulpine features; and another face and another, men who have lost their lovers, their girlfriends, their wives. Their faces revolve over me in rhythm with the sleep-drugged movement of my hand.

And then, as I'm almost there, I can't see his face at all. He could be anybody. His proportions stretch out impossibly, a shadow lengthening against a wall. He's no longer panting above me but is too far away, looking down from a distance and watching me. I'm sinking fast. He shimmers above me, a silhouette seen through the moving surface of the water.

I reach for him.

He steps away.

S he sleeps on the couch in her tight dress. Her hip slopes upward beneath the blanket.

I lean forward to catch her warm, sour breath. *"Wake up,"* I say.

She sighs and shifts.

"Wake up."

Her eyes flutter open. Ana sits abruptly, bracing herself with one hand. Her eyes take on a stricken wariness.

"You took him from me," I say.

Ana shakes her head, again and again.

"You didn't have to do that." The words emerge from my throat as if by a magic trick, an endless scarf pulled from the dark pit of my mouth.

She reaches for me, fingertips icy on my arm.

"You thought you won." I push her hand away. I'm gentle, but she flinches.

"Edie," she says. "You're having a bad dream."

"He's mine," I say.

"Of course he is," Ana says, soothingly. "Of course he is."

I'm silent. The living room is sifting into focus in the clean light that comes through the blinds. I'm suddenly exhausted, as if

I've been awake all night. I can feel more words congealed at the back of my throat, trying to push out.

"I'm sorry, Ana," I manage.

She smiles, but her eyes stay tense. "God, you scared me."

"I talk in my sleep," I say. It's a lie. But now that I've said it, it begins to feel real. I can convince myself that the words were sleep-clouded and indistinct. I can forget the actual sensation of speaking: my mind both outside my control and buzzing with clarity, fully awake.

"Really, I should have warned you." I stand, light and shaky.

Ana swings her legs over the side of the couch, reaching for her shoes. The tapered heels jut like weapons. "Isn't it early for that?"

"For what?"

"I barely recognized you." Ana slides her foot into the punishingly narrow mouth of the shoe. "You apply that in your sleep? Not bad for a sleepwalker."

I move into the kitchen, where a small mirror is one of my few concessions to decorating. My face in the uneven surface is startling: not my disarranged hair or puffy-lidded eyes, but Sylvia's lipstick. It's perfectly applied, as if I've been wearing this color all my life.

Ana's cautious footfalls move up behind me. "It's grown on me," she says. "It's really your color, Edie."

'm scared."

Ms. Young's eyes are leveled at mine. After a second, I decide that she's not one of the unpredictable clients who sometimes slip through the cracks, their calm exteriors hiding onslaughts of tears, accusations, grief-torn wildness. Instead, Ms. Young offers her confession with a thoughtful weight. It's as if she's just realized it herself.

"Someone should have spoken to you about this process, Ms. Young," I say. "There's no need to be nervous."

"Oh, I know," she says, voice shaded with apology. "It's not about . . . you, or this place, or anything. It's about me and her."

Ms. Young has cloudy black hair, a crisply ironed blouse. According to the forms, she's here to see her daughter. A young woman who died several years ago, at the age of twenty. This surprises me; Ms. Young strikes me as being in her late thirties. Not much older than I am.

"I was in high school when Tiffany was born," Ms. Young says. "Everyone said adoption was the best thing to do. It would give her a better shot at life than I could provide. I went back to school, and then to work, trying to make a life for myself. I'd only placed her for adoption because people told me I didn't have a real life yet. But I started feeling—I don't know how to describe it. Stuck, I guess." She considers this. "Stuck."

I can't look at my client as she speaks. Instead, I focus on the corner of the room, the uneven fit of the crown molding, the glossy-fine cobwebs wreathed there.

"I'd keep thinking—if I made a good life for myself, then I may as well have kept her with me," Ms. Young says. "It didn't make sense. But I couldn't let go of this obsession. I had to keep my life small and plain, because if Tiffany ever came looking for me, and she saw that I was successful, she'd wonder why I didn't let her stay."

With an effort, I bring my eyes back down to Ms. Young. She gazes straight ahead, lips pressed into a stark line. The seconds tick past us.

"It was an open adoption," Ms. Young says finally. "But I kept my distance. I didn't want to create any confusion. She sent me a friendship bracelet when she was nine or ten. The idea of speaking with her was too much. I put it off. I told myself I'd wait until her eighteenth birthday to reach out. Trust me, I'm not proud of this. But you'd be surprised how quickly life can go by when you're hiding from something."

I make a small noise of encouragement.

"When she was nineteen, I got a call from her parents," she continues. "Ovarian cancer. It's rare in someone that young. There are barely any symptoms until it's advanced. I found out later it had something to do with a mutation of the BRCA gene. From my side of the family."

Ms. Young tucks her hair behind both ears, a methodical gesture. I notice her hands trembling slightly.

"I got to know Tiffany," she says. "We all pulled together at the end. Her parents and me. It was hard on them to see her so changed from the person they'd known. But it was hard on me too. I'd never known a different version of her. I'd missed Tiffany during her healthy years. So much lost.

"And I'm scared she'll be angry," Ms. Young says. "Angry that it's me coming to see her and not her parents. They have no idea I'm here. I wanted to have this one thing between her and me."

"Don't be scared," I say. "This is a place where you don't have to dwell on the past."

My client reaches up and flicks a finger beneath each eye. She hasn't been crying; it seems like a gesture born of habit. "But what about you?" she asks, and it takes me a second to recognize that she's addressing me. "You're all right? You look a little pale, ma'am."

"I'm fine," I say. A braided friendship bracelet coils around my wrist, tight enough to lightly pinch my wrist bones. The pink and purple threads are frayed. When Ms. Young tucks her hair behind her ear, I watch for and catch the flash of matching colors beneath the cuff of her blouse: she wears the bracelet's twin.

I reach for the lotus, gripping its edges tightly between the pads of my fingers. "Let's begin," I say.

On Friday, I enter the bookstore right before the clock ticks over to noon. At the door chime, the man behind the counter looks up. "Just yell if you need anything," he calls.

Catching a flurry of movement through the bookstore window, I turn. It's an older woman walking a bouquet of lap dogs. My heart slows. Angling my body so that the window is in my peripheral vision, I slide a book off the shelf, eyes slipping unseeing over the words.

This morning, I bought a fashion magazine at a drugstore, as furtively as if I were buying pornography. After five years of helping people pretend I'm not here, I don't remember how to draw eyes to my body. The outfit I found at the back of my closet has gone unworn for years. A black blouse with pearly buttons, a gray skirt. Cheap, with sharp threads poking at the seams. But if I don't look closely, the outfit creates a paper-doll illusion of elegance. I've coated my mouth with red lipstick, a tube I bought alongside the magazine.

When I glance up, the man behind the counter is watching me. I can tell by the duck of his head that it was more than an idle gaze, and I surge with a mix of triumph and shyness. A sensation I'd nearly forgotten.

He walks past the bookshop window. I know it's him before I even turn my head. He's encoded in my memory now: his gait, his gestures. Patrick glances through the window. Our eyes meet. And just like that, he's gone.

I hold the words open in my hands, frozen and ridiculous. Then I push the book onto the shelf and hurry outside. The April air is damp and outrageously sweet, intoxicating.

Immediately, I spot Patrick's lean back.

"Mr. Braddock." My voice barely belongs to me.

Patrick looks back. He pauses, turns around to face me. We examine each other. As strange as I must look in my darkly gaudy outfit, he's different too. I've never seen him in the sunlight before, or in these clothes, his shirt open at the throat. The daylight carelessly reveals the folded wrinkles at the corners of his eyes, the bruised fatigue beneath his lower lashes. I've forgotten how appealing it is: a man whose body looks lived in.

"It's you," Patrick says, and the words sing through my body: *It's you, it's you.* "What are you doing in this neck of the woods?"

"Oh, I was just—" I gesture at the bookstore window.

"Did you find what you were looking for?" He glances at my empty hands.

"Not really," I say. "I was hoping to find a copy of"—I dredge the name from my memory—"*Villette.*" A book I read in high school; I remember almost nothing about it. "By one of the Brontës."

A funny distance opens behind his eyes. "What happens in that book? Something about a governess?" He doesn't wait for an answer. Whatever changed in his face is already gone. "Listen, I was just going to lunch, if you want to join me. If you're free."

"Yes," I say. "I'm free." As if I might as well. As if it's one option of many.

He props the café door open, gesturing cartoonishly to me, like a maître d': the quick bow at the waist, the extended arm. "After you."

As I pass, I catch the gleam of his wedding band.

Inside, the smell of fresh bread envelops me. Classical music plays overhead. The whole area seems doused in more sunlight than the sidewalk outside.

When we receive our food, arranged on delicate wicker trays, Patrick leads me to an isolated corner table. Our knees almost touch when we sit. I face the back of the café. Patrick is all I see. The distance between us is smaller than when we sit together in Room 12. I feel every inch in my bones. I measure it with the steady pump of my pulse.

He shakes open a napkin, drapes it on his lap. "I hope you enjoy," Patrick says. "I used to come here with my wife." His voice doesn't change when he says this. His wife could be a mutual acquaintance. A woman I met at a party once, safely ensconced at her desk job.

I slide a tongue of red pepper from inside the sandwich. My courage isn't flagging yet, but a worry worms its way in at the edges.

"Do you work around here?" I ask.

Patrick nods, swallowing. "Right down the block. It's a law office." He pulls his mouth at the corners, acknowledging an unsaid joke. "I know."

"You're a lawyer."

"I am." The grimace again; a pause. "Really? Nothing?"

Images from afternoon TV, melodramatic movies, flash through my mind; the hushed courtroom, the beleaguered lawyer pacing in front of the judge's bench, rearranging the world's inflexible patterns into something more forgiving. "You're giving people a second chance," I say.

"Nice way of looking at it." He's surprised and then pleased, like a teacher whose quietest student made a wise observation. "But I'm not the grand-speeches kind. Corporate attorney. It's more conference calls and document review than you want to think about."

"I see."

"It has its good points, its drawbacks. I'd been considering changing paths, but then it happened." A shrug. "I felt safer staying in a holding pattern."

It. It. I work a slice of tomato from inside the crust.

"So you're a bookworm," Patrick says.

I take a moment to connect this to our earlier conversation. "Well, I read when I can."

"Same," he says. "There's an unexpected upside to insomnia. Apparently you should avoid screens at night. Something about the circadian rhythm. So I've been catching up on books I bought years ago."

"Any good ones?" I ask.

"Nothing as highbrow as the Brontës," Patrick says. "I tried slow-paced stuff at first. But it works better if I'm reading something I want to be reading. If I'm fighting to reach the next chapter, it knocks me out quicker." He smiles. "There's my stubborn streak for you."

"That makes sense," I say.

"Now let's see what I know about you," he says. "I know that you like to read. You go for the classics. I know you keep up with the news. And you prefer the winter to the summer. Does that sound right?"

It's a sketched silhouette of who I am. Scarcely anything. But I'm overwhelmed that he's remembered these details.

"Yes," I say. "Just about."

"Good," he says. "I'm glad I remembered."

It occurs to me that he's waiting, inviting me into his life. I search for an innocent question to ask him. Engaging, flirtatious. A question that his wife wouldn't have had to ask. A black-and-white image of the Eiffel Tower hangs above our table, overwhelmed by an elaborate frame. "Have you been there?" I ask, gesturing at the photograph.

"To France?"

The note of surprise in his voice is small and politely suppressed. But I realize how foolish the question is, and how clumsy it must seem to someone like him. Such a broad question; not *when* or *which city* or *how did you like it.* The gap between his life and mine, so yawning that only the strangest circumstances could have closed it for us.

But if he notices my mistake, Patrick's kind enough to ignore it.

"I have," he says. "Paris. Not the Eiffel Tower, not since I was young. I've been back a few times. Enough that I've staked out my favorite spots. There are hidden gardens all over the city. Not too touristy, so it's a good way to experience local life. People on lunch break or out with the kids." A smile. "My wife always asked, what if everyone in those gardens is secretly a tourist? We're all from Idaho and Alabama, sitting on park benches with each other, thinking we're with the real Parisians."

This time, the mention of Sylvia doesn't bite as hard. I manage to laugh.

"And you?" Patrick asks. "Much of a traveler?"

I've never left the country. This seems like a pitiful flaw, suddenly, proof that I'm small and stunted. I've been satisfied with the same grudging slice of the world.

"No, I haven't traveled much lately," I say.

"Your job keeps you busy," he says, thoughtful now. He starts to speak, then hesitates. "Can I be frank? I have so many questions about what you do."

I could pretend that he's asking me about my work as a bank teller, as a teacher, but I can't keep up the fantasy. "It's a strange job," I relent. "You get used to it."

When he leans across the table, I blush. The heat of my own skin feels as if it's pouring off his body, like I've shifted closer to a fire. "How long have you been working there?" Patrick asks.

"A few years," I say.

"You like the work?"

"It has its good points," I say. "And its drawbacks."

We exchange smiles, quick and conspiratorial.

"Every time I drive away from there," Patrick says, "for the rest of the day, I can't stop thinking about you."

I freeze.

"About how hard it must be for you," he continues. "How can you do that all day?"

I make myself breathe again. "Well, I know how to separate myself."

He nods. "There must be a lot of jobs like that." A hesitation. "My wife was a photographer. Originally, she'd wanted to be more serious. Photojournalism. Before we married, she worked freelance for smaller sites, magazines. She gave a lot of herself to her work. Spending time with her subjects, getting inside their heads. Being close to other people's lives. She said you need a certain distance. Maybe you can relate."

My smile feels tucked into place with pins. "She sounds wonderful." I could have cut the words from cardboard and propped them in front of my mouth; I make another effort. "But she lost interest in the work?"

"Well, Sylvia"—the first time he's said her name, I notice— "she was very giving. When we first married, I was having a stressful time at work, and Sylvia shouldered a lot of that burden for me. It didn't leave her with much time to devote to her own interests. I know what a sacrifice it was," he adds. "Maybe I didn't appreciate it at the time, I was young and stupid. I should have worshipped her. You don't always meet people that selfless."

I glance around the café, making eye contact with an older man. Just long enough to be satisfied that he sees me. That I'm still here, wearing my cheap and obvious red lipstick.

"I know what you're thinking," Patrick says, quietly self-deprecating. "Everyone must talk about their wives this way. Nobody's going to talk about the bad habits or the arguments over dishes."

"People can certainly be more forgiving after a loss."

"I went to a support group," Patrick says. He stretches his arms over his head. Darkness blooms under his arms. "I noticed how we all talked the same way. Competitive: Whose dead wife had the brightest halo? Like we're fighting with each other over whose partner was least deserving of death."

"That's a normal reaction to grief, Mr. Braddock," I say.

"Call me Patrick. Please."

He lifts his sandwich to his mouth. When he lowers his hands, a dab of grease stays on his cheek. He flicks his thumb across the spot, then sucks his finger clean. I look at his glistening fingertip and cross my legs beneath the table.

"How did you hear about the Elysian Society, Patrick?" I ask, testing out the name.

"A friend told me. She used to go herself. Jenn's father passed a while ago."

A couple enters the café, trailing a jangling string of conversation. Patrick peers at his watch. He's suddenly all business, crumpling his napkin, asking me if I'm sure I'm finished. My sandwich is barely touched, tattered at the edge from where I've been picking at the crust. "I hate to cut this short, but I have a call," Patrick says.

Outside, we stand in front of the plate glass windows. A breeze pulls my hair over my eyes and I reach to brush it away. When my vision clears again, I see Patrick's hand move back, as if he'd been reaching for me at the same time.

"You look great," Patrick says. "I almost didn't recognize you in this outfit."

And I'm stupid with pleasure, my heart panting shamelessly at his heels.

"I don't even know what to call you. Out here. In the real world." He smiles, sunlight caught deep in his eyes.

My real name hovers on the brink of my tongue before I answer him. "Edie."

"Pretty. It suits you." He holds out his hand; I take it. "I'm glad I had this chance to get to know you better."

"I'm glad too."

He doesn't let go of my hand. I feel the easy strength and energy behind his grip. Everything in my body settles in the spot where our flesh touches.

Patrick holds my gaze. His lashes are ridiculously long, this close up. "Can I ask something? Are you supposed to see your customers outside of work?"

I can't tell if he's been wondering this the whole time or if it just occurred to him. "Not exactly," I say.

"I thought not."

"But I don't mind, if you don't."

"I don't mind at all," Patrick says. He lets go of my hand. "I'll see you again soon, Edie." And I can almost let myself pretend that it's really me he wants to see.

ELEVEN

A heaviness. *A swell that pushes into every part of me, like exploring fingertips. Far away, impossibly far, moonlight cuts through the surface of the water.*

I used to believe that drowning would be peaceful, second only to dying in my sleep: a slipping away, a death that would glide up behind my back. But my death was urgent. Terrifying. My lungs ached with the desire to do something as simple as draw in a breath, exactly what I'd done since the moment I came wailing into the world.

I remember that drowning includes a moment of pure and childlike betrayal, that an act so simple and necessary has been ripped away. There one moment, gone the next.

I n the waiting room, someone taps my bare shoulder. I have the idle impulse to move closer to this touch, the way I'd turn my face toward the sun on a cold day.

"Lee." Stepping back, I let his hand fall lightly from my shoulder.

"I've been trying to find a good time to talk," he says.

I remember our last interaction, the concern that pulled his features tighter as he leaned toward me at the bar. "Is something wrong?" I ask.

Lee hesitates. "I was hoping to talk somewhere more private," he says. "Maybe tonight. We could go somewhere close by, have dinner or drinks."

I'm opening my mouth to refuse, to make my excuses, but as if from a distance, I hear myself saying, "All right. Tonight then."

His expression opens up with an unguarded excitement that turns me almost guilty. "There's a place not far from here," he says. "Close enough to walk."

"I'll meet you outside," I say.

After he leaves, I stay rooted, staring at the TV screen. An autumnal scene, red leaves reflected in hot bursts against the surface of a pond. My mind turns back to the familiarity of Lee's touch. Usually, we don't so much as shake hands. As small as Lee's gesture was, there was an automatic intimacy to it. His hand on my shoulder. I wonder if some part of me is changing behind my back. Sending out a receptiveness, an openness. As if a long-locked door has swung open a fraction, enough to allow a thread of light inside.

don't expect the book to be new. I steel myself against dog-eared pages, pencil scribbles in the margins. But the cover is unmarked. A woman from some nineteenth-century painting stares out, her eyes lashless and heavy-lidded. In contrast to her prim dress, there's slyness brewing in the corners of her expression.

"She reminds me of you," Patrick says. "That girl on the front. I hope you take it as a compliment. It's meant as one."

I staunch my surge of pleasure the way I'd hold a cloth over a wound. "I do have to remind you that personal gifts aren't allowed," I say.

Patrick clasps his hands together, a sign of contrition. "I know. I explained to the woman, Jane, that the book used to belong to Sylvia. But if you'd rather not, I understand."

I run my thumb down the cover. I can't imagine parting with it now. *Villette*.

"Sylvia was reading this book when it happened," he says.

"I found it on our nightstand when I came back from the lake. Opened on its spine. Such a strange moment, seeing that book and knowing she'd never find out the ending."

I won't be able to bear it if he cries.

When Patrick continues, his voice is mercifully steady. "But all those books, they end pretty much the same. She falls in love with a guy, she changes him, they live happily ever after. Something like that."

"Something like that," I echo. "Thank you for trusting me with this, Patrick." I set the book on the end table, next to the pill.

"You should know how much I appreciate everything you're doing for me." Patrick reaches across the space between us, and he touches my thigh: he rests his hand on my knee. His fingers rest beneath the hem of my skirt, warm and firm.

He traces a single quick circle with his fingertip. There must be a singed mark left behind on my naked thigh. A symbol of his presence.

Then his hand is gone and we sit and face each other, his face closed off except for a knowing smile. I can breathe, which surprises me; I can breathe, and I do, in and out. I breathe even if I'm going to break apart, a piece of paper consumed by a flame in a second.

The restaurant stands on the northern edge of the Elysian Society's neighborhood, leaking toward the next stretch of civilization. Lee and I walked here with a buffer of space between us, the evening air still spiked with heat. Lee has changed into his own clothes: a button-up shirt and dark pants that he wears with a slight stiffness. I've draped a cardigan over my white dress and pulled my hair loose around my shoulders, but I'm careful not to make an effort.

The restaurant is on a quiet street corner, the windows a patch-work of laminated menus, bright flyers offering expired specials and discounts. Inside, the place is mostly empty: low ceilings, booths coated in red Naugahyde, gold-flecked plastic tabletops. A sleepy-eyed waitress plants pebbled plastic cups in front of us.

"This place is probably a drug front," Lee says, low. "But they have decent coffee." When I lay the book on the tabletop, he tilts his head to scan the title. "*Villette*. I've never read that. Any good?"

"I haven't read it in a long time," I say.

"A client gave that to you?" Lee asks. I blink, unnerved at how easily he can detect the presence of somebody else. "I ask because a client used to bring me gifts," he continues. "A woman who'd been contacting her son. He died young, a bad car crash that she survived. His mother brought me things that she'd purchased new, just for me. Expensive things. A watch, cologne. Concert tickets. I could never use any of it."

"What did you do?"

"I had to turn her away," Lee says. "I tried to convince her that it wasn't appropriate. I wanted to help her. But of course I couldn't take the risk." He shrugs.

The waitress looms over us, her eyes grazing my thin dress. She slides two ceramic mugs onto the table. The insides slosh with black coffee. I take a long drink; after the hollowing effect of the lotuses, the coffee is tart as poison. Shakiness zips through my bones.

"When I started at the Elysian Society, I was curious." Lee fingers the handle, turning the mug around and around. "I heard they had more trouble keeping male bodies. And I thought, you know, there must be people who can't connect with their hus-bands or their sons. Their fathers. I wanted to help. It seemed like a way I could step in."

I know that male bodies are scarcer inside the Elysian Society walls. Ana's scornful of them. "Poor boys," I heard her say once, flirting with a new hire. "Such a disadvantage. They don't have the training for this work that women do."

But sitting across from Lee, looking at the patience that plays like light and shadows over his features, I think he must have found some emptiness inside himself. An obliging blankness. Without fully meaning to, I shift Lee's face aside, slide a new one in its place. My mind pulls together the right mannerisms. The exact expression: the set of the mouth, the coolness in the eyes.

I have to turn my head sharply, staring instead at the froth of dust collecting between floor tiles. When I glance up, Lee is himself again.

"It's not always easy," Lee says. "That woman wasn't coming from a bad place. Turning her away before she took things any further—it might not have felt like helping. But it was."

"Helping yourself?" I give the words a slim edge.

"Helping her." Lee's eyes on mine remain steady. "You know it's true, Edie. Sometimes helping our clients means stepping away from them. Setting them free before they hurt themselves, or hurt us."

Through a gap in the neon flyers pasted to the window, the sky shows in a smear of darkening gray.

"Why did you really want to talk tonight, Lee?" I ask.

"It's been worrying me for a while," he says. "Ever since that night."

On the other side of the dining room, the waitress leans against the counter, so still she could be a prop. The empty booths lining the windows, the tables scattered in the center of the room with their listless bundles of utensils, give the impression of a hastily constructed stage set.

"Patrick Braddock might be dangerous," Lee says.

I'm not even surprised. "How is he dangerous?" I ask, voice pleasant.

"I looked up the details," he says. "The circumstances surrounding his wife's death. There's something strange, Edie. Something off."

"Off," I repeat, making the word subtly ridiculous.

"The details don't add up. The story is that she goes swimming alone in the early morning and drowns. She's drunk or exhausted. But if you look deeper, you see discrepancies. Did you know she was naked when they found her?"

I can feel my heartbeat held inside my chest, like an insect clutched in a fist.

"And it's not just that," Lee says. "I noticed that he apparently dropped the lawsuit against the resort. The whole thing vanished."

"He didn't want to go through that, right after his loss," I say.

"Maybe," Lee says. "Or maybe he didn't want a closer investigation. A wrongful death lawsuit could have uncovered details Braddock didn't want out in the open."

I take another long sip of the coffee, the bitterness setting my teeth on edge.

"All this could be nothing," Lee continues, "or it could point to a different side of the story. Foul play."

The two words roll through my skull, hard as marbles. "These are just pointless rumors," I say. "Mrs. Renard trusts Mr. Braddock. Why doubt her judgment?"

"You don't know what kind of life Sylvia led with him, what problems they were having. Letting Braddock continue to see her, to be around you—" He hesitates. "It could end badly."

When I glance down at the book cover, it's transformed: the woman's face has lost whatever wildness I detected and is instead unreadable, dumbly complacent as a dreamer's. "I've been working with Mr. Braddock for weeks now," I say. "He's been nothing but professional."

"Why did you become a body?" Lee asks.

"Same as you. To help people."

"When I tell you about myself," Lee says, "you don't offer anything in return. We've been talking for two years. You never say anything about your past. It's like you fell out of the sky."

I start to speak.

"It's not my business," he interrupts. "I know that. But I thought, how strange that she's doing this, seeing someone like Patrick Braddock. You never take risks. Then I realized that I don't know enough about you to make that call. Maybe there's something I'd need to know."

As I stand, a rush of light-headedness nearly pushes me backward. "Lee, if you care about me, you'll drop this," I say. "Please."

"Whatever you want." But his eyes remain unconvinced, as if I'm insisting I'm not hurt while holding my bleeding hand between us.

Without looking back, I hurry out of the restaurant. The evening sky is thick and low-slung, threatening rain.

Halfway down the block, I stop. A little girl waits at the intersection just ahead. In the gloom, her face is soft and diffused, a generic grouping of features. Her hair hanging flossy and straggling, the way she swings her arms: the sight of her passes through me like a bullet. She's too young to be out alone. She could have materialized here, brought to life by my gaze.

The girl's head is ducked, but as I stand and stare at her, she looks up. Her pale hair slides away from her cheeks. I won't be able to stand seeing her face.

Then an older woman walks toward her, appearing from behind the corner of a building. The girl whips her head around, skips over to the woman. The two of them start across the street, and I take a deep breath, following in their wake. From the back, the woman and girl are plain and unremarkable. Faces in the crowd. I don't know them, I remind myself. I don't know anybody in this city.

———————

L ake Madeleine. *August.*

I hesitate a second. *Foul play.* I delete the words, as if I can scrub the term out of my mind, and instead type: *Drowning.*

The results are sparse. Articles in local news sites, a handful of stilted blurbs in national sources. Some don't refer to her by name. *The 32-year-old wife.* Three pieces show her portrait, the same one each time. A professional shot, a smile as posed and unspecific as a stock photo. A few sources use an image of Sylvia and Patrick together at a formal event, her neck wreathed in pearls, his hand tight at her waist. A copy of the same photo lies on my bedroom floor.

I read and reread the articles, hungry for any detail. *Braddock was accompanied to the lake house by her husband and two close friends.* The friends' names are withheld, but I recall the wife's name after a second. Viv Damson.

Sylvia went swimming without telling anyone, breaking the resort's policies. Going into the water after consuming alcohol, in the early hours of the morning, nobody else around. Only one article echoes Lee's assertion that Sylvia was naked.

At this time, it is unknown whether Braddock was clothed when she entered the lake.

I remember Patrick's face when I reassured him that nothing was strange about his wife's death. His passing flinch of what could have been doubt, shame. Anger.

The raw and unfiltered information is restricted to forums populated by amateur detectives. People with cryptically anonymous names who seem capable of a weird arithmetic. Reverse division: they can take the slightest clues and dissect the details until they're bloated, page-long theories.

The Braddocks appear briefly, a scattering of mentions. I read with heat growing in my chest and tightening behind my ribs.

What do we think about this one? Couple of strange things, including the husband backing off from a lawsuit. Afraid? What do you think?

Yeah obviously no accident.

Guy is guilty as hell but seems to have deep pockets so I doubt he'll pay for it.

Reports say the autopsy doesn't show any signs of foul play??? Seems like the bitch just got wasted and thought she was too good to follow the rules.

Don't know. Don't care. They're smug as hell in their photos. Maybe she drowned to get away from him. Maybe he killed her to get away from her. Not worth discussing.

I stand, withdrawing from the quick, cold authority of those strangers, summing up Sylvia's death as if they were there. It's like finding a fragile keepsake smeared with a stranger's fingerprints.

They're outsiders. Tourists, gathering around something bigger than themselves, hoping for a cheap moment of connection.

I end up in the bedroom. I riffle through the photographs. Sylvia and Patrick rush past, one broad, gleaming grin and openmouthed laugh after another. She nuzzles her head into his shoulder. She links her arm through his. There's no sign of unhappiness, no sign of discord. I know exactly how to decipher other people's tragedies. I would recognize it.

I reach a photo and stop. The lipstick. Sylvia's high, round breasts and narrow waist are inviting, luminous. I turn the image over.

My dearest. The writing is a childishly elaborate cursive.

Faded blue ink. *It's not always easy, is it: being madly in love? But I'll be yours today and forever. Nothing can keep us apart. Love, your butterfly.*

I read the words again and again and again until the world steadies itself around me.

TWELVE

Locating her number doesn't take much time. A quick consultation with an online directory. Her basic information collected in one spot, splayed out thoughtless and cheerful. A person with nothing to hide.

I dial and wait for the voice on the other end. Already, I'm calm, becoming the woman I'll be once she answers.

"Yeah, hello?"

"May I speak with Mrs. Damson?" I ask.

"Speaking."

"Wonderful," I say, brisk and smooth. "I'm glad I have the correct number on file."

"Who is this, please?"

"I notice you were working with a grief counselor about a year ago, and I was wondering if you'd be interested in a follow-up session." I lift my voice, efficiently tamping down any questions. "It's part of a study about the long-term process of grieving and healing."

"Oh," Viv says. I hear the tug of uncertainty, her blank surprise. "How did you get my number?" she asks. "I don't remember—"

"My records show that you completed an exit survey and indicated that you'd be open to further studies," I say.

"Really?" There's a long silence, then an apologetic laugh. "That was a crazy time. I was signing so much paperwork, it just— I must have forgotten."

"Would you still be open to that, Mrs. Damson?" I ask.

"God, I don't know. When I was seeing a counselor, it was different. I'm at home with my baby now."

"Your baby," I repeat, softening my voice around the words. "How old?"

"He's eleven months," she says.

I calculate quickly. When Sylvia died, this pregnancy was new. A tentative secret, a negotiable slip of life unable to make itself known. I wonder if Patrick traced the passage of time after Sylvia's death by dutifully admiring photos of his colleague's wife, her belly swelling. "Eleven months is a wonderful age," I say.

"Anyway, I'm doing a lot better," she says. "We've been moving on from everything."

"Actually, Mrs. Damson, the purpose of this study is to address exactly that," I say. "The recovery process. When you first lost your friend—Sylvia Braddock, is that correct?"

A hesitation this time. "Yes."

"In the time following your loss, your counselor was impressed with your resilience," I say. "We're hoping to work closely with the clients who showed the most promising recovery process and use our research to help others in the same position."

"I'd have to talk to my husband," Viv says. But I can tell I'm getting through to her. Her politeness is shifting into a cautious relief. "How long would this last?"

"Just a few sessions," I say. And Sylvia's inside me, rounding out the words, turning my usual flatness and coolness into a warm invitation. I sound like someone the Damsons have known for years, someone they'd trust with their lives. "Two or three, maybe."

"Yeah, OK," she says. "That doesn't sound too bad. Henry wouldn't mind."

"I can make house calls, if that would be preferable." As if I'm offering a modest favor.

"That would be a big help," she says. "Can I ask your name?"

I hesitate, shrinking back into my old skin. "My name," I say. She waits.

"Lucy Woods," I say, the name presenting itself easily.

"All right, Lucy," Viv says. "Well, thanks for reaching out."

This morning, I sifted through Sylvia's belongings. My hands lingered over the pins, the perfume, before I lifted up the earrings, slipping them into my bag before I could change my mind.

Sitting across from my regular clients, I welcome the brief respite that each swallowed lotus provides. Every time I vanish and then reemerge, I'm closer to seeing him.

"Is something funny?"

"Not at all, Mr. O'Brien," I say, swallowing my smile.

"You seem amused all of a sudden."

"I apologize," I say. Mr. O'Brien is one of those clients who watches me closely, obsessively focused on any sign of individuality that pushes through. "It won't happen again."

After Mr. O'Brien, I retrieve Sylvia's earrings. The dark luster of the emeralds feels dangerous. The posts are needle-thick, and when I slide them into my lobes, my flesh protests.

When Patrick enters, he instantly fills every corner of the room. We sit across from each other. I turn my head and wait for him to notice, like a shy housewife showing off a new haircut.

"You're wearing them." His eyes move over my face, from my dark red lips to the thick twinkle at my ears, across the plane of my throat, and then back again. I see him retreat from me. It's as if these pieces of Sylvia have already conjured the rest of her into this room. Moths gathering around a single flame, blocking out my shape.

I stir, caught between jealousy and pleasure. Two heartbeats colliding.

"I've been meaning to ask you," Patrick says. "How long do people keep coming here?"

This takes me aback. "I'm not sure what you mean."

"I was talking to my friend," Patrick says. "She called yesterday, out of the blue. We usually don't talk about this place. Unspoken rule. But Jenn mentioned—she mentioned that she's still coming here." He watches me as if this should mean something.

"Our clients are loyal," I say.

"I thought she was done," Patrick says. "I'd assumed that she'd been—I don't know. Cured? Fixed. What is the right word? Learning that she's been coming here all along—" He shakes his head. "It surprised me."

"Everyone has a different timeline," I say.

"How long is typical? Weeks, months?" He's softly intent. "Longer?"

"Sometimes," I say. "Sometimes longer."

"Years?"

"Years," I concede. "Usually."

Patrick's expression is unreachable. Room 12 isn't my own anymore. The whole space belongs to him, and I'm an intruder, desperate, pleading for something from him. For too much.

don't leave me

"Shall we begin, Mr. Braddock?" I ask, as opaque as the first day I met him.

'm the last to leave. Against the dusk, the Elysian Society building rises like a monolith. The unlit windows turn into rows of shallow impressions, like indented fingerprints in wax. All day, I've been replaying my last conversation with Patrick. Fitting different words in our mouths.

It would have been so easy to reassure him that his grief would be eased soon, that his life would return to normal. It's an unspoken promise that defines every interaction with our clients: that they're working toward a discrete goal. A moment of closure, peace. And if this moment keeps receding like a hazy mirage, always the same distance away, we don't acknowledge it.

I should have lied to Patrick. Given him the hope that he's paying for.

When a hand closes around my elbow, I'm less afraid than relieved. It's him. He's come back for a second chance. I can explain everything.

I turn, already smiling.

"You're one of those bodies," he says. "Aren't you?"

I'm still smiling, a dumb and helpless impulse. The man is a stranger. Older, with seed-dark pores bristling along his cheeks, a thick vein marking a line across his forehead. He doesn't let go of my elbow. Though his grip is light and brittle, as if I'm being grasped by an empty glove, I can't move. His breath is acidic with menthol.

"I want to know why," he says. "I deserve that. I tried to get a good answer from those others and they brushed me off like I was nothing. So I'm asking you now. It's a simple thing to do, miss. Tell me why you people turned me away, without even letting me speak to my boy."

Anxiety constricts my chest. I'm not worried about what he might do to me. It's the awareness of what I'll have to do for him.

"I never said good-bye," the man goes on. "I didn't know it would happen. He was happier than he'd been in years. If I'd known, I would have done things differently. We could have done something fun together. But he was happy, and I was so relieved to get him back that I treated him like my son again. Hounding him about getting a job and settling down. Fighting with him over stupid things. All I want is a way to say good-bye, a real good-bye this time. I'll pay. I'll pay anything. It's not fair to turn me away."

"Your son took his own life?" I ask.

His eyes snap shut as if I've directed a shocking light at his pupils. "Yes."

"Well, I'm afraid it's true," I say. "We can't work with victims of suicide. I'm sorry."

"You hurt us again," the man says, voice surprisingly strong in comparison to his frail frame. "You look at people who are hurting and say we're not good enough. We're not like the other people who are grieving. We deserve to hurt. We deserve to be alone."

"It's not like that," I say, keeping my voice under control. "It's a policy."

"Then tell me why."

My bare forearm is pressed against the chilled window of the car; my hair, after the long day, has come loose in rough, prickling strands against my neck. The man's hand at my elbow has slackened, now hanging gently, almost politely. We could be a grandfather and granddaughter.

The usual way to answer these questions is to induce a clinical sense of danger, lay out the risks that the body faces. Deny responsibility. But I can't do that right now.

"When someone chooses to take their own life," I say, "we respect that. We don't force them to come back into a body they wanted to leave. It would be cruel."

The man opens his eyes, staring at a spot just past my shoulder.

"That's why," I say. "I'm sorry I'm not able to do more for you. But now you know." Gently, I step away, and his fingers slip and then fall from my arm like a dangling man letting go of a cliff's edge. "I hope that can be some comfort to you."

"Don't they ever change their minds?" the man asks. "Maybe it would be the best thing in the world to come back one last time."

"We can't know that," I say.

He nods and nods, mouth working as if he's preparing to speak.

"I really need to be going," I say. "Can I give you a ride somewhere? Can I—"

"It's no excuse," he says. His eyes lock on mine for the first time. The piercing clarity of his gaze makes me squirm. It's as if he's prizing open my forehead to look inside, poke an exploring finger into the coils of my brain. "People who died other ways don't want to come back either," he says. "You bring one back, you bring them all. It's only fair, miss."

touch my face. My cheeks are damp. My eyes are tight and swollen, painful around the edges. I sit up in bed, fumbling for the lamp. In my dream-blurred state, I imagine the water everywhere. Soaking through my mattress, pooling on the floor, dripping steadily into my lungs.

how could you do that to me

In the bathroom, I examine my reflection. I've been crying. My eyelids are a stinging pink, my skin tight and sticky from dried tears. The evidence of crying renders my features unfamiliar. My nose is narrower than I remember; a pale brown freckle above my lip is jarring. I peel back my top lip to examine my teeth. The incisors are crooked. It's as if someone reached into my mouth and nudged them askew.

It's been so long since I cried. I never cried, right after it happened. I never let myself.

Back in bed, I make myself as small as I can, curling up and clutching my elbows. The tears have stopped; they don't even feel like my tears, but like something dragged from inside my body by force. What disturbs me is the sensation that filled my brain during those first few moments after waking. The heavy knowledge that nobody would come looking for me.

Do you know what it's like to lose somebody before they're even dead?"

Beth Olsen's voice holds a dogged resolve, as if she's finally releasing words that have grown in the dark for too long.

"People have been so nice, since Amber died," Ms. Olsen goes on. "I've had all the frozen meals and flowers and everything. I appreciate it. I do. But I almost want people to stop talking about her." The quick glance at me, gauging my reaction. "Amber was exactly what people expected her to be. Her friends called her inspirational, or a fighter. Amber left the church when she was a teenager, but she'd started praying again. And anything that made her happier was fine by me." She looks at her hands, pressed together on her lap. "It's only now that she's gone that I can admit how miserable it made me sometimes."

Ms. Olsen has coarse auburn hair. Her serious face is lightened by freckles. In my favorite photo of her and Amber, they sit at the edge of a balcony during a party, the other guests hazy faces around them. I see the bend of Ms. Olsen's head, as if she's muting everyone else to focus on her girlfriend, and Amber's sweet, secretive smile.

I shift in my chair. Patrick hasn't scheduled a new encounter in three days. Since he first stepped across the threshold of Room 12, his presence has become the most consistent thing in my life. He's the point I wait for. And though my clients can be unpredictable, scheduling encounters based on their own private patterns of pain and optimism, the suddenness of Patrick's departure opens a deep pit inside my chest.

"We were outsiders together," Ms. Olsen is saying. "In high school, we were always on the fringes." She laughs under her breath. "We had a mean sense of humor, when you put us together. But that's what was so addictive. Even the worst thought that went through my head, Amber wouldn't just listen to it, she would understand it."

Her eyes take on the fixedness of suppressed tears.

"I really miss that side of Amber," she says. "It was her battle to fight. But God, I miss her, the way she used to be. That dark sense of humor. And the worst thing is when they keep telling me she's in a better place. What was so wrong with being here?"

Her voice holds a naked plea. I reach for the tissue box, extending it vaguely, as if I'm offering it to someone else and she just happens to be nearby. But Ms. Olsen smiles and shakes her head, holding up one palm.

"Listen, I'd give anything to spend an hour with her, being assholes again," she says. "It's like I lost time with her before she even died. I was cheated. Do you know what I mean?"

For the first time in years, the distance I've maintained between my clients' lives and my own has snapped shut, leaving us uncomfortably close, breathing the same suffocating air.

"Let's begin, Ms. Olsen," I say.

P atrick hasn't returned to the Elysian Society for over a week. Everything in my life has become an attempt at distraction. Evenings after work are the hardest. I remove the battery from my clock. I start drinking, burning swallows of whiskey, acrid glassfuls of wine. When I've been drinking, my brain is safer, as if someone has padded it with cotton. I can handle my thoughts more directly. Even the volatile ones.

I chased Patrick Braddock away. I was too greedy, reaching out to him too openly. Our last discussion must have clarified an ugly truth for him.

And Sylvia. Sylvia.

If Patrick leaves, I don't know what will happen to his wife. After it's clear that he's not coming back, she still might stay inside me, metastasizing through my organs until nobody can tell us apart, or she might leave. A parasite deserting a starving host; a stowaway swimming from a sinking ship.

Sylvia's presence in my life is both intimate and unknowable.

Even as I feel her stirring beneath my skin, there's a disconnection. I don't know whether she's drawn to me or whether her presence here is as inextricably attached to her husband as a shadow cast by his body.

And I'm not sure which fate I prefer, if it comes to it. To let Sylvia devour me or to be entirely alone again, abandoned inside my skin.

My outfit borrows the anonymity of my Elysian Society dress and merges it with bland respectability. Gray linen, boxy jacket. Paired with my colorless complexion, the clothes wash me out. I rub Sylvia's lipstick on my fingertip and then over my lips, seeing my face come alive.

The Damsons live in an area I don't recognize. A domesticated breed of wealth, hiding its privilege in a show of quaintness. Older houses, small flower gardens out front. A few colorful riding toys are posed on lawns, beneath gingerbread trim and ivy trellises. Tied to someone's front porch railings, a bouquet of Mylar birthday balloons stir and sway, just starting to droop.

Viv Damson opens her door a few dragging minutes after I ring the bell. She's wearing a baggy shirt with one button done wrong, leaving a buckling gap. Yellow-blond hair gathered in a topknot, her cheeks shimmering with a dusting of powder. "Lucy, right?" she asks. "Come in, come in, please. Sorry for the mess."

She leads me into their dining room, an open floor plan that spreads into the kitchen. Viv has to shift aside a sliding stack of magazines and chunky board books to clear a space on the table; I arrange a blank notebook on the table while she gets me a drink. It's a cheerfully untidy house, the air saturated with the lingering scents of old milk and hand soap and baby wipes. A doll lies on the floor, one eye cocked shut to show a stiff spray of lashes. A swift jealousy, something like homesickness, moves through me.

"Thank you for agreeing to be part of this study, Mrs. Damson," I say, when Viv returns with a diet soda.

"Oh God, I'm happy to do it," Viv says, waving her hand: mint-colored nail polish, a delicate shard of diamond in her ring. "This is happening at the perfect time. For some reason, I've been thinking about her these days. So it's super lucky that you"—she gestures at me, as if otherwise I won't know myself—"popped up when you did, Lucy." A pause. "It's fine to call you Lucy, right?"

"Of course." I hurry past the ache the name opens inside my chest. "It's been about a year and a half since your loss?"

"Well, more than that now. Um, a year and a half?" Viv crosses her arms over her chest, unwinds them and places her hands on her knees. Catching my gaze, she laughs. "It's hard to know what to do with my hands when the baby's down for a nap."

It's later in the day, half past four. I'd been wondering where the baby is, where Mr. Damson is. I'm hungry to meet Henry in the flesh. This colleague of Patrick's. Someone who must greet him every day, know a more consistent version of him than I do.

"When we lost Sylvia, I'd just found out I was pregnant," Viv says. She's hushed now, a purposefully somber tone. "It was weird. Something so good happening and then, a few weeks later, something so terrible. I was over the moon about the baby." Viv's hand flutters to her stomach as if a version of the child remains there permanently. "Then we ran into Sylvia that weekend. You know, she was the first person other than Henry to even know about the baby?"

"Is that so?"

"I asked her to be the baby's godmother," Viv says. Her eyes gleam, the familiar glazing of tears. All my clients have a different way of managing tears: banishing them, indulging them. Viv is the indulging type. Dewiness builds on her lashes. "I just wanted her to be part of Ben's life. Sylvia didn't have kids yet, but I saw the way other people's kids would gravitate to her."

"Being a godmother is an honor," I say.

Viv gazes at the ceiling. "God, I'm rambling. You need to tell me what to say."

"Could you share more about Sylvia, if it's not too painful? What she was like, her home life?" Seeing Viv's expression shift into confusion, I hedge: "It would give me a clearer image of your recovery process to know more about your loved one."

"Well, sure," Viv says. "Patrick and my big brother knew each other growing up. When Patrick and I ended up in the same area, my brother put me in touch. The Braddocks and I started getting together. Just casually. I clicked with Sylvia. And Henry, my husband? He works with Patrick. We met through the Braddocks. So, I really owe everything I have to them."

"Have you kept in close touch with Patrick since—?"

Viv presses her lips together. Her face tightens briefly. "We haven't seen him lately. Just the shock of everything. And the baby. It's been hard."

I make note of this. "That's understandable. Sometimes grief can push apart surviving relationships. Would you say Patrick and Sylvia were a happy couple overall?"

Viv waits for a moment before starting to answer, words caught in the damp hollow of her lips. I lean forward, magnetized by this clue into the Braddocks' lives. But there's a sudden noise behind us. The slam of a door, heavy footsteps. The atmosphere shifts to make room for the new presence. Viv's face brightens as if she's released from a spell.

"Henry," she says, tilting her head to look behind me. "This is Lucy, the woman who said she'd come by? Lucy, this is my husband."

For a strange moment, I don't want to turn my head. I don't want to meet his eyes. Then I do, putting on a professionally distant smile. Mr. Damson is dark-haired and bearded, bulkier than Patrick. Good-looking in a brusque way.

"I apologize for barging in on you ladies like this," he says.

We shake hands. His grip is firm and energetic.

"How's it been going?" He's addressing his wife, but Henry's gaze loiters on my mouth. I remember that I blotted my lips with Sylvia's lipstick. I shouldn't have worn such a severe color; Viv didn't seem to notice, but Henry's questioning look turns me into someone suspicious.

"She was just asking about Patrick," Viv supplies.

"You've worked with him for some time, Mr. Damson?" I ask, limply curious.

"Oh God, must be about four years," Henry says. "Four years this summer."

I imagine him scrawling his signature on a sympathy card passed throughout the office. A terse, inadequate message: *So sorry for your loss.*

"I was telling her, honey, that we haven't been in touch with Patrick lately," Viv says. She taps her nails on the tabletop. "Should we invite him for dinner?"

"Braddock? No." Henry's dismissal hurts for a second, as if it's aimed at me. "He wouldn't come. He keeps to himself these days. Barely talks to the rest of us."

Viv darts a sheepish look at me. "Yes, but he needs his friends now more than ever."

It feels like a belated show of compassion, mostly for my sake. Henry's at the fridge, leaning down, the front of his body washed pale blue. "Yeah, well," he says. "If you think it will help, invite him over. But I'd lay money he won't show."

Viv starts as if she's received a shock: "I have to deal with that," she says, and it's only when she's hurrying from the room and up the stairs that I hear the ragged cry of the baby.

Henry saunters back to the dining room table, standing nearby like a sentinel as I slip my notebook back into my bag. His presence turns me jumpy, aware of a slight charge in the air between us. I straighten to meet Henry's eyes squarely: he's shorter than Patrick, closer to my height.

"What did I hear you asking, anyway?" he asks. "When I came in."

"Oh." I trace back. "I believe I was asking whether the Braddocks were happy."

His expression shifts, almost too rapid to catch. Like a dark shape beneath the surface of water, gone before I can be sure I even saw its outline. "Strange question," he says.

"Understanding these dynamics illuminates the bigger picture of moving on from a loss."

His eyes on mine are steady. "So are you going to ask me?"

I look at him mutely.

"Ask me if they were happy," he clarifies.

I hear Viv and the baby in the upstairs room, Viv's soothing coos and murmurs. The sunlight streams through the windows to highlight the faint stains on the chairs' upholstery, a bowl of some gluey substance on the countertop. This monotonous image of ordinary life hurts. A throb of nostalgia that I haven't felt in years.

At the door, I turn, intending to thank him for the visit. Henry's watching me as if he's trying to place me; it's the type of intently open gaze that people usually try to hide once they're caught. But Henry doesn't falter.

The question pushes out before I can stop it. "Were they happy, Mr. Damson?" I ask.

"No," he says, just before he shuts the door.

FOURTEEN

There's something funny in the air lately, don't you think?"
Hazy, I look up at Ms. Mendoza.

"It's probably just the way people are after a long winter," she says. "They don't know what to do with themselves."

She's pulling on her cardigan; the sleeves stretch between her elbows like awkward bird wings. "I hope you had a pleasant encounter today," I say.

Ms. Mendoza hesitates before she answers. "Eurydice, dear, I may not be coming back soon. But I don't want you to think it's anything about you."

"If you'd like to work with another body—"

"Oh, no. I would never. It's just—" She looks away, fussing with the pearly buttons on her cardigan. "Personal matters. Financial."

"I know Veronica will miss you."

It seemed like a kind thing, but Ms. Mendoza's eyes brighten with tears. "I've tried to cut back in other areas of my life," she says. "I've been making adjustments for years. But I have medical expenses and bills to pay. I'm not getting younger."

I watch her go, shoulders hunched. I have an unwelcome flash of her life: a dingy apartment stripped bare of luxuries, counting down the pennies. The minutes.

"Ms. Mendoza," I call. She turns. "Do you find that your encounters with Veronica help you?" When she frowns, a polite confusion, I continue: "Do you feel happier after you see her?"

"Well," Ms. Mendoza says. "Well, of course I do. Always. That's why I keep coming back, you know. My sister will always be the best part of my life. But after all, I do have to live." Ms. Mendoza's chin lifts with a fragile defiance. "It feels selfish sometimes, but I do have to live."

Leaving the Elysian Society, I stop short. She's waiting for me in the parking lot, leaning against the side of my car, smiling too coaxingly.

"Dora." I move to unlock the car. "You need a ride again?"

"I missed the bus," she says. "My client couldn't stop crying after I woke up. I felt bad leaving her there alone. What was I supposed to do?"

Sliding into the car, I stretch across to unlock the passenger-side door.

"Anyway," Dora says, climbing in. "Remember what you said, about how we could go shopping together? Maybe we could do that now."

I'm about to refuse, but I know what waits for me at home. Silence, the heaviness of time pressing down in a slow crush.

When we're a few blocks from the Elysian Society, Dora rolls down the window. Fresh air whistles into the car. I take a deep breath, enjoying the coolness. "Where do you want to go?" I ask. "There's a consignment shop, not far."

"Consignment? Like secondhand?" The corners of her mouth twitch downward. "Nah, I'm getting sick of wearing other people's things."

We end up at a strip mall. Dora chooses the store on the corner: fake stone facade, headless mannequins staggered in the window. It's all wrong for us. The dresses are conspicuously formal. Prom gowns with beaded bodices like armored breastplates, puffy skirts that remind me of jellyfish. I can't imagine either of us having an occasion in our lives that would require one of these gowns, but I follow Dora inside.

The interior is bracingly cold, lit with hospital-bright fluorescence. Compared with the jeweled gowns, the surroundings are incongruously harsh. A girl stands in front of a display, yanking a bridal gown over the unresisting limbs of the mannequin. The mannequin's stiffly extended arm trembles helplessly. The girl turns as we enter, taking us in for a silent moment and then looking away without offering a greeting.

Dora moves deftly behind a circle of racks, hiding us from the view of the front counter. A red dress hangs in an alcove. The tightly banded panels remind me of blood-soaked bandages. "Do you think we look weird to her?" Dora whispers.

"I doubt she knows what we do," I say.

"Before you worked here, did you know about bodies?"

"I guess so." Memories nudge the back of my skull. "I was aware of the possibility."

"Did you ever think you'd work as one?" she asks.

"No." We're passing a wedge of mirror, and I catch our reflections from the corner of my eye. Dora, small and vivid, and me trailing after her like the pale blot reflected by a jewel. "Why?" I ask. "Did you?"

She pulls a lavender gown from the rack. When she holds it against her body, the hemline pools on the floor. "I wanted to do this for a while."

"Really?" I don't hide my surprise.

Dora replaces the dress. She's not meeting my eyes now, slowly circling the rack, reaching out to touch a sleeve here, a skirt there. "My mom used to go see this woman who'd channel for you in the back room of her bookstore. She was in another town. My mom had to drive for hours. She'd be gone all day. I knew not to talk about it with my dad. We pretended it wasn't happening."

The music overhead is a keen wail set over discordantly jaunty instruments.

"My older sister died when I was . . . nine? Ten?" Dora's tone suggests I might know better than her. "They were always really close, she and my mom. There was no room left for me. When my sister died, I even thought—" She runs her fingertips down a rose-pink bodice: all clear beads, silver sequins. "But. Then my mom found that place, and she was gone all the time."

"Dora . . ." I say.

But she twirls to face me now. Her expression has turned determinedly cheerful, almost flinty. "Hey, you should try something on," she says. "You never dress up."

I accept the gown she pulls loose from the clutter. Dora guides me to the dressing rooms, cramped stalls covered by curtains that scarcely reach far as my knees. The full-length mirrors are inescapable. I'm forced to look at myself from multiple angles as I undress, pulling my Elysian Society uniform over my head.

When the white fabric falls free of my face, I stop, shocked. The woman in the mirror is wrong. She's tall, her hair listless. Small, firm breasts, swollen like teardrops; the exaggerated curve of her hips, disproportionate against long and boyish legs. I take her in, this stranger.

"How does it look?" Dora calls.

"Wait a moment." I turn from the mirror, reaching for the green dress. Compared to my Elysian Society uniform, the fabric is densely luxurious. I thread my arms through the straps.

"That's why I wanted the job," Dora says. In the corridor that houses the dressing rooms, the music is muted. It's easier to hear her voice. I'm quiet; it's as if she needed to be separated from me by the curtain before she could continue. "I used to imagine what it was like for my mom. Some woman who maybe looked a little like my sister, sitting in a room, and my mom loved her. I wanted a chance to be on the other side of that."

I reach for the zipper. "Does your mother know you're with the Elysian Society?"

"No." She laughs, a sad, frayed sound. "We don't talk much these days."

I'm shocked at how well the dress fits, lightly grazing my hips, fitted across the chest. I run my hands over the slippery softness. I imagine standing in front of Patrick. How his eyes would move over my body: the softness of my breasts, the arch of my hips. I'm furious at the image, even as a spike of excitement moves down the length of my body.

"So you like the dress?" Dora asks. "Are you going to buy it?"

"I don't think so," I say. "It's not for me."

t's been nearly two weeks since I saw him.

After work, I lie on my bed with the Braddocks' photos. There's a voluptuous humiliation in being reduced to looking at his image like an outsider. I've moved through my days in a perfunctory way. Unlocking my mailbox and collecting the stray bills and flyers, cleaning dishes and folding laundry, turning down my sheets to enter my bed. The rote mechanisms of sustaining day-to-day life. I can't believe this was a life I didn't know enough to hate. Worse, a life I was grateful for. It's the sensation of a fog lifting to reveal that I've been standing right on the lip of a plummeting cliff.

I keep the book and the box of Sylvia's belongings right near my bed. Tangible proof that what I had was real. The woman on the cover of *Villette*, with her veiled, cunning face looks sometimes beautiful, sometimes ugly. I've tried picking up the book and following the dense thread of the plot. But each time, my mind slips off the words.

Without his presence in my life, I'm reduced to my old tactics. For five years, my access into other people's lives has been through the unwitting clues they've left behind. Their photographs offering an intricate but obscure code into their habits. Into the rhythms of their lives together, the quiet, tugging undercurrent they never noticed.

Tonight, I stare at Patrick's hand entwined with Sylvia's. His skin against hers. I can almost feel the heat of his palm pressed against mine, the small, thoughtless movements of his muscles as he shifts. A tiny flame sparks inside me, but I extinguish it, not wanting the pain of desiring him.

Moving to the second photo in the stack: Patrick's arm circles around Sylvia's waist. In another photo, he buries his fingers in her hair; in the next, she perches on his lap, cupped perfectly against him. Her lips pressed to his cheek, his hand on her shoulder. In nearly every photo of the Braddocks together, Patrick touches Sylvia. She touches him. They're like a couple in some urban legend, kept alive by physical contact with each other. Remove that touch and they wilt.

The space between the chairs in Room 12 must be a constant taunt. To be so close, held apart by that clinical distance. Even from the first day I met with him, Patrick was breaching these boundaries. That sensation of his knee against mine: maybe it wasn't an act of rebellion, but a deep and unthinking instinct, his body drawn automatically to hers.

I grow calm. The awareness of what I have to do comes over me so easily, so completely, that I know this plan has been waiting inside me all along, biding its time.

FIFTEEN

I come to the Elysian Society early, before I'm scheduled to meet with a client, and slip directly into Jane's office. I've brought money along, folded tight and moist inside my palm. My pulse is rapid against the knot of bills.

Jane barely glances up when I enter. "Can I help you?"

I shut the door behind me. "I'd like to talk in private."

Jane's office is ripe with signs of ordinary life. A birthday card pinned on the corkboard, a cardboard cup of pungent-smelling coffee on the corner of the desk. The framed photo of a graduating teenager, cheeks pebbled with acne.

"I need lotuses," I say.

"Oh?" Jane licks her thumb tip, turns over one page of a thin yellow sheaf.

"For my own purposes," I add, unnerved by her lack of interest.

"The lotuses are strictly controlled," Jane says. "You of all people should know that."

Her voice is neither surprised nor accusatory. She's like an actress reciting the expected lines, testing me with her coolness.

"I'm willing to pay," I say. "Whatever it takes, I'll pay."

Jane keeps her head bent. Her cheeks are too bright with blush, an unnatural layer over her skin, and she smells like laundry detergent, hairspray. I wonder if she wears these markers to remind the bodies that she's better than us. She goes home to a husband

and children and friends, secure that she's never been mistaken for anything other than exactly what she is.

"Five years," she says, at last, addressing her desk. "After five years of being the model employee, you want in on this? Why the change of heart?"

"I want to open myself up to new opportunities," I say.

"You want to open something," Jane says. "Don't get poetic about it with me. I've been doing this for years too, remember. I've heard all the excuses."

Her quick contempt is like a strike. I shut and open my eyes, letting myself become immune. "What do I have to do?" I ask. "Just tell me."

"There's nothing you can do."

"What does Ana do?"

Jane doesn't rise to the challenge. "I don't know what you're talking about."

"If you'll work with her, it only seems fair to work with me."

"Life isn't fair," Jane says.

"You're right." My spine lengthens. "For instance, what you're doing, it wouldn't look good if it ever got out. You might not be doing anything wrong yourself, but life isn't fair. Other people might not agree."

At this, Jane looks up. "You're not trying to blackmail me, are you?" She laughs once.

"How many other people know what you're doing here?" I ask. "I'm the only uninvolved person who knows. The others can't expose you without revealing their own participation. But if you won't sell me the lotuses, I don't have any motivation to protect you."

It's a flimsy argument, but in my mouth, the words are unflinching as weapons.

The silence builds between us. Then Jane stands abruptly, slides open a long drawer on the opposite side of the desk. "I suppose it doesn't matter, anyway," she says, brittle. "Suit yourself, if it means that much to you."

Glancing over the edge of the desk, I see the wastebasket, a nest of crumpled paper. And a pair of eyes. A photo that's been torn into pieces, leaving the strip of face from forehead to nose intact. I recognize the style of the portrait: I've assumed this pose myself, once each year. Hair pulled back, face scrubbed clean, standing against an unadorned white wall.

These images are arranged in a photo album for prospective clients, our faces collected between white leather covers. I've imagined strangers sitting in Mrs. Renard's office, suppressing tears, taut with that stubborn pride people draw on in painful moments. I imagine them examining me and deciding, *yes, she'll do*, or moving past me without interest.

The eyes in the wastebasket prick at my memory. I know her. Even from this small section of her face, I know her. Cloudy blue irises beneath eyebrows fine as pen strokes.

"Here we are." Jane's hand withdraws, clutching an orange plastic bottle. Thin silhouettes of lotuses cluster like fingerprints. "I'll give you eight to start with." She pauses, looking me up and down. "You've brought money, I hope?"

When Jane tells me how much it will cost, I know she's watching me to gauge my reaction, taking a mean pleasure in this. I duck my head to hide my face. It's three weeks' pay, easily. Ana hadn't mentioned this side of the arrangement.

"Don't worry," Jane says. "You stand to earn it back and more, if you're smart."

As she counts the money, I glance again at the eyes. They hold a hint of a smile, a faraway quality. The closed-off wisdom of an old morgue photo or a marble saint.

Jane tips the lotuses off the edge of the desk into the mouth of an envelope. "The one rule I expect you to follow above all others, Eurydice, is this." She pauses to lick the envelope flap, her tongue a startling wedge of wet pink. "Watch out for yourself," she says. "You go into this with your eyes open. Don't come crying to me if it's not what you expected."

"Of course," I say. "I won't. I wouldn't."

Jane holds the envelope out to me. After the briefest hesitation, the knowledge of everything I'm about to do teeming in my head, I accept.

"The real shame is that you're not cut out for this kind of work," Jane says then. She speaks so flatly that I can't tell whether she's making a prediction or a threat. "I always hoped you'd keep away from this. You're going to be eaten alive."

I call his office. It's seeping into evening, but calling him while he's at a public space feels like a safe compromise. The phone rings five times before he answers. "Hello?"

I was expecting the buffer of a secretary. For a moment, it's as if my lips have been sewn shut. "Mr. Braddock?"

"Who is this, please?"

He doesn't recognize me. "Edie," I say. "From the Elysian Society."

Patrick is quiet. Then: "Right. Of course. Hello."

I want to hold his voice inside my mouth and savor it. "Is this a bad time?"

"No, you're fine." A rustle on the other end. A creak, as if he's adjusting his weight in his chair. "So what is this about? Just a social call, or am I in trouble?"

It's the carefully cheerful tone that keeps other people at bay. Politeness as armor. "I wanted to—" I start, but the words lodge in my throat. "I want to make sure you're doing all right," I say instead.

"Well, I am, thanks."

"We haven't seen you lately."

"Things have been busy at work." There's silence for a moment, and I bite the slippery underside of my lip. "I wasn't aware that I'd been gone long enough for anyone to notice," Patrick says.

"We've missed you at the Elysian Society," I say.

"How long has it been? A week?" His voice lightens even further, that false friendliness as sharp as a needle.

It has been two weeks. It's nearing the end of April now. Once, I would have agreed with him that fourteen days is nothing. Since I met Patrick, though, the passage of time has taken on a startling weight.

"Mr. Braddock—" I begin.

"Just Patrick. We don't have to get formal."

"Patrick," I repeat. "I'm calling because our last conversation concerned me, and I wanted to address that."

"All right."

"When you asked how long people stay at the Elysian Society, I could tell you were disappointed in my response." It could be risky, saying it aloud. It's possible he wasn't disappointed at all, and that my words will plant that seed in Patrick's mind.

"I wouldn't say disappointed," he says after a moment. "Surprised. Maybe."

"You don't feel closer to Sylvia," I supply. "And you're afraid you never will again."

A long silence. "I guess that's true." He laughs under his breath. "Am I that transparent?"

"I'm calling you because I have an idea." And I tell him, presenting everything to him as cleanly as possible: a business proposition. A legal contract.

When I'm done, there's silence on the other end. I rub my thumbnail against my thigh while I sit cross-legged on my bed, pressing the nail down hard into my flesh. I close my eyes and colors flower against the back of my eyelids. I open them again and look at the indented circles on the tender insides of my thighs.

"I'd like that," Patrick says at last.

The next afternoon, I find Ana in the waiting room. She's slumped and staring at the TV, dark brown eyes catching a reflected hint of the rushing waterfall on the screen. She runs a lock of hair through her fingers again and again; I watch the shiny black strands slide through her fingertips in a hypnotic rhythm.

When I sit beside her, Ana starts, looking at me as if I've woken her from a deep sleep. "How have you been?" I ask.

"Oh, fine, thank you." She matches my formal tone with enough exaggeration to slip from sincere to mocking.

I study the fine fan of her lashes, and her short, blunt hair held back with pins. She looks exhausted, shadows collecting underneath her eyes. "What happened with your client that night?" I ask, dropping my voice to a hush. "Are you still seeing him?"

"God," Ana says. She laughs under her breath. "One favor and you're my mother?"

"If he's still bothering you, you can go to Mrs. Renard. I'd vouch for you, I've seen the way he acts."

"And you think she'd help me?" Ana asks. "Thanks anyway." She sighs. "It's not a big deal. Rob just wants more from me than I can give right now."

"What more could he want?" I ask.

Ana visibly shakes herself, a quick movement, as if she's working an ache out of her muscles. "He wants me to go full-time," she says. "Go permanent. He's been riding me about it for a while, but it's worse lately."

On the TV screen, a vast field of yellow flowers lies ringed by distant mountain peaks. Thousands of blossoms, so uniformly bright that they hurt my eyes.

"He wants me to be her," Ana continues. "Live with him. Wear her clothes. For a few months. Enough that he can be with her day in, day out, not just for a night at a time."

"Ana—" On the screen, a breeze blows across the surface of the blossoms, stirring them into a froth. Like waves moving over the water.

"I need the money. I can't even answer my phone anymore because I'm afraid of creditors, and—" Ana stops, a stubborn look pulling over her face. "Anyway. That's why we fought. Now you know. Happy?"

Ana, her hair dyed dishwater blond or flashy red, curling up next to a stranger at night and waking to kiss his cheek, changing into a too-small blouse that she never chose for herself. A wild sensation overwhelms me: too many doors flung open at once.

She's watching me. "Well, you look awfully calm," she says. "Aren't you going to tell me not to do it? That I have so much to live for, that I shouldn't throw my life away for some heartbroken asshole?" When I don't answer, she tries for a smile. It comes out a wince instead. "Yeah, I guess not," she says. "Maybe it is a good plan for a girl like me."

"I never said that."

But Ana's lost to me, her mouth crimped into an inflexible line, staring at the TV screen. After a second, I rise and leave, and it's not until I'm moving back toward Room 12 that I realize I meant to ask her about the pale blue eyes, discarded in the wastebasket.

SIXTEEN

I sit on Patrick's sofa, my bare feet tucked beneath me. It's evening, the final day of April. I could reach out and wipe everything away: the cream-colored living room, Patrick's body beside me, the dusky world beyond the window. But I'm here. The world is here.

I wear a new dress, the one I tried on with Dora. I returned to purchase it just this morning. The fabric is the green of a furled bud, the neckline plunging low enough to expose my breasts. My mouth is dark and full with Sylvia's lipstick.

Patrick holds the slim stem of his wineglass. His fingers are long and thin, the fan of bones clearly visible. I lift my gaze to catch him watching me. He smiles and I turn away too quickly.

The Braddocks' house has enormous windows dominating the front, like a dollhouse with one side opened to the world. It's a showy home, valuing pride over privacy. Where we sit now, anyone could look inside and see us arranged here. An ordinary couple. A man and a woman after a first date. A husband and a wife with a baby upstairs asleep. Lovers reconciling; lovers breaking apart.

Up close, the rough edges show. I can tell that Patrick is attempting to make it a home again, and to a casual observer, nothing is too obviously out of place. It's as if Patrick is a museum curator, rebuilding a convincing replica of a past he only knows through books. But the telling details present themselves one by one the longer I gaze around the room.

The house has an unused smell. The light bulbs in the hallway don't work; we had to pick our way through the gloom. The hard, shiny shell of a dead wasp, ruffled with legs and wings, curls against the leg of the coffee table.

When Patrick lowers his wineglass, there's a light stain on the chapped skin of his lips. I have the impulse to press my mouth against the mark.

"Do all of your coworkers make house calls like this?" he asks.

I smile, unsure, but his eyes over the edge of his wineglass are light and conspiratorial, inviting me in. "What I'm doing this evening is a service I'm providing on my own time."

"Well, I respect a woman who can take initiative." Patrick lifts his glass in a brief toast.

Framed photographs scatter across the bookshelves and against the wall. Sylvia smiles at me in duplicate. Music playing in the background covers the brief silence that hangs between us.

"Your home is lovely," I say.

"Sylvia is responsible for most of the decorating," Patrick says, glancing around as if noticing his living room for the first time. "I can't take credit."

I imagine what Sylvia must have felt, during parties, during quiet evenings, surveying the home she'd designed. A child with a dollhouse, choosing the decorations she liked. And the husband smiling beside her.

"Should I give you the grand tour?" Patrick says. He sets down his wineglass; it's already empty. "I probably remember how to do this."

The entire house is beautiful, though I spot needling signs of neglect. In the kitchen, a cluster of amber bottles stands on the counter, a single fly buzzing greedily around one open mouth and then the other. A cupboard door hangs open, revealing empty shelves. I notice a thick pile of mail on an end table, envelopes flaking onto the floor.

But I focus on the monuments to Sylvia's taste that still stand: the rug so exquisitely soft that I shiver when I cross it in my bare feet. The windows are tall and bare, slicing up the outside world into private works of art.

My mind returns to the photographs. The way I first saw the Braddocks' lives, offered up in small pieces. A corner of a doorway, an edge of a window. I spun together my own version of their home. Walking through the reality now, the differences keep catching at me. The living room is larger than I expected. In the kitchen, the hallway branches off to the left instead of the right. I feel the other version of their home flickering, fading.

I reach out and brush my fingertips along a wall to reassure myself.

We reach a second hallway. Patrick flips a switch and the recessed lights glow like flat halos above us. We stand together, his elbow nearly touching mine. My breath comes quick and shallow. I feel an uncoiling inside me, something tight and inflexible finally loosening.

"These are all photographs she took," Patrick says in a hushed voice. It's as if Sylvia is sleeping nearby and we might wake her. "Every year, we went on vacation right around our anniversary. Sylvia picked her favorite photo from each vacation."

The six framed photos take up half of the hallway, trailing off like an unfinished sentence. One photo shows terracotta soldiers, their faces static but alive and alert. In the next photo, the ungainly lines of Stonehenge rise against a mute gray sky.

Patrick stops in front of a narrow cobblestone street, wet red pansies in the windowsills. "I wanted to show her everything she'd missed before we met." He reaches out to wipe dust from the lip of the frame, leaving a streak of shiny darkness.

When he speaks, his voice is careful. "Anyway. To finish the tour."

There's a door at the end of the hall, hanging open. I follow

Patrick, but he pauses at the threshold, pushing the door so that it swings inward. I see a bed that seems to take up most of one wall.

If there's a moment to turn back, it's now. Patrick and I look at each other. We don't look away. I feel at once as if I'm not here at all and as if I'm the only woman who's ever lived on this planet. In my years working as a body, I've forgotten what it feels like to be desired.

And I want him back. It's a pure greed that cuts through everything else. I want him. It seems impossible that I could channel what I feel into any other pursuit, any other direction, without destroying everything in its path.

Patrick pulls me into his arms. For a moment, the fierceness of desire fades, and I'm astonished by the simplicity of being held against another body. My contact with other people has been so stingy, doled out in accidental touches. This close, I can feel Patrick's heart beating through the fabric of his shirt. His chin is rough against my cheek.

I'm the one who kisses him first.

When I pull back, he stops me, holding onto my wrists. "Where are you going?" he asks. Although I'm already breathless, his voice stays soft and unhurried.

"I thought you wanted her."

"I want to be with you first," he says.

I hesitate. "That wasn't part of the agreement."

"But it's what you want?"

"Yes," I say. "It's what I want." It feels as if I've never said anything this true before. Even just admitting that I want something is arousing.

Patrick's grip tightens. He pulls me toward him. "If it's what you want, then you should have it," he says, as if it's always been this simple.

———

My shorn dress on the bedroom floor is iridescent green, like the husk an insect leaves behind. We're on the bed. The sheets are thick with his scent. The pillows indented, blotchy and misshapen. I can't get enough. It's thrilling how used everything feels. Compared to the cool anonymity of Room 12, Patrick's bedroom is opulent with odors and clutter.

In the mirror across from the bed, my hair is tangled and my eyes are wet and luminous. I'm feral. A creature awakened from a long slumber.

Afterward, I lie across the bed. I'm dazed and pulsing, someone cast up on an unfamiliar shore and slowly returning to consciousness. When I glance down the length of my body, I could be encountering a stranger. I didn't recognize the voice that issued from my throat while we were together.

Patrick strokes my hair away from my forehead. When he kisses me, I catch an unfamiliar taste on his lips and realize that it's me.

"I liked that." I'm still unguarded enough to say such naked things.

He laughs, low and intimate. We lie together, Patrick loosely embracing me. The uncurtained windows overlook the backyard. An impression of thick foliage, the night pressing up against the glass, as if we're alone in the middle of an enchanted forest. I'm tired, suddenly, my eyelids weighted.

Dark water leaks at the edges of my consciousness, then swells from a trickle to a roar, rushing over my head.

it can't last

it never does

"Edie."

With effort, I open my eyes. Patrick looks down at me, face half in shadow.

He doesn't say anything else. He doesn't have to. I remember. And while I was compliant before, now there's a glimmer of stubbornness. I don't want this to end just yet. The two of us.

I rise from the bed, Patrick's arms falling from me. I walk past the mirror, my reflection a long, willowy apparition crossing the darkness, and retrieve a single lotus. "I'll need water."

Patrick lifts himself up on one elbow. "You're taking that?"

"It's the same as when you visit the Elysian Society."

Patrick rises. His elbow brushes me roughly as he moves by, and I'm jarred. In an instant, I have been reduced from his lover to something inconvenient, a mere obstacle.

When he comes back with a glass of wine, I'm sitting on the edge of the bed, covered with the sheets. He hands me the wine. "Be careful," he says.

His concern feels as tender as a bouquet of roses. As romantic a promise as a diamond ring. Emboldened, I touch his hand.

I slide the lotus between my lips. Maybe it's the wine that makes the lotus work more quickly than usual, or maybe it's my lusty, drowsy state, but I recede almost instantly. My last image is of Patrick's face, his eyes looking down at me, lips parted slightly, waiting. Waiting.

It's early in the morning when I leave, the predawn sky creamy and pale. When I see my reflection in the entryway's mirror, I'm rumpled. My already clumsy eye makeup is smudged.

"How much do I owe you?" Patrick asks from behind me. He doesn't meet my eyes, his voice cool.

I turn from the mirror. He's counting a sheaf of bills from the depths of his wallet. It's impossible to think that he's the same man whose head was between my legs just hours ago, so that I could look down and notice, as if from a great distance, the way the hair was beginning to thin at the top of his scalp. His exposed scalp felt as intimate a revelation as the presence of his mouth against me.

"What are you doing?" I ask.

"We already discussed this," Patrick says.

"You're right," I say. He hands me the money. I accept, holding the bills like a wilted corsage. "Thank you."

Now that this ugly part of the evening is over, tucked away, Patrick relaxes again. He reaches out to slip a strand of my hair behind my ear. Even after everything else we've done, the smallness of this gesture brings my heart speeding. "I'll see you soon," he says.

t's as if I've been allowed into a secret world and then forced to reemerge, unprepared for the narrowness of my reality. I move through the confines of my apartment, astonished at the apparent connections between one life and the other: the glass of stale water that's been sitting on the kitchen counter for days; my toothbrush propped inside the medicine cabinet; a brush with golden hairs curled through the tines. These remnants of my presence are the only way I can connect the woman I am now with the woman I was before I walked into Patrick's house.

One thing still troubles me, an ache I can't place. It doesn't come to me until I go into my bedroom and lie down on my colorless bedding. The photo doesn't fit anymore. The Polaroid of Sylvia, naked, in the too-dark lipstick. Unconsciously, I always filled out the details with the bedroom from the photo. Compared to this, the actuality of their bedroom seems too pale and too ordinary.

Later, I remind myself. Later, later. I can think about it later.

SEVENTEEN

Again, I wake up on the floor. Crumpled against the wall as if I've been pushed.

My lungs stretch tight as bruises inside me. I wait to come back to myself fully: my hand resting against the floor, my legs folded at an angle beneath me. My left knee stinging. Cautiously, I rise. I have to cling to the top of the bureau to steady myself. Dizziness blazes through me.

I wonder what Lee would think, what he'd say, if he could see me lying here, still damp and soft and almost bruised from Patrick's touch, like overripe fruit. The idea brings a dutiful shame. But stronger than that, a triumph. A thrill.

Lee only knows the version of me that exists within the Elysian Society walls. A woman ruled by caution. Controlled and wary, never asking for more than I can safely allow into my life. He hasn't seen just how quickly caution can turn inside out. Desire turns me reckless, hungry. I have to relearn how to control my lust, how to partition it off like a dangerous beast that could ravage the other areas of my life.

Meeting with Mr. O'Brien, I will my brain to stay calm, ignoring the turbulence that rushes beneath. He's come to see Margaret nearly as frequently as Patrick has seen Sylvia. Today, I try to imagine how he'd react if he knew what I could offer. If he realized that the access to Margaret he has now is as stingy as what he had during her lifetime.

All this time, I've been sitting across from my clients as they speak to their lovers, held apart. I used to feel generous, letting them borrow my body. Now that I know what else I could give them, my denial feels close to power.

As the lotus slides down my throat, I think of my own private stash back home. Visualizing that envelope of slim pills is enough to throw me off. As I start to sink backward into the darkness, I can tell that it's wrong. All wrong.

'm naked. The night air is humid against my skin. The lake spreads out, dark and glittering; the moon over the water is suspended like a drop waiting to fall.

I rise and float to him, light as a butterfly. When I'm next to him, his hands against me, the heat and energy of his touch nearly press right through the fine layer of my skin. Even though I'm close enough that his breath slips into my mouth, his face stays shadowed.

I should go with him, leave this place. But a tug of dread holds me back.

When I look again, the window consumes half the sky. Patrick lies in bed, his back to me. I recognize the spare constellation of freckles and moles across the span of his shoulder blades, the dulled white-gold of his hair in the moonlight. Hidden from me by his body, on the far side of the bed, there's a woman. Her hand rests on Patrick's waist.

The hand stirs. Her body rises into view. Hair tousled. Her features have a plainness that turns her too familiar. As if she's a minor actor in a play, the same insignificant face reappearing throughout the story. The maid, the nun, the lover, the fool. The woman stares directly into my eyes. She's me; I realize it with a dulled shock.

At the edge of the lake, I'm trapped, unable to move, not certain whose body I occupy. I watch as I lean over Patrick, my mouth set in a smile. My hand slides down the length of his chest, pausing just above the curled lip of the sheet. Then, so quickly that my head swims, my hand has moved to Patrick's face. I press my palm down against his nose, his mouth. One quick flinch of life passes over the length of Patrick's body, a protest. Then he's gone.

I watch myself press my cheek against his, my face transformed from blankness into a specific and wild beauty. The face of the woman who has everything she's ever wanted.

W ho's Patrick?"
The electrical crackle of anger wakes me immediately.

"Who is he?" His face is pinched. "I've never met anybody by that name."

"I'm sorry," I say. Mr. O'Brien is subdued for now, but his stillness is just a layer over a bristling tension. I have to control this before Mr. O'Brien's anger seeps through the building like smoke. "Am I to understand that Margaret mentioned that name?" I ask.

"Yes," Mr. O'Brien says, mocking. "You are to understand that. Everything was normal and then it's suddenly Patrick, Patrick. Patrick." The name falls from his lips with a wrong-sounding thud. "Who the hell is he?"

I survey my client for a second, running my tongue over the slick backs of my teeth. "Perhaps a friend of Margaret's," I say. "This process can be inexact, it can—"

"Margaret and I were always open with each other," he says. "She never would have kept a secret from me."

The solution comes to me swiftly, passed to me as if a hand in a crowd slipped something into my palm. "In that case, Mr. O'Brien, I have to apologize. It seems there's been a mistake."

"I pay a lot of money to avoid mistakes," Mr. O'Brien says.

"And I can appreciate that," I say. "If you're willing to let this indiscretion slide, I'd be happy to lessen that burden for you."

He blinks hard. "Meaning?"

"I'd be willing to meet you again, without any extra cost to you." I can spare one lotus. One lotus is nothing. "We could make up for the time you've lost."

He runs his tongue over his lips. "Here?" Mr. O'Brien asks.

I hesitate. If I schedule another encounter inside these walls, it could draw too much attention. Throughout the years, there have been bodies incapable of emptying themselves enough, or bodies who have emptied themselves too completely. I've heard the stories: spitting out the wrong words during encounters, garbled names and misplaced details, meaningless as radio static rising from dead airwaves. None of these bodies have lasted at the Elysian Society.

"We'll meet privately," I say. "At a location of your choosing."

"That's allowed?" he asks.

"It can be." My body is tense with the waiting, prepared for a sudden knock at the door, Jane's presence swooping down like a triumphant bird of prey.

"Fine," Mr. O'Brien says, at last. "That sounds like a fine solution to me."

I listen for footsteps in the corridor beyond Room 12. But Mr. O'Brien isn't done yet: "And in case you're interested, when you said Patrick's name, you sounded terrified." He narrows his eyes at me. "You sounded furious."

In the entrance to the waiting room, I pause. Bodies cluster at the far end, faces craned forward, washed in the unflattering glow of the TV screen. Several people have arms knotted around chests or hands clamped over mouths, poses that strike me as theatrical.

I approach, scanning the faces for one I recognize. Lee meets my eyes and breaks from the group. "Edie," he says. "Don't worry. I'm sure it's nothing, really."

"What's happening?"

Lee touches my arm. "It's nothing," he repeats.

The TV screen is still hidden from me by someone's broad back. I imagine what they're looking at. Patrick and my body sitting in Room 12. His hand reaching for me, my body unmoving, accepting whatever happens next.

I shift into the center of the group so that I can see the dusty TV set. A reporter speaks into the camera, eyes darting across unseen cue cards. The trim cadence of her voice refuses to fall into intelligible words. She stands in direct sunlight, posing in front of a building that's starkly familiar. The white brick walls, the trimmed hedges rising in the background.

"It's not a live broadcast." Lee hovers behind my shoulder. "It's just a segment."

The murmur of the reporter's voice stops. She smiles into the camera too long and then vanishes. The group of bodies breaks apart immediately. A body leans behind the TV set to adjust something. A second later, a pristine forest at dawn replaces the news channel.

"I don't understand," I say.

"A body from the Elysian Society worked with someone," Lee says. "Some woman trying to get information about the Hopeful Doe case. Apparently, she just went to the authorities."

Betrayals like this are what Mrs. Renard has guarded against for years, and the fact that it's finally happened is more of a surprise than it should be. The blow that lands as the muscles relax. I glance at the cluster of bodies, now talking in low voices. It could have been any of them. Beneath their cultivated emptiness, there must be dozens of seething secrets.

"Her name is Candace Fowler," Lee adds.

My mind freezes for a second, trying to figure out why the name is so familiar. She comes to me: the woman in Room 12, the one whose daughter found the body. I stifle my surprise, keeping my expression flat. I didn't expect Mrs. Fowler to try again; she seemed like the type to make a self-righteous show of tenacity and then give up with secret relief.

"Which body worked with her?" I ask. "Did they mention any names?" Names wouldn't even do any good, I realize, with a misplaced desire to laugh. I don't know the birth name of anyone who works here.

Lee's face grows careful, as distancing as if he's holding me back by the shoulders. "We don't know," he says. "They haven't said. It could be anyone."

I search his features, hearing an unexpected coolness in his voice. "You don't think I could have done it, Lee?" I ask.

"Like I said, nobody knows." He hesitates. "But I did hear that you were the first body that Fowler approached."

I take a deep breath. "I see."

"The only body she approached, that we know of."

"But that's just it," I say. "I sent Fowler away. I told Jane. I'd forgotten about her completely until now." My words are unconvincing. I should have remembered: a single secret contaminates everything around it, turning honest moments into things to be guarded. "You have to believe me," I say.

Lee's resolve hovers and then loosens. "I do."

"I'd never endanger the Elysian Society," I say. Then I add, "Lee, it's me," as if this means anything anymore, as if it's even true.

EIGHTEEN

Laura Holmes. That's Hopeful Doe's true name. The only detail Mrs. Fowler could glean from the encounter, the only information Hopeful Doe provided. It makes me strangely sad that this was all she could say about herself. A detail that a lost child, trying to find her way back home, would offer in desperation. *This is my name. This is who I am. Help me.*

Laura Holmes vanished from her life at the end of last year. She lived in a town eighteen hours away. Her rent checks stopped, she missed too many work shifts as a drugstore cashier, her scattering of acquaintances stopped hearing from her. Laura's disappearance was less one recorded moment of absence and more a gradual fading. *Further details about Holmes's death are still under investigation at this time.*

I spot several discrepancies in the saintly Hopeful Doe narrative. Laura Holmes was nineteen, hovering on the brink of womanhood. She was aloof, maintaining only shallow relationships. Trying to reconcile wistful Hopeful Doe with the blunt reality of Laura Holmes is like laying two transparencies on top of each other. For every feature that lines up neatly, there's an unruly edge extending out, a curve that doesn't match. The result is looking at two people at once, neither of them quite themselves anymore, but neither one completely the other.

Viv asks me to hold the baby, thrusting him into my arms without waiting for a response. The baby is a bundle of con-

tradictions: heavy and damp, yet astonishingly light. He's muscu-
lar, kicking at me with froggy legs, but also disjointed and loose
inside his chubbiness.

In the baby's face, there's a trace of Henry's broad nose and
Viv's tidy, crimped chin. Impulsively, I visualize a child with my
austere blond hair, Patrick's greenish eyes and haphazard freckles.
Embarrassed by the image, I nearly let the baby slip. He braces his
feet against my thighs, drools a fine sheen along his chin.

"Come back over here, Benny-bean." Viv stretches her hands
out for the baby.

I hesitate. My hands tighten around the baby; I can feel the
quick pump of his breath through his belly. An unfamiliar impulse shifts through me. I'm not sure if it's violence or tenderness.
I don't want to relinquish the baby.

The moment stretches on, seeming to grow thicker and deeper
than the actual time passing. Viv's expression shifts from polite
expectation to impatience, then confusion.

don't try to take him

he doesn't belong to you

My muscles loosen and the moment becomes normal again.
I smile broadly, stretch Ben across to his mother. She skillfully
removes the baby from my hands.

"You have kids, Lucy?" Viv's carefully sunny, hoping to blaze
away the oddness.

"Me? Oh, no. No," I say. "Not yet."

Viv settles the baby on her lap. Ben pats at her arm: quick little
touches, as if his mother's skin might hurt him. She reaches down
and kisses the baby's head, and I look away.

"You want kids one day, though?" she asks, lifting her face.

"As soon as I get my life in order." I match her brightness.

"No point putting it off too long," Viv says. "So many people
think they can wait for the perfect time. You have to make the
leap. I've known women who waited and then they ran into

trouble." Viv sucks in her breath, widens her eyes. "God, I'm sorry."

"It's fine," I say. "You can speak freely."

We sit in their living room across from a lineup of the Damsons' wedding-day portraits, photos of infant Ben. I'm working harder than usual to slip into my role as drab Lucy. Now that I've been with Patrick, that knowledge lies sparkling and hot under everything.

"Sylvia was like that, you know," Viv says. "She wanted kids, but they kept putting it off. Then it was hard for them to get pregnant. I know it upset her."

This new knowledge slides into place in my understanding of the Braddocks, pulling open more spaces than it closes, skewing everything out of line. Patrick hasn't even mentioned children.

Viv tucks her arm tighter around Ben. "I hate thinking that she never got her baby." The words are humid with the threat of tears. "I couldn't stop obsessing about it. Then I thought, but what if she *did* have a baby, and now the baby didn't have a mother? I can't figure out which is worse. Would I rather die without knowing Ben, or would I want him to be alone without me?"

I'm suddenly furious at Viv. At how effortlessly she glides from Sylvia to her own life, as if Sylvia is just a mirror for Viv to stare into. Measuring her own sadness against the immeasurability of Sylvia.

"It's natural to dwell on these questions after a loss," I try. But my anger grows, sparking like a match dropped in a trail of gasoline. I find myself staring at the baby's head. His bones are clearly outlined beneath the fuzz of his hair; the light catches the slightest indent at the top of his skull. Again, that wild mix of greed and rage and loss grows inside me.

"Viv," I say, "I should really be going."

Uncertain, she stands, bouncing the baby on her hip. "I'll see you later?"

"Yes," I say. "If you like."

Outside, in the Damsons' driveway, the strangeness of pregnancy is all I can think about. Sharing a body with an unseen being, crowded aside to make room for a separate mind. I place my hand on my lower stomach. There's a single shudder somewhere inside, and I yank my hand away as if I've been pricked.

Did you ever finish that book?" He strokes his hand through my hair. I'm lulled by the movement.

We're in his backyard; a high fence surrounds the property. Trees grow close to the border, offering enough coverage that we could be alone, except for the rising second-story windows and small balcony of his next-door neighbor's house.

With effort, I remember which book he means. "Not yet."

The patio chairs are scabbed with rust. Patrick had to wipe away a soupy layer of stagnant rain and dead leaves from the hollows of the seats. He excused himself by saying he hadn't been back here since last summer. Though the yard holds the lingering shape of something planned, it's overgrown, grass shabby and higher than my ankles. Flowers brim over the edges of the beds.

I was worried when I came over this evening; worried that our time together was a singular moment, unrepeatable. That Patrick would lose his nerve, or I wouldn't be able to reenter Sylvia's bed. But we'd barely greeted each other before he was kissing me, my neck, my shoulders, with a hunger as keen as my own.

A creak catches my attention. Turning my head so that Patrick's wrist presses my ear, I look toward the neighbor's house. A woman stands in the balcony doorway, her face framed in the shadows. She's youngish, about my age. Pretty in an expensive, upholstered way.

"I should try to turn this place around," Patrick says.

He hasn't followed my gaze. I turn back, face tight with embarrassment. It's as if Sylvia is gone, somewhere across the globe, and this woman, her ally, has spotted me with Sylvia's husband's hand in my hair.

I dip my head until Patrick's fingers slide free.

"Sylvia was always out here in the evenings. With a book and a drink." He inhales. "I'd love to see this place thrive again."

The balcony door clicks shut.

"When we first looked at this house," he says, "I remember Sylvia saying we could put a swing set in." And he points, closing one eye, at a corner of the garden. The spot suddenly looks lop-sided and bare, crudely excavated.

"You wanted kids," I say.

"One day," Patrick says. "You ever thought about kids?"

"Maybe," I say. "I was with someone when I was much younger and we—" I hesitate. Talking about this is prizing open a half-healed wound, picking at the tender edges. I force myself to speak casually. "We joked around. Named our future kids."

"What names?"

"Lucy," I say after a pause. "That was his favorite."

"Pretty."

"We weren't together long," I say.

"That's the point of people you date when you're young," Patrick says. "You build futures with them knowing it won't work out. I had a girlfriend like that. The last one before I met Sylvia. We invented a dozen futures. Living along the Seine. Famous artists in New York."

I try to imagine this precursor to Sylvia. If she had Sylvia's relentless, unshakeable beauty or if she was more like me, saved from ordinariness only through exhausting effort.

"I still think of her sometimes," he says. "Wonder how she's doing."

"Why did you end things?" I ask.

There's a long silence. I'm on the verge of repeating the question when he speaks. "She ended it," he says. "But it was my fault. My relationships before Sylvia, I was too jealous. Once I liked someone, I put a lot of pressure on her. Asked for too much."

A quick shiver runs through me. I rub furiously at my forearms.

"We should go inside," he says. "It's getting dark."

In the house, the chilliness and the silence wrap themselves around me. A contrast to the fading heat of the day. It's like hanging at the edge of a drop-off: the warmth still clinging to one half of my body while the rest is steeped in the coldness of what's ahead. I close the door, trying to forget the neighbor's expression as she watched us. That lack of surprise, as if she was used to seeing Patrick with unfamiliar women. As if I'm just one more body in a long line of them.

urydice," Mrs. Renard says. "I'm glad you could find the time to see me."

I stand in front of the desk, hands clasped. I'm aware of all the traces of Patrick that remain on my body. My sleep last night was thick, waking up a pleasant struggle. I barely had time to splash water across my sleep-rumpled face. Now, the sheen of sweat drying on my neck, his saliva lingering on my lips and body: it all feels like it's glowing, lighting a detailed map of my transgressions.

"I plan on meeting with each employee individually," she says. "It's not what I'd prefer to spend my day doing. Playing at principal, meeting with naughty students. It's a waste of time. But unfortunately, I don't have much choice."

I keep my shoulder blades tucked back, my gaze calm.

"Naturally, I'm aware that Mrs. Fowler approached you first," Mrs. Renard says. "I'm also aware that you reported her to Jane. You're not on trial here, Eurydice. But I need your help. You're my eyes and ears."

Behind her desk, a bird flies past the window, a rush of darkness.

"The others will see this as merely disciplinary," Mrs. Renard says. "It's true that I don't tolerate employees who break the rules. Whoever worked with Mrs. Fowler is dragging us into the media frenzy and misrepresenting what we offer." She laces her fingers together. "But it's more than that, Eurydice. Whoever did this, whether she knows it or not, she could need my help."

"I'm not sure I understand."

Mrs. Renard tilts her head, squinting at me. "You know what happened in Room 7?"

I didn't expect this question. "Yes," I say after a second. "I've heard rumors."

"Tell me."

"I've heard that there was a client who lied about his wife's death," I say, reluctant. "The version I heard was that he claimed she'd fallen down the stairs, broken her neck, but in reality it was his fault. He'd been abusing her." I look to Mrs. Renard to see if she'll confirm this, but her face stays immovable. "When the body swallowed the lotus in Room 7, everything went wrong. She smashed the water glass. She attacked her own body. She attacked the client."

Hearing the story in my own voice, it sounds overblown and childish. A retroactive cautionary tale attaching itself to a detail as innocuous as using paper cups instead of glass. But there's something inside the exaggerated details that's unnervingly real, like glimpsing the coldness of human eyes behind a gaudy Halloween mask.

"That's all I've heard," I finish.

Mrs. Renard nods. "When I was a young woman, there wasn't anywhere like the Elysian Society. A safe, respectable place to reconnect with your loved ones. Channeling was a dirty secret. A disgusting act for desperate people. And dangerous. Terribly dangerous. I heard stories of clients mistreating the bodies in horrible ways while they were gone. Bodies channeled for far too long, vast stretches of time. They'd end up broken, more often than not. I looked around at all this and I wondered why such a gift had to be so dangerous. So illicit."

It's not the first time Mrs. Renard has sketched out the history of the Elysian Society. She paints its origins in misty terms, dotted with flowery details. The same ones every time, like a well-worn fable. But I listen today as if I'm hearing it for the first time.

"Establishing the Elysian Society took trial and error," Mrs. Renard says. "Years of heartbreak and hard work. I had to fight tooth and nail to make people take this place seriously. For twenty years I've poured my energy into this place. I've helped thousands of grieving people. Healed thousands of broken hearts. But I lie awake sometimes and wonder if I've overstepped. Perhaps I've made things too safe. I've declawed the monster. Now people look around and they don't have the consequences breathing down their necks. The rules start to seem old-fashioned."

Her voice has a closeness that turns back in on itself, not extending to me. I could be overhearing a private conversation.

"In a perverse way, I'm grateful that story about Room 7 has survived," Mrs. Renard goes on. "Crude though it may be, it's an effective warning for the new hires. The clients are a different matter. We'll always have to guard against the questions: Why do we turn our backs on the souls most desperate to communicate?"

A flash of the lake. Sylvia's naked body curled up like a sleeping child, wrapped in weeds. Her dark hair glittering with a million tiny bubbles, eyes unseeing.

"Look at this whole sordid case," Mrs. Renard says. "Laura Holmes. We know her name. Barely anything, but even that much is surprising. This isn't the first time that clients have gone behind my back. They're arrogant. Certain that they'll sit down and hear a perfect confession: Professor Plum in the study with the knife." She laughs. The sound curdles in my ears. "Our clients don't realize what it does to someone, dying violently. Forcing the dead to solve their own deaths is like interrogating sleepwalkers at best. At worst, it's awakening a monster."

"You think Mrs. Fowler's information is false, then?" I ask, not sure whether this disappoints me or produces a grimy relief.

"Whether it's false or not," Mrs. Renard says, "she'll keep trying. That's why it's crucial to discover who worked with Fowler. Each time this body channels Laura Holmes, she comes closer to losing herself."

The sunlight has been creeping steadily up the windowpanes. Now it presses into my eyes like a searchlight.

"None of the bodies have left the Elysian Society since the news broke," Mrs. Renard says. "I suppose they know how suspicious that would look. That's quite lucky for us. I need you to be vigilant, Eurydice. Watch the others for any unusual behavior."

"Like what?" I ask.

"Well, anyone who seems different," she says. "Anyone who seems not herself."

I'm woozy from the light. Mrs. Renard turns into a dark shape in front of me, her features obscured. I can't make out her expression.

"The signs will be subtle," she continues. "Room 7 serves its purpose well enough as a warning, but if you look for blood and gore, you may miss what's right in front of you."

I can't say anything. My mouth has gone dry.

"Eurydice?" she prompts.

"I'll do my best," I say.

He walks through the dark hallway with the unthinking confidence of someone who knows every inch of this space. "Care for a drink?"

"Please," I say, keeping pace as if I'm also exactly at home here.

In the kitchen, Patrick reaches to open a cabinet above the fridge, his shirt lifting to expose the surprising darkness of the hair at his navel. I look away, shy as if I've never seen him undressed before.

When we pass into the living room, I instinctively straighten the edge of a tilted picture frame, pushing Sylvia's brilliant wedding-day smile back into alignment.

"How have you been holding up?" Patrick asks.

I pull both my legs up beneath me on the couch, aware that my dress's short hemline will slip up my thighs. "What do you mean?"

Patrick sits next to me. I watch the purposefulness that comes into his eyes as he keeps them focused on my face, not edging downward to my exposed skin. "The publicity your place is getting lately," he says. "This woman who's gone to the authorities."

I lift my glass to my mouth to avoid answering. I hadn't planned to broach any of this with Patrick. When I'm with him, I feel so separate from the rest of the world that there could be fires blazing outside the window, floodwaters bleeding up the road, and I wouldn't notice.

"You seem to stay away from the spotlight," Patrick says, and it takes me a second to realize he means the Elysian Society as a whole, not me specifically.

"I thought you said you didn't watch the news," I say.

I was trying for mild teasing, but he doesn't smile back. "Jenn mentioned it," he says. "It's been bothering her too."

"Patrick, it's nothing," I say. My whole body tenses, as if I'm preparing to run. "This story should fade any day now. We'll protect our clients' confidentiality."

"It's not that."

"Then what?"

Patrick reaches for me abruptly, running his thumb down the length of my hand. It's more soothing than sensual, his warm, rough-skinned thumb stroking my skin over and over. I can't tell which one of us he's trying to calm.

"This woman didn't even know the dead girl," he says. "Is that right? She brought back a stranger."

It's so quiet on Patrick's street. A steeping silence.

"She's breaking the rules," I say.

"Yeah, but it's a possibility," he says. "One I hadn't considered. Is a stranger going to pay to bring back my wife?"

"That won't happen," I say quickly. "We won't allow it to happen." But I'm thinking of the accusations I read, the careless sense of ownership that surrounded the speculation, as if these strangers deserved to know Sylvia's story by mere merit of their curiosity.

Sylvia's voice emerging from a different throat, her words sliding from a different tongue. Somebody asking her: *What happened to you? Tell me. Tell me.*

You can trust me.

His touch gains speed and pressure, almost painful. I resist the urge to move my hand.

"It could happen and I wouldn't even know," Patrick says. "She'd be helpless. A stranger could say anything to her. Do anything to her." He pauses. "Ask her anything."

"Patrick," I say. "You're worried for no reason."

He doesn't answer.

"This woman is only bringing back Laura Holmes because it's a murder case," I say. "Laura's a piece of a puzzle, something to be solved. It won't happen to someone like Sylvia."

Though I keep my words flat, there's a plea hidden inside. I want Patrick to agree. I want him to say: *You're right, you're right.*

There's no mystery to her loss.

"How can you guarantee that?" he asks. He lets go of me. When he drops his head, staring at the floor, the bumps of his spine stand out beneath the smooth skin of his neck. Even this utilitarian part of his body excites me. I want to trace each separate knot. The desire presses up under the gravity of the moment.

"I'm so sorry," I say. "I hate to think of you worrying."

He lifts his head, face bleary but slackening into a smile. "No," he says. "I'm being unfair. You have nothing to be sorry for. God, you've done so much already. Don't let me take my frustration out on you."

A jolt like an electrical current runs through my nerve endings. I ignore this; I reach for his hand again, intertwining my fingers through his, and then I move against him, pressing my face into his neck.

"I want to protect her," he says. "I failed once already."

"She's safe, Patrick," I say into the warmth of his skin. "She's yours."

His grip on me tightens, his fingers move to the small of my back. He's like a man under a hypnotist's sway, accepting without fear or question whatever he finds in front of him. Patrick's breath quickens. He murmurs a name, and I kiss him, kiss him again, not letting myself register whose name he said.

interpret my body differently with him. Before, I'd focus impassively on my flaws, the silvery stretch marks etched along one hip. Anything I could smooth or trim to blankness, I have, for years. Even the parts of my body that my clients never see.

With him, my body turns complete. I admire the flatness of my belly, the raised tenderness of my areolas. Flaws transform into markers of who I am. When Patrick idly traces a small maroon birthmark on my inner thigh, when he cups the fullness of my hips, he's experiencing a singular version of who I am. In these moments, it's easy to think that nobody else could slip into his bed and take my place.

There have been a few small, startling moments of panic or doubt. When I undressed in front of him, after the first wildness of being together had softened, I paused, suddenly exposed. If Patrick looked at my body more carefully, more critically, would he notice? Would he see the scars my past left on me? But he didn't say anything, and I let myself relax again. The marks have nearly vanished by now; my fingertips know where to go by memory alone.

Patrick's body is completely familiar to me. I'm least shy, most bold and possessive, when we're in bed together. I think nothing of taking him into my mouth, or of kissing the length of his thigh with its layer of pale hairs, soft and wiry at the same time. I crave the concentration that comes across Patrick's face as he pushes inside me.

When I wake into the watery darkness of the bedroom tonight, I turn my head to find Patrick awake. His arm is threaded beneath my cheek, his pulse against my skin, slightly out of rhythm with my own. "I'll get her for you?" I ask.

After a second, he nods.

Leaving the bedroom, it strikes me again. A fleeting realization. How open the bedroom is, how different from the dark, low-ceilinged room in the photograph.

At night, the shadows wash away the kitchen's abrasive edges. I can pretend that the lights would work if I tried the switch. I can pretend that the refrigerator is brimming with food. Last night's rinsed dishes are lined up inside the dishwasher. That there's life waiting just beyond, like a stage before the curtain lifts. I fill a glass with tap water.

he doesn't love me anymore

Someone slides his arms around my waist and leans his cheek against the top of my head. Fear moves through me. I hadn't known he'd followed me. Then I relax into Patrick's arms.

"I was dreaming about the lake," he says, muffled by my hair.

"Was she there?" I ask.

"No," he says. "It's always the same. I'm alone in that cabin. Waiting for her, and she never shows up. It's like a bad joke."

My mind stalls as I search for something comforting to say.

"I was only there once," he says, "but I remember that place better than I remember my childhood home. Where's the fairness in that?"

"Have you ever considered going back?" I ask.

His grip around me tightens. "Going back," he repeats.

"To the cabin," I say. "Maybe it would help." In the moonlight, the glass of water is silvery as a potion.

"I'm not sure it works that way."

"You've never wanted to go back?"

"No," he says. "I don't see a point. It wouldn't change anything. It wouldn't . . ."

I wait to see if he'll finish the sentence. When he doesn't, I'm relieved, as if the edges of something huge have brushed against me and then retreated. "Looking at it again could take away some of its power," I say.

Patrick doesn't answer for a long time. "What would you know about it?" he asks at last.

My heart contracts. "Nothing," I say. "You're right."

"Some things should stay in the past," Patrick says.

The words fill the kitchen around us, all the implications. Outside the window, the sleeping neighborhood feels like a glimpse into an entirely different world.

"You don't need to do that tonight if you don't want to," Patrick says, voice soft, and I look down at the lotus still clutched between my fingers.

"I know." And I slide the lotus between my lips. I swallow. In the moment, it's a relief to erase myself. Right now, I'm the discrepancy in this house, the dark thing disrupting the Braddocks' life together.

TWENTY

W elcome to the Elysian Society, Mr. Rogalski," I say to my newest client. "You're hoping to reach your daughter, is that correct?"

My mouth is greasy and candy-scented with pink lip gloss. In the photo he provided, Mr. Rogalski's arm is tucked self-consciously around a thin adolescent girl, her grin bristling with braces, dotted with gummy pink bands.

"As a matter of fact, I'm here to contact you."

Mr. Rogalski fits the mold of the semi-anonymous bachelors that pepper my clientele. Late middle age, eyes drooping like a dog's. I'd pegged him as divorced, latent problems with his wife triggered into action by their daughter's death. But his voice, that knowingness pulled taut as a wire, makes me reconsider.

"I'm here to ask a few questions," he says. "No need to take that." He gestures toward the lotus. "I'd like you to be fully present. Think you can manage that?"

"I'm afraid you may have misunderstood the services we offer here," I say.

Mr. Rogalski exhales, reaches inside the front of his jacket. He pulls out what looks like a slim back wallet, opening it and presenting it to me. I pretend to know which signs of legitimacy to look for, studying the somber police portrait against a pale blue background.

"I see." I settle back in my chair. I'm fully awake now, caution buzzing through me. In spite of myself, I'm curious. "I'm not sure I can be much help, Detective."

"Let me be the judge of that," Rogalski says. "First off, what's your name?"

"You can call me Eurydice."

A lift of the eyebrows, a low whistle. "That's from a myth, isn't it?" He doesn't wait for an answer. "Do you know the story behind it?"

"I'm familiar with it," I say, though I've forgotten. I can't remember if she's the one who eloped with a swan or the one who ate fruit seeds in the afterlife, dooming herself to stay imprisoned.

He glances around the room with a considered weight, as if he's just noticed where we are. "How long have you been working here?"

"Five years."

"What drew you to this job, if you don't mind me asking?"

"I needed work," I say. "The Elysian Society was hiring."

"Simple as that?"

"Simple as that." The lie comes easily.

"And you enjoy it," Rogalski says. "You're treated pretty well by your boss, by, ah, Mrs. Renard." He squints as if checking invisible cue cards.

"She's a wonderful employer."

"You'd really say so? Someone who asks you to do this?"

I'm silent.

"When you see clients, it's only talking, right?" he asks. "No physical contact."

"Correct," I say.

"Forgive me for being blunt, Miss Eurydice, but this job, it's not sexual?"

"Of course not," I say, heat rising through my veins.

"I've heard this place is supposed to be classy or something. All on the up-and-up. But to be frank, there's a potential for something a little—" He searches for a word. "Untoward. It never bothers you, having men use your body for their girlfriends and wives?"

"No," I say. "It's not like that at all."

"So what are your clients like, the men? Do you ever notice violent tendencies? Possessive, obsessed, yeah, I know all that."

"Our clients are not possessive," I say. "They're not obsessed. They're here to reconnect with their loved ones."

"Your wife dies and you don't move on? You keep on dragging her back, sitting in a room with a pretty girl in a dress that barely covers her, pretending you're getting closure?" His eyes move pointedly to my breasts.

I resist the urge to tug at my neckline.

He smiles as if my mere silence has settled something. "When you're sitting here, in this room, you must overhear lots of private information. Strangers spill their guts to you."

"The information our clients share in these rooms is confidential. I don't hear any of it."

He tilts his head down, looks at me from beneath his eyebrows. "But aren't you sitting right there?"

I'm an endless expanse of ice. "Can I ask why you're here?"

"I'm here about Laura Holmes," he says. "You've heard of her?"

"In that case, Detective, I think I can clear up some confusion," I say. "Whoever worked with Mrs. Fowler was doing so unauthorized, without our knowledge. That case doesn't have anything to do with the Elysian Society."

"Well, look at it from my angle," he says. "What we have is a lead that sounded like the work of your typical nut job. Half the time, when someone comes in with a tip like this, it's useless. This time, though, the joke's on us, because it turns out to contain some valid information. But it doesn't mean that everything is aboveboard."

I clasp my hands so tightly that I feel the interlocking bones.

"There's nothing conclusive yet, but Fowler's given us enough information to push the investigation ahead. Better than what we were working with before. So the question is: Does somebody inside these walls know more about that girl's death than they want to let on?"

Curling my fingers inward, I press my fingernails into each opposite hand until my flesh burns.

"The workers here could be sitting on some big secrets," he continues. "You squat here all day, hearing people's private thoughts. Deep dark confessions."

"As I've explained," I say, words brittle under the weight of my impatience, "the conversations they have with their loved ones stay between the two of them. Nobody else."

"Maybe," Rogalski says. "Or maybe somebody here overheard a juicy secret, a nice piece of information, and then fed it to Fowler."

"If you don't believe that what we do here is real, there's not much I can say." My heartbeat is shuddery and too quick. "We've never wasted time pandering to the skeptics."

"That's real noble of you." Rogalski laughs once. "People get all scrambled up by grief, they want to throw their money at whatever will make it all better, and you're here waiting in your little tight dress. Taking advantage of the grief-stricken, that's—" He turns his hand into a gun, thumb erect, pointer out, and jerks his hand once. "That's shooting fish in a barrel."

Impulsively, I reach up and wipe away the lip gloss. "May I speak plainly?"

"Please. That's what I expect."

"If I were you, I wouldn't judge what happens between these walls when you've lived a life so untouched by death." My anger is unwieldy, forcing the words out.

"And what makes you think my life has been so untouched, Miss Eurydice?"

"If you'd experienced loss on the same level as our clients, I don't see how you could come here and try to twist what we do into something"—I reach for the right word—"predatory."

Rogalski folds his arms over his chest.

"The girl in the photograph you gave me," I say. "Is she a friend's daughter? A niece?" I glance down at the lurid streak on my hand. "I assume you bought the lip gloss yourself."

"I bought it on my way here. It's called, ah, Sugarplum Fantasy. Nothing I'd ever let my daughter wear, personally."

I touch my lips. "I'm going to need you to leave."

Rogalski studies me for a second longer before he rises to his feet. His unhurried, shuffling movements are out of place in this room. I'm suffocated by his presence: the lunch on his breath, his uneven fingernails, the missing button on his jacket pocket.

He pauses, extends his hand toward me, something white jutting from between his fingers. I accept automatically. A business card. "If you're ever feeling in an honest mood, don't hesitate to be in touch. I'd like to hear your side of things."

I place the card on the end table.

At the door, he hesitates and then turns. "You should know that you're wrong about one thing," Rogalski says. "That really was Madison, in the photo. Her eleventh birthday party. She would be twenty-one this year. She'd be grown up, a real adult. Madison was crazy to grow up. Always in a big rush for it."

I sit very still. "What happened?"

"What happened doesn't matter," Rogalski says. "Folks pretend to be sympathetic, when they ask, but there's an ugly part of their brains that just wants the story. We all have it."

I'm a still ocean. A starless night.

"I got to apologize for my role in what happened, and I'm grateful for that. I'm not grateful for much in my life, but that," he says, "I'm grateful for." He opens the door. The corridor beyond is muted as the backs of my eyelids.

"Detective, I'd be willing to help you contact your daughter," I say. Sitting in Room 12 in my white dress, I suddenly and desperately want him to try. I want the predictability of swallowing the pill and waking to that brief moment of a stranger looking at me as if he loves me. "Maybe then you'd understand what we do here. Then you'd believe."

But Rogalski smiles patiently. "I'd rather not, Miss Eurydice," he says. "Thanks for the offer and all, but saying good-bye once was more than enough for me."

I wait for Jane. When she walks in, I have to make myself speak before I lose my nerve. "Jane," I say, "you should know that the client who was just here, Arnold Rogalski, was here under false pretenses. He's with the authorities."

Jane sucks her breath in through her teeth, a sharp hiss.

"I suppose we should have been guarding against something like this." She sits down heavily in the client chair. "We'll have to be more careful," she says, as if to herself. "Stop taking on new clients, at least for a while." She looks at me. "What kinds of questions?"

"He was looking for problems between the bodies and clients," I say. "He seemed concerned that we might be preying on clients. Taking advantage of their private information."

Jane smiles with one side of her mouth. "A skeptic," she says. "That's a relief. At least he's focused on protecting his own ego. He won't poke around too deeply." She sighs. "I hate this, Eurydice. I can't tell you how much. All this negative attention."

Something about her weary, confiding tone makes me trust her. Or maybe it's the fact that she's sitting across from me, dressed in a short-sleeved blouse that shows off her sunburned shoulders, looking exactly like one of my clients.

"Have you told Mrs. Renard that I bought lotuses?" I ask.

She glances up at me, gaze whetted into a point. Her harmlessness falls away. I regret saying anything. "No," she says.

"Thank you," I say.

"Don't get all comfy," she says. "It's for my own sake that I've kept quiet. But Renard's not a patient woman. We're running out of options. When it comes right down to it, I might have no choice."

"I'm afraid it would look bad," I say. "If she knew I'd bought lotuses right before the story broke."

"It would look bad," Jane agrees. "Especially considering that Fowler came to you first."

I lick my lips.

"If you want to prove your innocence, you need to figure out who worked with Fowler," Jane says. "There's no two ways about it. You're hardly a social butterfly, but it shouldn't be that hard. Did you tell anybody else when she first came to you?"

The day unspools in my memory. Mrs. Fowler's derisive smile over the heart-shaped zipper pull; her sickly sweetness as she tried to bribe me into channeling Hopeful Doe; and afterward. I remember a tendril of cigarette smoke, a laugh. My mind clicks and clicks again. The obviousness of it is clean and swift, so pure that it feels like a solution. It's only after a second that I begin to see its true shape as a complication.

Jane watches me, her eyes keen behind the lenses of her glasses. "Anything?" she asks.

I shrug, give a rueful smile. "Nothing," I say. "That day's a blank."

"Well, too bad," Jane says. "I thought we were on to something."

In the waiting room the next day, I wait for Ana. Before she has a chance to sit down, I stop her in the doorway. Her eyes are still blurry from the lotus, her skin cool against my fingertips when I touch her shoulder. "I need to see you alone," I say, low.

"God, Edie," she says. "I always knew you had a thing for me, but this is pretty forward." Her teasing isn't quite right; it has a tinny flatness that makes me embarrassed for her. When I don't respond, her voice becomes more subdued. "All right," she says. "Follow me."

I think she'll guide me to the restroom, but I trail her down the corridors, past Jane's office, past the block of encounter suites, until we reach an unmarked door that's tucked off to one side. Ana makes a show of looking around, mouth drawn into an O and eyes too wide, before she opens the door and slips inside. I hesitate, seeing only a shadowy gap beyond the door frame, and then I follow her.

Darkness. The air against my legs is prickling cold; a musty odor presses against my nose and eyes, thick as a wet cloth. The combination sends panic rippling across my skin. I'm drowning, not able to draw a full breath. A name streaks across my brain like a primal scream. A soft click ahead of me. A watery light spills out. We're standing on concrete steps, the edges clotted with cobwebs. Ana smiles up at me from two steps below. "You didn't know this was here?"

I make myself breathe normally, though the air is clammy and earthy, too heavy.

"I don't come here often." Ana sits down on the step, bringing her knees to her chest. "But it's the best way to get privacy around here. Used sparingly." She lifts a lacy strip of cobweb between her thumb and forefinger, examines it, then flicks it into the darkness at the bottom of the stairs. "You said you wanted to see me alone. So here we are. Alone."

I sit. The cement is so cold against my exposed skin that it burns. "Did you work with Fowler for the money?"

Ana stares. Before she can pull her usual armor back into place, I see raw emotion on her face: a blend of relief and surprise, as if she's finally been unburdened of an immense heaviness.

"I told you about Fowler right after I turned her away," I continue. "She mentioned to me that money was no object. She must be paying you well. And I know you need the cash."

There's a deep silence as we study each other.

"Well, look who finally woke up," Ana says. She gives a rough scrape of a laugh. "What brought about this miracle, Edie? Did you get laid?"

"I know you've broken other rules, Ana. I just want to hear it for myself."

"God, you're seriously falling for this bullshit?" Ana asks. "I know you're a sycophant, but I thought you were at least smarter than this."

"Don't distract from the real issue," I say.

"This is all an act, Edie," Ana says, jagged with impatience. "Renard calling us into her office, the big sad eyes, boo-hoo: it's a smokescreen. She wants us to be distracted, a bunch of tattling kids, so we won't notice what's happening."

"And that is?" I ask.

"There's more to this story than she's been telling us," Ana says. "Think about what Laura Holmes was wearing when they found her. A sundress. A single diamond earring."

A brief, ominous note rings at the back of my skull. "That doesn't mean anything," I say. "A dress and jewelry? That could describe nearly any woman in this city."

"Well, it could describe you," Ana says. "It could describe me. A shitty dress and then one nice thing, something we could never afford ourselves."

I imagine Laura in a gauzy dress, bare-shouldered, her eyes snapped shut. "You worked with Fowler and now it's out of your control," I say. "This is how you're justifying it? Making up your own theories so you don't have to be held accountable?"

Ana's expression stays chilly as stone.

"Our clients have been hurt by what Fowler's doing," I say. "It makes us look irresponsible. It makes us look sloppy."

"You're going to run right to Renard," she says. "Aren't you?"

"I don't want to," I say.

"Oh, but you will," Ana says. "You will because you think it's the right thing to do. And you're always so quick to do the right thing."

I shut my eyes against her contempt. "What will you do, anyway?" I ask. "If you leave the Elysian Society, will you go with Rob? Will you—" I can't finish the sentence. The possibility still feels too huge, tantalizing and terrifying in equal measure.

"Will I be forced to go permanent?" Ana asks.

After a second, I nod.

"Maybe so," Ana says. I hear the rustle as she rises, the neat tick as she turns off the light. Even with my eyes closed, I sense the darkness deepen and lose texture. She moves past me, stepping over my legs as roughly as if I'm an inanimate object. Her sole meets my thigh, rolling clumsily against the bone; I wince with pain, but I don't move.

"You'd like that, wouldn't you?" Ana asks, her voice now floating above me. "You'd love to see me brought down to your level. More dead than alive."

sent Henry and the baby out of the house," Viv says. "This can just be a girls' talk."

She's poured pink lemonade into two champagne flutes. The stinging sweetness lands in a bubble at the back of my throat. Viv Damson surprised me today by calling to request another visit. After last time, I didn't trust myself to reenter their home. But when Viv called me herself, it felt like a sign.

"I've been having a rough time lately." She picks up her glass, swirling the pink into a froth. "The second anniversary's coming up at the end of the summer."

"How did you handle the first anniversary?" I ask.

"Ben was tiny at the time," Viv says. "He wasn't sleeping. We were in and out of the pediatrician's office. We didn't even re-member the anniversary that year. What would we have done?"

It takes me a beat to understand that this is a genuine question. "You might have shared memories of her with each other," I say. "Looked through photos." The lemonade leaves a sweet skin on my teeth.

Viv shrugs. Looking more attentively, I register her tense posture, one arm hugged across her body, her legs knotted. Her eyebrows aren't darkened today. Their natural color is a nearly invisible blond, giving her whole face a formlessness, as if she's gradually vanishing.

"Would it help to talk about it now, Viv?" I ask. "Your experiences during that weekend, and the last time you spent with Sylvia before it happened."

"Oh, I don't know," Viv says. She gives an odd bump of a laugh, as if she's trying to recapture a levity that didn't exist to begin with. "God, I don't remember much. Henry and I were just married, and then the pregnancy. It felt like—like everything was beginning, you know what I mean? Just like, oh, here it is." She looks at a spot beyond me, at the window with its construction paper snowflakes, leftovers from the winter. "My life. Starting."

The Damsons' living room has yellow walls, a potted fern, a scattering of stuffed animals watching me with lopsided glass eyes from their exile on the floor. I wonder how the Braddocks' house would look now if they'd never gone to the lake that August. If they'd have moved toward the same clutter of parenting magazines, graham cracker dusted into the rug.

"What I remember from that weekend is that I felt bad for her," Viv says.

"How so?" I ask.

"Patrick and Sylvia seemed tense," Viv says. "For Henry and me, it was an impromptu trip. We were celebrating the baby. I thought Patrick and Sylvia would be there for some similar reason. It's a romantic place, like for anniversaries. But they were unhappy. I didn't get it."

I watch her hand on her lap, fidgeting with the hem of her blouse; her fingers tug at the silky material as if she's trying to tear away a piece. "They were fighting?" I ask.

Uncertainty flutters across her features, as if she'd forgotten I was here. "Oh, not really," she says. "They weren't doing those couple things, touching each other, inside jokes. Henry and I were newlyweds, and the Braddocks had been together for years. Maybe that's all it was." In the distance, machinery whines faintly. "It makes me grateful to have somebody like Henry. Does that sound awful?"

"Not at all," I say.

Her fingers still. Viv unwinds her arm, face brightening. "He's been my rock. After Sylvia died, he was there for me, one hundred percent. If losing Sylvia taught me one thing, it's that—" She pauses. "That I need to appreciate my husband."

I finish the lemonade. Some part of her must have been secretly thrilled when Sylvia died, finally allowing Viv the chance to pity a couple like the Braddocks.

"Do you have someone special in your life, Lucy?" Viv asks.

The question wakes me up. A familiar apology rising behind my lips, *I'm single right now.* "I'm in a new relationship," I say instead. "We've only been seeing each other for a few weeks."

"Oh, that's the best stage. You haven't got sick of each other." She laughs, revealing pink tongue, too-white teeth. "It doesn't surprise me. You seem like a woman in love. That glow."

I glance at my arm, as if my flesh might be lit up. Little needles of light shooting up through each pore.

"With your line of work, it must be especially big." She goes on before I can react. "Working around people who are grieving must make you so aware of needing to cherish the moment."

The front door opens, a crash and clatter in the foyer. Viv rises immediately; a moment later, Henry pushes a stroller into the living room. A big complicated structure of canvas and metal, the wheels muddied and flecked with grass. In the center of the stroller, Ben stares at me imperiously. When Henry catches sight of me, his face takes on a restrained wariness.

"Well, I should be going," I say as Viv kisses Henry. She's theatrical in the way she reaches up to throw her arms around his neck, the childish rise onto her tiptoes.

"Lucy is in love," Viv announces.

"Congratulations," Henry says, voice somewhere between polite, for her sake, and a shade too dry, for mine. Viv, sensing she's being teased, swats at his arm.

The baby releases a tangled loop of syllables.

"Did Ben behave himself?" Viv asks her husband.

"He was fine," he says. "But I'm spent. You're going to have to take the reins for the rest of the night."

"Hard day at work?" Viv asks, all sympathy.

"Oh, same old, same old," Henry says. "Picking up the slack, as usual. Fixing other people's mistakes." He's sweaty, his cheeks ruddy and hair ruffled; I can smell the sharpness of the outdoor air on him, the tang of his sweat.

"Because of—" Viv stops, darting a sidelong glance at me.

"Not because of Braddock, for once," Henry says. I've been going through the vague, lingering motions of preparing to leave, smoothing my skirt, glancing back at the couch to see if I've left some trace of myself behind. But I look up sharply at this mention of Patrick, such an obvious gesture that I'm sure they've noticed.

"He's doing better?" Viv asks.

"Just different these days." Henry squats down to unbuckle his son from the stroller. His hands are hairy at the knuckles, his fingers broader and stubbier than Patrick's. "Maybe he's in love too. Maybe it's contagious."

Standing in the Damsons' living room, I feel both vulnerable and conspicuous. My body is taking up too much space.

"It's too early for him to be in love again," Viv says.

Henry rises in a surprisingly fluid movement for his frame, holding Ben close against his chest. I'm stunned by the sight of Henry Damson with the baby. Something gluttonous and clawed unfolds inside me, wanting to reach out and take everything inside this house.

"Is it too early?" Henry asks; I twitch back to attention. "I mean, you should know," he says to me. "Being an expert in this."

We hold eye contact for a long moment until Viv starts chirping and fussing at Henry's elbow, plucking at the hem of Ben's shirt.

"Everyone has a different timeline for moving on after grief, Mr. Damson," I say. "But it's certainly possible."

I go to his home. It's dusk. After I left the Damsons', I was nearly home before I made a wrong turn at an intersection, and then another. I drove in the opposite direction of my own life.

As I enter Patrick's neighborhood, a deep ease settles around me. I know his neighbors' homes. The fusty gables on one side, the sterile lawn on the other, treeless and unadorned. And there's his house. Our house. The enormous front windows stand darkened and bare this evening.

I pull up on the opposite side of the street.

Across the street, a window lights up. Patrick comes into the room, as if walking onto a stage. I know the details that soften his edges. The long lashes that tangle together, his habit of clearing his throat in short coughs. But from this distance, he's a handsome stranger again. Intimidating, unknowable. I watch him cross the floor, stop next to the drape pull. He turns his head, saying something. He laughs.

Before I can make sense of this, someone else walks into the room.

It's her. Me. Hair black as an inkblot, pulled back with a tortoiseshell clip. Her long neck and her pastel dress are as shocking to me as if she were dripping wet, stark naked, insects sliding from her lips and weeds trailing her like a bridal train.

I sit back as if I've been physically pushed, my mind a hot blank.

Patrick begins to pull the drapes shut over the windows. As the visible wedge of the room shrinks, the woman comes to stand behind him. She clutches a wineglass clumsily. I can see her more clearly from this angle. She's less beautiful than Sylvia, her face highlighted too heavily with makeup. And she's shorter, older. An unsatisfying substitute.

Yet there she is, with him. The drapes swing shut, swaying from the momentum. Patrick is hidden from me.

L ate at night, I hang in a blurry exhaustion that refuses to plummet into the relief of sleep. Sitting in the bluish cast of the TV screen, I look through the Braddocks' photos again. After being inside their house, I recognize the backgrounds more easily. It's a disconnected intimacy. I've sat on the same couch that Sylvia curls on, smiling, with a plate of birthday cake. I've passed through the same doorway that she poses in, her dark hair tumbling back.

The house in the photographs is different. It's larger. Brighter. As if Sylvia's presence filled the rooms, demanding more space, drawing the sunlight to her. The house I know now is subdued and still. I don't seem capable of bringing it back to this former glory.

From above me, a rushing clatter of footsteps, the starry jangle of dropped keys. Muted laughter, then the bump of bass. I glance up at the ceiling, the noises moving across it. I could be buried beneath them. Listening in on the music and life of another universe.

The low cadence of the newscaster's voice pricks at my attention. I listen for the name again: *Laura Holmes.* I turn up the volume, the reporter's voice strengthening by small degrees and then suddenly blaring.

. . . Authorities have verified the identity of the body discovered in March. The victim is nineteen-year-old Laura Holmes, who has been missing from her last known address since December. Following new information about Holmes's

murder, Candace Fowler, whose tip helped authorities un-
cover the victim's identity, has publicly announced that she
will no longer be involved with the investigation.

I wait for more details, but the screen goes dark. A commercial
replaces the newscaster. A drab office-dwelling redhead drinks
a soda, transforms into a busty blonde on a beach, face giddily
empty.

arrive at the motel Mr. O'Brien has specified on a gray morning, the air laced with rain so fine it's invisible. I was hoping for an expensive place: a room with a sweeping view of the city, a concierge with averted eyes. But instead I recognize the name as a cheap roadside motel poised to attract tired families. I find a quiet parking lot; the fenced-off swimming pool collects water in its tarpaulin.

When Mr. O'Brien called this morning, I let myself hope that the recent coverage had scared him away. But he told me the room number and had me repeat it twice, instructing me to meet him here at *noon sharp*. The exaggerated hush of his voice left me feeling grimy. I imagined his sweet-faced wife somewhere else in the house: washing his dishes, folding his clothes.

Room 2B is tucked into the corner of the motel's layout, rooms pressed tight on either side. I try the doorknob. It's unlocked; I step into the room.

As bare-bones as it is, the space is cramped. A bed with its quilted bedspread, a framed watercolor of a meadow. Something isn't right. I reach for the doorknob, fumbling. The woman rises from the chair.

"Please," she says, softly urgent. "Don't leave. I need to talk to you."

She's shorter than me, her stomach pressing against the front of her blouse. I take her in. I feel like I already know her, although this means nothing. Everyone seems familiar these days.

"My husband couldn't make it," she says.

Of course. "Mrs. O'Brien," I say, although my mind fills with her first name. Lindsey.

Lindsey stays standing, awkward and shifting. "Can we just talk? That's all I need to do, ma'am. I'll leave you alone after that."

I sit on the edge of the bed. She positions herself back in the chair with an uneasy stiffness. I cross my legs. Lindsey glances at my bare knees once, her eyes wide and prim like a child sneaking a glimpse at a pornographic magazine.

"Did your husband send you here?" I ask.

"No." Quick, as if defending his honor. "It was my idea. I figured out where he was going, all this time," Lindsey says. She twists her fingers together on her lap. I spot the busy sparkle of a wedding ring, too ornate for her blocky hands. "He said he was getting grief counseling. I wanted to believe him, but I knew it was wrong. He was so angry after Margie died. He only seemed to be getting worse. I can't remember the last time he's even touched me. Even a hug or a peck on the cheek."

I clench my hands against my thighs.

"When I saw that place on the news one night, I just—I just knew. They were saying it's a place where people can communicate with the dead? Stay in touch with their loved ones? And that's when I knew what was happening."

The walls seem to be closing in.

"At least Ken didn't fight me on it. He confessed right away. And he said—" Lindsey squints at me. "He said this was the first time you two were meeting like this. Is that true? You have to be honest with me. I'm not going to do anything. I just need to know."

Red patches are leaking up her skin from beneath her neckline. I look directly into Lindsey O'Brien's eyes. "He's being honest," I say. "This was the first time we've met here. Every other time, your husband has been with me at my place of work."

"Oh God," she whispers. I can't tell whether she's relieved, or whether the ridiculousness and humiliation of her relief is hitting her. "Oh God."

"Everything that's happened between your husband and me has been innocent. He just wants to talk to your friend again."

She stares into her lap.

"I'm sorry, Mrs. O'Brien."

"You don't have anything to be sorry for, ma'am," she says. "It's your job, isn't it? You have to do your job."

I focus on the watercolor painting above the bed: meadows that appear bubbled, like burning plastic, a segment of sea as black as rotting fruit. It's a landscape cobbled together from other pieces, a crude representation of a place that's never existed.

"Margaret didn't love him," Lindsey says. "It probably doesn't matter to you. But I wanted to tell you."

This startles me.

"Ken loved her," Lindsey says. "I knew that within a month of dating him. It was obvious to everyone."

"You know she didn't return the feelings?"

"She told me she didn't," Lindsey says, with a painstaking gentleness, as if I'm the one who needs protecting. "Margie and I got along better than Ken knew. There were plenty of times we'd confide. We drank way too much one night and it all came out. She didn't want to embarrass me or Ken. She had a kind heart. But she told me how she felt."

"You never shared that with your husband," I say.

"No." Lindsey's eyes widen. "No, why hurt him?" She looks at my body openly then, her gaze traveling from my ankles to my neck in a slow once-over that could have been sexual, except for the rueful appraisal in her eyes. "It's a good thing you're so thin," she says.

"Why is that, Mrs. O'Brien?"

"Well, not for his sake," she says. "For Margie's."

I shift against the bedspread, stray threads pricking against the flesh of my inner thigh. In the photos, Margaret was all angles and hollows.

"Margie worked so hard to be thin like that," Lindsey says. "I have my mother's genes. I could starve myself forever and never get that thin, so I thought, well, why not enjoy myself? But I know Ken wishes I applied myself."

I inhale the thick, stale smell of the motel room. Cigarettes layered over cleansing agent layered over cigarettes, gumming up the air.

"I wonder if it bothers her," Lindsey says, "that he's bringing her back. She thought she'd escaped her body, and here she is again, right back where she started. That's why I'm glad you're thin, ma'am. Just so it feels familiar to her."

"Mrs. O'Brien," I say, standing from the bed. "We'd both be better off leaving this place behind for good and getting on with our lives. Agreed?"

She shakes herself as if she's just waking up. "Oh, yes," she says. "Yes, agreed."

Mr. O'Brien entrusted a lifetime of hope to this room, his chance to be with Margaret. I'm closing the door on it all, the bedspread taut over the mattress, the plastic seals pulled meticulously over the mouths of the glasses. Despite everything, I feel a quick throb of regret as I walk away from all this, knowing that I've pulled Margaret out of his grasp just as his fingers started to close around her.

At Lindsey's car, a boxy SUV with a plastic flower on the antenna, she opens the door and then looks at me, hesitating. "I should thank you," she says, half a question.

"For what?"

"For making this whole thing not as terrible as it could be," Lindsey says. She rubs at the back of her neck, looking up at me through blond hair muddied with highlights. "You must think I'm pretty pathetic. My husband wants a dead woman more than he wants me."

I resist the impulse to reach out and touch her hand, push her hair behind her ear. Some gesture that would remind her of her own specificity, her tenacious, beautiful existence.

"Well." Lindsey's sigh is channeled from a place deeper than I can access. "I don't blame you if you do." When she opens the car door wider, I spot a scatter of plastic toys across the passenger's seat, a bottle with milky white inside. My heart stutters. I hadn't realized that the O'Briens were parents. "You'll never be seeing my husband again," she says.

"Never," I agree.

A re you free tomorrow night? Come over. I want to have a real date, a nice dinner."

His easy warmth thaws the resentment that's been growing inside me since the other night. But I hold back. I almost didn't answer the phone when I saw his name trapped inside the screen. The accusations push at my lips: *I saw you with her. She was there, in our home.*

Who was she?

Who is she?

"If you can't make it, though," Patrick says, "I understand."

"No, Wednesday night sounds perfect," I say. "I'll bring the ingredients. Let me cook."

"I didn't realize you cooked," he says.

"Maybe I haven't mentioned it yet."

"There's a lot I still don't know about you," Patrick says. He sounds genuinely surprised at this.

O n Wednesday morning, Dora comes to find me. I've just ended an encounter with Ms. Milroy, a wistful, diluted woman who lost her mother as a child. I'm dazed from the lotus, a floating sensation just behind my eyelids. When Dora taps on the door frame and then comes into Room 12 uninvited, I focus on her as if she's a figure in a dream, conjured inexplicably into the wrong scenario.

Dora sits in the client chair. She hovers on the edge, knees loosely together, one leg jumping. She gives a tentative smile. "Mrs. Renard wanted to see you," she says. "I volunteered to get you."

As the lotus wears off by degrees, I look at her more closely. She's different, her cheekbones more pronounced, her curls limper and flatter. She's growing less specific. A face in a crowd. "Thanks for letting me know, Dora."

"There's something else I wanted to talk to you about." She whispers now, words rushed. "How long did it take you to move out of the apartment?"

"The apartment," I repeat. I piece together what she means. "On Sycamore? Maybe a year. Not long."

Dora's eyes flick toward the ceiling as if she's calculating.

"Is there a problem?" I ask.

"No," she says, too fast. Then, after a pause: "It's just— I keep finding stuff left behind by the girls who lived there before me. It's spooky. Like there's no room for me."

A spark of impatience awakens inside me. I want to tell her that she might never have a chance to free herself from other people's lingering influences, that some of us are destined to crawl inside the shells of lives others have left behind, never deserving a place of our own. But I bite this back. I remember how lonely the Sycamore apartment was, like a child's clumsy drawing of a home: bed and table, chair and lamp.

"I understand that you'd like your independence," I say, making myself speak gently. "Keep in mind that Mrs. Renard is looking out for you. It's not the most glamorous place to live, but it's cheap, and it's safe."

Dora bites at her lower lip, eyes unconvinced.

"Just be patient," I say. "Keep focusing on your work here."

"Yeah. Well. Beggars can't be choosers, right?" She slips off the chair and moves toward the door. "Anyway. You better go see what she wants."

M rs. Renard glances up as I enter her office. I instantly register another presence. Jane stands to the side of the desk, hands clasped in front of her body. I almost turn back, an instinctive desire for escape.

"You wanted to see me?" I ask. A throb of anxiety runs through me.

"Come in," Mrs. Renard says. "Lock the door behind you."

I slide the lock into place with a solid click, a punctuation mark in the silence. Jane won't look at me. Every time I try to make eye contact, her eyes slide away from mine.

"Sit," Mrs. Renard commands.

The chair is overstuffed, overwhelmingly soft. I could sink into the upholstery and never emerge, a crumpled white dress and strands of blond hair spat out in my wake.

"I'm sure you have some idea why I've called you here today, Eurydice. I placed a significant amount of trust in you," Mrs. Renard says. "Imagine how much it disappoints me to hear it was misplaced."

Her voice is only mildly reproving. It's as if we're discussing someone we barely know.

"I've always been generous with you," she continues. "But when I learned that you purchased lotuses behind my back, for your own purposes, I knew it was time to start treating you like any other employee. Like someone I can't trust."

I look at Jane again; she's gazing at the floor as if she has no part in this conversation.

Mrs. Renard examines me without speaking for a long, tense moment. "Do you have anything to say for yourself?"

"I bought those lotuses for a different client," I say. "You have every right to be disappointed in me, Mrs. Renard, but—"

"Are you meeting with Patrick Braddock?"

I shut my eyes, barely even surprised.

"That's what Leander has suggested to me," Mrs. Renard says.

Resignation moves sluggish through my veins. Lee: of course. Lee, saving me from myself. Backing me into a corner for my own good.

"You've removed a paying client from inside these walls and started meeting with him on your own terms," Mrs. Renard says. "You think you know better than I do what our clients truly need, what they want from you, but you're wrong. These things never end well. You're hardly the first body to betray me."

"Are you going to fire me?" I ask.

For a moment, leaving the Elysian Society holds an appeal so strong it surprises me. But then Patrick moves back to the forefront of my mind. I don't know what our relationship would look like without the Elysian Society between us. Taking it out of the equation feels too soon and delicate, like moving an injured person when the wound is fresh.

"Try to see things from my perspective," Mrs. Renard says. "You've been soliciting lotuses behind my back. If you'd betray the Elysian Society on one level, who's to say you wouldn't go further?"

"Fowler's not even working with the authorities anymore," I say.

"But the damage is already done," Mrs. Renard says.

The words come out of my throat, shoved along by my own desperate momentum. "I know who worked with Mrs. Fowler," I say.

"Is that so?"

I'm silent. My pulse pounds in my ears.

"Give me a name," she says, low.

"It was Ananke. Ana. She admitted it to me." And I'm prepared to justify this. To point out that Ana knew about Mrs. Fowler, that she needs money, that she has a history of working with clients outside these walls.

But instead: "I suspected as much." Mrs. Renard leans back in her chair. "I only wish she had told me herself."

Jane reaches up to scratch at the back of her neck, still not meeting my gaze.

"Mrs. Renard, Ana was only trying to help," I say.

"Possibly," she says. "But Ananke's shown an unforgivable disregard of what we do here. She's endangered this institution, and for what? Nothing." She smiles with a thin triumph.

"You said she needed protection," I say. "Isn't that why you wanted to find out who worked with Mrs. Fowler? Not to punish her, but to help her."

"She'll be helped." Mrs. Renard is distracted; she reaches for the phone on her desk. "Thank you, Eurydice. I'm glad to see your loyalty hasn't changed as much as I feared."

I watch as she brings the phone to her ear, her fleshy cheek pouched against the receiver. And I understand that Mrs. Renard isn't going to press me about Patrick Braddock. This is my reward for being faithful to the Elysian Society: being allowed my small vices. Being allowed him.

All of Ana's hints, her pointed focus on the sundress and the earring, clutter my head. I study Mrs. Renard behind her desk. She runs the entire operation from this hidden perch, pulling the strings, soothing the clients, dispatching the bodies. I can't believe I ever thought she was unaware of Ana in hotel rooms, of Jane selling lotuses. Of me and Patrick.

"Jane," Mrs. Renard says, "will you please show Eurydice out?"

In the hallway, Jane won't speak. She starts down the corridor to her own office until, desperate, I step in front of her. I think she might walk right into me. But she finally looks at me, examining me with chilly blankness. As if I'm a mere obstacle in her trajectory.

"We need to talk," I say.

"I told you that I couldn't protect you if it meant risking my own position here. Surely *you* can understand that." There's a nasty undercurrent in her voice.

Ignoring this, I say, "I need more lotuses."

"You're out of luck," she says. "Renard's tightening the reins around here, didn't you notice?"

The implication of this hits me hard, full as a fist. "How will I get more?"

"That's not my problem," Jane says.

"Please," I say. "It's not what you think, Jane. It's not about the money. I'm in love with him."

The words between us are clear, bright, as if I could take them into my hands and watch them light up the shells of my closed fingers.

I'm in love with him. I'm in love with him.

"Love?" Jane repeats, almost reverent. I think she feels it too: in the middle of this space, the air stifled with strangers' grief and the muted ache of loss, there's something exquisite with life and promise.

"Jesus," Jane says. The mood snaps, neat as a twig under a heel. "If you knew how many times I've heard that, you'd understand why I don't care."

TWENTY-THREE

'I've brought a bottle of wine to Patrick's house tonight. Glossy pink chicken under plastic, a glass bottle of brined capers, two lemons, olive oil.

"What are you making?" he asks.

"It's a recipe my mother used to make." I open one of the low cabinet doors beneath the oven range, searching for a pan. All the dishes inside have a furred skein of dust settled in their depths; a spider scuttles away from the sudden press of light.

When I straighten again, Patrick watches me. "Are you and your mother still close?"

I realize that I've mapped out a portion of my distinct history, diverging sharply from where I first met Patrick in March. I remember myself as a little girl with a long, melancholy face, hair so pale it looked white, like a photographic negative of a dark-haired child.

When I don't answer, Patrick speaks up, tentative: "I said the wrong thing."

I smile an apology, shaking my head. "She lives far away," I offer. "We don't talk often. Not for any reason. Just life getting in the way."

Patrick's eyes turn thoughtful. "I haven't seen my family in a long time. You look up one day and it's been a year. More. It's easy to lose track of people." A pause. "Easy for them to lose track of you."

He speaks lightly, but the very lightness of the words is wrong, as if he's so accustomed to this isolation that it's no longer strange. Standing in the kitchen, I think of the photographs, my first introduction to the Braddocks: so many faces spread across those images. A whole rotating cast of bit players, supporting roles. All those people thickened out the Braddocks' lives, reflected their beauty and happiness back at them. Eyes like mirrors.

In contrast to those infinitely populated photos, Patrick's current life is astonishingly empty. His echoing house; his solitary body moving through the rooms. No photographs displayed on the walls other than Sylvia's. No envelopes bearing return addresses in the intimate handwriting of friends, parents. This must be why the sight of the dark-haired woman hit me so hard. She's such an anomaly that she's forced into uneasy significance.

Patrick picks up one of the lemons, rolling the pebbled neon yellow between his palms.

"It's not so bad, losing touch with people who aren't there for you anyway," I say. The Damsons flash through my mind. "I find it's better to focus on the future." I peel away the plastic veil clinging to the chicken: the pink meat shimmers with crystals of ice.

"Wise woman," he says.

I'm silent, thinking of those faces. Something else occurs to me, a hard punch of a realization. Each smile in those photographs must mean something specific to Sylvia, a trail of beloved memories. Her friends, cousins, college roommates—they're scattered across the city, across the globe, mourning her. Navigating the flat, unending landscape of grief, running into unexpected reminders of her absence. Sylvia is coming back into a world without these other lives. Her life, this time around, is narrower. Only big enough for the two of them. Him and her.

Patrick leans over me to reach for a glass. His body tight against my back, his breath in my ear, and I'm penned in. I can't move. His arm presses tight against my shoulder.

The bathroom has high ceilings, eggshell-pale walls. A trace of ammonia sours the air, and the bar soap next to the sink is hardened and warped.

The muffled rush and clink rises through the floorboards as Patrick washes dishes downstairs. He still hasn't mentioned the stranger. I've been looking around, furtive as a suspicious wife, for some remnant that could open up the conversation. Blotched lipstick on the rim of a glass, a black hair curled on the sink drain. But it's as if she was never here. She walked through these rooms without shedding a trace of her physical presence.

I open the medicine cabinet, the mirrored doors cutting my reflection in two as they swing open. On the shallow shelves inside the cabinet, I find a razor, an empty prescription bottle. A sleep aid. Crouching, I pull open each drawer beneath the sink: nothing, nothing, nothing. And then, at the bottom, a lone object. The movement of the drawer has sent it rattling wildly from one corner to another. A single earring, a simple gold stud.

I reach for it. This proof that a woman was here, in this house, intruding on my space. I imagine going downstairs, laying this piece of evidence between us, forcing Patrick to account for her: *Who is she? Why is she inside my life?*

But confusion washes through me. Maybe the earring is mine. Maybe I wore it a few weeks ago, forgot it here. Or maybe it belonged to Sylvia, a leftover, neglected for years. I drop the earring back into the drawer.

When I go downstairs, back into the kitchen, Patrick glances around from the sink. "Get lost up there?"

"I'm sorry," I say.

"You know I'm only teasing," he says. "My home is your home."

I can't speak. I go to him, wrapping my arms around his waist and feeling him still at my touch. Leaning my head against Patrick's shoulder, I'm shocked at how neatly we slide into place. As if I've worn grooves in him, as if he's carefully shifted the shape of my body during my sleep.

I wake up in a stranger's bed. His face next to mine is gaunt and somber; his eyes shift beneath the tissue-fine membrane of his eyelids. His hand on my hip is heavy enough to pin me down.

I struggle to my elbows. A hard thud of panic slams over and over into my brain: *get out get out get out.*

I look for the door. Beside me, the stranger mumbles, shifts.

The sleep dissolves from my brain slowly, then quickly, and I'm back in Patrick's room. I'm naked, the covers wound around my ankles like weeds. On the bedside table, the envelope of lotuses is half open. Only two left. The depletion of the pills is as steady as an hourglass, ticking down until the moment I have nothing left to offer.

Out in the hall, I breathe more easily. Pulling Patrick's discarded shirt around my shoulders, I move past the kitchen, past the living room. I automatically shift my hips to avoid the protruding corner of a side table. My foot knows which creaky step to avoid on the stairs.

And I know which unassuming door to open and enter on the second story of the house. The room is overcrowded. Boxes stacked haphazardly in one corner, disgorging a clutter of paper. I could open the boxes and find Sylvia's body parts, labeled and bubble-wrapped, neat as a mannequin's. Her slim torso, tiny waist, beautifully sculpted face, ready for assembly.

The first box holds a tumble of clothes, elegant colors and delicate patterns. Silky dresses, sweaters soft as fur, shoes dainty as a doll's. I've never realized how tiny Sylvia was. Photographs gave me an abstracted sense of her body, but holding her clothes is a shock. Placing a lacy shirt against my own body, I see exactly where I diverge from her shape, the bone and flesh I'd have to trim away, stitch to my frame, to match her. The clothes release a light floral scent of detergent. At the edges, there's the bitter breath of clothes that have sat untouched.

I look through the other boxes. Expensive jewelry tangled together, jewels choked by chains and earrings snagged like fish-hooks. Cases for DVDs. Hardback novels: classics, titles that I vaguely recognize. A defunct phone, screen smeared with finger-prints. Everything looks as if it's been swept into the boxes uncer-emoniously. In one box, a glass bottle of nail polish has cracked, leaving a red crust against a white sweater.

And I find a square book with a satiny cover printed with pastel daisies. I flip through the pages. Bare, marked with tiny motifs and scraps of words. *First Memories. People I Love.* A baby book. Something slithers out from between the pages, drops to the floor. Small and flat, shiny plastic. I reach for it, sliding it into Patrick's shirt pocket.

When the noise comes in the doorway, I'm not even startled.

"There you are." His voice is thick with fatigue, but holds a splinter of alertness. I suspect Patrick is pretending to be groggier than he is. He moves closer, crouches on the floor next to me. "I haven't been in here for months."

"You put all this in here?" I ask.

"Her mother was supposed to help me," Patrick says. "After a while, I did it by myself. I couldn't keep walking into the bath-room and finding her toothbrush." The boxes hulk over us, their lids askew. "She left behind so much."

I wonder if Ana's client Rob has a room like this in his home. All the little pieces of his dead lover collected in one spot, wait-ing. Waiting for Ana to give the objects a purpose again.

"What are you doing in here?" he asks.

"I was looking for the room in the photo," I say. "The one with the lipstick."

Patrick searches my face. "She wore lipstick in a lot of photos."

"It was a certain color," I say. "The darker color. The color you gave me."

Patrick shrugs, impatient.

"She was naked." It's only then that I understand just how much this has disturbed me: an itchy anxiety, a need for an explanation. "I remember it. A Polaroid, not like the rest. Most people don't include photos like that. She was naked. Wearing that dark lipstick."

Patrick drums his knuckles against the edge of the nearest box, a muffled staccato that worms into my head. "She was naked when they found her," he says. "After she drowned."

In the silence of the room, the moon and streetlight mingled white against the curtains, his words are exactly wrong. They're heavy, abrupt as thrown punches.

"I didn't identify the body," Patrick says. "I didn't want that version of her in my head."

"Who did?" I ask.

"A friend," Patrick says. "Her family hadn't come out to the lake yet. I didn't want to tell them until we knew. Henry had stayed behind after Viv went home. He volunteered."

Shock moves through my skull. I imagine Sylvia's bloated body, her face puffed into cartoon proportions, ugly for the first time in her life, and Henry staying with her in this vulnerable state. Recognizing her for the last time, giving her the dignity of a name. I'm suddenly furious at Patrick, that he couldn't be the one to do this for her. The betrayal is as shocking as cold water rushing into my lungs.

how could you not look at me?

see me

"When I collected photos to send you," Patrick says, "I was barely paying attention. It was too painful. I gave you whatever Sylvia had lying around. She always had too many. Our whole life documented." He stands, stretches, the skin stretched against his ribs for a second. "Bring me that photo? Maybe I can figure it out."

The anger still tight in my throat, I can't speak.

In the doorway, Patrick pauses. I take him in: the long planes of his torso. The wiry muscles beneath his shoulders. Beneath the coldness of the fury that has grown over me, rooting me to the spot, I melt. I give, cracking open like ice.

"Are you coming back to bed?"

"Of course," I say.

TWENTY-FOUR

The home hid its secrets well, but the attention has tapped at the weak spots. Now, everything comes to light. The house that sheltered Laura Holmes's body was abandoned, but not empty. At night, the echoing rooms sometimes took on a temporary pulse of life. Drifters, the perpetually or temporarily homeless, runaways landing in the city before moving on: all of them would gravitate to the house, moving through its silence. The rooms held leftover furnishings. A floral sofa with its guts nibbled out by mice, a dining table wearing thick doilies of dust.

The house was a squat. But according to the teenage boy who recently came forward, it was an innocent place. A refuge. The visitors cleaned up all traces of their time there, avoided attention. After the subdivision began construction, the pilgrimages to the abandoned house continued, though more cautiously, and then trickled to an eventual halt.

I watch a video of the news report. The boy's hair is dark red and ragged with split ends; he insists that nothing dangerous ever happened there. The discovery of Hopeful Doe was as much a betrayal to everyone who'd ever set foot inside the house as it was to the wealthy and self-contained neighbors.

"I was scared to come forward sooner." The boy's eyes dart anxiously. "But once they started using her real name, it felt more— I don't know. More real."

I understand now why Mrs. Fowler backed away, even after her fervent insistence on solving the case. Hopeful Doe was nameless, an angelic girl sprouting from thin air, her death such a mystery that it carried every potential danger along with it; Laura Holmes is a specific woman, a sullen misfit drifting from city to city. And now it's turned out that her body showing up in the house is less an anomaly than the final, visceral consequence of many smaller transgressions. I imagine how chagrined Mrs. Fowler must be at her own involvement in the case. Her piety turned to rage, that she'd waste her time on someone like Laura. A woman who must have fallen in with the wrong crowd. Discarded in an abandoned house.

Snapping off the TV, I move into my bedroom. It lies on top of my dresser, next to the wedding portrait. The remnant that fell from the pages of the baby book. I took it home with me, not telling Patrick. Of all Sylvia's leftovers, this is the only object her husband hasn't given me himself.

A thin plastic wand, wrapped in a plastic bag. At the tip of the wand, a little indented window shows two blotchy pink stripes. One of them is faded as old ink; the other bleeds slightly into the surrounding paleness. A pregnancy test.

Two lines for positive.

Two lines indicating a second presence.

I can't tell how old the test is. Whether Sylvia watched these two lines develop years and years ago, or whether it happened only recently. Only a month before she left for Lake Madeleine, or a week, or a day. I don't know if she ever told Patrick; maybe it's been lying tucked within the book, swept inside a box, trapped where his gaze can't reach.

All I know when I look at the two lines is one simple reaction. The small, soft agony of a lost chance.

've been spending my time between clients half asleep in the waiting room. I'm tired these days. Whenever I swallow the lotus in Room 12, I feel the additional toll it takes. The pill has to push aside the gentle weight of Sylvia: prying loose her fingers, dulling her curiosity. I'm exhausted afterward.

Today, I feel someone hovering just in front of me. A funny sadness shifts over me like a passing cloud. I open my eyes. "Lee," I say.

"It's been a while, Edie," he says. "How have you been?"

"Why did you do it?" I ask. Lee inhales, nods, as if he's been expecting the question. "I told you that Patrick Braddock wasn't a threat."

"For what it's worth, I never mentioned you when I went to Renard." Lee sits next to me. "I was only asking about Patrick Braddock. I hoped she could reassure me about him."

"Did she?"

He hesitates. "She looked into his records. Patrick hasn't scheduled an encounter for several weeks."

"There you go," I say. "Nothing to worry about."

"I'm sorry, Edie. I know you cared about him as a client."

"He's not the first client to leave the Elysian Society," I say. "He won't be the last."

Lee's skin must still hold a trace of cologne from a recent encounter. His scent is rich and textured. I glance at his hands on his thighs, at the slight hollow of his throat, and heat stirs under my skin. It's disorienting to feel this way for Lee, the wrong reaction transplanted into my chest like a stranger's beating heart. I imagine what Patrick would think if he knew that my hunger for him was spreading, indiscriminate, attaching itself to the nearest body.

"Just know that I'm here for you," he says. "If you need anything."

"I do know that, Lee," I say. "Thank you."

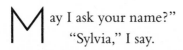ay I ask your name?"
"Sylvia," I say.

The receptionist's face stays placid as she rises. I relax; there must be a thousand women named Sylvia in this city. "I'm an old friend," I add, wanting perversely to establish specialness.

She smiles, uninterested and polite.

I follow the receptionist down a hallway. Tiled floor, stone-colored walls lined with framed newspaper clippings and embossed plaques. Out of the corner of my eye, Sylvia's face dots the wall. Just once or twice, but I slow to study the images.

In the first clipping, the Braddocks pose together on the steps. In this photo I haven't yet memorized, Patrick's youthfulness stands out with a flare of unfamiliarity. I assume it must be a much older photo, maybe from the first year of their marriage. But the caption suggests that the image is only two years old. Taken a mere six months before he lost Sylvia.

The other photo holds the colorful blurriness of a candid. A tableful of people lifting their glasses, eyes caught shiny and unfocused. I see Henry Damson, face distorted with motion. It takes me a second to pick out the Braddocks, and I realize why: they're separated, sitting on opposite sides of the table. Patrick gives an abstracted smile, as if automatically obeying a command. Across from him, Sylvia's grin is too hectic, as obvious as a mask held over the lower part of her face. Her eyes hover thoughtfully above the smile, looking directly into mine.

The receptionist opens a door. "Mr. Braddock, someone to see you. A Sylvia?"

When I step into the office, Patrick is very still behind his desk, leaning forward as if he's on the cusp of rising. He doesn't speak. I'm barely aware of the receptionist shutting the door behind me. I smile, wanting to make it all into a joke. Not because of the fading shock clinging to Patrick's features, but because of what I saw there just a second before: hope.

"It's you," he says finally.

"It's me."

"You told her your name is Sylvia?"

"It was the first name that came to mind," I say.

"You know better," he says. "People here knew Sylvia. They'll notice, Edie."

What's happening between us is so close to politeness that I try to convince myself we're fine.

Patrick rubs his forehead. "I just——" He stops. "I don't think you appreciate how much trouble you could make for me."

"I'm sorry," I say.

"No, you're not."

"Of course I am. It was never my intention to upset you."

He doesn't answer for a long moment. "This is all a mistake," he says.

"What do you mean?"

"Asking you to be her, like this, it's——" Patrick makes a sudden and frustrated gesture, lifting his hand. "It's wrong. Hearing you with her name, here, in a place like this. In the real world. I don't know. What am I making you do? What am I doing to myself?"

When I sit, the leather is slickly cool on my bare thighs. Patrick's office rises around us, tall and narrow, lined with bookshelves. The book spines are too uniform, like cardboard stand-ins. A fern browns on the windowsill.

"Patrick," I say.

He looks at me, eyes holding a trapped glimmer of wariness.

"It's all right," I say. "I won't do it again. Don't worry."

"Why are you even here?"

It's a weak excuse, but I'm glad to have it now. "I brought you the photo," I say. "Of Sylvia. You asked to see it."

Patrick lifts his folded hand to his mouth, his eyes flicking to the closed office door. "Fine," he says. "Let me see it."

I slide my bag open, disentangle Sylvia from the darkness. I hesitate before I pass her over the desk to her husband. In this harsh lighting, Sylvia's naked body is too vulnerable. When he takes the photo, Patrick is brusque and businesslike. His face doesn't betray any emotion. He could be examining courtroom evidence, a legal document.

Patrick turns the photo around, reads the message on the back. A strain comes across his features.

"Do you recognize it?"

"Not entirely." He hands the photo back to me. I accept, not sure whether I'm pleased or hurt that he doesn't want to keep her. "The room," Patrick says. "That room is familiar."

"She could have left the photo behind for you," I suggest. "A gift."

"Maybe." Across the desk, Patrick shuts his eyes as if something has hurt him.

Outside, in the hallway, somebody calls good night. There's a trail of muted voices and fading footsteps.

"You can't show up where I work," he says.

"Nobody knows who I am. I just said I was an old friend."

He laughs, and I understand. The idea of the Braddocks being friends with someone like me, pale and uninteresting, a vague ghost of a person: it's funny. It's a joke.

"Why don't you want to be seen with me?" I ask. "Am I a secret?"

"I'm not ashamed of you," he says.

"That's not what I asked."

A muscle near his jaw jumps. "So do you talk about me?" Patrick stands, his chair scraping against the floor. He comes around the desk. In the evening light, his downturned features are heavy. "Your friends and family. Do they know what we do together?"

In answer, I reach my hand toward his face, and Patrick intercepts the gesture, holding my wrist. He pulls me to standing. I feel how fast his breathing is. My own speeds up. I move to wrap my arms around him, but Patrick pushes me down until I'm on the edge of the desk. He slides a hand up my thigh.

Up close, his eyes are blurrier than usual. He's been drinking. It's taken me a moment to recognize the smell of alcohol here, in his office, in the late afternoon.

His hands against me feel thick and clumsy, lacking their usual precision.

"Don't you want her?" I ask.

Patrick hesitates. He shakes his head, swift, without speaking. When he tips my mouth up to his, his breath is acrid and warm. I have to make myself ignore this.

When it's over and I'm gasping, my knowledge of my body coming back in pieces (the sore spot on my back where I was pressed into the desk, the slight headache behind my eyes), I also ignore the steep loneliness that winds itself around me.

Patrick moves around the desk, opens a drawer. I watch as he retrieves his wallet from the jumbled depths.

I've immunized myself to the shame when this happens. I've learned to navigate seamlessly between the two layers of our relationship: the immediacy of our time together, the distance of being paid for services rendered. I haven't spent any of the money he gives me. I slip the bills in a dresser drawer, hidden from view, and I forget about it. A peace offering on the altar of Sylvia's heart.

But today I reach across the desk to still Patrick's gesture, gripping his wrist hard enough to feel the bracelet of bones underneath. "Don't."

He looks at my hand, follows the length of my arm to my face, my eyes. "You're sure?"

"You weren't even with her, Patrick," I say.

"Well." He moves his hand from the wallet, seeming to consider what I just said. "Next time, then."

I watch him on the other side of the desk, buttoning and zipping. The bite of alcohol still clings to the air around him.

"You'd tell me if something was wrong, wouldn't you?" I ask.

Patrick doesn't answer, and I don't ask again.

O utside, the evening sky is muddy. The streetlights push through the shadows with effort.

"I know you, don't I?"

I turn, heart wedged in my throat. My impression is that he's been waiting for me, standing in the mouth of the alley. He moves into the light now, keeping his eyes fixed on me as if I'm the dangerous one.

"Mr. Damson." I wonder if Henry was in the office when Patrick and I were together. If he heard anything.

"Hello, Ms. Woods," he says. I detect a slyness in his voice, but it could just be a shadow cast by my guilt. "I wouldn't expect to run into you here. Were you looking for me?"

"As a matter of fact, no."

Henry glances at the building I just left. "What brings you here, then?"

I don't answer.

"I want you to stop coming to our home, Ms. Woods."

His voice is so casual it takes me a moment to make sense of his words. "Is there a problem? I was making good progress with Mrs. Damson."

"Viv's been getting worse since you started showing up," Henry says. "We'd left the past in the past. And then you come into our home, making her think about it. Forcing her to answer pointless questions. She's getting depressed again. It's even affecting Ben. I'm not going to do this again, not when we were reaching the light at the end of the tunnel."

My lungs tighten. "My impression is that your wife's appreciated the chance to talk," I say. "It's better to address these issues than to hide from them—"

"Nobody is hiding," Henry says. "Don't tell me what's best for my wife. I've already been through this with her. I know what she

needs. If you come to our house again, there will be a problem."
He shuts his eyes; when he opens them, he's forced himself back
from the brink of his anger. "I'll tell Viv that you completed your
study. We'll all move on from this. Agreed?"

There's a noise somewhere behind us. We both turn, alert as
deer. The street beyond is dotted with lit windows. When I left
the office, Patrick was still working, claiming vaguely that he
needed to catch up on a project. I have a sudden vision of him
coming down the steps, seeing me and Henry together.

"Very well, Mr. Damson," I say. "I respect your wishes."

He turns to go and my brain surges with panic. Sylvia rushes
through my body like a prisoner, hammering at the windows,
trying all the doors, scratching and pounding.

don't turn your back on me

don't leave now

"Mr. Damson," I call, "could you do one favor for me?"

"What's that?" he asks, reluctant.

"A while ago, you said the Braddocks were unhappy. I wish
you'd explain what you meant by that."

"You already know what I meant."

We stand a few feet apart, the distance between us crackling.

"He treated her badly," Henry says. He's careless with this
confession. It falls from him, swift and meaningless as a dropped
coin. "Cheating on her. Not uncommon."

"I see," I say. The surprise that should be there isn't, just an
empty space opening up behind my eyes. "Well, thank you for
your time."

"Of course." Henry smiles almost politely. "I hope I could be
some help, Sylvia."

The world around me stutters violently, then picks back up.
"I'm sorry?"

For a moment, his face in the shadows shifts. I see Henry

Damson as if I'm lying beneath him, his features washed too bright in the coldly clinical light that surrounds us, burning away details. I'm pinned down like a butterfly.

"That's your name, isn't it?" His shrouded eyes hold a hint of knowingness. "Have a good night, Sylvia."

only remember a single clue about where Ana lives. Poplar Avenue is a long row of gas stations and strip malls, dreary under the sun's fading fluorescence. I pass a stretch of weed-choked fields and undeveloped lots before I pull up to an apartment complex, shutting off the engine. The complex reminds me of my own. Layers of identical doorways marked with halfhearted attempts at individuality. A plastic chair, a stroller, a dog-eared welcome mat. Idling near the curb, I scan the silent eyelids of the windows for some sign of life.

The sun deepens behind me, coating red and orange against the side of the building. Glancing down, my eyes snag on the pale underside of Sylvia's photo. The corner sticks out from inside the glove compartment.

I hesitate, then work the Polaroid loose. After all that's grown between us, Sylvia still turns me stunned and breathless for a moment. Such a pure representation of the difference between a plain woman and a beautiful one. That luminous skin, her black hair sliced against her shoulders. The too-dark lipstick turning her mouth heavy as a secret.

And I see it, this time. A shadow on the bedspread leaks up the edge. Against the deep purple sheen, the shadow is subtle. But I understand that there's a specific body blocking out the light. The shadow is wavy and elongated.

Someone was with her.

A noise outside my car window distracts me. I drop the photo, turning in the direction of the sound. A woman walks across the edge of the curb next to the apartment complex, both arms wrapped around a trash bag. I'm struck by her quick gait, the lift of her chin. As if she's proving to anyone watching that she's fine. It's a defiant aura that I recognize instantly and instinctively.

Hurrying from my car, I call to her. "Ana?"

The woman keeps walking with a slight waver in her steps, as if I'm a voice in a crowd, talking to anybody. She's heading toward the alleyway.

I touch her shoulder when I reach her. "Ana."

She turns. I take a step back, searching her features for a recognizable landmark. Her features resemble Ana's, but older, exaggerated by her blunt red lipstick. Her hair is a brighter blond than my own, and stiff and shiny as a doll's.

She moves closer to me. One step, another. The lost, empty look in her eyes makes me want to beg her forgiveness: *You shouldn't be here.*

When she's right next to me, so close that my skin warms with the breath unspooling from her mouth, she laughs. It's Ana's laugh, and I relax, feeling both foolish and furious.

"God, you look like you've seen a ghost." Ana shifts the trash bag in her arms. "Do you mind if I take care of this? It's heavier than it looks." I watch as she slides the bag over the lip of a dumpster and then steps back, wiping her hands along the tops of her thighs.

"I've been cleaning out my closets," Ana says, returning to me. "So many things I'm never wearing again. There's something so freeing about just"—she sweeps her arm—"letting it all go." She looks me up and down. "Anyway. What's this about?"

Now that I've found her, everything I could say gets knotted on my tongue. "We need to talk."

"A little late for that."

"It's important."

"How do I know you're not here to do her dirty work again?" Ana asks. She pushes her hair off her forehead with both hands.

"It's not about Mrs. Renard."

"She knows you're here?"

"Of course not."

Ana studies me a little longer. Depending on which feature I focus on, I can make her a stranger again. The near-white hair or the red mouth, she's a stranger. Her fierce dark eyes, she's Ana again.

"Fine," she relents. "God only knows why I still trust you. But make it quick."

Her apartment looks as if it's been abandoned. A couch lies along one wall. Besides this, there are only boxes, shopping bags, a greasy paper plate in the center of the floor. A darkened square spreads across the wall above the couch: a sunless scar from a poster or painting.

Ana collapses onto the couch, tucking one foot underneath her body. "You better be here to beg my forgiveness," she says.

"I'm sorry for any role I played in what happened." I mean it, but the words are so stiff in my mouth that they turn insincere.

"Maybe I've got it wrong," Ana says. Her bare knee pokes out from beneath her red dress. "You came to see me paying for my sins. You wanted to make sure that I don't have a future anymore."

A future: the bulging bag of clothes tossed into the darkness, the dyed hair, the abandoned apartment. "So you're going with him," I say. "With Rob."

Ana looks down.

"I'm sorry," I say. "I know you wouldn't be doing this if I hadn't forced your hand."

Her head comes up, and it takes me a moment to piece together her expression. Bright eyes, flushed cheeks. She's laughing at me. "No way," she says. "I'm never going to see that asshole again. I'm leaving town." She gestures around at the apartment, as if it proves something undisputable. "New city. Blank slate."

For a second, I can't manage a response.

"I'd be insane to keep up with this," Ana continues. "I'm insulted. In a sick way, you did me a favor, pushing me out when you did."

I sit cross-legged on the floor. The carpet is threadbare and scratchy, burping up stale nicotine. My real reason for being here keeps nudging at me.

"You know, I didn't do it for the money," Ana says. "Out of everything, that bothered me the most. That you thought I did it because I was broke."

"You're right," I say. "I shouldn't have said that."

"I never worked with clients like Fowler," Ana says. "People looking for publicity. The guys I was with, they had more to lose than me if word ever got out. Vigilantes are different. You go into it knowing they'll blab. There's not enough money in the world."

"So why Fowler?"

She bites down on her lip, leaving a fleck of bloody lipstick on her canine. "That police sketch. Every time I saw it, it nagged at me. I brushed it off, brushed it off, but when you told me about Fowler, it was like fate. I had to take the chance."

I'm curious, but my curiosity is a muted thing, half smothered under my instinct to be cautious. My awareness that it's better not to know.

"I came so close," Ana says, a sudden blaze of frustration. "But it wasn't enough. Fowler ditched me before we could get anything useful. Just turned her back on me." Ana's eyes flutter closed. "Three encounters, two lotuses each time. It was awful. I couldn't stop throwing up when I came back. Even now, I get these memories. Moments of feeling *wrong*. I'm working through it, but it's slow. I have to be hyperaware of who I am all the time.

It's like relearning how to walk. Staying so conscious of something that's always been effortless."

Almost without wanting to, I look down at my hands in my lap. My hands, ordinary enough to be invisible to my gaze. For a second their bareness, the lack of a ring, the naked, unpolished nails: it all flickers into strangeness.

"Fowler recorded the sessions so I could listen. We got her name. The whole city knows her name," Ana says. "Big fucking deal. We couldn't get much else. Laura couldn't remember anything. Not how she died. Not who killed her. Mostly gibberish. Fowler was asking stupid questions, detective shit she'd heard on TV: *Tell us who killed you, what did he look like.* There was one thing Laura said. When Fowler was getting pissy, screeching about *how'd you die, how'd you die,* Laura said—" Ana snaps her head forward, opens her eyes to look right into mine. "She said, 'I wasn't there.'"

I shake off my uneasiness. "Ana, the police are saying it could be drug-related. That house apparently attracted addicts. Maybe somebody killed Laura while she was high. Blacked out. It would make sense, right? She wasn't there when she died."

"God, you're as bad as Fowler," Ana says. "You're as bad as the cops. No. Worse. Because you, of all people, should know better." She launches herself off the couch, moves over to one of the boxes, scrabbling through the papers inside.

"OK, look at this," Ana says. She comes back to thrust a crumpled piece of paper at me. I accept. It's a printout, a gray-scale girl staring directly into the camera. Her hair is a shabby black. She wears too much makeup: eyes heavy with liner, brows shaped into apostrophes. "Do you recognize her?"

"Should I?"

"That's a photo of Laura Holmes." Ana's eyes have a manic luster. "When they found the body, though, she was blond, like in the police sketch. Imagine her blond. No makeup. Come on. You *know* her."

Almost against my will, I rearrange the girl's features. I wash Laura's hair into paleness, turn her eyes bare and soft, her eyebrows sketched fine and light. Posing against a plain background. Hair pulled back. Barely smiling.

"Well?" Ana asks.

I look at Ana, seeing the desperation in her face, her naked need for me to believe her. The torn photograph in Jane's office; the knowingness in those disembodied eyes.

"Thisbe," I say. "You think Laura Holmes was Thisbe."

Ana lets loose a quick gasp, as if she's been released from some crushing weight.

"Did Thisbe ever tell you her name?" I ask.

"No," she says. "Never. I didn't think to ask. But you see what I mean? It's too much to be coincidence. Sundress, earring, police sketch. And Thisbe was in trouble. I sensed it. I just didn't know it was so serious."

"What do you think happened?" I ask.

"Some asshole killed her," Ana says. "We've all had those clients. Someone who pushed his wife around until she escaped him by dying. He can't take that, he goes after her again. Or someone whose relationship was fine until he brought his girlfriend back, but then he can't take it, buying her affection by the hour. I've had more than a few clients tell me they hate thinking of me with other men."

There's a rushing at the edges of my consciousness. For a moment, I can't fight it off. It's like trying to rise against a great pressure, a vastness between me and the life and light above.

"Anyway, it doesn't matter now." Ana sounds infinitely tired. "I had my chance to get answers and I couldn't do it. The one time I've actually given a shit about something at that freak show, and look what happens." A bitter smile. "Maybe there's a lesson there."

I'm reminded of why I came here originally. "Ana," I say, "I need to know if you have any lotuses left."

She blinks, startled. "Yeah. Rob pressured me into it. He wanted them on hand in case we went through with his plan."

My relief is followed instantly by a cold focus. I need them.

"I'll pay, Ana," I say. "Just name the price."

She looks at me as if I'm a stranger accosting her on the streets. "Are you serious? What would you even do with extra lotuses?"

"I wouldn't ask if it wasn't important," I say.

Ana studies me. "So you're here because you want a favor," she says, as if to herself. "I should have known."

"You don't have a use for them anymore. It would work out for both of us."

"I never said I didn't need them," she says.

I realize that I've performed a dark little magic trick. I've driven away the version of Ana who was my confidante and instead summoned the woman I knew inside the Elysian Society walls. Calculating and careless. She surveys me with arms akimbo, elbows harsh angles.

"So maybe I'm not using the lotuses anymore," Ana says. "But they're valuable. Renard must have competitors who'd love to get their hands on these things."

"I already told you I'd pay anything," I say. "Just take this offer. Please."

"Will you tell me why you need them?" Ana says. "Little Miss Perfect. It has to be something juicy."

I'm barely listening. My mind is rushing ahead, the idea unraveling in front of me, almost too fast for me to keep pace. "All right," I say. "What if I don't pay you for the lotuses at all?"

She laughs, a thin sound that folds quickly. "Your negotiating skills need work."

"I'll help you channel Laura," I say. "The right way this time. So that you can get your answers."

Ana drops her head toward her chest as she considers this idea, examining it from all angles.

"I knew Thisbe," I say. "I know the Elysian Society, and I know our clients. If you're right, and Laura worked as Thisbe, then I'll be able to ask all the right questions. Who else could do that?" When she continues to hesitate, I press on: "Did Mrs. Fowler have anything that belonged to Laura?"

"Of course not," Ana says. "What, you think she raided the evidence room?"

"I know where to find something that belonged to Thisbe," I say. Uncertainty plays across her face, along with a half-buried shimmer of hope; I dig my fingernails into that hope. Leaning forward, I catch Ana's eyes and don't look away. "Ana, this is your chance. If you walk away, you'll always wonder. You can't make a clean break until you have your answers."

She runs a hand down her face, gives a weak and perfunctory laugh. "God," she says.

I wait.

"I can't believe I'm saying this, but fine."

Ana vanishes down the hallway. When she returns, she holds a small plastic bottle. A stark and utilitarian orange. A month's supply of lotuses. More. Every nerve in my body is honed on that bottle.

Ana shakes the bottle so that the lotuses rattle together. "We don't have a lot of time to carry out this little plan of yours," she says. "I'm leaving town, remember?"

I stretch out my palm. "We'll do it tomorrow, then. Meet me at 801 Sycamore. It's an apartment complex."

"All right," she says. "But I'm holding onto these until then. Leverage." As I open my mouth to protest, Ana cuts me off, voice tightening: "Don't push me on this, Edie. I'm already second-guessing this whole plan. Just take what you can get."

Reluctant, I withdraw my hand.

She moves to the apartment door, holding it open for me. Dusk leaks inside and turns her red dress the color of old blood.

"Listen," she says. "Whatever you're planning to do with those, watch out for yourself. I hope it's not what I think. I hope you aren't running off with some Mr. Lonelyhearts to be his dead sweetheart. Because after I've told you—"

"Don't worry," I say, rising. "I'll be careful."

Ana smiles with one side of her mouth. "Of course you will," she says. "What am I saying? It's you."

W
e need to talk."

"Viv?" At the sound of her voice on the phone, my tiredness turns into a sharp crack of wariness; I remember Henry's warning to stay away from his family. "I'm not sure we should be—"

"Henry was overreacting," Viv says. She's speaking in a half whisper. I wonder if the baby is sleeping nearby or if she's trying to hide this conversation from her husband. "He's been overprotective since what happened with Sylvia. It's sweet, but sometimes it drives me crazy."

"Even so, I need to respect Mr. Damson's wishes," I say.

I'm in my bedroom, preparing for sleep. On my bureau, the Braddocks' relics are arranged like a skewed timeline. The wedding portrait, the lipstick, the pregnancy test. And then the envelope of lotuses. The one object that I can fit into the timeline with confidence.

My future.

"Henry said he saw you at the office," Viv says. "Are you working with Patrick Braddock?"

I sit on the bed, my free hand gripping the edge of the mattress.

"There are things I haven't told you," Viv says. "Maybe I'm crazy. I haven't been able to tell anybody. Not all this time." Her breath has a quick, wet rhythm, like the aftermath of tears. "But if you're spending time around Patrick, you should know."

Still, I'm quiet.

"Lucy?" The desperation in her voice is like a child waking up in a dark room, grasping for a nearby presence.

"I'm here," I relent.

"Patrick was my friend for years," she says. "I—I used to play in his backyard. I'd never hurt him. But I also care about Sylvia. She was my friend too. She should have been Ben's godmother. Instead, Ben never even knew her." She pauses. "I'm supposed to accept the whole thing was an accident, but part of me can't stop thinking that it wasn't."

My reflection lies trapped in the darkening window. A tree branch cuts through my torso, the spidery limbs fanned like veins and arteries spreading outward from my heart.

"I had trouble sleeping at the lake," Viv says. "We'd come back from the restaurant. Sylvia had gone to her own place. Henry was still awake, in the other room. I couldn't get comfortable. I have a hard time falling asleep without Henry around. When he travels for work, it's terrible."

This is as much for Viv as for me. There's a lulling quality to her voice that reminds me of my clients recounting their loved ones' deaths, sitting in Room 12. Memories that have been worried over in secret, handled until they've grown a calcified layer of fear and doubt. It's a relief to put a story like this into words, to feel a stranger's eyes dissolve the thick coating and reveal the raw, soft core.

"The shouting wasn't clear at first," Viv says. "Like a TV in the other room. I'd fallen asleep and woken up. Maybe they woke me up. I don't know what time it was. And I was lying there, listening, and I started tuning in to these angry voices. The words weren't clear, but I recognized the voices. Sylvia's, mostly." A shaky breath. "It was hard to tell if they were somewhere outside my window, or if I was hearing them all the way from their own cabin. Sound was different near the lake. You could hear everything."

I see the flat expanse of the water, the words glancing across the surface like tossed stones.

don't do this

you don't have to do this

we can still fix it

"The next morning, when everything happened, I was in shock," Viv continues, and I snap back to focus. "I couldn't stop thinking about it. About the fight. And I wondered . . ."

"Did you tell anybody else about this, Viv?" I ask when it's clear she won't go on.

"No," she says. "I still don't know what I heard. It could have been my imagination. A dream. And Patrick had just lost Sylvia. How could I point fingers?"

My apartment complex is so quiet tonight. As if everyone else has been spirited away behind my back, leaving rows upon rows of empty rooms. Stretching high above my head, sinking below my feet. My body solitary in the center.

"I tried to be there for Patrick for the first few months after it happened," Viv says. "I hated turning my back on him. But every time I was with him, I'd wonder and wonder. I felt like he could see right through me." She pauses. "He's withdrawn more and more. It makes me feel better, as bad as that sounds."

Visible through a crack in the blinds, a car slides into the parking lot. The silhouettes of the passengers are revealed as the interior light comes on: stiff and unmoving, propped inside the car like dolls. Then they start moving, their gestures casual as they unbuckle their seatbelts. The light inside the car fades into blackness.

"Can you think of a reason the Braddocks would have been fighting?" I ask.

"I don't know," Viv says. "No. Not really. Henry has told me—he's told me the gossip. That Patrick wasn't faithful to Sylvia. I never would have guessed. Sylvia was good at putting on a brave face. It never even seemed like an act."

Standing from the bed, I move to the bureau, touching each object in turn.

"Now I'm looking back on everything else," Viv says. "That one memory ruins the others. Was any of it real? I'm so stupid I couldn't even tell." A damp, wrung-out laugh. "I wish I could go back to remembering them the way I used to. I want those memories back."

I shift the objects from one place to the next, rearranging them like a slide puzzle. Wedding photo, pregnancy test, lipstick, lotuses. Lipstick, wedding photo, pregnancy test, lotuses. Wedding photo, lipstick, pregnancy test, lotuses. I run my finger over the envelope of lotuses, then move it from its fixed position at the end of the Braddocks' story to the beginning.

"Can't you do anything?" Viv asks.

"Do you want me to help him?" I ask. "Or find out what happened?"

She must catch the anger in my voice. The line goes dead.

TWENTY-SIX

My client scratches at his exposed forearm, leaving thin white trails along his skin; I find myself staring at them, mesmerized. "Four years," he says, half to himself.

I glance at him. "Since your wife's death, Mr. Deehan?" I ask.

A curt, distracted nod. "And since I started coming here. To you." He scratches at his chin this time, plucking at a reddish mark just beneath his lip. A wound from shaving, maybe. Mr. Deehan's dressed less formally today, switching out his generic jacket and tie for jeans, a T-shirt. "It's our anniversary, in a way," he says.

I smile, trying to match his levity without acknowledging the undercurrent of desperation I hear in his voice. "In a way," I say.

"Barbara and I were only married for three years," he says. "That means I've been coming here longer than I was with her."

"Yes, I suppose so."

"I was thinking how strange it is," he says. "We met later in life than some of our friends. The relationship was always rocky. We'd both dated around a lot. We got used to always looking for something better. I'd see Barb looking at me sometimes and I figured she was thinking, why him? Out of all the men she could have been with." Mr. Deehan clasps and unclasps his hands, winds his fingers together and then grips his knees.

"Before the accident, we weren't doing so well. She would take off for a weekend with her parents or her sister. A few times every month, we'd discuss divorce. She even scheduled a meeting with an attorney. But then we'd make up. It got to be part of our routine. I stopped thinking it would change. It had turned into a waiting game, almost. When would one of our fights stick? When would I come home and find all her stuff gone?"

On my wrist, the diamond tennis bracelet glimmers with rows of stones, tucked together tight and sharp as a zipper. A row of tiny teeth.

"If the accident hadn't happened—" Mr. Deehan says. He pauses, running the blade of his thumbnail against the red mark. "I don't know where we'd be now. I don't know if Barbara and I would have kept hanging on. Maybe she'd be long gone. Maybe I'd be walking around the house and it would be as empty as it is now, and I wouldn't even know where to find her. This place—" He looks around Room 12, bleary-eyed, as if I've pulled off his blindfold after a long journey. "Well. When she's here, I always know just where to find her."

The clear sparkle of the bracelet makes me think of crunching ice chips between my molars. The freezing, painful sting of it.

"It's a real comfort," he says.

"Shall we begin?" I ask.

The word *comfort* lodges in my head as I swallow the lotus.

knock. The night air is deep and warm, leftover humidity tacky on my skin. In the distance, a police siren wails before dropping off into a series of short chirps.

Ana waits at my elbow, jittery, a large canvas bag slung over her shoulder. Her hair has already started to darken at the roots, a fine line spilling along the part. She wears her Elysian Society dress like a child forced into itchy formal clothes; she keeps plucking at the straps.

"I don't know how I ever put up with this thing," she says to me, catching my gaze.

The peephole flickers. A second later, Dora unlocks the door, leaning in the door frame with her arms crossed over her chest. She's unfamiliar: sweatpants, a T-shirt with an unraveling hem. Her gaze moves blankly over Ana's newly blond hair before her eyes click with recognition.

"Thanks for letting us come here, Dora," I say. "I promise we'll be quick."

"It's not a problem," she says. She opens the door wider. I understand how she feels: that this space isn't hers to control, that its boundaries are negotiable. I was relying on this. "I thought you were gone," Dora says to Ana, uncertain.

"Almost gone," Ana says. "Not just yet."

Standing in the living room, I absorb the Sycamore apartment. It all looks the same. Taupe walls. Cloudy light fixtures that produce a weak glow, like ambient light straggling in from somewhere else. The same wilted couch, the same cardboard-thin dining table. I realize with an ugly pinch that my current apartment isn't any more substantial than this one.

Behind me, Ana clears her throat. "Edie tells me that you've been finding things around here," she says to Dora, slipping the bag off her shoulder and resting it against the wall. "From the previous tenants."

Dora's been collecting everything in a bathroom drawer. Now, she lines her findings on the Formica countertop like sacrificial offerings on an altar. Two bobby pins, one green-gold, the other black. A tube of antibacterial ointment. A bottle of nail polish. Looking over Ana's shoulder, I relax. None of these items ever belonged to me.

Ana's fingers hover over the objects; she reaches for the nail polish bottle. She turns it around and around in her hand, as if searching for a tangible sign of its previous owner. The bottle is small, containing barely enough to cover all ten fingernails.

"That was stuck in an air vent," Dora volunteers. "I found it when I got the AC to work."

"You moved in during March?" I ask her, and she nods. "Thisbe left not too long before that. Just a month or so. There wouldn't have been many tenants between her and you."

Ana unscrews the cap, begins painting the nail of her left pointer finger. The polish is gelatinous and tarry, forming small bubbles and sliding clumps. When Ana's finished, her single red nail looks like a wound: clotted with red gore, as if the nail has been yanked out.

In the living room, Ana takes the two flimsy chairs from the table and places them, facing each other, in the center of the floor. She sits with her knees together, her back very straight. I start to sit across from her.

"What are you doing?" Ana asks. "Aren't you forgetting something?" When I stare, she tilts her chin toward the bag she brought with her. "Tie me up."

"You're joking," I say blankly.

"I brought rope," Ana says. "Not exactly glamorous, but it'll get the job done. We don't need to be all formal. It's just us girls." She winks, but there's a paleness to her skin, a layer fine as frost. It's this sign of fear that makes me realize she's serious.

"Ana, there's no need—" I start.

But Dora has brushed past me. She stoops to retrieve a coil of cheap rope from inside the bag: shiny yellow, slithering through her hands. I watch mutely as Dora moves to where Ana sits. Brisk as if she's rearranging a piece of furniture, she pushes Ana's left forearm against the back beam of the chair. Ana doesn't resist. Dora begins looping the rope around her arm.

"I told you, I'll be taking two lotuses," Ana says to me. "And whatever happened to Hopeful Doe—well, it wasn't pretty. It's safer this way."

After a second, I join them, tying Ana's other arm against the chair. Her arm is so thin, the skin so soft, that it surprises me. She's always seemed more solid than this, all coiled and restless strength.

Maybe Ana catches a change in my expression. She makes eye contact with me briefly. "Don't try to cop a feel, Edie," she says. "This isn't a date, you know."

I tie an efficient knot and move back to sit across from her.

Dora holds the lotuses up to Ana's lips, one at a time, and slips them inside. She reaches for the glass, tilting it against Ana's mouth. There's something gentle about the ritual, like a bedtime between a mother and a child. I watch the jump of Ana's throat as she swallows.

"Think of Thisbe." I recognize the smoothness of Ana's voice. It's the tone I use with clients. A voice from nowhere. "Think of Laura."

I think of her. Thisbe's face running with tears. Her wispy hair, earnest eyes. The police sketch, with its soft beauty showing through the inexpert lines like a miracle; the photo Ana showed me, the drab gray scale of heavy makeup.

The temperature in the room gutters. The hairs on my arms rise. I'm cold, then too hot. The air is drawn tighter around my skin, clamping down. Dora hovers near the door. I should tell her to go to safety, but selfishly, I want another ordinary body in the room with me, someone singular and rooted to the same world I am.

"Laura?" I ask.

Across from me, the body stirs. The eyes open. They're unfocused, blinking at the room around us. The lips wilt open: the darkness inside is layered and deep.

The mouth opens wider as she shifts her jaw experimentally. I imagine another woman's fingers creeping up her throat. Gentle and exploring, prodding the inside of her mouth and then retreating, pulled back to where the other woman is waiting.

"Laura," I say again.

The eyes meet mine with a slow, dragging effort. *"I know you,"* she says. A voice that's unsettlingly familiar, like a stranger performing an uneven imitation of Ana. A flawless syllable followed by a skewed one. I hadn't expected her to sound so much like Ana; it would be easier if she spoke in a voice I'd never hear again.

"I know you," she says again. *"You never talk to me. But I see you."*

"And I've seen you," I say. "Do you know this place we're in?"

"It's where I stay," she says, throwing a weaving glance around the apartment. Her gaze catches on Dora: there's a strange moment of silence as they study each other. Then the body in the chair moves. Just a shudder of movement, jerking her arms forward until the ropes restrain them.

Dora and I look at each other.

"Is it your home?" I ask, trying to redirect the body's attention.

"Not home," she says. *"But where I stay."*

"What do they call you, Laura?" I ask.

She shakes her head, pressing her arms against the restraints again.

I try again. "Does the name Thisbe mean anything to you?"

Her eyes drift down to her lap.

"Thisbe?" I ask, more insistent.

"I hate that name." Her anger flashes across the room. Dora cringes.

"I'm sorry. I'm sorry." I hesitate. "Laura, can you share a memory with me? Try to remember if there was anyone who threatened you. Anyone who frightened you."

"These aren't my hands," she says. *"Whose are they?"* She rolls her wrists, her hands twisting with the movement. *"Doesn't she want them back? Tell her that I have them for her."*

"Was there anybody who made you feel scared?" Desperation rises in my chest.

"*I just want my own hands back,*" Laura says. Her voice is shifting, rising. Higher pitched and younger. And it's as if her voice is a visible presence in the room, a shimmering heat wave that distorts her face, turning Ana's features too soft.

"I understand," I say. "I'm a body too."

"*She took them.*"

"Who took them?" Dora, this time. Her voice is small and fragile.

Again, the body jerks against the ropes. I realize how thin the restraints are, and how halfheartedly the knots have been tied. Dora and I were still seeing the whole thing as a game.

"Please," I say. "We're helping you."

She stops moving. "*She took them,*" Laura says. "*She wouldn't take my body off. And nobody would help me.*"

"You channeled a client's loved one," I say. "Something went wrong. She wouldn't leave. Is that it?" I remember the rumor that grew after Thisbe, so insubstantial I could brush it away like a cobweb. "You were possessed," I say.

"*It's my fault,*" she says, shutting her eyes.

"It's not your fault." I'm surprised at the roughness of my voice. "This wasn't supposed to happen to you."

Her eyes snap open. "*It could happen to you too.*"

"Who hurt your body?" Dora asks. "Was it a client?"

Coldness runs down my spine. "Dora," I say, a sharp, instinctive reprimand, and the air around us stretches and strains.

"What?" She's wounded, surprised. "We need to know."

In the chair, Laura tilts her head with a slight smile, confused as a child as she listens.

"You're right," I relent, forcing myself to focus. My mind becomes clear as a winter sky, still as deep water. "Try to remember," I say to Laura. "Remember his name."

"Leave me alone," the body says.

"We need to know," I say. "It's important—"

"It's too late."

She wrenches against the restraints. One of the ropes sags loose around her arm. It slides to the floor with a loose rustle, a thump. Dora makes a strangled noise that I feel inside my own throat. The body looks down at the snake-like yellow coil on the floor.

I force myself to stay seated, not showing my panic. "We're on your side," I say to her.

"It's too late," she repeats as she stands. In one quick movement, she wrenches her other arm free.

"Who did this to you?" I ask, and the answer is just inside my mind, pounding like a headache. I will her to say it, to say the name, push it out into the room. Put it between us.

"You know," she says. *"You must know."*

She closes the space between us, reaching out an experimental hand to graze Ana's blunt-cut fingernails against my skin.

Fear tightens everything inside me. Though Ana's body seemed small and light a few minutes ago, the woman in front of me brims with chaos. Laura has no stake in the world I occupy; she's all animal confusion, brimming anger.

She takes a step toward me. Then another. She falls into a kneeling position next to me. Her skin against mine is cold. My fear rises to a shrieking peak, and then, just as suddenly, it dissolves. I feel a strange tenderness.

"You can help me," she says. *"Help me take it off."* She holds out her arm, running the opposite hand down the fine skin of her forearm. I think she's left a deep scratch in Ana's flesh until my mind unscrambles the image. Streaks of nail polish, that's all. *"Help me,"* she repeats, her gauzy pupils focused on mine.

I could peel her like fruit. Slip my fingernails under Ana's skin and tug the flesh aside neatly to reveal Laura Holmes. Thisbe, in her white Elysian Society dress. Or a living version of the sketch,

Hopeful Doe, face deformed with the subtle misinterpretations of the artist.

Who would I find beneath the thin surface of my skin? Bridal Sylvia or the Sylvia in the lipstick? I'm overwhelmed by the thought of all the women who would pour out of me if I were cracked open: swarming like insects, bubbling up out of my mouth. The women who have collected inside me over the years, filling up my insides until there's no room left for me.

Laura collapses against me. The body heaves. She hides her face in my lap, hair tumbling against my thighs. I reach down to touch her scalp. Her hair is stiff under my touch, sharp with chill, as if she's been outside in freezing air.

"I'm so sorry," I say.

"Why would you bring me here?"

"To help you," I say.

"There's no helping somebody who doesn't want to be helped." Laura lifts her head toward my touch.

Our gazes lock. It reminds me of making eye contact with a stranger in a reflection, a bus window or a restroom mirror. A silvery, palpable layer of disconnect. Then her eyelids start sinking again, lopsided and heavy, like uneven curtains.

The air in the room is wrapped vacuum-tight around my body. In my peripheral vision, I see Dora against the wall, making herself as small as possible.

"Laura?"

She doesn't answer. Her shoulders slump.

"Laura."

The air above us seems to loosen, like a needle puncturing the tension.

I stand, letting her body slide away like a doll's onto the floor. I watch for her to rise again. She's still, only the faintest throb of breath moving through her. When I'm satisfied that the body on the floor belongs to Ana again, I go to the kitchen, not looking at

Dora as I pass. Leaning over the sink, I vomit. Again and again, my body jackknifing from the pressure.

Patrick and Sylvia. I've visualized the two of them together, sometimes: Sylvia conjured in the flesh, as if she stepped out of one of their photographs to join her husband. A stupid image. Idiotically romantic as a teenage crush. Now I'm forced to see them. My own face animated with another woman's expressions, my body crude and slow and wrong as it tries to accommodate the impulses of someone else's muscles. And Patrick with her.

I scoop a mouthful of water from the running tap, swish it through my teeth and over my tongue, spit it down the drain. There's soft pressure on the inside of my skull, like a soothing hand on my forehead during a fever. Slowly, I relax.

When I return to the living room, Dora's still in her same place, face drawn. Ana's sitting cross-legged on the floor. She smiles at me as I lean in the door frame. "That bad, huh?" she asks.

"I know it was worse for you," I say.

"Hey, I'm sturdier than I look." Ana's skin is pumped back full of color, her flesh damply golden. Wet stains spread beneath her arms. They strike me as beautiful, like dew on fresh fruit. "So," she says. "Anything useful?"

I hate the hopefulness etched on her face. Dora looks down at her feet, silent.

"Laura was working at the Elysian Society, as Thisbe," I say. "I verified that much. Something went wrong. She must have worked with a risky client at some point. The rumors were right, for once. She lost her body and couldn't get control of it again."

Ana's breath is soft and shallow.

"But—I'm sorry—Ana, she couldn't tell me if there were any violent clients, anyone threatening her. She still doesn't know who killed her," I say. "She left the Elysian Society at the end of January, the body wasn't discovered until March. If she was possessed, then weeks of her final memories are gone. Her body could have been anywhere in that time, with anyone." I pause. "Doing anything."

Ana takes this in, running her tongue over her lower lip. "But we've proved that she was working at the Elysian Society," she says. "That counts for something."

"We could go to the authorities," Dora cuts in. "If we tell them that Laura worked as Thisbe, they'd follow up, right? They'd have to."

"The least they could do is look at clients with a history of violence," Ana says. "Guys who have been too attached to the bodies. Anyone who's been paying for extra services."

"They probably wouldn't help us," I say. "They're not on our side. I spoke with a cop at the Elysian Society a while back. They think we're freaks. Untrustworthy."

"We have to try," Ana says. "Jesus, I'm risking everything here. If it's all for nothing—"

We survey each other without speaking. The air in the apartment is like a burst balloon. Tattered and exhausted.

"What is this really about?" Ana asks. "I know you're attached to the Elysian Society, but this—" Her eyes on me are flat and hard as coins. "I'm disappointed in you."

"Fine," I say. "I'll do what I can. But I can't promise anything."

Ana sighs deeply and then stands, her movements as stiff and clumsy as if she's waking from a long sleep. In the muted light, her single red fingernail holds a gory luster. She crouches down to reach into her bag; when she withdraws her hand, I see the familiar orange sheen of the bottle. I'd nearly forgotten about the lotuses.

"Here you are," Ana says, holding out the bottle to me. "I wouldn't want you to leave without it. It's the whole reason you did this, right?"

234 · **SARA FLANNERY MURPHY**

I hate the depth of relief that opens inside me as my fingers close around the bottle. When I glance up, Ana is diminished, replaced by the shadow of the other girl. I have to blink several times before she's herself again.

"What's wrong, Edie?" Ana asks, voice quiet.

"Nothing." I rise, keeping the bottle close to my heart. "Thank you."

"He's a lucky guy." Ana nods at the bottle.

stand in front of the screen, not moving. I didn't mean to come into the downstairs office, one of the rooms Patrick and I usually ignore when I'm at his house. But when I saw her face glowing out at me from beyond the half-open door, I moved toward her without thinking, caught in a trancelike curiosity.

I'm just another girl looking for my soul mate.

I read the words over and over again. Instead of softening my reaction, the alcohol amplifies my dizziness, sending me spinning into every corner of the room.

She looks so much like Sylvia. A younger, riper Sylvia; a cheerfully sexy version. Sylvia born into a different life, with a pinkish suntan, a tie-dyed sarong. She grins into the camera without a gleam of doubt about her own charms. The disembodied arm of a friend lies draped on her shoulders like a stole.

"I thought I'd find you here."

I turn, smarting at the faint hostility in his voice. Patrick comes into the office to stand beside me. He reaches out and clicks the window closed, leaving me staring at the desktop.

"I was married to Sylvia for six years," Patrick says. "We were together for three years before that. People stop counting that when you're married. Those years vanish. Marriage resets everything. But we were together for nine years. I can't remember what it's like to do any of this." He gestures at the screen.

What hurts isn't that he's been looking at photos of girls with heart-shaped faces and generous mouths, poring over their breasts and hips like toys in a catalog. It's his lack of apology. I crave the fumbling explanations, the defensiveness. But instead he's vaguely chagrined, as if I'm someone with no stake in his future.

"She's pretty," I say, voice stiff with an attempt to match his casualness.

"Sure," Patrick says.

"She looked so young, though," I say, not moving. "Isn't she too young for you?"

"I don't know," Patrick says. "How old are you?"

The slow shame unfurls in me, even though his voice was serious when he asked. Almost kind. I'm aware of being alone in this house with a stranger. It's a broad shock yawning beneath me, like missing a step.

"We always said, if one of us lost the other, we wouldn't be martyrs," Patrick says. "Sylvia wanted me to find someone new. She wanted me to be happy."

As he speaks, I can remember. The words, sweet and hot, and the expanse of the bed around us, white sheets binding us together loosely. At the time, saying this to my new husband was a gift I could give freely. There was so little chance of anyone collecting on it. Promising him a blank silhouette, waiting in the wings, seemed like proof of our everlastingness.

"Who was she, Patrick?"

Patrick doesn't say anything. In the flat radiance cast by the screen, deep hollows stand out beneath his eyes, his eyes sunk back farther into his face. He looks old.

"I saw you, that night. There was a woman," I say. "I was going to surprise you, but then I saw her. Who is she?"

"You must mean Jenn," Patrick says at last. He's careful, picking out each word as if sifting through glass. "She's the only person who's visited me in a long time. She was only here for a couple of hours."

"Jenn," I repeat.

"You remember. A friend from way back. She dropped by unannounced. Trust me, it wasn't a welcome visit. It wasn't anything I planned." He looks at me sideways, through the denseness of his lashes. "She's worried about me. Trying to be a good friend."

Patrick moves from the office. I follow, watching his body pass through the shadows and back out, until we reach the kitchen. He works the cork free from the bottle. "Jenn said I don't seem like myself anymore." He pours a glass; the wine splashes over the edge. "She'd read some study that men, widowers, they start dating again within a few years of a loss. I'm coming up on the second anniversary. Two years." He swallows, eyes searching the room restlessly over the rim of the glass.

"You're going to start dating?" I ask.

"Maybe," Patrick says. "One day."

My heartbeat stumbles in my chest. I wrap my arms around my body as if I can soothe the movement. "What about Sylvia?" I ask.

"Sylvia," Patrick says. "I've been thinking about that."

That. Not *her.* A mere complication, a roadblock to his new life.

"Jenn meant well," Patrick says. "She's one of the only ones who makes an effort. The only one who sees potential for a normal life. I was trying for her sake. Seeing if I could imagine a normal life with any of those women."

The grinning girl from the photo transplanted into this kitchen, light and life trailing after her like a bridal train. She'd replace Sylvia perfectly; from the back, faces hidden, they'd be identical. She could use Sylvia's old photographs as her own, slipping seamlessly into someone else's history.

"I can't—" Patrick starts. He presses his palm briefly against his mouth, as if preventing the words from forming. "Whenever I think of going on a date, a candlelit dinner, a movie, whatever you're supposed to do—it's impossible. I can't sit across from women and pretend I'm someone I'm not, pretend I can be a normal husband one day."

"So instead you sit across from me," I say.

Patrick makes the gesture of a smile, no emotion behind it. "Sure," he says. "I guess so."

"Whatever you do," I say, "just don't turn your back on her again."

"I never turned my back on her," Patrick says. He's looking at me as if I'm a stranger he's discovered in the middle of the night, rifling through his medicine cabinet, running my hands over his silverware. "You don't know anything about our lives," he says, half a question.

"You won't let me in."

"I've let you in," he says. "God, you're in my house, you're in my bed—"

"Then why can't you be honest?" I ask.

"About what?"

I shake my head.

"About what, Edie?" he asks.

It all rises onto my tongue. The questions I could ask him; the strange discrepancies that have floated to the surface of his life without his knowledge, the debris of his marriage that I've been examining. The anger that Viv overheard, the two lines on the pregnancy test, the deep wilderness of isolation that Patrick has built around himself.

"Did you ever do this before?" I ask instead. "With someone else?"

His face is blank. "I don't know what you mean."

"Am I the first body you've used?" I ask. "To see Sylvia."

A trace of coldness tautens the air around us, moving swiftly through the room.

"Of course." A strange laugh, barely recognizable as a laugh at all. "Why would you ask that?"

"You never went to the Elysian Society before?" I ask.

"You're my first," he says, with a small, sharp edge of mockery. I can't speak.

"Edie, what is this about?" he asks. "You really think I've used other bodies?"

Thisbe's face stitches itself together in my mind, then dissolves.

"Even if I had, what would it matter to you?" When I don't answer, Patrick goes on: "She's my wife. Whatever happened before I came to you, it doesn't involve you."

"So you did see someone else," I say.

"No," he says. "But I didn't make any promises to you. If something happened between the two of us, there would be nothing to stop me from going to another body."

The anger is as heavy and tangible as a new organ, squeezing under my ribs. "I know you cheated on your wife, Patrick," I say.

He shuts his eyes against the words. "I can't do this," he says, as if to himself.

"Why would you hide that from me?" I ask.

Patrick shakes his head, eyes still closed. "I never cheated on her." The quietness of his voice gives me a crawling sense of unease.

"I know about it," I say. "And if you'd do it to her once, then I shouldn't be surprised you'd do it to her again."

I want him to be angry. I want the screaming, the hot, shocking burst of rage, the wildness of a fight. I want him to look at me. But when he does open his eyes, he's already gazing beyond me. I feel as if I'm not even in the room.

"You have no reason to trust me," he says. "It's easy to forget that, doing what we do together. I keep thinking it doesn't matter when I'm with you, because you're—"

The beat of silence is a neat summary of my place in his life. Outside the window, a bird calls and then calls again, a piercing string dipping into a melancholy lilt.

"What did you say, that night?" Patrick asks. "That I need to look. That I can't keep running from the past."

Across the kitchen, in the mirrored surface of the night-dark window, I see us side by side. Time-lapsed versions of us, older, thinner, tense. The stretch of space between us is disproportionate, as if we're standing on opposite sides of a vast gulf.

"It's true," Patrick says. "I can't avoid it. It hasn't worked."

I already know what he's going to say next.

"So we'll go to the lake," Patrick says. "You and me. We'll leave tomorrow morning."

The words come from my mouth, but they don't belong to me. It's a ventriloquist's trick: a woman's voice coaxed from the opposite corner of a room, from an empty chair, a birdcage, a vase. From thin air. The source of the voice is a formality, a mere vessel for the words. And what I have to say is, *"Yes, yes, I'll go with you."*

TWENTY-EIGHT

Lake Madeleine is farther from civilization than I expected. After the exit from the freeway, we've only been driving for a few minutes down the narrow, tree-lined road before I feel a shift in the air, sparking against my skin like an electrical current or the first hint of rain. Patrick's in the driver's seat; the tree branches cast a shifting veil of shadows over his skin.

It's been years since I left the city. The slender trunks cluster close together and, glimpsed just beyond, more trees and then more, rolling out like an ocean.

This morning, I rescheduled my upcoming encounters at the Elysian Society, shifting everything aside for the next two days. I'll lose some of my regulars. My clients love me for my predictability, the way I'm always waiting on the shelf. This is the first time in five years I've betrayed them by denying them access to their loved ones.

I should feel guilty over this. But every time I try to imagine my life beyond the next few days, my mind finds blankness. A wall of fog, as if my future has been steadily rubbed away.

"Are you afraid that the people here will remember you?" I ask.

"You think that's going to be a change?" Patrick asks. "The only people who remember are stuck way out here?" His hands on the steering wheel tighten.

The water shines through the trees in a quick, dark glimmer.

"Anyway, I'll use a fake name," he says.

I look at him, but he's still gazing ahead, expression distracted. After a second, I decide that he didn't mean anything by it.

Patrick guides the car into the parking lot. Only a few other vehicles share the space with us. I wait in the car as he goes to the front office, taking in the curved strip of grainy beach, the single-file row of triangular cabins glimpsed through the trees. The cabins' gray siding is weathered too cleanly, like props. On the boat rack, the bottoms of the boats stand out like blanched rib bones.

In the daylight, Lake Madeleine is beautiful. Gemstone blue, sun-gorged and glittering. From its banks, the trees feather upward in a gentle slope, or sink back to shadowy alcoves. There's a brutal innocence to the water's beauty, as if it doesn't understand its own dangers.

A shadow falls across my lap; Patrick taps on the window.

Following him down the path that winds through the trees, I study his body. We've been civil with each other since last night. Polite but distant. Two strangers bound by something bigger than either of us. We slept next to each other without touching. When Patrick's hand brushed against my arm as he reached for a glass this morning, we pulled apart as if we'd received a shock.

Only two cabins display any signs of life. Crumpled sunscreen bottles on the porch railings, next to the damp neon of draped towels. In a window, the blinds lift in a crooked arc. Each time I think we're going to stop, Patrick keeps moving. Then I see it. The second cabin from the end of the row. It's identical to the others, with its A-frame design and the outcrop of the porch. The steps are dusted with pebbles. I veer toward the cabin as if I've come here a thousand times, my muscles guided by an automatic impulse.

Patrick calls my name; I stop, confused. "We're the next one," he says.

"I thought we'd be staying in the same one," I say. Only a few yards away, the lake laps at the bank, patiently rolling over the grasping twigs and pale pebbles. "The same one as that August."

"This is the one we stayed in," Patrick says, gesturing ahead at the last cabin of the row. When I don't answer, he says, "Edie, trust me. I remember."

When we enter the cabin, I stop in the doorway. Nobody else has been inside this space since Sylvia and Patrick left two summers ago. The cabin holds the oversteeped stillness of a house in a ghost town, shrinking at the sudden intrusion. Once, it must have been quaint: a dutiful honeymoon suite. A glass butterfly hangs over a fireplace, wings fuzzed with dust. The floral wreath above the sofa breathes out the memory of sweetness. Each separate piece of furniture, each decoration, feels immovable inside its own space, like a wasp preserved in amber.

Patrick pulls up the shades. Dust rises into the air, a glittering veil in the sunlight, then drops and vanishes. In the generous light afforded by the huge windows, the place shifts back into ordinariness.

I move down the narrow hallway that opens beyond the kitchen. Three doors spread out along the left side. I open each in turn. A small pastel-colored bathroom, the shower encased in frosted glass; a closet; and the bedroom. White walls, floral coverlet, a spidery antique bed frame.

I was so sure that I'd find the bedroom from the photograph, ready to reveal its secrets. Instead, I've found this unfamiliar space. It's like a cruel magician's trick. The other bedroom must have been here as I approached, dematerializing the moment my eyes touched it.

When Patrick comes in a few minutes later, I'm curled on the bed. I'm silent as he lies next to me. As his weight shifts the mattress, pulls me closer into the dip he creates, I think: this is the last space where Patrick and Sylvia spoke together in their own voices. The last space they touched each other with their own bodies.

Turning, I rest my hand against Patrick's chest. The rapid rhythm of his heartbeat fills my palm.

He shifts until he's above me, pinning me on the bed. His hand moves down my stomach and lifts the hem of my dress. When he touches me, I'm amazed at how immediately he stirs up desire, a pinch deep beneath my skin. I hold myself back with an effort. It's as if I'm hanging in a corner of the room, watching two strangers.

But the faster my breath comes, and the surer his touch grows against me, the more fully and firmly I sink back into the shape of my flesh. At the same time, Patrick transforms back into himself. The man he was when I first met him. I cling to him, finally, wrapping my arms around his back, feeling the quick, easy movement of his muscles.

Afterward, we lie breathless, staring at the ceiling.

"What is it like to be here?" I ask.

Patrick pulls me against him until my skull nestles against his jaw, clicking into place like a puzzle piece. "Strange. Not strange." A pause. "It's like everything that happened between then and now hasn't even been real. I've only been waiting to come back."

From outside, a burst of laughter punctures the silence of our bedroom.

"Patrick," I say. "What really happened, that night?"

His hand strokes a slow circle on the small of my back. "You know what happened," he says. "I came here with my wife. We wanted to spend time together. Get away from it all. One night, she went swimming alone. She wasn't a drinker. She wasn't much of a swimmer. So I lost her. A stupid mistake," he says. "And I lost her."

"There's more to it than that," I say.

Patrick doesn't answer.

"You didn't want anyone to investigate her death," I say.

His hand on my back slows and then stills.

"You couldn't look at her after she died," I say. "You couldn't look at your own wife. You've withdrawn from everybody in your life. You can't explain the room in the photograph. And people—people heard fighting. Shouting. The night Sylvia died."

Patrick's breathing is low and even against my belly. "How do you know all this?"

"It doesn't matter," I say.

"You've gone behind my back." He doesn't even sound angry. "Is this what you meant by letting you in?"

The truth is that there's more than what I've said. This spread of accusations is only a thin layer floating over the true evidence: the dark beat of another woman's heart in my chest, the sticky caul of her presence that clings to the folds of my brain.

"Things weren't perfect between me and Sylvia." Patrick's voice buzzes from his throat into my scalp. "When you love somebody and you're afraid you'll lose them, it can change you."

I shut my eyes. "I know that," I say.

"No, you don't."

I'm quiet.

"How could you?" Patrick asks. "You don't know what it's like to lose someone. I've spent every waking moment with you and you've barely told me anything about yourself. You're just—" His grip on me tightens.

I open my eyes to find Patrick looking down at me, searching my features as if he's trying to recognize someone who's been gone a long time. "You're not my wife," he says, half wondering. "You're not even yourself."

I don't move. "Do you want her?" I ask.

His pupils expand, spreading points of darkness. Fear or desire—I can't untangle them. He shuts his eyes. "No," he says. "Right now, I just want to sleep."

I watch Patrick until the heaviness of his breathing and the droop of his lips convinces me that he's gone. Only then can I sleep. I've been holding my exhaustion at bay, and now it's huge, rushing over my head and taking me down.

But there's space for one thought to slide swiftly through my brain, carried in on eddies of sleep. When Patrick told me I wasn't myself, what I felt wasn't rage or humiliation or even loss. It was a deep sense of comfort.

I wake. The light in the bedroom has shifted from thin afternoon brilliance into the density just before sunset. All the shadows in the room are slanted, as if cast by a lamp knocked on its side. I sit up. The bed next to me is empty. I touch the sheets: cool under my fingers.

"Patrick?"

No response.

I slip my dress back over my head, the sheer folds briefly muting the world. Going to the bureau, I kneel next to the lowest drawer and slide it open. I reach inside. Emptiness. The next holds only a Gideon bible, a folded hand towel. I'm not certain what I'm searching for. All those nights I've woken up on my bedroom floor without explanation: there must be a reason, trailing behind the events. But I reach the final drawer and find it empty.

For a second I see myself. A ridiculous woman in a too-young dress, kneeling on the bedroom floor. Looking to patterns in dreams, sifting through the leftovers of someone else's tragedy. Hoping to find answers in benign and meaningless places because I'm too afraid of looking directly into the source of pain.

I stand up. That photo. Her body on the bed in the lustrous lipstick, her naked body, the directness of her gaze against mine.

In my mind, her body transforms. Her skin blue-tinged, the hollows of her hands and her fingertips thickly dimpled, her features darkened with veins of rot.

I walk out into the threadbare light of the evening. Standing on the porch, I look across at the cabin next to ours. It's set back farther into the pines, retreating from the water. The windows holding the particular darkness of an empty house at sunset, as if the shadows inside are a solid weight pressed against the glass.

My feet carry me across the strip of grass and up the stairs. My approaching reflection sharpens in the front window as I approach, like a face slowly emerging from underwater. When I push my shoulder against the door, it gives way easily.

The inside is nearly identical to the other cabin. Only a few details are switched. The windows facing the opposite direction, a landscape painting instead of a wreath. The back of my neck goes cold and buzzing.

I already know what I'll find behind the final door on the left. I switch on the light and the bedroom is revealed. The darkness of the bedspread, the lines of the walls. It's the room in the Polaroid. The one Patrick claimed not to recognize.

She must be here. Passing the bed, I drag my hand over the slick fabric. Her shampoo on the pillowcases, inky hairs woven into the fine tapestry of dust and detritus along the baseboards. Phosphorescent fingerprints on the bathroom faucets and the drawer pulls.

Crouching, I slide the empty drawer out of the dresser, leaving a gap in the row. I lean down, head bent against the side of the bureau; I reach into each corner, groping at the floorboards. My fingertips brush against something. Small and sharp-edged. I manage to slide my fingers beneath the shape, drawing it loose.

A photo. The displaced companion to the one that still lies inside my apartment. A Polaroid; the same blocky border, this one dust-darkened.

That picture with the lipstick was my first introduction to Sylvia's mystery and her hidden ferocity. Here, finally, is the second scene. The next step. The room around me takes on strange dimensions, reflected back at me in the photograph. Like nesting dolls. The room within the room, the space around me and the past version of it trapped and shrunken. Sylvia on the bed, so vivid that I could turn my head and see her.

And him.

The source of the shadow, stripped to his flesh, exposed, finally, at the core of her life. Henry Damson. Sylvia's laughing, naked. She's on her knees, as if caught while changing positions. The mirror exposes the curve of her back, the rope of pearls of her spine. In the reflection behind her, there's a clear view of Henry. Shirt unbuttoned. His smile beneath the mask of the camera.

know where to find him.

It's dark now. The moon is gauzy, partially hidden by clouds. The stars are starting to spread in little puncture wounds. The lake seems to throw off its own pale, fractured light.

I walk along the rocky shore, then onto the path that winds through the trees. The coating of pine needles slips under my bare feet, a few of them cracking beneath the weight of my soles.

The trees seem to draw closer as I go deeper and deeper, venturing farther from the negotiable sense of civilization back at the cabins. The insects and tree frogs create such an overwhelming layer of shrieking and pulsing that I feel hidden by the noise.

It takes me twenty minutes to reach him. Patrick sits near the water, back against a tree trunk. He's on a small tongue of land that extends from the main path. He doesn't seem distressed; he could be transplanted here from a hazy summer day, surrounded by crowds of people. Only the chalky spotlight of the moon reveals the scene's true strangeness. He doesn't startle when I come up behind him.

A floral memorial wreath hangs on the tree trunk. The flowers are stiff fabric, the cruelly cheerful yellow of birthday cake icing. Its tattiness stands out. Layered water stains, petals torn and shedding.

"This is where they found her?" I ask.

A long moment passes before Patrick answers. "One of her friends must have left that," he says. "Or her parents."

From this point, there's a clear view of the lake. The expanse between us and the opposite shore is vast. Next to the enormity of the water, the wreath is inadequate. This attempt to take Sylvia's death and condense it into one discrete marker.

I sit beside Patrick, careful not to touch him.

He turns to me finally. "You know," he says. Calm, but leaving no room for argument. "Sylvia had the same look on her face, that night."

"Patrick," I say, "why didn't you tell me?"

"You've never trusted me," he says. "You came into my home, you slept with me, but you started doubting me. So you drag me here to find out what happened." He looks back at the water. "As if finding out will fix anything."

"You're the one who wanted to come to the lake, Patrick," I say. "Not me."

"None of this was your idea," he says. "You've been careful about that. When I first left the Elysian Society, you pulled me back. You made it look like my idea. I should have known then. I should have run." He leans his forehead against his fist. "I've wanted to end this. Sometimes I'm disgusted by the whole thing. Every time, you're right there, convincing me to stay. You won't let go."

Even in this moment, I want to reach out to him. Some vitality in Patrick has diminished since I met him. Or maybe it's a transformation inside me, the spell ripped from my eyes to reveal him in his true form. But despite everything, my fingertips are restless with the desire to stroke his hair off his forehead.

"Seeing a person the way they really are—it's not simple."

"What did you do to her?" I ask.

Patrick smiles, quick and indecipherable. He holds out his hand and opens his palm, as if he's going to release a trapped firefly. In the gloom, my brain lags before I can make sense of what I'm seeing. A lotus. That thin white pill, more familiar to me than the air I breathe.

A heart-sized knot swells in my throat. I watch my hand reach out to accept the pill. Patrick's eyes are on my mouth as I slip it between my teeth. The world is still and deep and quiet. In the moonlight, the boundary between the water and the land is a thin glowing stripe. I imagine sliding my fingers under that edge, lifting the water open like a trapdoor and slipping down into a light-filled space.

The pill is heavy on my tongue. I swallow. Before I'm even gone, I can feel her stepping into my skin. So easy now, so expected. Like a woman pulling on a glove. I'm not being chased from my skin. I'm relinquishing it to its true owner.

I'm gone, gone, traveling through the body, the bulging knots of the spine and the red swimming thump of organs, the underwater *whish-whish-whish* of the heartbeat. Silence.

And then nothing.

TWENTY-NINE

I wanted to come here.

It wasn't the other woman's idea to come to the lake. Not really. It wasn't even his doing, though I know he's been dreaming of this place ever since that night.

At first, we were in that plain little room. Unrecognizable enough to be anywhere. Then we moved deeper into our old life. He took me into our house. Our shared possessions laid out in the same patterns; all I had to do was touch one and it released a trail of memories. None of it felt right. Even the places I loved the most—the backyard with its canopy of tree branches, the pale sprawl of our bedroom—have been disorienting, suffocating.

I came to the lake exactly eight times during my lifetime. I kept careful count, each visit a strange and shining thing that I savored for weeks afterward. It should have been seven times. But I couldn't resist coming here that August. Even as I knew it was wrong. Even as I understood what would happen—that it would be an ending, that something in our lives would have to change—I came here one final time. I never left.

I want to make him watch what he did. Make him look this time.

Everything is the same. The lake, the moon, the layered silence, his body beside mine. The past is implacable, time twisting around on itself. Not softening or yielding to reveal new chances, but narrow, holding our exact shapes. Forcing our bodies through the same actions.

As we move into the waiting mouth of the water, one thought surprises me. A rush of compassion for the silent mind and heart that shares this space with me.

I wish she didn't have to be here.

THIRTY

My ears are filled with water. My arms float next to me. Distantly, I see the surface of the water. A mantle spun from different material. A layer of ice.

The surface is floating farther and farther from me, as if it's ever-rising and I'm the still, fixed point.

I can come up. I tell myself this. My lungs are swollen inside me, pinched and burning at the edges. It's so quiet down here that I forget I'm anyone. My stomach jumps hard. My lungs stretch until they don't fit the confines of my body. I'm already relenting. Blackness leaks in at the edges of my vision. I shut my eyes.

It's all happening again.

I've missed this. I've kept it out of my mind, refusing to let myself remember. But now that it's here, I know how deeply I've wanted to feel it again. Just one more time. The peacefulness of inevitability. Everything shedding away, piece by piece. Faster and faster. Weightless, I'm stripped of my past and my future, stripped of my choices. I'm a hanging heartbeat on the brink of being extinguished.

A name forms on my tongue.

It jolts through me. An awareness of my body around me, everything electrified with the urgent desire to draw a breath.

I open my eyes.

It's a deep impulse, foreign and completely consuming, filling every part of me: *Go.*

I don't have a chance to examine the sensation. I'm moving up, up, toward the faint streaks of light that signify the world above. I'm so swift, so assured, that it feels as if I'm being pulled in a current. I see myself as if I'm watching from a distance. This small, pale life against the darkness.

That layer of light is just above me now. Close enough that I could put out my fingers and break through it.

And he's here. His silhouette blocking the moonlight. He reaches for me; I feel the strength and solidity of his hands, completely wrong in this place composed of softened sounds and floating impressions.

I barely have time to register his grip, and then we're above the surface of the water. The air is sharp as a knife's blade, thin and spare. Each lungful is brutally tender, as if I'm exposed to air on an undiscovered planet. I cough and choke.

He's moving, clumsy and slow, back to shore. Everything is tilted and trembling, a world sent spinning like a marble across the floor. Pressed awkwardly to his body, I can feel the strain of his muscles, and, miraculously, the weight and stretch of my own body. My consciousness still tethered to my limbs.

We're approaching the shore. The moon in the sky rights itself. The water is as high as his shoulders. When he stops, I lean against him, clutch at him. The other name dissolves on my tongue.

"I'm sorry," he says, close in my ear. His voice is burning and clear; it's as if I'm hearing a human voice for the first time. "I'm so sorry, Sylvia."

THIRTY-ONE

The earth under me and the tree trunk behind my back are gloriously real. The pine tree's reptilian bark, the thick soil. I want to reach out and grasp everything, drinking the world in. I'm intoxicated by my body: my skin and bone and blood, the humidity and shivery pulse of me. I could stay here forever.

Far away, on the other shore, sparse glimmers of light cut through the trees.

Patrick leans against the opposite tree trunk, his hands clasped between the peaks of his knees.

"Things had been going wrong," he starts, as if in response to a question. "When I married Sylvia, she was the most vital person I'd ever met. She made me a better person. People responded to me differently when I was with her."

"She was pregnant," I say.

Patrick breathes in sharply, as if bracing against physical pain. "She was. Once."

I lay my palm along the ground next to me, relishing the soft give of the earth beneath my hand. I slip my fingernails into the damp loam. For a moment, I'm about to speak—then he continues, and I swallow the words back down.

"We'd been married for a few years," Patrick says. "There was no reason not to have kids. One day she came into the bedroom, smiling, crying, showing me the test."

After the Elysian Society, my brain has developed a specific quietness. The ability to walk inside a stranger's story without being touched by it. Tonight, I'm stripped to a primal state. Sylvia's story is as intimate a landscape as my own memories.

"She started bleeding," Patrick says. "On the way to the doctor, I kept telling her, it's nothing. But she already knew what was happening. She wouldn't look at me. She didn't even let me come to the exam room with her. That was our hardest month. I kept saying the wrong things. Once, I told her that at least we knew she could get pregnant. We'd just try again. Sylvia reacted as if I'd . . . struck her. I couldn't understand.

"It didn't happen, and it didn't happen. We were trying everything. Spending so much time and money and energy, constantly failing. It was like that first pregnancy had been our one chance, and we'd lost it, and now we'd never get it again. I saw a whole new version of my wife. All this sadness I hadn't even realized she'd had inside her. She was barely leaving her bed. Do you have any idea what that's like?"

I curl my fingernails deeper. "No," I say.

"We don't know what happened," Patrick continues. "The doctors could never give us a straight answer. That's what I wanted. One thing we could fix. One problem we could focus on. But there was no real explanation. Her body just . . . didn't want to do it. I'd rest my hand on her stomach at night and imagine reaching right through her skin to fix something. She was so small, and everything was right there under my hand. But I couldn't do anything for her.

"We were exhausted. It was hard to have that same warmth around other people. People talked. I hate myself for it now, but then, I resented Sylvia for not being stronger and happier. I looked the other way. I waited for her to change back into who she'd been before."

The stars are different out here. Dizzy sprays of light, more star than sky, whorled and textured like the wind-churned surface of an ocean.

"I got lost in work," he says. "Sylvia made an effort to focus on other things. She was thinking about returning to photography, taking it seriously again. I'd still catch that sadness in her. But she was trying to hide it, and I let her. I wanted her to hide that side of herself from me." Patrick opens his eyes. "This went on for a year. When Sylvia asked to come to the lake that weekend, I took it as another sign that things were getting better."

The photo. It slips into my head, every detail crisp and alive. I'm grateful for the image: proof that arrived ahead of its explanation. Preparing me for what comes next.

"The Damsons were here," he says. "That changed things. We were doing our old song and dance, playing the happy couple. Even when we were alone together, it felt like we were being watched. I couldn't go to dinner with them that night. Sit there and be the charming husband. When they came back, she'd been drinking too much.

"She said we hadn't been honest with each other in a long time, and she wanted to change that. But she needed to be honest. She didn't want any secrets between us." Patrick pauses. "Being with Henry, it was a chance to be somebody different. With him, she wasn't failing at anything, she wasn't thinking about the future. She could be her old self. Or maybe—maybe she said she could be someone new. I forget which. Both."

I rise and go to him, wrapping my arms around Patrick. The chill goes deep: his body drenched down to his center, the coldness seeping outward.

"All my wife wanted was for me to see her at her most unhappy and broken," he says. "She wanted me to see her that way and still love her."

"You never knew about her and Henry?" I ask.

Patrick makes what sounds like a muffled laugh, a noise I feel in his chest. "It's like I'd been waiting for her to tell me. Once she did, I could look at it directly. The Damsons being here wasn't a coincidence. She'd followed him. When I went to confront Henry, he was waiting for us. Whatever she'd said or done earlier that night, he must have known she'd tell me."

I tighten my arms around him.

"Viv was asleep," Patrick says. "That's when Sylvia told me Viv was pregnant. I stood in that place with my wife and with him. I couldn't say or do anything to make it right. Henry kept saying we should move on. I felt this huge difference between us. Henry and Viv—somewhere behind my back, they'd become so real. And Sylvia and I were broken. When Henry told us to forget the past, he was gloating. He knew that he'd move on, with Viv and their baby. And he knew that we couldn't. He was chasing us out of our lives."

"Sylvia still wanted to be with you," I say. "She told you that she wanted a new start."

"I didn't believe her," Patrick says. "If Henry had been willing to walk away with her that night, she wouldn't have looked back once. I told her I was leaving her. Told her she was nothing. Worthless. I was glad we'd never had a child, because I wouldn't want my child growing up with a mother like her."

The pain is like a knife meticulously slicing open the outline of a scar.

"It was a blur, after that," Patrick says. "Sylvia wasn't crying. She wouldn't speak above a whisper. All the color just gone from her. Her eyes were— I couldn't look at her directly. Like she'd already stepped out of our world and into another place. She just turned around and left."

"You didn't follow her?" I ask.

"No," Patrick says. "One of us should have gone after her. She was out of her mind with sadness, she'd been drinking. She wasn't a strong swimmer. I left a few minutes after she did. I saw her, on my way back to our place. She was already waist-deep, pulling off her dress. Seeing her from a distance, doing something like that, she could have been a stranger. This beautiful woman standing in the water. She didn't even seem real."

Looking out across the water, I can see Sylvia coming toward us. Submerged to her waist, torso cutting an elegant line through the darkness, bare breasts streaming with lake water. Her eyes locked on us. On me.

"Henry and I never made a conscious choice to hide what happened," Patrick says. "Viv was with him the next day. The lake was swarming with people. We couldn't even make eye contact without someone noticing. It was a silent agreement. Henry seemed to think I'd leave. Leave the firm, leave the city. Vanish, like she did. I can tell he hates having me around."

"He identified her body?" I ask.

"I let him," Patrick says dully. "What did it matter? I remember Viv acting like he was a hero for doing that. Like it was a kindness. I always thought it was his way of showing that she was more his than mine. I didn't stop him."

The way Henry has spoken about Patrick, that quick dismissiveness and impatience; he must see Patrick as a ghost, circling the edges of the life the Damsons have created, carrying the bitter memory of Sylvia with him into every room he enters.

"And her family wanted to blame this place," Patrick says. "They wanted something to explain her loss. I was the one who discouraged them from pursuing a lawsuit. I didn't want people picking over the details. Her family respected my wishes, but that was the beginning of the end. We stopped seeing each other. Everyone who'd been part of our lives together fell away. I didn't do anything to stop it."

The knob of his collarbone presses into my cheek as I lean against him.

Patrick turns his head toward me, his startlingly warm breath catching at my skin. "Now you finally know everything about me," he says. "You know me better than anybody else alive. So what about you?" he asks. "Any deep dark secrets?"

He's teasing, weary and rueful. Sitting next to him in this moon-glutted place, I realize how easy it would be to tell him everything. To open myself to him: show him the parts of myself so scarred and strange and distant that they barely seem to be me at all.

"My life has been very quiet," I say.

"You're lucky," he says. "A quiet, honest life. You don't know what it means until you don't have a chance to lead it anymore."

I can't answer.

"I pretend all the secrecy is for her sake," Patrick says. "Sylvia wouldn't want people knowing what really happened. Better to let them think it was a freak accident, one of those senseless tragedies they can obsess over. But people sense my guilt. And I did kill her, just not the way they think." He shifts restlessly. "It would almost be better that way."

"You were heartbroken, Patrick," I say. "You weren't thinking clearly." When he doesn't answer, I ask, "You've apologized to her?"

"No," he says. "At first, being with you, with her—it helped. Talking with her felt like the first few years. The years we were falling in love. We've never discussed that night. I couldn't risk ruining what we had. Then you started mentioning the lake, pushing me to come here. I gave in."

"We were in the water together," I say, half a question.

"Usually there's enough of you to soften her," Patrick says. "Tonight, you swallowed the lotus and she was here completely. You were nowhere. I'd thought if we relived that night, I could undo what happened. I'd go to my wife, the way I should have that night. But she was in the water. She was strong. She fought back. There was a point where you went under the surface and I knew you wouldn't be coming back. Sylvia would hold you there until you were gone too."

It returns to me, a confused jumble of soundlessness, fractured darkness, the sensation of his hands against me. His arms wrapped tight around me. And I realize: Patrick doesn't know what happened while I was tucked deep inside the belly of the lake. When he found me, he couldn't have known that I was already caught in a relentless trajectory toward the surface, my body bright with the desire for breath. If he'd looked for me before, he couldn't have found me. I was so far beneath his reach. Too far.

There was that moment when something changed inside my brain. A stubborn spark that spread to my limbs, propelling me away from the blackness I'd been sinking into.

I examine Patrick. He followed his wife, this time; he pulled her from the lake. I see all the tired relief, the cautious triumph, collected in his eyes. His past finally erased and rewritten.

"But you saved me, Patrick," I say. Strong, as if there's not a doubt in my mind. I brush his hair behind his ear. "You saved Sylvia."

THIRTY-TWO

I n my apartment, I survey the place through new eyes. I've neglected my own home these past few months. A discarded blouse droops over the back of the couch, arms splayed like a crime scene outline. The TV plays an upbeat commercial jingle to the empty living room. The dishes in the sink give off a curdled smell.

In the shower, I shut my eyes. Fear jolts through my muscles: the memory of my time under the water. Then I relax, feeling her retreat like a watchful animal.

Patrick and I parted this morning without any mention of when we'd next meet. It didn't occur to me to ask whether we'd see each other again. It feels natural now. A given part of my world. I caught the tenderness, almost reverence, in the way he'd look at me, the gentleness when Patrick kissed me good-bye.

I have dozens of lotuses. Enough to retrace a portion of a life. Erase the ugly parts and restart, step back into the sweetest moments. In my bedroom, drying my hair, I catch sight of the photograph that lies next to my bedside table. The Braddocks' wedding portrait, all that hope shimmering behind Sylvia's smile. It feels like the truest version of her, trapped behind the other women she became. The scared and frustrated and angry incarnations. The grieving mother, the fierce and heartsick woman wrapping her arms around Henry to forget everything else.

That first woman, all optimism. She's the one I could bring back. The one I could lead from the darkness. I remember last night, in that distant universe we occupied at the lake. When Sylvia carried my body up to the surface of the water.

The moment she pushed back against the press of time, refusing to let this second body sink into the same lonely space as the first.

I press my hand against my cheek, the skin hot and beaded with moisture from the shower. I'm filled with gratitude that she would give me this chance. As much as I've been exposed to her secret heart, Sylvia knows mine too. She knows what I've done, the parts of myself I've hidden from everybody else. And yet she pulled the air back into my lungs. She strummed my pulse back into my veins; she breathed warmth onto my eyelids, coaxing them open like petals.

After my day at the Elysian Society on Monday, I'm tired. Even being gone for two days has damaged my ability to sink fully into the work. I feel like a new employee again. My clients' steady stream of hope has sapped the oxygen from my brain. I'm ready to return home and sleep. When I see the silhouette of a man standing next to my car in the evening light, his face turned from me, I stop.

He looks up. It's only Lee. He instantly adjusts his demeanor: shoulders back, a smile beneath serious eyes.

I move closer, fishing for my keys. "Hello, Lee," I say. "What are you doing out here?"

"I wanted to talk." The light is an uncanny sunset mix of dimness and brightness, everything brilliantly obscured. "I looked for you yesterday and I couldn't find you."

I slide my car key into the lock. "You must have just missed me," I say.

"Tell me it's not about Patrick Braddock," Lee says.

I freeze.

"Maybe you aren't seeing him here anymore," he continues. "But I'm not naïve. I know that what goes on doesn't always happen inside this building."

I should go, leave Lee with his question unanswered on his tongue. But something holds me back. My heart blossoms with an unexpected affection for him. All these years, he's been one of the few people to try to understand a version of me that extends beyond this white dress.

"I have been seeing Patrick," I relent. "At his home, as his wife. As Sylvia."

"And that's what you truly want?"

I'm opening my mouth to say, *Of course it's what I want*, but the certainty isn't there. My desires betray me. Once I get what I've wanted, all that's left is more wanting, the next desire slipping seamlessly into place like a demon jumping from host to host. I should have remembered that wanting is like this. Always leading further and further down a path of new complications, endlessly hungry. For a moment, I miss the former version of myself: the woman who'd taught herself how to stop wanting.

Lee's face, backlit, is emotionless. "I hate seeing you caught up in this," he says. "You're better than what he can offer. You're cut from a different cloth than the Braddocks."

"Maybe you don't know me that well," I say.

"I know you're in love with Patrick."

I can't open my mouth to deny it.

"And I know that Patrick might not be able to feel the same way."

I consider hurting Lee, squeezing my hands against the dip in his throat. I'm shocked at the vividness of the image, unfolding colorfully inside my head. The streak of unexpected violence leaves me almost queasy.

"One of my clients worked with me since I first started," Lee says. "A while back, she told me she was getting married. I wished her well and said my good-byes. The wedding was a few months ago. She's come back a dozen times since to talk with her husband. Her first husband—I guess that's what he is now. I don't ask questions, but I worry. I'm not sure her new husband knows about her visits. Maybe he approves of it. Maybe he just tolerates it."

A group of bodies leaves the building, moving close together, silent and bowed. One of them, an older woman, glances pointedly at me and Lee together.

"So what would you do?" Lee asks, soft. "If Patrick moves on, he remarries. Has children with someone new. If he kept on coming to see Sylvia, you'd be all right with that?"

"He wouldn't do that," I say.

"You have your own life, Edie," Lee says. "You don't need to share somebody else's." He touches my hand.

Lee is an ordinary life. An ordinary lover, unattached and undemanding. I stare at Lee's hand on my skin: the absence of Patrick's golden freckles. The absence of Patrick's wedding ring. Uncertain and small, something comes awake inside me. Not the lust I feel for Patrick, engulfing me in a second flat, but a warm and vulnerable spark. One I'd need to nurture.

Quickly, I pull my hand away. "I need to go."

'm glad you came tonight," Patrick says, shifting against me. "I wasn't sure you would. After."

"I wanted to come."

Laughter rises in a fluttering peak from outside. Patrick's neighbors are hosting a party; I noticed it when I parked. The burn of paper lanterns, the hum and jumble of voices.

It seems like an event that the Braddocks might have attended as a couple, walking over arm in arm. All charming smiles, light jokes about how long the journey took, *stuck in traffic.* For a wistful moment, I wanted to join the party. I wanted to slide into my green dress and wrap my throat in jewelry, feel Patrick's hand at the curve of my waist. All those eyes registering us together, their idle curiosity as they examined Sylvia's replacement.

We lie in bed alone now, beneath a canopy of fractured, colorful light from the lanterns outside, splayed at an angle across the ceiling. When a breeze blows outside, the gem-bright blobs shift and wobble.

"I'd understand if you hated me," Patrick says. "Knowing what you do."

My heart squeezes. "I don't hate you, Patrick."

"It's weighed on me." He continues as if he didn't hear. "This wall between me and other people. I can't get close without imagining what they'd think if they'd heard me say those things."

"You didn't mean any of it," I say. "It's what you said in the moment. A terrible moment. It doesn't define everything that came before it."

Patrick's silence is restless, tinged with doubtfulness.

"Can I ask you something?"

He stirs and smiles, half distracted. "Yeah, yeah, of course."

"Have you forgiven Sylvia?"

He lifts himself up on his elbows, staring down at me. "For what?" he asks. "For Henry? Or for leaving me the way she did?"

"Either," I say. "Both."

He lies back down with an impatient gesture, flinging his arm across the pillows. "For a long time," Patrick says, "I was obsessed with her forgiveness. I thought I'd make it up to her and move on. But—I wonder. If I'd said those things, that night, and Sylvia had woken up the next morning, would I have forgiven her for what she did? Maybe I only forgave her to bring her back."

I make myself face the thought calmly, the one that's been strung through my brain since I learned about Henry. It's possible that I've never been in love with Patrick. My heart is so plain and foolish that it only wants what someone else has. I'm attracted to desire itself, not the human that lies beneath. Even someone else's borrowed lust will do. And now Sylvia's love for her husband has diminished, leaving me alone.

But even his smallest detail, the dark knot of a mole near the base of his throat, opens desire in me.

"What you want—" I stop to collect my thoughts. "What you want is a chance to fall in love again. On your own terms. Without the past hanging over you, without those mistakes."

"Isn't that what everyone wants?" He speaks quietly, ruefully. He has no idea, yet, just how weighted this moment is.

"Patrick, I can bring Sylvia back for a longer period of time," I say. "You could spend more time with her. Not just a few minutes at a time, but every day. The way you used to be."

Next to me in the bed, I can sense his body grow tense.

"If that's what you want," I add, when he doesn't speak.

"I don't understand." Patrick's careful as a man negotiating with a gun to his temple. "Bring her back for good?"

"Not permanently, but for a while. A month," I say. "Longer. Enough so that you'll have her with you again, uninterrupted. You can hold her at night. Wake up to her in the morning. Do the things you thought you'd missed."

"But you'd be taking hours off your life," he says. "Weeks. Months, maybe. I don't understand why you'd do this."

"Because I know what it's like," I say. "I know what it's like to lose somebody you love. You lose all the possibilities that went with that person."

From outside, a voice crests suddenly above the mutter and drone of the partygoers. The voice has a desperate joviality, as if the speaker has been trying for too long to make this point and has only one chance: *The heart wants what it wants.*

"How would you know that?" Patrick asks.

"What?"

"How could you know what it's like to lose somebody?" He's mildly confused, as if I've made a tiny clerical error. Misspelled my name, recited the wrong digit in my birth date.

I can't answer. I've been so meticulous. So constantly careful that the carefulness itself has turned invisible, as if I've never known anything but caution. As if I was born hiding. And now I've spilled the dark core of myself as casually as I might tip over a glass. It's such a clumsy mistake that it seems to stem from someone else.

"Because of my clients," I say. "I've been surrounded by death for five years now."

To my relief, he nods. I let myself relax again. In his eyes, this indiscretion must scarcely matter, overshadowed by the main point.

"If I can give that to you and Sylvia, then I will." I turn to him. "I'll be happy to."

On the ceiling above him, a red light pulses and shivers. A woman's laugh exhales through the room like a breeze.

"Will you think about it, at least?" I ask.

"Yes," he says. "I'll think about it."

know just when to go to him. The time of day when he's left unguarded. Late Friday afternoon, the sky piled with distended, bruise-dark clouds. I park down the block and walk to their home. Approaching, I notice that the stroller is gone from its usual spot next to the door. The driveway is empty. A dog barks nearby, over and over.

Instead of Lucy Woods's muted costume or my Elysian Society uniform, I've chosen a tight black dress. The backless design is webbed with delicate straps. Sylvia's lipstick coats my mouth.

I ring the doorbell. Muffled music throbs from inside the house, the bass line cut through with an angry, slurring voice. I ring again. After a second, the sound drops off abruptly. Footsteps approach; the door swings open.

He's been expecting a sales pitch, a nosy neighbor. He's smiling too politely, hands curled into fists on his hips. Beleaguered as he stands in the doorway. When he recognizes me, he stiffens.

"Can I come in?" I ask.

"Viv isn't here right now," he says.

"That's fine," I say. "I need to speak to you."

Behind him, the spidery coat rack dangles with objects. Ben's puffy blue coat, a crisp sun hat, an umbrella printed to resemble a frog. A colorful foliage of grocery flyers spread near the mail slot. It's a sweet, simple backdrop. Inside this space, Henry feels all wrong.

"I told you to stay away from us," he says.

"It's about Sylvia."

He's quiet for a beat too long, as if purposefully suppressing any reaction to my mention of her. "Frankly, I don't have anything to say to you about Sylvia Braddock." I note his formality in using her last name. "And I don't have time to—"

"I was at the lake."

He looks around quickly, an instinctive check to see if anybody has overheard. We're alone; the neighboring houses are quiet except for the relentless staccato of the barking.

"Just come inside," he says.

I pass close enough to catch the musk of his deodorant. Henry closes the door behind me. Without speaking, he guides me to the dining room, where he hovers near the doorway, creating the impression that he's on the brink of leaving. As if this is my house, and he's a nervous visitor. I sit in one of the dining chairs. A bowl of cereal is on the tabletop, pinkish rings ballooned and crumbling inside a pool of milk.

"How is your family these days?" I ask.

He laughs. "Seriously?" Then he squares his shoulders back, playing along. "My wife's fine," he says, showily polite. "The baby's fine. Everyone's doing quite well."

"I'm glad to hear it," I say.

His exaggerated smile drops away, revealing his tension. "Let's get to the point," Henry says. "Get this over with."

"I need to know about your relationship with Sylvia Braddock."

"She was a friend." Fast and casual: rehearsed. He was anticipating this. "A family friend. You knew that."

"That's what you've told me so far, yes," I agree.

Henry shifts his balance on his feet. "You're not a PI or something, are you? All your questions. You need one of those lights." He opens his fist toward me, the flung fingers suggesting the probing rays of an interrogation light.

"Henry, I know," I say. "You don't have to hide it anymore."

He stares.

"You can tell me what happened between you and Sylvia," I say. "It can't hurt you now."

Maybe it's my years at the Elysian Society that give my voice the right weight, the coaxing pressure of a truth serum. Henry seems almost relieved. It occurs to me that he hasn't been able to talk about this with anyone else.

"Start at the beginning," I say.

"We met through Patrick," he says. "We clicked, but we were only friends at first. The Braddocks had been married for years. They treated me like a younger brother. A bachelor. Nothing happened. Flirting, maybe. Innocent stuff. She was being nice to a guy without a date.

"Things started about three years back. Right after I started dating Viv. I know how that sounds. It wasn't on purpose, not on my end. Sylvia introduced me to Viv. And Viv's great, we got along immediately. But it was like seeing me with another woman clarified things for Sylvia. She had to see me with somebody else before she knew she wanted me. Her attention was flattering," he says. "Flattering as hell. You've seen her, right?"

"I've seen her."

"Lake Madeleine was her idea. Far enough away that nobody would recognize us. We made excuses. Work trips, weekends with friends. Sylvia almost wanted to be caught," he says. "She was sloppy. We took photos. Again, her idea. Polaroids. I was always terrified that one of them would find its way into the wrong hands, even though she kept hold of them. She'd destroy most of them right in front of me, on the day we left. Nothing was real for her until she saw a picture of it. The reverse of how it should be."

Outside, the dog continues to bark at an even pace, a machine producing an automated noise. The smell in the dining room—

sharp basil, sickly tomato—lingers from last night's dinner. I think of the two remnants of their time at the lake that have survived without Henry's knowledge.

"Things with Viv got serious," Henry says. "We got married after a year or so and made it official. I couldn't live a double life. I'd seen inside someone else's marriage and I wanted it for myself. The real thing. Not borrowing theirs."

A hard flutter of outrage. I'm not sure on whose behalf.

"I tried to break things off," Henry says. "Sylvia kept saying she was already married, why should it stop me? Was my marriage more important than hers?" He runs a hand through his hair. "It all feels like something other people did. Strangers."

The contrition in his voice is too pointed. Carefully engineered to sound authentic, but with a prodding note underneath: Henry looking around to be noticed, to be admired.

"And then the baby," I say, refusing to rise to this.

"The baby." He hesitates; when he speaks again, his voice has cooled. "The baby changed things. I stopped answering her calls, stopped seeing her. And I planned a weekend with Viv at the lake. I wanted to send a message to Sylvia."

"She followed you," I say. "With Patrick."

"Only fair." Henry's quick smile is uncannily detached as a sawed-off limb. "She was out for blood. She was all over us the whole weekend. It drove me crazy. Patrick was useless. I ended up alone with Sylvia and my wife, pretending everything was normal."

I've barely eaten today. My stomach and head are scooped out with hunger.

"Viv announced the pregnancy to Sylvia," he says. "That wasn't part of my plan. We'd only known ourselves for a couple of weeks. We came back, Viv went to sleep. She was still adjusting to the pregnancy. She slept like the dead. Thank God. She didn't have to know when the two of them came pounding on the door, trying to drag me into their fight."

"Their fight," I repeat.

Henry must catch my subtle emphasis on the first word. His mouth twitches. "I stayed out of it," he says. "It wasn't my battle. I couldn't step in and fix a relationship with that many problems. They seemed fine, but talking to her, I realized how much they'd been hiding. I couldn't take that on. I had my own life." A pause. "I *have* my own life."

I glance around. A framed photograph of infant Ben, his body curled tight as a bud. Viv's discarded sandals, the foot beds darkened, tossed carelessly near the doorway. This is what required Sylvia's absence: the suffocating enchantment of ordinary life.

"Why didn't you follow her?" I ask.

He knows what I mean at once. He runs both hands over his face. "Following Sylvia would have sent the wrong message. I would have been pulled right back into it."

Dark water spreading around my waist, expanding outward in shimmering circlets, ringed by moonlight.

"Every day, I've thought about her out there," he says. "Alone. Waiting for somebody to follow her. But I had no idea. You have to believe me. I had no idea what she'd do."

A warning at the back of my head, too small and swift for me to fully examine its implications. "But it worked out for you, didn't it?" I ask instead. "If Sylvia had woken up the next day, you would have always worried that she'd expose you. She might have told Viv or mentioned it to a friend. With her gone, you don't have to worry."

Henry watches me, eyes cloaked.

"A while back, you told me Patrick was unfaithful to Sylvia," I say abruptly.

He shrugs.

"You lied to me."

He seems annoyed by this sudden change of topic. "It doesn't matter anymore."

"It's the lie you've been telling yourself, isn't it?" I'm so calm I sound almost sweet. "Telling anyone who will listen. It's not enough for you to destroy them and get away with it. You also have to get rid of your guilt. You have to shift it to Patrick."

We stare at each other. My gaze is twice as dense as his. It's the unevenness of a roomful of people staring at one subject. He must sense it too; he breaks eye contact to look at the floor.

"What do you want me to do about it?" he asks, rough and low. "Sylvia wouldn't want me to ruin my life. She knew what family meant to me." The dog falls suddenly silent outside. "Patrick doesn't have anything to lose," Henry goes on, voice louder in the emptiness around us. "Nobody knows why he's still here. No friends. No attachments. He should have left by now. He's dead weight at the firm, doing work that should go to teenage interns. I'd leave if I were him. I'm the one with a life to protect."

I laugh. The sound startles both of us.

"Are you going to tell me who you are?" Henry asks, hostile now. "You come into my home. You're stalking my family. For what? To find out I cheated?"

I lick my lips, catching the slight sharp taste of the lipstick.

"Now you know," Henry says. "You know what I did, you know that it's over. Whatever you're doing, you can move on."

There's the sound of the car in the driveway. Tires crackling against the pavement, the hum of the engine that cuts to silence. A door swinging open.

"They're home," he says. Then Henry moves toward me roughly, as if he's chasing away a wild animal. "They can't see you here." He grabs my elbow, pulling me to my feet.

The car door slams. A second later, a creak as another door opens. I picture Viv leaning over the car seat, murmuring to her son as she unbuckles Ben and lifts him free.

Henry's hand is a hard knot at the small of my back, guiding me to the kitchen. A door stands at the end of a small hallway.

I shake Henry off, turn to face him. His expression is fist-tight with tension, eyes wet and harsh. Our bodies are so close that I feel the heat rising off him.

"Maybe they should see me here," I say pleasantly. "How much have you told her?"

"Don't do this," he says.

The sound of footsteps up the stairs. Viv's muffled voice, singing, talking to the baby.

I study Henry. The close-cropped beard; the startling fullness of his mouth; the clear, shallow brown of his eyes, like weak coffee. Sylvia must have gazed into this face with love.

The click and jingle of keys in the front door.

"Go," he says. "Please."

I step so close that we meet, grazing at the hips and the chest. Henry grows still, breath suspended. We listen to the door swinging open, the flat thump of heavy bags dropped on the floor. "Anybody home?" Viv calls.

I slide my hand down his body. Down his stomach, past his waist. I press my hand against him and feel him stir in response. Henry grabs my waist, pulling me closer with the urgency of a man inside a dream. Her name is caught at the very tip of his tongue.

Viv's footsteps come through the living room, bright and clacking against the floors.

I step back from Viv's husband, slipping out the door. I'm down the back stairs; I'm walking through the gate, not securing it behind me, so that it clacks and bounces against the side of the house; I'm going down the driveway, past Viv's sedan. I don't care, right now, if Viv looks out and sees the rude shock of the past, brushing right up against her future.

'm about to enter Room 12 to meet with my first client of the day. Mr. Watts, who lost his younger sister so long ago that his only photo of her is age-cracked and sepia-stained. A hand on my shoulder stops me. I turn, confused.

Jane's businesslike as she reaches out and scrubs her thumb hard over my lips. I can taste her skin, a trace of acerbic hand soap. It's such a surprising moment that I stand completely still, an obedient child being tended to by an impatient parent.

Jane pulls her hand away and holds up her thumb as if she's showing off courtroom evidence. Her finger is bloodied with lipstick. "Still wearing your favorite lipstick?" she asks. "Your other clients won't much like that trashy color."

Instinctively, I touch my mouth. "I forgot. I'm sorry, Jane. It won't happen again."

"Why are you here?" Jane asks.

I'm very aware of how vulnerable we are, standing in the doorway of Room 12. Anyone could spot us. Down the dim corridor, a few doors are snapped shut, but others stand ajar, waiting for clients and bodies. I catch the edge of something from Room 10: a plea, a sob.

"Even after all that mess with Ana and Renard, you just keep coming back. You vanished for those few days and I thought you were gone. But here you are."

"I'm not going to abandon my clients," I say. "They rely on me."

She makes a noise deep in her throat. "And what about you?" she asks. "Do you rely on your clients?"

My face is hot with embarrassment at how easily she's figured me out. Jane's right. There isn't any reason for me to return. But I'm not sure how else to fill my days. All that stretching space, staying inside my skin without the reliable relief of the lotuses.

Jane reaches out and pats my upper arm, a gesture without warmth. "You're not the first person to use this as a place to hide," she says. "And you won't be the last. But you're certainly the longest standing. I admit, I'm curious to see what it would take to chase you out."

I'm fixated on *hide*. My body feels as if it's been turned inside out, everything dark and protected revealed to sudden and corrosive light. "Mrs. Renard told you?" I ask.

"Told me what?"

I can't tell whether there's a challenge beneath her voice. "Nothing," I say. "Whatever you think about me, Jane, I'm here for my clients. That's all."

She glances at the smear of lipstick on her skin, then wipes her thumb along her skirt. "I'll send your next client in, Eurydice," she says.

t's not much of a home," I say. At the threshold, my key in the lock, I stop, balking. "I've never gotten around to decorating, or—"

"Edie, it's fine," he says, and touches me between my shoulder blades. "I'm just glad you invited me."

I let the door swing open. Such a small apartment that we can take stock of it from the doorway. I cleaned recently. Somehow it makes the space feel sadder, the harsh scent of lemon cleanser floating out. This sign that I've tried to impress him, and how inadequate the space still is. The space I occupy is a mere fraction of his home.

Patrick follows me in. Over our heads, a neighbor's music jud-
ders like machine gun fire.

"How long have you lived here?"

"A few years," I say.

"You still haven't unpacked?" He's teasing; he gestures at the
tidy row of boxes that lies against one wall.

"Oh," I say. "That's my clients' information."

Patrick's face tightens into purposeful seriousness. He glances
again at the unmarked boxes. When I imagine the scene through
his eyes, the boxes multiply. So many other lives and other deaths
and other bodies. I wonder if he's discomfited by this visual evidence, summing up how much time I've devoted to strangers'
loved ones.

"Would you like a drink?" I ask. On the way home from work
this evening, self-conscious, I sought out and purchased the same
label of wine that Patrick keeps at his house.

"Sure," he says, producing a smile. It's almost as if he's doing
me a favor. I feel like a child hosting a tea party for an indulgent
adult.

But when I return from the kitchen, he's gone. Clutching the
pair of wineglasses, I hurry down the hall to find him in my bedroom. My heart blanks. He stands in the center, surrounded by
the spread of photographs. Photos on my bureau, on my nightstand; fanned on the floor and the windowsill. I didn't think to
hide them. They're such a natural part of my life's landscape that
my eyes don't register the Braddocks' memories anymore.

"Patrick, I'm so sorry—" I start.

"Why would you be?" he asks.

"You're not upset?"

He seems puzzled. "I gave these to you."

The bright orange of the lotus bottle stands out on my bureau.
It's been nearly a week since we left Lake Madeleine. We've been
avoiding the subject of when he'll next see his wife.

Patrick leans to retrieve a photo from the center of my unmade bed. He examines it before turning the Polaroid toward me. "Where did you find this one?"

Sylvia and Henry. "At the lake," I say. "She must have left it behind by accident, during one of their visits."

He lets go of the photo. His wife drifts to the floor.

My hesitation only lasts a second. "I went to see him," I say. "Henry."

Patrick stares. "You're not serious." And then: "Does he know who you are? What we do together?"

"No," I say quickly. "No. He knows that we know each other, but—he doesn't know about her." I don't mention that I've been visiting the Damsons' home on a regular basis, that I've sat with Viv and pored over the dregs of Patrick's private life.

"Edie," Patrick says, and inhales, letting the breath out again in a heavy sigh. "You can't do that. He's not part of this. Going after him is only going to get me in trouble."

"After what you told me, I had to talk to him."

"Don't be stupid." He's tired, irritation worn so thin that it doesn't hold any roughness. "Henry and I have been avoiding each other. It's shitty, but it's a truce. Now you've gone to him, I don't know how he'll react, what he'll do—"

"Something he said bothered me," I say. "He said that he hated to think of Sylvia out there in the water, all alone. But you left the cabin right after she did. You didn't tell Henry where you were going. How did he know you didn't go after your wife?"

Patrick rubs his hand over his mouth.

"What if he followed her?" I ask. "He knew she was alone. He knew you weren't with her because he came after her. Maybe Henry had more to do with her death than he admits."

"No," Patrick says. "Don't go down this path. We know what happened." He pauses, and when he speaks again, he's gentle. "I know why you're saying this. You don't have to."

"Why am I doing it?" I ask.

"You're trying to help me," Patrick says. "Take away my guilt. But I know what I did. I hurt her and I lost her. It was my fault that she died that night."

I consider this, too surprised to argue.

"Or maybe you're doing it for yourself," he goes on. "Proving that I didn't drive Sylvia away. You can't be with me until you convince yourself that she wanted to live, and that she wanted to live with me." He tucks my hair behind my ear, the unexpected intimacy of his fingertips warm at my temple. "If you've changed your mind, I'll understand."

"About our plan?" I ask.

"I want to do it," he says. "I was going to tell you tonight. But if I'm too late—"

"Patrick," I say, and everything else falls away.

"We'll go," he says. "Leave this place behind. There's nothing here for me, hasn't been for a long time. If Sylvia had stayed with me, we would have moved away and found a fresh start somewhere else. It's what we can do now." He pauses. "Unless you have a reason to stay."

The Elysian Society; Room 12; my faithful white dress. My clients. Will any of them really miss me? Or will they shrug, sigh, resigned to the minor inconvenience, moving on to the next body? I imagine a world without other people's perfume and jewelry. Without the love of strangers constantly surrounding me and not quite touching me.

"I want to go," I say. "Of course I do."

Her office is empty this morning, door nudging open at my touch. It's the first time I've come to Mrs. Renard's office and found it abandoned. Without her presence, the space seems shrunken. A rib cage without a heart. The book spines transform from mystical artifacts to shabby discards; the windowpanes are dust-dulled.

When Mrs. Renard returns, I'm waiting. She pauses in the doorway, eyes blank and then widening just a fraction. I can tell she's disturbed to see me. I sit up straighter.

"Eurydice," Mrs. Renard says, clicking the door shut behind her. Taking her place behind the desk, her hands float briefly over the spread of papers and pens, as if checking that I haven't touched anything. "I'm not prepared to meet with anyone today."

"I'm here about Thisbe," I say.

No change in her expression. "I don't recall a Thisbe."

"She only left at the end of January," I say.

"January?" she repeats. "Eurydice, we'll go to the waiting room right now and I'll ask you to name the bodies there. Bodies who have been working for years. You won't be able to."

"I have reason to believe that Thisbe was killed by a client," I say.

The moment stretches out. I want her to comfort me: lift away the guilt that's been winding through me, erase this other version of the Elysian Society. But Mrs. Renard smiles, sudden and ingratiating. It's eerie on her, contradicting her usual imperiousness.

"Laura Holmes worked as Thisbe," I continue. "It was her body they found. Laura was possessed when her body died. My fear is that she ran away with a client while she was overcome. She didn't even know what was happening. And he killed her."

Abruptly, Mrs. Renard leans over her desk, hands knotted together. I can see her pulse in her neck, fast and hard.

"I need your help," I say. "You can look up the clients who worked with Thisbe and find out who might have done this to her."

"I couldn't protect her," Mrs. Renard says. "I tried. Trust me."

I sit back in the chair. My fingers twitch instinctively, as if

I'm trying to grab hold of a steady surface at the beginning of an arcing fall.

"She was running away from herself," Mrs. Renard says. "I've seen quite a few of those types pass through our doors. People hoping to make quick money before they move on to the next place. I was happy to give Thisbe a chance, but she was sniffing around in the wrong places. Dangling too much in front of her clients. I've always been careful to give clients just enough, you understand," she says. "Give them too much, and who knows what will happen?"

I have a vision of Mrs. Renard sizing us up judiciously, weighing us like cuts of meat. Slicing off a pinkie finger or the crook of an elbow, arranging a pair of lips or a single glistening eyeball on a plate. Serving us to clients with a brisk smile.

"Thisbe—" she starts.

"Laura," I say. "Call her Laura."

A startled blink. "Laura, then," Mrs. Renard says, as if humoring a child. "Laura wasn't strong in her own identity. She was easy prey. When someone else wanted her body more than she did, there wasn't even a struggle. It all happened so quickly."

Nausea pulls tight along my jawline.

"I was sloppy," Mrs. Renard says. "I can admit that. I go to great lengths to protect my bodies. But I've been exhausted. This job, it may weigh on you, Eurydice, but you have no idea how it weighs on me. And sometimes I fail. Sometimes I let the wrong clients through. Laura paid the price for that. It's something I'll always have to live with."

A woozy sensation rushes across my scalp. "Who was it?" I ask.

She doesn't answer, eyes narrowing slightly.

"The client," I say. "Who was the wrong client?"

"Oh, well," she says. "It scarcely matters, does it? A man whose wife wasn't the woman he pretended she was. His wife was deeply troubled, a fact he hid from me quite cleverly."

"Tell me his name," I say.

A knowing smile. "Mr. Richards," she says. "A new client. You've never met him."

The relief I feel is watery and thin, spiked with an awareness of the betrayal I just committed. I shouldn't have needed to ask. I should trust Patrick completely by now.

"Why didn't you help her?" I hope Mrs. Renard can't sense the chagrin that pushes this question out too fast.

"I did what I could," Mrs. Renard says. "I turned Mr. Richards away. I made sure Laura stopped taking the lotuses. Some people might have sent her onto the streets. Those smaller operations, I've seen them do that—abandon the bodies. Let nature sort them out. Wandering and unnoticed. It's a cowardly way. I took her with me. To my own home."

Her voice holds a steely defiance, as delicate as a wire. That frightens me more than if she'd been angry. It's a sign that she's been defending herself in her own mind, all these months.

"What else could I do?" Mrs. Renard asks. "Laura came to me with no family, no background. I wanted to help her. I've never done that before. Taking a body into my home."

There's disgust in her voice, as if she opened her life to a creeping contamination.

"I kept her in my bedroom," Mrs. Renard says. "I treated her like a normal person, trying to get through to the poor creature. She was calm enough at first. I brought her food and water. I gave her a new outfit. A sundress, not much different from what you girls wear here. So that it would feel familiar to her. But that damn earring—I couldn't take it off. Any time I tried, she'd react as if I was trying to cut off her ear. I let it stay. That chintzy little bauble. Taunting me.

"Sometimes I tried to talk to her as Laura, to see if she was still there. But God knows Laura was a stranger to me already. I couldn't tell one woman apart from the other. And the look in her eyes, Eurydice. Like talking to a wild animal. She'd seem to see me and understand me and then—poof, she'd be right back to her own world."

"You could have helped her," I say, my chest tight. "Laura didn't deserve that."

"What about the other woman?" Mrs. Renard says. "It's easy to feel sorry for Laura. But consider the other woman. She comes back into a body to find that it's all wrong for her. All the rage of her past life poured into a new envelope and it's splitting at the seams. I had to watch this. I had to watch her for weeks, unraveling. After a while, she tried to escape when I opened the door. Tried to attack me. She stopped eating. I did what I did out of mercy, Eurydice."

I can feel each separate bead of sweat sliding from my skin. "It wasn't a client who hurt her at all," I say. "You killed her."

"No," Mrs. Renard says, calm, as if she's just now considering and then dismissing the idea. "No. She was already gone. Both of them were gone. I couldn't very well let it continue on. I ended the whole thing. There was no other option."

The details of Hopeful Doe's murder—ones presented by sleek newscasters, peppered throughout news pieces—come back to me now. Blunt force trauma; a clinical term, when I first heard it, so simple that it became a contradictory euphemism. Now I fill in details, flesh out the scene with fingernails and teeth. Mrs. Renard with Laura's body: taking her, unresisting, by the throat, knocking her head against the wall. Again and again, her skull giving like tapped eggshell. Or slamming some heavy household object, a shovel, a bat, against her chest.

The intimacy of the death, the necessary violence involved, is a woozy shock. I can't look at Mrs. Renard's hands where they lie on the desk, bare and obscene.

"I'd heard about that house from other bodies," she says. "I gleaned scraps here and there, during interviews over the years. I didn't even know that the house was scheduled to be torn down. It was perfect. An act of fate. Or so it seemed," she says. "I've tortured myself since then. The what-ifs. If the house hadn't been scheduled for demolition, that neighborhood girl wouldn't have gone nosing around where she didn't belong. If that Fowler bitch hadn't decided to take justice into her own hands. If. If. But it doesn't matter. The danger has passed."

"You have to tell somebody," I say.

"Why?" The genuineness of the question makes my heart sink. "Everyone has moved on. There's no mystery to her. A girl like Laura, found dead—it's not a tragedy. Nor a rarity."

"And if it happens again?" I ask. "Another body ends up possessed?"

"It was a single mistake," she says. "Weigh all the good the Elysian Society has done over the decades, my dear, and then weigh it against this. One casualty. A girl with nobody in the world to miss her."

I look around the office, hoping to find something to anchor myself here. But everything slides away, refusing to fall into familiar territory.

"If you're wondering whether to be a hero, I'll ease your conscience," Mrs. Renard says. She sounds almost kind. "It won't do any good. They can look, but they can't prove anything. Your testimony won't hold water. You're not exactly a respected member of society. Besides—do you want the authorities investigating our clients? Think of all the innocent people who will come under the microscope."

I understand at once what she means. His face comes back to the forefront of my mind.

"If you're threatening me," I say, "you should know that Mr. Braddock has done nothing wrong. I'm not concerned." But my desperation from earlier, when I asked, *Who was it?*, still hangs in an oily film in the air.

"Oh, Mr. Braddock is an upstanding citizen, at the end of the day," Mrs. Renard says. "The kind of man a woman like you would never meet without doing what you do. It's lucky for you, isn't it, that he's favored you with his attention?" She settles back in her chair, runs her tongue over her lips. "I take it your relationship with Mr. Braddock is becoming more personal. You must know everything about him at this point. And he knows all about you."

"He knows enough," I say, the lie so obvious that silence would have been less incriminating.

"I wonder if he'd be interested in knowing more?" Mrs. Renard asks, crisp and conversational. "In my experience, clients often come here because they have limited room in their hearts. A limited capacity for embracing new people. But maybe Mr. Braddock is different. Maybe he'd love to get to know you. Learn where you came from, what you've done."

My silence expands, big enough for us both to understand fully what it means.

"You'll stay uninvolved," she says. A command.

"Yes." I hear myself say it, flat and grudging.

She sighs as if she's survived a small crisis and is ready to move on to something more important. "Don't torture yourself over this," Mrs. Renard says.

I look at her dully.

"Remember that most of the people who work for me don't have lives to speak of," she says. "They're lonely. They don't have their own loved ones to miss them after they're gone. What kind of person would agree to be the vessel for the love of strangers, day in and day out?"

My mind turns to my childhood bedroom. The lawn under my feet, the taste of birthday cake, the scent of my mother when she hugged me, her hair floating in my peripheral vision. And I remember the memories from later, the ones I've hidden.

Letting the layers upon layers of other people's stories smother my own.

Mrs. Renard addresses the crooked square of afternoon light that lands on the opposite wall. "Really, it would have been the best thing for that girl if we'd let her stay Hopeful Doe," she says. "When she was Hopeful Doe, people were interested. She was someone worthy of love. Never make the mistake of thinking that one's true identity is necessarily the best one. You know better than that by now, Eurydice."

THIRTY-SIX

There are arrangements to be made. Patrick has asked for a week. My apartment lease expires in three months, a lifetime from now. I walk through the rooms, assessing which parts of my life I'll bring along. Everything feels expendable, as if I was waiting for a chance to get rid of it.

I research cities to disappear to. There's the predictable spread of places, more fantasy than reality. Sun-drenched beaches in California, the endless movie set of New York City, watercolor towns in Europe. I skim past these, unable to fit ourselves into other people's dreams. Instead, I look at unremarkable places, places people move to out of necessity. I imagine us living in a split-level on the outskirts of a run-down city, a freeway roaring past our bedroom window. I imagine us tucked inside the graying snow for months at a time in a northern state.

When I come to the Braddocks' house tonight, I find him upstairs. He's in the room that holds Sylvia's belongings, looking at a stretch of gauzy white spread over the top of the boxes. I come to stand next to Patrick. Her wedding gown.

"I don't know what to do with all of this," Patrick says. "I should have thrown it away a long time ago. Or donated it. It felt like turning my back on her." He glances around the confines of the room. "It's impossible, but there's more in here than there used to be."

The unfairness of it hits me: that this pointless piece of Sylvia's life should have survived longer than she did. All the possessions that my clients have brought to me over the years, each one out-living the person who loved it.

"Just keep the things that were most important to Sylvia," I say.

"I have," he says. "I already gave most of that to you."

We exchange smiles.

"Patrick," I say, "why did you bring me that lipstick? The first time you came to the Elysian Society. Sylvia barely ever wore it in her photos. And she—" I hesitate. *She clearly chose it for Henry Damson*, I want to say. Her lips were darkest in those photos from the lake.

"I can't really explain it," he says. "I walked through the house that day, trying to choose the right object to bring. It was still surreal, like a joke. I was trying to remember what she wore, what jewelry she liked or what perfume she'd put on. I found that lipstick lying at the bottom of her closet. I remembered seeing her in it, once. When she was getting ready to go out of town. She was looking at herself in the mirror, and she was different. Beau-tiful, but different. It was a moment of realizing how little I knew about her. How separate she was from me."

I touch his arm. "Do you want to see her?" I ask, and his ex-pression opens up as if he already knew that I was going to ask, as if he's just been waiting for a chance to say yes.

In the bedroom, after I apply the lipstick, Patrick reaches out his thumb to wipe away the excess. The lotus lies on the bed next to me, nearly lost in the rumple of the sheets.

"Are you nervous?" I ask; briefly, a memory of that infinite, soundless world beneath the water fills my skull.

"No," Patrick says. "Not really. Are you?"

I slide the lotus between my teeth, swallowing without water. The dry clot of bitterness brushes the tender back of my throat, and then I'm gone.

T he moon is full tonight. So heavy that I imagine it falling right out of the sky, landing with a wet thump at our feet.

"She wasn't supposed to do that," he says. "It was a shock to me too."

It's not exactly an apology. I just shake my head, afraid that if I speak I'll embarrass myself. An undignified lurch of a sob. A spiraling shriek of accusations.

When it's clear I won't respond, Henry sighs and reaches into his pocket for his phone, making a show of checking the time. Viv is still inside the restaurant; she excused herself as we were leaving, fluttering at the two of us to go on ahead, go on ahead. I wondered if this was the way it would be from now on. Viv flaunting her status, fussy, secretive needs that a barren woman can never understand.

The restaurant has ivy-choked trellises, sparkling lights strung along the gutters. Music playing soft and tinny, barely discernible on the outdoor speakers. We're the last diners leaving tonight, alone in the parking lot. Blandly romantic violins twirl overheard. Everything feels like a mean punch line at my expense.

"Of course," Henry says, as if we're continuing a conversation, "you can't blame her. She shouldn't have told you. But you weren't supposed to be here."

"You wanted me to follow," I say.

A soft, disbelieving huff of breath.

I see us as if I'm observing from a distance. Leaning against the car like people half our age, the strangeness of the evening and the alcohol hitting us at once. Patrick and I have always looked good together. We complement each other: my stark coloring against his sunniness. But Henry and I are similar, almost like siblings, with faces that tend toward melancholy when we aren't making an effort to charm, with dark hair that snaps up all the light.

"You could have told me about the pregnancy yourself," I say.

"Jesus, I only found out a few weeks ago," Henry says, impatience clouding his words. "You're not supposed to tell anyone except close friends. Family."

A joke swirls wildly through my brain: *Can you tell your mistress?* It's the kind of joke I could have made, a month ago. Henry liked my irreverent moments, and I'd play this up, half guilty, knowing that it separated me from Viv's sweet, wide-eyed humorlessness.

"I deserved to know." I'm too exposed in my white dress. "It matters to me too."

"Fine," Henry says. "I'll report every detail of our lives to you. I'll make sure you know what we do together. Every time she picks something new for the nursery, every time we have an appointment. Do you want me to send videos from the delivery room? Tell you each time our kid scores a goal, gets a laugh from the audience?"

It's a keen hurt. He knows I don't just want a baby, a newborn, but everything. The whole tedious and beautiful life that child would bring along. I've used those exact examples, achingly ordinary. The soccer matches. The school plays.

"I know why you introduced me to her," Henry says. "So you could watch us fail."

"That's unfair," I say.

"You didn't expect I'd start a life with her," he says. "You didn't expect the baby. That's what gets to you, huh? You wanted a baby for so long, and now here I am, in a relationship that was supposed to be a joke, and—"

When he stops talking, it's not out of discretion or a desire to shield me from the pain. It's because his point is already made. After so little time, he's created a vision of a family that I've been chasing and losing. As if it's truly this easy, and it's just fatal stubbornness on my part that's preventing me.

A light in the window near the front of the restaurant snaps off, and then another, closer. The insects are shrieking all around us. Beyond the parking lot, the roads are dark and quiet this late in the evening. I think of Patrick, back at the lake, miles away. Waiting for me. Waiting.

For the first time, I regret it. The pain is almost a relief, if only because it's a fresher pain than the same aches I've been worrying over, pressing like bruises that won't fade. I regret letting my heart be devoured by this imaginary child. I regret ignoring Patrick, the flesh-and-blood reality of the two of us. Who we were. Who we could have become.

"I have to tell Patrick about us," I say.

I expect him to protest. I brace for his anger. But after a moment, he says, "No, you won't." Perfectly calm and assured.

"I don't have a choice."

"He'll leave you," Henry says. "What have you been telling me about your husband? He can't look you in the face when you've been crying, he ignores you when you're in bed all day—he's not going to shrug this off."

My tipsiness is a woozy layer just behind my eyes. "Maybe he won't," I say. "But whatever happens, I was honest. If Viv is happy with you, it's because she doesn't know you."

"My wife knows who I am," Henry says.

The restaurant door clatters open, and then Viv is walking toward us, grinning with exaggerated apology, waving like a parade-float queen. Henry reaches around me to open the car door; I understand I'm supposed to get inside. I panic like a hostage.

"Forget this," Henry says to me, a quick whisper. "I don't want to be looking over my shoulder and waiting for you to do something stupid."

She's coming across the parking lot, her body highlighted by the street lamp and then dimmed in the shadows. If she can detect the tension that surrounds us, she doesn't show it.

His sudden anger closes the space between us, yanking us together like a string pulled taut. "I could lose everything," he says. "You don't understand what that feels like."

"I have as much to lose as you do."

He laughs.

I slide into my seat, away from him. Heart hammering, I watch through the window as he turns to his wife, all warmth, all solicitousness, opening his arms. Her face appears over his shoulder as they embrace. And I'm watching them from far away, trapped in a world beneath their feet.

E die."
      who is that?

who is she?

Across from me, in the mirror, I see her: a strange woman in our bedroom. In our bed. Her coarse hair, startled and pale-lashed eyes. His arm around her; his hand tipping her chin to seek out her gaze.

"You're all right, Edie?" he asks.

I want to tell him that's not my name. But I remember, slowly, that it is. My name for this life with him. One name for each life.

"I'm fine." My voice is hoarse; I clear my throat. "Could I please have a glass of water?"

After Patrick's left, I sink back against the pillows. When I learned that Sylvia had brought us back to the surface of the water, I was grateful for a presence inside me that saw my body as something worth rescuing. But I know, right now, that it wasn't a pure gift, freely given. It was a bargain, a truce, and she'll ask for something in return.

THIRTY-SEVEN

Four days until we leave the city. I've gone through my typical routine this morning. White dress. Hair pulled back; skin scrubbed bright pink in the shower. In the parking lot, I look up at the ashen brick walls and the curtain-blinded windows.

Behind each pane of glass, a body in white, a static chill, a household artifact. A stranger leaning across the space that separates them, searching for a way back to the beginning. Each room a time capsule.

Coming to the Elysian Society has the ugly undercurrent of an obligation now. After our conversation, Mrs. Renard will be watching for me. My obedient presence here is an implicit absolution of what she did to Laura Holmes. If I didn't show up, my sudden disappearance could trigger her cool and swift revenge. I'd lose Patrick just as we're about to walk away.

I step out of the car and move toward the building, trying not to remember Laura's eyes staring out of Ana's face, or the feel of her fingers against me as she begged me to peel her down to the most fleshless part of herself.

Ms. Olsen, I wanted to let you know that I may not be coming back," I say.

Beth Olsen has only been with me for a few months, but I've

come to like her. When she visits her girlfriend, she's so reverent and serious, like a student contemplating a difficult question.

She squints at me. "What do you mean?" she asks. "Is something wrong?"

"No," I say. "Not at all. I'm just . . . moving on."

"You're going?"

"When you joined the Elysian Society, someone should have explained to you that bodies sometimes leave," I say. "If you'd like recommendations for a replacement, I can—"

"No, no, I knew all that," Beth says. "They mentioned it. But I picked you because they said you weren't going anywhere." She pauses. "If I'm honest, I wanted you because of that."

"Things do change," I say. "I'm sorry."

Telling her was a mistake. I wanted to test out the sound of it. But Beth's eyes brighten and expand with tears. "Jesus," she says softly, as if to herself. "I can't believe this."

"You'll find a new body, Ms. Olsen," I say. "Nothing will change."

"Everything will change," Beth says.

I'm quiet, startled by the grief exposed in her voice.

"I'm sorry," Beth says. She squares her shoulders back, shuts her eyes and opens them again, clearing away the tears. "You don't owe me anything. I know that. But it's like you're asking me to say good-bye to her all over again."

The exhaustion laps at my heels. After my day at the Elysian Society, it's as if the final lotus I swallowed never fully wore off. At home, I sit on the couch, my skull heavy, listening to a shouting match between the neighbors above me. Their voices crash and ebb like waves.

The tiredness seems to grow more solid around me. Not a prelude to falling asleep, but a force that's gaining strength.

There's a hollow thump from above me, the rise of a wordless yell.

Finally, I shuffle through the contents of my medicine cabinet. I find a small bottle of over-the-counter sleeping pills, bought years ago and never used. The little tamper-proof seal is still in place; underneath this, a layer of cloudy cotton.

I tip two of the tiny blue pills into my hand and bring my palm to my mouth.

t's dark. The night lit only by the street lamps, by the crisp pools dotted along the street. The snowflakes taped to the front window are coming loose. One or two dangle crookedly from single pieces of tape, dead leaves on a branch.

Through the frosted crescent of glass in the door, the security system blinks red.

The porch holds the stroller, a tiny pair of rain boots, a ceramic swan overflowing with fern fronds. Stooping, I lift the potted plant from the hollow in the swan's back. Something glints in the darkness of the dusty cavity. Of course: no matter what illusions of safety they might create, they're secure in their lives. Sure that nobody can take it from them.

I unlock the front door. The alarm starts a thin series of chirps as soon as I enter, but I know which numbers to press. Their wedding date. The alarm goes silent. The red light resumes its neat, reassuring blink. I shut the door behind me and ascend the stairs.

Their bedroom door is on the right. Tightly shut. I walk past quickly and softly. The room I want is on the left. The door hangs open, and through the wedge I can see pale blue light spread on the wall, cast by a miniature lamp. As I slip inside the baby's room, I spot the broad black eye of a monitor, positioned to look through the bars of his crib.

The baby lies on his back. His pajamas cover his feet, zipped up to his neck. Too warm for the summer outside, but the house purrs with frigid air-conditioning. The baby's eyelids are so fine, like veined insect wings.

His stomach jumps in a hard bubble. I reach down and stroke a finger against his cheek. Poreless skin, fine and unused.

If Ben hadn't come into the world when he did, Henry might never have left me. More purely than Viv, it's Ben who came into Henry's life and left no room for me.

He should have been mine. Could have been mine. There's a particular cruelty to being replaced by him.

I slip my gift beneath the mattress, leaving a single edge showing.

The overhead light comes on, washing the shadows into flatness. I don't turn from the crib. Ben winces, his lips puckering, but he doesn't wake.

"Please," Henry says. His voice is quiet. "You don't want to do something you'd regret."

I don't answer.

"If Viv wakes up, you're going to terrify her," Henry says. "Get away from our son." He's barely holding back his rage. It's there beneath the surface of his words, like the rush of water beneath the surface of ice.

I turn to him. He must detect me in her features: her plainness fleshed out with my beauty. He steps back, his eyes moving over me, piecing me back together.

Memories filtered through someone else's brain are strained and stale. But I'm lucky. She's so austere. Everything is pushed to the very sides, leaving my memories with more room.

I remember Henry before we were ever together. A party. He told me about the death of a classmate when he was a child. For months afterward, he said, strangers would randomly remind him of this boy. A child who'd never seemed noteworthy to Henry before, now multiplied in faces in the crowd.

He must be haunted by me. These past eighteen months populated by sudden flashes, swift and cutting. A black-haired girl at a restaurant; a woman with my slim back and long neck sitting in a parked car. My laugh rising disembodied from a group of strangers. He's grown used to it, I'm sure. He knows how to hide these moments from other people. But now I'm looking right at him, daring him to see me.

Henry turns off the overhead light. The blue lamplight spreads against the wall like a patch of frost on a windowpane.

"They're not part of this," he says. "Come with me. Leave them alone."

I follow Henry out of the nursery, down the stairs. He guides me into the living room. The curtains are drawn over the window, backlit by the street lamp. From this angle, the shadows of the snowflakes lie in an uneven pattern across the fabric.

"So." He faces me, arms coiled over his chest. "You're in my house in the middle of the night. Give me one good reason why I shouldn't put an end to this right now."

"Have you told your wife?" I ask.

"Told her—?"

"You've been lying all this time."

Henry doesn't speak for a long moment. The heavy light slices his face in half. One eye exposed wetly, the other sunk deep in shadows. "I don't know what you're talking about."

I retreat then, letting her take over. As I break apart, her uncertainty moves through the cracks. I feel her muscles seize, her arms crossing over her chest, as she looks around and understands where she is.

H enry and I examine each other. Being left alone in the Damsons' house is a shock. Henry seems to grow assured, taking up more space. I shrink; Sylvia and Henry were two animals circling each other. In contrast, I'm small, cornered by a larger beast.

"What's it going to take to get you to stay away?" Henry asks me. "Am I going to be looking over my shoulder every day now? Every night?"

"Mr. Damson," I say, "I'm afraid I don't—"

"Tell me something," he says. "Are you from that place?"

"What place?" A useless bid for more time.

"It was on the news a while back," Henry says. "Contacting the dead. You're one of them?"

My denial wilts in my throat.

"You've been lying from the start. You got to Viv, but I never trusted you," he says. "Be honest for once."

"Yes," I say. An ache of exhaustion pulls at the back of my eyes. "Yes, I'm from the Elysian Society."

Henry's gaze is tinted with both fear and disgust now. "What is he doing with her?"

"It shouldn't matter to you," I say. "You won't see me again. Patrick and I are leaving the city together."

"Going where?" he asks. And then, more quietly but more urgently: "Going as who?"

"All we want is a new start," I say. "Surely you can understand that."

"Sylvia's gone." We're standing so close; I catch the sourness of Henry's interrupted sleep. "She's not coming back. What you're doing with him isn't a new start. It's sick."

"You're getting exactly what you want," I say. "Your family. Your job, your reputation. You'll never have to worry about Patrick again."

"And what are you getting out of this?" Henry asks. "Whoever you are. Lucy. What are you really getting out of this, Lucy? The chance to be someone's dead wife?" The repulsion in his voice is wet and bitter. "Something's wrong with you. You can't be with Patrick as yourself because there's nothing there." He flicks his fingers against my forehead, hard; the pain rings through me. "You need Sylvia to be anybody. To be a whole person. Is that it?"

I don't answer.

"Or is it something else?" he says, almost to himself.

I stare at him, lips pressed together. I'm still wearing only my thin nightgown, the silky material worn thin and drab. It slips off my shoulder.

"Henry." His name floats down to us from the top of the stairs and we both turn. "What's happening?" Viv stands high above us. She clutches her bathrobe closed, fist at her throat, the fabric ruffled into a bouquet—an old-womanly gesture. Her down-turned face is lotion-greasy, eyes wide and fearful. "Who is that?"

"Go back to bed," he calls up to her. "Don't worry." To me, he adds, "You need to get out." Henry opens the door wider, allowing me to pass through.

I step out into the hugeness of the night. "Promise you won't tell Patrick I was here."

"Right now, I want to forget this ever happened," he says, low enough that Viv can't hear us. "If Patrick wants to play some twisted game with you, turn you into his wife, that's his business." Henry starts to close the door. "That's what he was doing with Sylvia already."

THIRTY-EIGHT

We meet at a park. On this dazzling, heat-doused evening, the park swarms with bodies, everyone still working out the caged restlessness left behind by the long winter. I arrive early to wait for him, spreading a blanket on the grass. I would feel conspicuous, sitting alone, but I've arranged two wineglasses. When strangers' eyes graze over the blanket, they acknowledge that second glass and seem satisfied. As if a suggestion of someone else is enough to legitimize me.

Teenagers roam in packs, flirting aggressively, or sprawl out, as entangled as if they're alone in the universe. Twenty-something couples walk arm in arm, trying on decorous adulthood like costumes; a bride moves down the sidewalks with her photographer, trailed by shuffling bridesmaids. Oblivious parents run after their children. Older couples pick their way through the crowds, steady markers, like lines on a map cutting through the wilderness.

When he arrives, I watch him register and dismiss woman after woman until his eyes land on me. His whole face comes alive with a smile. He lifts a hand.

When he sits next to me, the sun behind him, I take in the muscles visible in his forearms. He's freshly shaven, smelling like laundry detergent and spicy cologne. Already, he looks fuller.

I'm unprepared for what I feel. In a way, I needed my desire to stem from Sylvia. I needed it to be inherited, passed on and well-worn. It's a shock to be alone with this all-consuming thing, even more shocking to realize that it originated from me all along.

Then Patrick reaches across, lays his hand warm and light on my thigh. I relax again. "Will you miss this place?" Patrick asks when we're drinking.

It's champagne; the bubbles sizzle down my throat. "Maybe," I say. "In a way."

A couple walks so close to us that the strap of her sandal catches on the edge of our picnic blanket, tugs it lightly.

"You look wonderful today," he says.

I tuck my hair behind my ear, murmuring a protest. I've worn a new shade of lipstick, streaking each color on the back of my hand in the drugstore and then holding my hand up against my cheek. A rosy nude that brings out my best features. Full mouth, strong nose.

"I dreamed about you last night," Patrick says.

Looking up, I laugh. It's such a vulnerably tender thing to say, offered without apology.

"I was in our bedroom, in the morning, and I went to the window. You were there, in the yard. You weren't doing any-thing. Not that I can remember. It was more a sensation. This huge sense of—" He hesitates. "Peacefulness. Everything right with the world."

I consider this, taking a burning sip of my drink.

"You have that quality," Patrick says. He lifts his glass to me, a little toast. The bubbles have settled, shifting and sparkling, along one edge.

"That's very kind," I say.

"I mean it. It's hard to be open to other people," he says. "The fact that you are—well, it's a strength."

A group of girls pass us, hair long and streaked with sunshine, dresses floating above the tops of their thighs. One of them turns her head toward Patrick, her eyes resting on him as if I'm not here. When she shifts her gaze to me, she smirks as if she's figured something out.

"Patrick," I say.

He must catch something in my face. "What?"

Everything I could say to him is right there. Not just on my tongue but down my throat, inside me, as if I've been hollowed out to hold what I feel for him. But I can't find the words.

"Excuse me."

We both turn our heads, attentive and startled. A girl with hair colored pink at the ends, as if she's trailed her hair in wet paint, stands at the edge of the blanket. Her eyes are big and blank, and I think she's going to accuse us. *There's something wrong with you two. Why are you pretending to be like the rest of us?*

Who do you think you're fooling?

"Would you be interested in a photo?" the girl asks. A bag is slung around her chest, and she reaches into it now, pulling out a chunky camera. "Five bucks. It's a great souvenir."

"Do you have a license for this?" Patrick asks.

I think he's serious, but the girl laughs, throwing her head back. Looking at him, I see the responding smile on Patrick's face, friendly and indulgent. "We'd love one," he says.

"All right, lovebirds," the girl says, and she holds up a camera. "Ready? Say cheese."

Patrick shifts close enough that our hips press together. He slips his arm around my waist, pulls my body in close to his. His cheek hovering just next to mine. I can feel the light humidity of his sweat, the movement of his muscles against me.

The camera gives off a weak snap of light, cold against the lavishness of the sunlight. After a second, a slim Polaroid shoots out one side of the camera and hovers like an extended wing.

She passes the photo to me. "You're a cute couple."

I stare at the couple captured inside the photo. I'm surprised: we're not mismatched. We're a cohesive pair, each picking up details in the other. The glints of deep gold in his eyes, the slope of my shoulder against his. We tilt our faces toward each other.

I imagine Sylvia looking at this image. If she'd experienced some lightning bolt of prescience one evening two years ago. Maybe she would have looked at us and thought: *How happy they are.* The uncomplicated happiness she wanted for her own marriage. All our rough edges flattened into a still and perfect moment.

We arrive home clinging to each other, punch-drunk from our time together. The house burns with the late afternoon that punctures through the windows. This is what I've been waiting for. My life's been thrown wide open all over again, revealing a dizzying blankness. It's as if I've been picking my way through a dark tunnel, only the path in front of me illuminated, and now I finally can see everywhere. See everything. It hurts my eyes.

"You're OK?" Patrick touches my cheek.

"I was thinking—" I say, and stop. Over his shoulder, a detail pulls at my attention. The living room, visible through the kitchen's far entrance, lies bare. A stretch of beige marked with paler squares. He's removed the framed photographs of Sylvia. Without her smile repeating across the room, the wall is unmoored.

"Edie?" he prompts.

"It's not too late to have a child," I say.

Patrick's brows flinch downward. "You mean it?"

I remember the book I found in the upstairs room, locked away. "I want to do this for you." And then add, realizing how much it sounds like an afterthought: "For us."

On the porch, later, I stand with Patrick. In the evening light, the creased wrinkles at the edges of his eyes stand out. "Your hair," he says.

I touch my hair without thinking.

"It's glowing," he says.

In my peripheral vision, the sun catches hot in the strands. I think of Sylvia's black hair. "I could make it darker," I say.

"Darker?"

"If you wanted."

"No, I don't want that," Patrick says, stepping closer. He slides his hand into the hair at the base of my skull, weaving his fingers in deep. I feel the shift of him against my scalp.

Later, I take a final walk through the apartment. I'm trying to leave everything clean, as if I'm only departing for a vacation and planning to walk back into this space. The TV set is unplugged, floors vacuumed. I've wiped away the nests of dust and insect husks inside the light fixtures. I've been sleeping on top of my bedspread, not disturbing the freshly washed sheets.

I imagine the landlord moving through the rooms when it's clear I'm not returning, assessing the leftovers of my time here. Later, he'll tell his wife that he can't believe I stayed here for four years. He can barely tell anyone lived here at all.

The Braddocks' photos are still scattered through my bedroom. I collect them into a shoebox, not sure what I'll do with them in our new life. I can't abandon them, these years and years of the Braddocks' history.

As I'm collecting the photos from the corners of my life, something nags at me. I can't find the photograph from the lake. The one of Henry and Sylvia. I leaf through the images and find only Sylvia and Patrick, the Damsons an occasional and minor backdrop to their happiness.

I do find the card Detective Rogalski gave me. It lies at the bottom of a stack of unopened mail; I'm about to throw it away, rip it into shreds and deposit it neatly with the other trash. Instead, I dial, not letting myself think about what I'm doing.

"Hello?" Bored, impatient already.

"May I speak to Detective Rogalski?" I ask.

"Speaking."

"This is the woman you met with, at the Elysian Society. Some time ago." I wait for him to acknowledge this, but he's silent. "Maybe it doesn't matter anymore," I continue, "but I want you to know that Laura Holmes worked at the Elysian Society. She went by the name of Thisbe."

A stretch of silence. I think he's hung up on me, and I'm disappointed and relieved at the same time. Just as I predicted to Ana, just as Mrs. Renard warned me, he sees this as a joke. Nothing I say holds any weight in the world of the living, not anymore.

But then he exhales, the sigh of a disappointed parent. "Well, you took your time," he says. "You couldn't have told me about this a month ago?"

"I can give you an address," I say. "An apartment on Sycamore, owned by Mrs. Renard. Her workers stay there sometimes. That might be why you haven't found any record of Laura Holmes living in the city."

Again, he doesn't answer for so long that I'm sure I've lost him.

"I'm telling you this because Laura's death involved the Elysian Society," I say. "It wasn't a coincidence that she worked there. You should talk to Mrs. Renard about what happened."

"You'd be willing to testify about this?" he asks. "Come down to the station so I can get an official statement?"

Panic needles under my ribs. In my mind, the station is a sterile territory, flat and benignly hostile. A place where I'd walk in and immediately be exposed for who I really am. No false name. No Elysian Society disguise. My whole history trailing behind me.

"If it's all the same, I want to stay anonymous," I say.

Rogalski laughs softly. "No real surprise there, I guess."

By tomorrow, I remind myself, I'll be long gone. I'll leave no trace of myself behind.

"Well," he says at last, "I'll see what I can do. But it could be too little, too late. It's important to be up front right away, young lady. You can't assume you'll get a second chance."

"I understand that," I say. "Thank you."

THIRTY-NINE

My last day begins with soft, clean sunlight filling every room. I walk through the space, hesitating over her belongings. The book Patrick gave me to finish for her. Earrings and perfume. So many tiny pieces of Sylvia have gravitated to me.

I discard my clients' old files. Their neatly typed stories, the photographs of weddings, holidays, family reunions. I release them, boxful by boxful, into the dumpster outside the complex. At the end, I add my white Elysian Society dresses, watching them drift to the grime.

I arrive outside Patrick's house as the sky burns into sunset. In the trunk, I've packed everything I care to bring. So few items that they rattle in their solitary box. A coffee mug with a watercolor lily peeling off one side; a framed postcard of a woman in an orange dress. A retroactive attempt to give these past five years some kind of meaning.

On my mouth, I wear Sylvia's deep and vibrant lipstick.

The Braddocks' house has changed. It's smaller, or thinner. Less substantial. Although the house has been creeping into disrepair for months now, the shingles tattered and dislodged like missing teeth, the windows cloudy, it looks abandoned for the first time this evening.

My heart hurts at the idea of leaving their home behind. The backyard that I could have trimmed and nurtured, ruthlessly slicing the weeds to make room for new blossoms. The shelves of

books I could have finished or reread on Sylvia's behalf. The bed
I could have filled.

I ring the doorbell, pressing my lips together. Sylvia must have
had her own set of memories attached to this shade of lipstick.
Now her memories share space with my own. Seeing Patrick in
the doorway of Room 12. Patrick's fingers and mouth, urgent
between my legs, coaxing me up into myself from where I'd been
hiding.

The unlocked door swings open at my touch. The room
beyond is so fierce with evening light that I can't make anything
out.

"Patrick?"

I step into the Braddocks' home, closing the door behind me.
Then I instinctively lock it. I call his name again. No answer. The
house has an underwater stillness to it.

A dull glint on an end table catches my eye. I pick it up. Patrick's wedding ring. It's smaller than I expected. On his hand,
the band has always seemed heavy enough to root him here. I'm
surprised at its actual weightlessness. I turn the cold metal over
and over in my palm.

I straighten. I slip the wedding ring into my pocket. "I'm
here," I call.

Nothing. In my bones, I feel a sudden absence. It's as clear as if
I'm sinking, the water shutting over my head. Down here, in this
landscape beneath reality, everything looks the same. I can't find
my way back to the surface.

Even though I'm calm as I approach their house, every movement precise and constrained, the Damsons react to my presence with a sudden, stricken tension. Viv, turning from the car
door with Ben in her arms, freezes, pupils darting between me
and her husband.

Henry's jaw clenches. He hesitates a second before he starts toward me, heading me off in the middle of the driveway.

I understand that there must be something in my expression. That beneath the surface of my silence, I'm blood-streaked, screaming, wild-eyed.

"What did you say to him?" I ask Henry when he's close enough.

"You need to go," he says.

"He wouldn't have left without me," I say. "He wouldn't have done that unless you did something, unless you—"

I stop, realizing that Viv has come up next to us. She's different from the brightly tidy housewife I've been visiting. Today, she's stripped and unadorned: wrinkles showing at the corners of her eyes and around her mouth, hair pulled back roughly. She looks older, strangely more beautiful. For the first time, I feel intimidated by her.

"Are you seeing her?" she asks her husband, not even looking at me.

My brain scrambles the question. *Are you seeing her?* As if Henry might not be able to register my physical presence. As if I'm invisible to human eyes.

"Of course not," Henry says. "This isn't the time. Take Ben inside. I'll deal with her."

"I'm supposed to trust you?" Viv asks.

Henry waits, gazing at the cracked cement of the driveway, at the weeds trickling through. The baby murmurs, tugging at a strand of his mother's hair. Viv finally looks at me. We make eye contact for a long beat. I feel a strange moment of sadness pass between us, disappointment and betrayal, all three of us pulled together by it. Then she turns and walks back to her house, closing the door behind her with a quiet click that's more startling than if she'd slammed it.

"She found the photo," Henry says to me. "She knows."

The Polaroid from the lake; I realize what must have happened, the memory shifting back into place. That night that I woke up in the Damsons' home.

"I'm sorry," I say, impulsively. The vengefulness that thumps inside my chest belongs to Sylvia, not me. I would have been content to walk away and leave the Damsons. Let them tend to the tangled undergrowth of secrets on their own terms.

"It's what you wanted, right?" he asks.

"You didn't have to do this to us," I say. "You could have let us go."

"It wasn't because of that," he says. "I was already going to talk to Patrick."

I can't tell whether this is true or not. It would be a relief to dissolve the chain of events that led to Patrick's absence. To think that I couldn't have stopped it, couldn't have changed anything. But already I'm looking for a moment that could have pushed the events in a different direction.

"What did you do?" I ask.

"I told him who you are," Henry says. The evening is deepening purple around us, windows breaking into illumination up and down the street. "You've been lying to him."

"I wasn't lying," I say. "He never asked."

Henry shrugs. "Same thing," he says. "So I told Patrick. What he did with that information isn't my business."

"How did you find out?" I ask.

"Your boss didn't want anything to do with me," Henry says. "She seems to care about you a lot. You should be flattered. But the other woman—Joan? Jane? Anyway, she was happy to talk. If it makes you feel better, it wasn't cheap to get your real name and your hometown. She didn't know much else, but that was enough. The firm used to hire a private investigator for background checks. We stayed on good terms. It only took a few days to get your story."

Whatever exists out there in medical records, paperwork, newspaper articles, is only the parched surface of the story. The stripped bones. Patrick still doesn't know the parts that only exist in the deepest, most tender pit of my memory. But I'm not sure if revealing this to him would pull him back into my arms or send him spiraling further from my grasp.

"I would have told Patrick," I say. "When he was ready, I would have told him."

"You wouldn't have," Henry says. "You knew he'd leave you."

It must have happened this morning. I was at home, going through my day, stupid with hope and fantasizing about my escape. Ready to step into my new life. And all that time, Patrick and Henry stood together, miles away, and Henry opened me up without my permission. Laid me bare and defenseless.

Look at her.

"I couldn't let him take Sylvia," Henry says. "He had his chance with her. He had no right to drag her back." His eyes surprise me, even in this moment: the sudden streak of grief. "Patrick doesn't get to do that. Nobody gets to do that."

"He's her husband," I say. "You don't know what Sylvia wanted."

"I saved her from Patrick," Henry says, as if he didn't even hear. "From you, trying to crawl into her life because you can't stand your own. You ruined your life, now you want someone else's." We face each other in the gloom. "I feel worse for Patrick than for you," Henry says. "There's no love lost between us, but even he doesn't deserve this."

"Where did he go?" I ask, my voice leaden.

He shrugs. "I wouldn't tell you if I knew."

The Damsons' house is all warmth, all light. Lit like a diorama, windows uncovered. The spread of framed photographs against the wall, the mantelpiece with its staggered candleholders, a stray shirt slung over the back of a chair. Viv walks through the rooms with the baby; I catch fractured glimpses of them. In the living room, the dining room. Then they're lost to us. Viv doesn't glance out the windows. She's a woman moving calmly through her evening.

My mind turns to what I learned this morning. What Patrick doesn't know yet; what Henry doesn't realize. The piece of the equation they haven't yet considered, still a secret.

"That place," Henry says. "They're all like you, aren't they?"

I look at him as if he's separated from me by layers of glass.

"All the workers are like you," he says. "Rejects. Recycled from lives you hated."

Mrs. Renard rummaging through a pile of discarded bodies, stiff mannequin torsos, angled knees, cloudy glass eyes. Taking us home, dusting us off. Propping us in chairs, painting on the right expressions. Making us useful again.

Mind spinning, I turn to leave.

"Wait," Henry calls. He's not angry now. There's a resignation to his voice, a grudging truce. That's what stops me in my tracks.

He goes to their car, opening the passenger-side door and stooping to retrieve something from beneath the seat. I stay at the end of the driveway. Down the block, children shout and laugh, colorful loops of sound against the evening. A young woman, ponytail whipping, jogs past without looking at us.

Henry returns. "Here." He extends something toward me: a thin yellow folder.

I hesitate before I accept. "What is this?" My hands are shaking. The paper vibrates lightly in my hand, as if something inside is alive and fighting to come out.

"I'm forcing you to face up to what you did," he says. "Who you are. Think of it as a favor."

I open the folder, already knowing what I'll find. My past self. Offered to me by a stranger, after all this time; dragged from her hiding place by a distant bystander. For a second, I'm overcome with resentment at Henry for walking into my life and doing this to me. He has no right. I'm homesick for the existence I built so carefully these past five years. A world tiny and controlled enough to hold inside my palm, where nobody else could ever access it.

But Henry never came to me, I remind myself. I'm the one who guided him into my life. I invited him in. I opened the door to an enemy and then turned my back as he ransacked my private possessions.

FORTY

The knocking at the door works its way into my dream, insistent as a heartbeat. As I rise from the couch, the stove clock marks the time as four in the morning.

I open the door. He stands in the hallway. Eyes bleary with exhaustion, jaw set. I watch his gaze move along my length. Patrick doesn't hide the fact that he's staring. I'm wearing a cheap silk bathrobe, the hem brushing the middle of my thighs. He's memorized my naked body, but right now, I'm more exposed in front of him than I ever was in his bed.

This time, he knows what I did. He's meeting me for the first time.

Everything in my body rearranges itself around Patrick's presence. The wildness of desire and relief, but following this, its inevitable shadow: the fear that I'll lose him, and how foolish I was to have wanted him at all.

"Come in, Patrick," I say, and open the door wider.

The apartment is saturated in darkness. In the shadows, he looks as grainy as a memory.

"I drove for five hours before I turned around," he says. "I should have kept going. But here I am." He keeps distance between us; I can sense the heavy restlessness of his body from across the room. "I wanted to hear it from you. I owe you that much."

We sit on opposite ends of the couch, stiff and careful, keeping our posture very straight and our hands tucked on our laps.

"I know your name," he says. "Your real one." A pause. "I always liked that name."

"I wish you'd keep calling me Edie," I say. The thought of hearing my real name in Patrick's voice is unbearable right now.

"Would you have told me your name, at some point?"

"I left it behind," I say. "It doesn't belong to me anymore."

"And Edie does belong to you?"

"For now," I say. "Yes."

From the corner of my eye, I sense him turning to face me. I think he's going to ask another question. But he's silent for long enough that I realize how hard this is for him. Any single question will come along with a trail of others, tangling together, each question marring the blankness he's relied on for months. I have to be the one to reach down into the cold and depthless place where I've been waiting.

In the end, I have to be the one to drag myself back to the surface.

"I can't really remember the first time it happened," I begin. "Other people had to tell me what I'd done. I was only thirteen or fourteen. A child. I'd been shy, a late bloomer. Everyone thought I was nice. Quiet. The kind of girl nothing would ever happen to. It just woke up in my brain one day. I was fine, and then there it was. I didn't know how to handle it. I was completely unequipped against something that huge. The first time, I wasn't trying to do anything. I wanted to take a break from everything, that's all. Sleep for a while. I had a vision of sleeping for days and waking up different. I'd go back to how I was before. Happy and calm.

"When my mother found me, she didn't believe that it was an accident. I still think sometimes that if she'd believed me, I could have moved on from everything."

That other life I could have led unravels, so gentle and ordinary and impossibly far away that I can't let myself think about it too closely.

"My mother treated me differently. I just wasn't her little girl anymore. Other people found out, the way things spread in a small town. They changed too. I went from being a nice girl to being suspicious. People talked to me as if I might explode. I wasn't part of the sleepovers or the birthday parties anymore. They weren't trying to shun me. Not really. They just saw me as a different type of person. Someone who wouldn't be interested in those things. Someone who didn't want to belong to that world."

Patrick's shape in the darkness is unyielding, impossible to interpret.

"Things went on that way most of my teenage years," I say. "Every single morning, I woke up thinking that it would be better. I'd be happy again with no warning. Really, it made sense. There wasn't a good reason to begin with. Who's to say it couldn't vanish the same way?

"But it became part of me. I couldn't remember a time when I wasn't like that. I withdrew from other people. My mother tried to be there for me at first. But after a while, she got impatient. I'm sure I frustrated her. I worried about being a burden. I tried to be as independent as I could, relying only on myself. I made OK grades, got accepted into a decent school. It seemed like a chance to make a clean break."

My mother's face pulls together in my memory. The careful restraint in her expression when we interacted, a chilly politeness that hurt more than anger would have. At the time, I thought it was her choice to withdraw, but now, I wonder if I was at fault too: holding her back by the shoulders and then resenting her for not embracing me.

"When I was about eighteen," I say, "after I started school, I tried again. This time, it was more intentional. Nobody found me. My roommate was out of town. I woke up in my bed as if nothing had happened. It had snowed that day, and the light in the room was so bright. I thought I was in a dream until I found the empty pill bottle. My body had pulled itself back. Despite everything, it was still there. I was still there."

I keep waiting for Patrick to say something.

"It was almost a game, from then on," I say. "Seeing if my body would ever give in. I tried twice more. Each time I came back, everything seemed more distant. Like I was returning to a fuzzier copy of life. I couldn't find my way back into a clear version. After my roommate found me, she forced me to see a therapist. I took medication. I went through the motions. But even when things became a little easier, I worried that it was only a matter of time. And so I didn't let myself want things. I was afraid of how it would feel when I couldn't have a normal life. Trying to keep my expectations small—it was the kindest thing I did for myself."

There's a comfort in listening to the story unfold without tears or rage. I could be telling a story that belongs to a stranger.

"After school, I moved away," I say. "Only a few hours. Everything even looked the same. Same architecture, same weather. But nobody there knew who I was. It was like resetting myself. I started to wake up. I still held myself back from wanting too much, but I was learning to be content with a small life. Only big enough for me. Manageable."

The other half of the story is approaching. I sense it deep in my body: a kernel of apprehension, as if I'm walking across ice toward the patches that will give under my feet.

"Daniel worked across the street from me," I say. "We sometimes had coffee or lunch at the same diner. I liked him for months before I even realized what was happening. For most women my age, it would have been a small crush. Not even worth noticing. But for me, it was . . . enormous. I didn't know what to call it. It was like everything inside me coming alive. By then, we recognized each other enough to say hello. I could pick and choose which parts of myself to reveal to him. Telling him about my life in these little pieces, I started seeing myself differently.

"Being interested in Daniel rearranged all my plans. Wanting this one thing, letting myself want it, had turned everything into a possibility. The type of life I'd never let myself want—it wasn't anything glamorous or exciting. A husband, a house, a baby. But letting myself want it after so long thinking I couldn't have it? It was intoxicating."

I keep waiting for the room to brighten. It stays sketched in the vagueness of early morning. In a way, it's easier to talk while I'm hidden, a mere silhouette.

"Daniel and I started spending more time together. I kissed him one night when we'd been drinking." Slipping backward, I see the girl with optimistic makeup, a dress both too cheap and too formal. Prissy office casual at a dive bar. "I wanted to see what it was like to act on something I wanted. He kissed me back. After that, we were together. Just like that. As if it had always been that easy."

A long exhale from the other side of the couch. I wonder if Patrick's hurt by this memory. An entire history that's been buried under our feet all along, sharing space with Sylvia.

"People didn't understand why Daniel would want me," I say. "He'd lived in that town his whole life. Everyone had predicted who he'd marry since he was a kid. I was a newcomer. Maybe it seemed unfair that I could come in and take him. I didn't care. I was selfish. I wanted him, he wanted me back. It was perfect. I never told him about my past, of course. I didn't want Daniel looking at me differently. And it didn't feel like lying. I really was a new person with him. The two of us didn't have to worry about what another girl had done during another life."

Footsteps in the hallway outside: the bad stage whispers of a tipsy couple playing at discretion. Laughing, a wet kiss, a playful, mumbled scold. I wait for the click of the closed door before I continue.

"In the summer, I found out I was pregnant." I say it evenly and firmly, not letting myself linger. A simple truth: *I was pregnant.* "We'd only been dating for a few months. People said I'd tricked Daniel into it. But it was a decision we made together. I was tired of holding myself back. I wanted to just reach out and take this life, before it slipped through my fingers. And Daniel was so young. I didn't think of him as young back then, but I see it now. He was in love with me and I was wild. Full of life. How could he have known that that brightness was only one side of me?"

Patrick starts to speak, a quick and uncertain syllable. Then he stops.

"The pregnancy was fine at first," I say. "I was healthy. The baby was healthy. The first few months passed quickly, and I convinced myself that I could do it. When I was four or five months along, I started getting flashes of my old self. It scared me, but I thought once I had the baby, I'd be better. It would change things. People told me it would. I'd look at her and feel the most intense love I'd ever felt, and it would make everything OK again."

"Her," Patrick repeats. "A girl?"

"Yes," I say. "By the time I found out that she was a girl, things were already going wrong. Daniel was caught up in work, but I'd been let go from my job; I was home alone all day. I wasn't much fun anymore. He'd started making excuses to spend time with friends, people I didn't know. We hadn't been together long, and maybe we were both realizing how—how big this thing was. How permanent. I had trouble sleeping. The doctor discouraged me from taking medications. When I was depressed, sleep was everything to me. It was a break from the heaviness and sadness. I'd look forward to it all day: that moment when I could forget everything for a while. So when I couldn't sleep anymore, it all piled up. Days and nights were the same. Too much time for my mind to obsess over the same questions, turning things over and over. Every time I'd settle a fear, there'd be a moment of relief, and then I was right back at it.

"After a few weeks of this insomnia, I was out of my mind. I was worried Daniel was cheating on me. I was worried he didn't love me anymore. I thought his parents would try to take the baby from me, because clearly I couldn't be a good mother. Then I'd worry that nobody would want anything to do with me. All the fear and sadness I'd left behind came back so much stronger. I'd tried to take a life that didn't belong to me. Things couldn't keep on like that. Fate had to restore the balance."

Patrick makes a movement as if he wants to come closer.

"Daniel noticed," I say. "I was an entirely different person. Trapped and desperate. I'd take it out on him, he'd take it out on me. I'd catch him watching me sometimes. As if he'd just walked into his house one day and found this strange and terrifying woman. We tried to get ready for the baby. We went shopping for clothes and a crib. It only made things feel more real. All these other couples shopping, they seemed so solid and happy—it felt like Daniel and I were the impostors. Playing at a real life."

Patrick must already know. Henry must have brought evidence: printouts of the news pieces, the mug shot from when I was taken into custody. That image that's haunted me all these years, a woman who wasn't really me. Skin drained of texture and color, eyes hollow and unfocused. He must know what I'm about to say: I sense him stiffening, braced for a blow.

"I bought sleeping pills," I say. "By then, I was seven months along. It was obvious to anyone that I was pregnant. I was afraid they wouldn't sell me the pills. The cashier asked me when I was due, but she didn't stop me. I was prepared to tell them the pills were for somebody else. At home, I hid the pills in a drawer. It comforted me just to know they were there. When things got really bad, when Daniel didn't come home all night, I'd think of them. I wouldn't use them, though. I promised myself. I'd wait until after the baby was born."

Abruptly, Patrick leans forward, elbows between his knees,

clasped hands pressed into his bent forehead. He's very still in this pose, eyes directed at the floor.

"It was late at night," I say. "I'd gone too long without sleeping. Probably thirty-six hours or more. I tried to cope by focusing on one moment at a time. But there was always this awareness of the time waiting for me beyond that. I started cracking. It was like I forgot where I was. I was alone again, detached from life, and I only had myself to worry about. I wasn't pregnant. I'd never met Daniel. That night, I was my old self, all my choices erased, and I got the sleeping pills. At first, I promised myself I would take one or two. Just enough to take the edge off and let me sleep. But once I'd swallowed a few, I started panicking that they wouldn't work. So I took more. Too many. I don't know the exact amount."

Silence. Patrick doesn't say anything. He doesn't react at all.

"I still don't know how long it was before I woke up," I say. "I was in the hospital. Daniel had found me. I was in a hospital bed, surrounded by wires. I couldn't move without something beeping. The baby was OK, they said, but they'd have to monitor us. Daniel wouldn't come to see me at all. Not once. His parents came to visit. They were worried about the baby. I thought they'd be furious at me, but they were forgiving. Maybe they realized how hard things had been for me. His mother even sat down and chatted for a few minutes. She wanted me to know that she'd be willing to help out after the baby came. It made me feel a little better. I was still trying to piece everything together. The nurses and doctors would tell me how lucky I was, that what I'd done hadn't hurt the baby. I'd gotten away with it. I almost started to believe it.

"It happened a week after I first woke up in the hospital. Late at night. Everything seemed fine, then suddenly it wasn't. I was bleeding. There was so much of it. Maybe it seems strange that I'd be shocked by blood. But I wasn't used to it. The pills took me out of my body. This pain was holding me there." I hesitate. For the first time, I'm not sure if I can go on. "It was an emergency delivery," I say. "She was already gone. I didn't even get a chance to look at her. They must have assumed I wouldn't want to see her. And I understand. I killed her. It was my fault." I pause. "It is my fault."

The pain isn't as deep as I thought it would be. After being stifled for five years, it should be enormous, unbearable. A neglected wound hidden under a sleeve, the infection seeping into the bloodstream. But instead I've found a mere scar. My pain has healed without me. I feel cheated, almost panicking. I want the freshness back.

"Lying there after," I say, "people wouldn't even look at me. Their eyes would go right over mine, no matter how hard I tried to make eye contact. Like I was just a blank space in the room. A broken machine. I had to eavesdrop to find out what had happened. A placental abruption, they said. I didn't know what that meant. It hadn't hurt me much—I was recovering, at least physically. I must have been lying there for days, and it was the strangest thing. While I was pregnant, I didn't notice the baby's movement much. But once she was gone, I felt so still and so flat. I kept wondering, where is she? Why isn't she moving? And then I had to remember, over and over again. This instinct I hadn't even realized I had—now it was haunting me."

Patrick's posture hasn't changed: the sharp angle of his back, the slope of his neck.

"Weeks passed, and I wasn't sure what would happen next," I continue. "It was impossible to imagine. I was completely detached. The drugs made me even more numb. When the officers came into the room, I barely understood what they were saying or doing. It took me a long time to piece together that I was being charged for the loss of the baby. Daniel's parents wanted me to be prosecuted for what I'd done. The baby would have survived if I hadn't overdosed; that's what they were saying. After that, everything was a blur—being in the holding cell wasn't much different from being in the hospital. These strange, lonely places where I wasn't quite real. I was just a problem to be solved."

The mug shot. Staring incuriously at the dark eye of the camera suspended above me. My face blank, my gaze indifferent. It would only be later that I'd wonder about the implications of that photo. I found it, attached to my true name, on a local news site: I scarcely recognized the person in the photo. A face captured at its most raw stage and preserved forever. All I wanted, back then, was to escape that girl and everything about her.

"It must have been Daniel who convinced them to drop the charges," I say. "A placental abruption can happen to anyone. It can happen to women who've done everything perfectly, who've been careful the whole pregnancy. That's what helped me. But the case had already caught the attention of the media. Enough to get my name out there. Maybe you heard about it—six years ago, maybe. I don't know how far the story spread."

He shakes his head, a barely perceptible motion. I can't tell if he's denying it or if he can't speak.

"After they released me, I went back to the house," I say. "Daniel wasn't there. I walked through those rooms and took a few things I might need. Clothes and toiletries, cash. The crib was still in the bedroom. I couldn't pass it without thinking of her. My poor girl."

The words shock me, forming without my awareness. *My poor girl.*

"And then you came here," Patrick says. His voice is hoarse, as if he's the one who's been talking all this time.

"I tried a few different cities. Temporary jobs, whatever I could get. Nothing was exactly right. When I heard about the

Elysian Society, it seemed like just another job. But it was exactly what I needed. Taking the lotus, I stepped outside my skin and everything was more bearable. One day I looked up and it had been a year, and then two years. I haven't been happy as a body, not exactly. But I've been safe, all these years."

"He never came looking for you?" Patrick asks.

"I used to think he would," I say. "It wouldn't have been too hard to track me down. For the first few months, I imagined him walking in the door. Coming back for me. By now, I don't think it will happen. He doesn't want anything to do with me. I don't blame him. I hope that he's forgotten me. I hope he's happy with someone else."

Patrick straightens. A diver breaking above the surface of the water, trying to find his bearings in this harsh-edged world. "So do you believe it?" he asks.

"Believe what?"

"That you would have lost the baby anyway," he says.

"I don't know," I say. "I'll probably never know."

"Did you pick out a name for her?"

"Lucy," I say.

His throat jumps as he swallows. "I don't understand how you could do that," he says. "Do you know what Sylvia would have done for a chance to be a mother? You had it, and you—you destroyed it."

"Patrick, I was desperate," I say. "I wasn't thinking of the baby. I wanted to be gone. I didn't even know I was pregnant when I swallowed those pills. It was a moment of such panic that I would have done anything to end it."

Outside, the darkness is backlit with creeping pink.

"You've hidden so much from me," Patrick says.

I don't answer. I'm not sure I have any words left inside me.

"I was hoping you'd tell me it was a mistake," he continues. "Even after I saw the photo. I came to your door thinking—

maybe Henry invented everything. One last way to hurt me and Sylvia."

My chest hurts, an ache through my muscles, as if expelling the words from my body required a physical force.

"But he was being kind to me," Patrick continues. "He was more honest with me than you've ever been."

So early in the morning, the traffic noises are scattered: the occasional roar and rumble of a truck that's been driving all night. Passing through quiet towns, cities suspended in sleep.

"I don't know how I didn't see it before." Patrick's voice verges on wondering. "You're exactly like her."

Even now, the words bring an instinctive rush of pleasure. Being compared to her. Taking on the dark-haired woman in the photos, her uncomplicated beauty. But I know what he really means.

"That night at the lake," he says. "Was that her? Or you?"

"I'm not sure." My voice is very quiet.

"You'd do it again," he says. "I can't live with that fear. Waiting for it to happen."

"I'm different now," I say. "It's been five years. I'm a new woman."

"But something like that—it won't just go away."

The faintest light slides across the floor. It's an optical illusion: indistinguishable as I watch, but brighter every time I look away and look back.

"I shouldn't have done this with you," Patrick says. "It was a fantasy, trying to get my wife back. You made it feel possible. Like something I deserved."

I pull the bathrobe's thin and chintzy fabric tighter around my body.

"You wanted to have a child with me," he says, and his voice is thick with both awe and disgust. "Jesus."

Without thinking about it, I touch my stomach. Just as

quickly, I pull my hand away, trying to hide the gesture. I imagine where we'd be if we'd left the city together yesterday evening—if we were already hundreds of miles away, curled together on a hotel bed. The early morning landscape outside the window completely unfamiliar to us, waiting to reveal itself in the dawn light as we pulled away, on to the next town. If we'd left, I would be telling him now. I'd wanted to wait until we'd escaped the city.

I only found out yesterday morning. I was curious about the heaviness between my hip bones, the dizziness that briefly dissolved my edges when I stood too quickly. Sensations that had nothing to do with Sylvia. I knew; before I even saw the second line, I knew. Another chance. I've saved the test, a tiny piece of proof. But now that my past has leaked into the present, all the hope I could have offered Patrick has grown tarnished and ugly.

If I tell him now, I'm afraid that he'll react with anger, disappointment: a cruel parody of what I'd wanted for us. I remember the undercurrent of reverence in his voice when I suggested that he and Sylvia could have what they'd missed. I open my mouth to tell him—but I can't make myself form the words.

"Patrick," I say instead, "there's nothing keeping us in the city. We're as free as we were yesterday. We're the same people. I can still do this for you and Sylvia."

For one more moment, I let myself believe that he'll be convinced by this. That he'll say: *You're right. Everything is forgiven. We'll go.* And we'll walk into the future together. The past falling away. Once we're in a new city, I can tell him, and he'll look at me with new eyes, see our future with eyes unclouded by what came before us.

But: "I can't," he says.

In the dusty shell of the TV screen, I can make out our shapes, side by side.

"I blame myself for this too," he says after a silence. "I let you lie to me."

I'm silent, words stuck to my tongue. There's nothing I can say. He'll leave. I feel his absence already, shifting closer with each breath I take. I realize that Patrick doesn't know how purely he'll be turning his back on his wife. He believes she's curled in the bottle of lotuses, confined like a trapped spirit in a fairy tale. Summoned only by the swallowed pill.

He doesn't know that she's with me. She'll watch through my eyes as he walks away from us. And though I haven't examined my reasons for hiding this from Patrick, I'm suddenly and deeply grateful that I've kept our bond a secret from him.

He rises. I stand too; I'm weak for a moment, exhaustion tunneling up through my throat and stomach before it pops in my brain. He's a stranger again. My familiarity with his body, his mannerisms, the sound of his voice: it's all been drawn back into him and locked away.

At the door, we hesitate.

"Will I see you again?" I ask.

Patrick brings his gaze to mine with an effort. "No," he says.

"Where will you go?" I ask.

"Anywhere," he says. "It doesn't matter."

After a second, Patrick grips my waist. He pulls me toward him until we press together. I feel his quick, hard pulse at every point in my body. Bowing my head, I rest my forehead against his chest. He kisses the top of my head.

Neither of us speaks for a long time.

Then Patrick lets go of me. He turns from me and walks away. He doesn't look back.

I stay in the empty doorway. I remember my time at the lake. Lying in bed. The scent of that cabin, like withered flower petals, treacly and dusty at once. The planes of the ceiling above us, the bedspread curled around my thighs. Patrick's hand on my belly. He'd said: *You're not even yourself.* And I'd assumed, then, it was an accusation, or the rising horror of realization.

It's only now, standing with my back to my empty apartment, that I can see it for what it truly was. A declaration of love.

FORTY-ONE

The first time around, it was inevitable. The easiest thing in the world to ignore.

I tried. I'd read gently chiding magazine articles that promised to teach me how to love my body, step-by-step. I'd listen to the cautionary tales about the human body breaking down in intricate ways, and I'd vow that I'd no longer take my health for granted. I'd revel in the miracle of my sturdy lungs, smoothly muscled legs, chugging heartbeat.

But at the back of my mind, I knew these were illusions. Attempts to make living inside my skin as toothless and luxurious as slipping on a new dress. The actual experience was too enormous and too ordinary to distill down to abstract platitudes.

My body, that first time, was so constant that I had to break it into tiny pieces to experience it at all. A knot of pain in my temple on waking. A prickling itch in my sole. Patrick's hand on the small of my back. A bead of sweat trailing slowly down the nape of my neck. The hairs on my arms rising in response to a breeze. Strangers' eyes shifting over me.

Photographs helped. Photographs let me step back and examine myself impartially. I'd run my finger down the length of myself, trapped in the still image, and all my thoughts would fall into line in response.

And then I became a cautionary tale. My body betrayed me, sinking further from my grasp. I reached down as far as I could and still my fingers closed on nothingness. My interior refused to make itself known to me. That was the time of sitting in sterile rooms in thin paper gowns, an object to be assessed and weighed and plucked over. A time of averting my eyes *from the firmly swollen bellies in the waiting room, their ripe roundness a sign of some perfect and tightly wound clockwork deep within them. While I was all rattling gears, loose coils.*

After this, I turned into something else. Someone else. A body that behaved in a way I never thought I could. Doing things I'd never let myself want to do. Henry's mouth an electric shock on my thighs, his fingers a stubborn reminder that my flesh still had other uses. Other sources of pleasure. I'd watch myself as if from a distance when I was with Henry, thinking: Can this really be me? Can I be this woman? Never certain whether I felt terror or delight at the thought.

It was too painful for me to touch my husband. Together with mine, his body was part of that unfixable equation.

Even as the oxygen leaked from my blood and water trickled into my lungs, during that one shining, brutal moment when I accepted what was happening, I still didn't know how to miss my body. I missed the world: warm pavement under bare feet, music fluttering from a passing car, the strange wildness in the air whenever seasons changed. I missed Patrick, the way we were before and the way we should have been. But I didn't miss my body in the moment that I left it.

It's taken all this.

I've come back into different flesh, shocking in its newness. At first, I was only in her for brief stretches of time, confused and sickened. Too much sensation: too much queasy closeness. The wrongness of being so intertwined with a stranger. Words formed with an effort on a huge, wet tongue, thrust out between the heavy stones of her teeth. The frantic pounding of blood in her ears. The maddening awareness of so much skin, itching and throbbing and hurting without relief. I pushed through it. I made myself stay and speak.

Settling into her skin took time. It was a primal instinct. Blunt, chaotic flashes of being inside her, interspersed with nothingness. Over time, though, I blinked awake more and more fully. I stretched.

For a long time, she was merely functional. I found myself with a body again and I wanted the simplest second chance. The impulse overrode ev-

erything else: to go back to my final moment. To make them see me, this time, when they'd been looking past me for so long. But over time, the vengefulness faded and thinned.

I wanted more. I wanted to walk through life again. If I miss the people I loved the first time, it's a forgivable ache. I can't see them again. But this new body, with all its limitations, has the strange, wild freedom of a second chance.

I've had to learn her. Patient and painstaking, I've felt out her boundaries. This time, I can't ignore the specificity of having a body. It's always a wonder. An astonishment.

With her, I view the world from a different vantage point. Everything lower than I remember. I've learned to grip objects with hands both finer-boned and longer than my previous ones. Our tongue responds to salty tastes more vividly, dampens sweet flavors: the opposite of my first body. At night, our dreams are bursting with color instead of black and white.

When we embraced Patrick, our mouth lined up with his. Before, I had to stand on my toes like a child. It was a revelation to be evenly matched with him. Everything in him aligned with everything in me. He turned smaller, easier to understand, and I could forgive him.

Now.

Now: he's gone again. He walked away from her, just like I knew he would. He's never learned how to look without flinching.

But I'm here. I'm here, I'm here. I'm in love with the tastes and smells and sensations that cut through the ordinariness of occupying a body, bright shocks. I want to soak everything in. Whenever I feel that darkness edging against her, dulling her brain, muffling her vision, and I know that she wants to escape, I share this wonder with her. This gluttony.

Want it, *I tell her.*

Want everything.

And she listens.

FORTY-TWO

W ithout anything to interrupt the cold, clean February sunlight, it comes through the bare windows to land in evenly paced squares across the length of the room. I stop just past the entrance. The place is dingy, holding all the stubborn dignity of a home long neglected. But the pure clarity of this room—the white walls, the slanted symmetry of the sunlight along the wooden floorboards—opens up something huge in my chest. I'm alive with the knowledge that I'm making the right choice. Moving into the right future.

"It's a quiet street," the real estate agent says. She's been hanging back, a vaguely polite presence, asserting herself at just the right moments.

I turn and smile. "Yes, I noticed that right away."

"There's not much traffic noise. The park we passed gives you some privacy, but you're only a block or two from the closest neighbors." She walks deeper into the room, heels clattering. Her shadow makes a swift blot across the sunlit squares. It's a small disappointment, like the first messy footstep in fresh snow. "It's a balance between residential amenities and that nice secluded feel," she says. "My impression is that you want something like that?"

"That's exactly what I want," I say.

"This home has been on the market for a while," the agent says. She's neutral: black dress; short, neat hair; makeup in subdued colors. I can see her getting dressed every day, making sure she's nonspecific enough to complement whatever space she enters. "It's one of those unique places that needs just the right person. I have a good feeling about you."

The house is old, two stories tall. White paint weathered grayish, like pencil shadings and idle scribbling on the margins of paper. The screened-in porch slightly lopsided, as if it's sinking gradually into the ground. Trees grow thick and close on one side, so that every east-facing window is cloaked with a lacework of branches.

I reach out to brush my fingertips along the walls. The layout inside is airy but close at the same time, rooms connected like a half-completed puzzle. Large rooms with unexpected angles and sunken nooks. I flesh out all the details. It wouldn't need much. Sweep away the ellipses of mouse droppings, repaint the walls, and wash the windows until the glass is cleanly invisible. The house is old enough to feel like a memory, something half remembered from anybody's childhood. It has a generous quiet: *Come in.*

Welcome home.

"You're new here, am I remembering correctly?" the agent asks.

"I moved last week," I say, gazing out the closest window. Through the layered grime, the view is perfect. A winding street, a tiny public park composed of overgrown shrubbery and a few concrete benches. The closest residence is just a roof's peak, edging over the treetops. In the warmer weather, with the branches thick with leaves, even this much will be hidden.

"Ah." The agent sparkles a smile at me. "New job?"

"In a way," I say. "I'm hoping to start my own business."

"Oh, an entrepreneur," she says. "You have family and friends in the area?"

"Not really," I say. "But I'm hoping to make connections." I smile. "As a matter of fact, that's why I'll be leaving earlier than we discussed. I'm meeting someone this afternoon."

She waits a second for me to elaborate, but I'm silent. "Well, I hope you're enjoying our town so far," the agent says, a brisk tamp of a conversation ending. "Now, since we're pinched for time, I'd like to show you the bedrooms. You'll be amazed at how much space you're getting for the asking price. More space than you know what to do with, I imagine."

I follow her up the steep, broad staircase, the dark-stained wood dully gleaming in the sunlight. I'm barely listening to her lively stream of details and selling points. She doesn't need to say anything else; in my head, this house is already mine. Ours. I reach into my coat pocket, my fingers automatically finding the lotus tucked inside.

've kept the photo from that light-dazzled evening at the park. I used to take Sylvia away and leave only the two of us. Patrick and me. Meeting a decade ago, or more, when we were both scrubbed bare of the future. I'd try to calculate what we might have brought out in each other. What we could have had, while there was still time to become different versions of ourselves.

But the fantasy was never right. Over time, I came to understand what really would have happened. We would have been vacant and too young, crossing paths without noticing each other. There would be nothing there to latch onto, smooth surfaces slipping past. We met when we were both roughened and torn, our hearts tattered enough to snag on each other's.

Even if Patrick thought he loved me for my infinite blankness, there must have been a part of him, hidden even from himself, that responded to our similarities. To the matching trails of destruction we'd left in our wake. What happened stayed with us, a force that guided my steps to this point.

To this house. To these movements, like a dreamer's, under my skin. To Sylvia.

Sylvia.

She's stayed with me. I've stayed with her. It's pointless to untangle us. I've stopped questioning which impulses come from me and which come from her.

There was a while, right after he left, when I thought she'd abandoned me too. I spent my days in an interrogation room, my shell-shocked reflection a blur in the corner of my eye. I talked in rote detail about the Elysian Society. About Mrs. Renard; about Thisbe. The lotuses.

The words fell like leaves from my mouth, dry and brittle. I was shockingly alone in my skin. Nothing but space. The people who filtered in and out of the interrogation room must have known why I was there. Their casual curiosity wasn't unkind, but it glanced sharply at my skin. My role at the Elysian Society had been protection for so long. It was disorienting to have it turned against me, my blank mask pulled inside out to reveal a freakish face.

I tried to apply Sylvia's lipstick one morning, hoping it would bring a comforting reminder of when the Braddocks were entirely new to me. When my world was lit up and crackling with that strange possibility. But the lipstick had soured, leaking out a smell both soapy and rotten. Eventually, I threw it away.

She came back the first time I felt movement. It was only a month or so after Patrick had left; the fluttering was a small shock, happening just as I fell into sleep. A brief stirring, outside my control, deep beneath my navel. Half dreaming, I pictured a goldfish swimming. Its fins brushing the sides of the glass. Then I remembered what it really was. It was happening much earlier than last time. My body's muscle memory waking up, reminding me. And for a second, I panicked.

I couldn't do it again. I couldn't face it. With Patrick, I was so sure I'd changed, but I hadn't. Not enough. The same impulses would pull me under, leaving no way back.

In the numb tilting of that moment, I felt her again. Another presence soothing my muscles. My dread dissolving into a sense of quiet as everything opened ahead of me.

Ahead of us.

I think about Laura sometimes, transformed into Thisbe, transformed into Hopeful Doe, floating further and further from her own identity. I don't know how we avoided her fate. It's easy to imagine Sylvia eating me alive. Fighting me until we merged into emptiness, canceling each other out. My dreams, the first few months, were heavy with these images. My body with Sylvia's face, discarded in an empty house. I'd wake up cold-skinned and screaming, the room pulsing around me.

But I'm here. She's here. There's a comforting weight to Sylvia's presence inside me, the empty places in me that she's filled. The cracks that I used to slip down into, where my body became something depthless and hollow, have turned into sources of warmth. All I have to do is reach for her; when I'm exhausted, Sylvia takes our body and lets me rest.

By now I wonder how I ever could have lived alone in my skin. It seems like an impossible loneliness.

We walk out onto the porch. This town has a milder climate than the city I left behind. Though it's still the middle of winter, the layer of snow on the ground is as thin as a fallen handkerchief, already melting in patches. A flock of birds takes off from a nearby tree, a sudden ink spray swooping across the sky. As the agent fumbles with her overloaded keychain, I look up at the still and quiet rows of windows. Everything just waiting to begin.

"Will anybody else need to see the house before you make a final decision?" she asks, turning from the door.

She's too discreet to lower her gaze, but I bring my hands to my stomach, acknowledging the unspoken for her. "No," I say. "It's only us."

The movement comes, responding to my touch. A swift kick near my rib cage, followed by a flutter like a trapped moth.

"Of course," she says. "I understand." Then she smiles, coaxing. "It would be the perfect home for a little one," she says. "So much room to run and grow."

"I think so too."

"We'll be in touch, then?" she asks.

"Definitely," I say.

The real estate agent beams. She reaches out to touch my shoulder, her fingers light and familiar. People have been this way since the pregnancy started to show: an easiness with my body. "Well, I admit, I have a soft spot for this house." Her voice softens to a ruefully confiding tone. "A few prospective buyers have passed it up. You should know how happy it makes me that you'll be breathing new life into those rooms."

I look back once as I drive away, trying to see the house through a stranger's gaze. The rising white walls, the bare branches etched against one side. The windows that already brim with something close enough to life.

When the idea came to me, I only wanted to talk to one person. I worked up the nerve to call him the evening before I left the city. I'd been living in a motel room, unable to return to my apartment. Afraid that if I walked back into those rooms as if I still belonged, even for just a day, I'd never leave again. The motel room was small, with upholstery-thick beige drapes that blocked out all light. I could curl in bed and imagine it was any time of the day. That anything was happening outside.

Six murky, impossible weeks had passed, going too fast and then too slow. Six weeks since Patrick walked away from me.

It was very late at night or very early in the morning, and I was groggy, furious, about to tip the bottle of lotuses into the mouth of the toilet. The idea came into my head. It was so simple and complete that I almost laughed.

I pulled the bottle close to my belly, pressing it tight. Carefully, I looked at the idea again, circling it to gauge its size, its layout. *Why not?* I thought, and then again, *Why not?* And each time I knew more surely that I'd do it.

Lee answered on the second ring. "Edie?" His voice tinged with caution.

"It's good to talk to you again," I'd said.

"I didn't think—" He stopped, and in the small stretch of silence I heard him sitting down. "When I gave you this number, I didn't think I'd hear from you," Lee said. "You're doing well?"

"Yes," I said. "I'm doing fine."

"You're with him." A statement.

I was about to say that I was living alone, but the untruth of this struck me. "No," I said simply. "I'm not with Patrick anymore. We parted ways."

"I see," Lee said. He hesitated. "Well, I've been thinking about you," he said. "I've been hoping you're all right. I should have come forward, but I was—"

"It wasn't so bad," I said. "The authorities did what they could. There wasn't any reason to get more innocent people involved."

"They treated you all right?"

"They were kind enough," I said.

"It was brave of you, to try and help Thisbe," Lee said. "It's still hard to believe what happened, but I should have suspected something. We all should have." He paused. "You don't know what happened to Renard?"

Mrs. Renard vanished not long after my call to Detective Rogalski. She slipped away quietly. The Elysian Society building locked up tight one morning. It was as if she'd always had one foot outside her own life, merely waiting for the signal to run into the next one.

A few weeks after the police told me I couldn't be any more use to them, I let my curiosity overtake me. I drove past the Elysian Society building. It had already started to fade into the same gentle disrepair as the other buildings in the neighborhood; it felt as if Mrs. Renard had provided all the building's weight and vitality, and without her at its core, the whole structure deflated inward. I thought of my clients. Tried to imagine where they were, scattered across the city, their grief once again hot and fresh.

"She didn't say a word to me before she left," I said to Lee. "She's out there somewhere."

We were quiet, considering this.

"Do you miss it?" I asked.

"In a way," he said. "Within a week of leaving—less—it didn't seem real. There are those things you do that always make sense. But something like that, the moment you leave, you look back and it doesn't seem possible."

I sat on the edge of the motel bed. "Lee," I said, and I told him. Clutching the bottle of lotuses to my heart, I told him. Of everyone I knew, even Ana, he was the only one who'd understand what it could mean. What was at stake: both the promise and the dangers.

Lee listened, his silence an attentive presence on the other end. "I'm not sure, Edie," he'd said after I finished. "You think it's wise? Maybe it's time for the Elysian Society to end. You have other talents, you could—"

"I'll be different," I said, cutting him off. The calm was so deep and clean and cool that I never wanted to leave it. "It won't be the same place. I'll make it more personal. Fewer rules. Better rules. Mrs. Renard lost sight of what the Elysian Society meant at its simplest level."

"Which is?"

"Connection," I said.

He didn't answer, but Lee's silence had turned yielding. I'd cracked the motel's heavy drapes, and the headlights of a car in the parking lot slid along the wall. They landed in two glowing spots on the wall, shining like an animal's pupils, before snapping off.

"I've saved money for years," I said. "There was never anything I wanted to spend it on. And I have nothing in the world but time." Across from the bed, in the broad mirror that spanned all sides of the motel sink, my reflection was faceted like a diamond.

"You'd continue to work as a body yourself?" he asked.

"No, I'm done with that," I said. "If I'm honest, it's time to move on from that side of things. I'll run the place. I can offer the bodies and the clients something Mrs. Renard couldn't. I know exactly what it is to be a body."

"And the lotuses?"

"I've kept a few," I said, fingers tightening around the bottle. "I'll find another supplier."

"You'd be taking on so much responsibility," Lee said.

There was a gentle challenge in his voice. It was exactly what I'd wanted from him. Something to push back against, forcing me to clarify the sudden and overwhelming wildness of my plan into a straight and clear-cut path.

"Lee, I understand if you don't want anything to do with this," I said. "But I'd be happy to have you."

"That's why you called me?" he asked.

"I also wanted to talk to you again."

I could almost hear his smile, though there was a sadness to the silence that hung between us. "Where will you go to open it?" he asked. "You won't stay here. Not after all this."

"No," I'd said. "Not here. I'll pick a new place. Anywhere. A fresh start."

The pregnancy is different this time. Nothing like the un-mapped panic of the first time. I'm clearheaded and purpose-ful; most of the time, my body is light with energy. I'm generous. Not overtaken by something beyond my control, but powerful. At first, I waited for the old helplessness to eat at my brain. Every morning, I'd wake up and brace myself for the slipping away.

But it never happened. And I've grown more confident, more assured. I understand my own boundaries. I'm able to enjoy the sensation of pregnancy. Relearning the changing landscape of my body. Feeling the glimmering movements that are gently out of sync with my own, a quiet pattern dotted throughout my days and nights.

Sylvia's amazement is a soft and steady rhythm. When she slips behind my eyes or into my fingertips, I'm overcome by the knowledge of what this means to her. Her astonishment blends with mine. I'm moved by Sylvia's pleasure, marveling at it, and then she slips away and my wonder is suddenly centered on myself. I'm in awe of my own ability to exist, unafraid, inside this life.

I arrive at the time we agreed on. I let her choose our meeting spot: a small café. Curtains with crochet trim covering a plate glass window. The interior is warm, competing with the flat gray glow of the winter sky, and crowded with bodies on this weekend morning.

As I slide out of the car, I move with the carefully calibrated grace I've developed during these past few months. The baby stirs, a rolling knot like a hand beneath a blanket on waking.

The girl is a contrast to the people around her, most of them slouching or chatting, lost in conversations, staring into screens. She's alert, posture tense and careful. She scans the crowd, her gaze lingering on each stranger in turn. But she doesn't seem to notice me until I've paused right next to her table, patiently waiting.

"Oh," she says. "You're—?" The girl half stands, then stops, flustered. "I'm sorry, I'm sorry. For some reason, I just didn't expect you to be—"

"It's fine," I say, sitting across from her. "Jessica, isn't it?"

"Yeah. Yeah, that's me. We spoke on the phone?" Jessica's in her early twenties, her bright red hair braided down her back. She's worn a clumsy approximation of a professional outfit: plain blazer over a lacy tank. "Thanks for meeting with me today," she says.

"You seem nervous," I say gently. "There's no need to be."

She laughs, touches her hair, both sheepish and relieved. "I didn't know how to prepare for something like this," Jessica says. "You didn't say much about it."

"Don't worry," I say. "This isn't a traditional interview. It's a way for us to learn more about each other. Just to see if our goals are the same."

Jessica nods and nods. I notice her picking at the edge of a paper napkin, and she must catch my gaze. Her fingers still.

"To be honest, I was surprised to hear from anybody," I continue. "I only just placed the ad. Why did you reach out to me, Jessica?"

"Well, I've been looking for work for a while," she says. "Nothing really inspires me. But when I saw your ad, I got curious. It sounds different, I guess."

"You know what the job would involve?" I ask.

"A little," Jessica says. "I have a general idea."

"And you believe you're suited to this kind of work?" I ask.

"Maybe." She makes faltering eye contact with me; I notice the coppery quality of her eyelashes, so pale they're a glittering suggestion. "I think so," she adds.

"I have to ask you a personal question, Jessica," I say, leaning over the table. "Are you happy in your life?"

If she's surprised, she hides it quickly. She gazes at the coffee-blotted rim of the mug, seeming to truly consider the question. "Yes," she says. "For the most part."

"Some people will use a job like this to hide," I say. "But I don't want that. I want people who are strong. Confident. People who don't see this as a way to escape their bodies or their lives, but as a way to help others while staying true to themselves."

After a second, Jessica smiles. "You know something—when I saw that ad, I thought it could really be a way to make a difference. Reach out to people who are grieving."

Her other responses so far have been tinted with hesitancy. She's been looking to me for cues like a nervous child. But this time, her voice grows stronger and brighter, her self-consciousness shedding away.

"This shouldn't be a temporary job." Leaning back, I instinctively press my palms to my belly, relishing the weight and warmth. "I want to get to know my employees. Work like this can take a toll on you, if you're not careful. I'd like to change that."

And we sit together as I look into the future, describing it to her, describing it to all of us, already letting myself want everything that waits for me there.

ACKNOWLEDGMENTS

Thank you so much to my enthusiastic and clear-sighted agent, Alice Whitwham, and to Zoë Pagnamenta. Many thanks to my wonderful editor, Jennifer Barth, for guiding this novel into a much braver, bolder place. Thank you to the team at Harper.

I'd like to thank David Jauss, my earliest creative writing professor. Much gratitude goes to the MFA program at Washington University in St. Louis. Thanks to Marshall Klimasewiski, Kellie Wells, and all my other thoughtful teachers. Thanks to all my inspiring colleagues who influenced my creativity and curiosity. Special thanks go to Kathryn Davis, who has so generously helped me find enduring confidence as a writer.

Thanks to Franklin Sayre, who read and responded to an early draft of this novel when my belief in the project was starting to falter. Thanks too to Janelle Barr Bassett, for your warm, witty friendship throughout this process.

Thank you to my in-laws, Tim and Karen, for being supportive of my family in big and small ways. Thanks to my many siblings and siblings-in-law for being fun, smart, and always willing to chat about books. Thanks to my sister, Anna, for being an early reader. And thanks to my grandmother for her pride and support.

Thank you to everyone who has supported and encouraged me throughout this journey.

Heartfelt thanks to my parents. To my father, Russell: thanks for fostering my love of reading and writing by being a passionate writer and scholar. To my talented mother, Teressa: thanks for raising me in a home where pursuing a creative life was an expectation.

To Miles: you're the funniest, cleverest kid, and I'm forever proud of you.

And finally, I'd like to thank Ryan with all my heart. You've been instrumental to making this novel what it is, with your keen insight and your unfailing, astonishing belief in me.

ABOUT THE AUTHOR

SARA FLANNERY MURPHY grew up in Arkansas, where she divided her time between Little Rock and Eureka Springs, a small artists' community in the Ozark Mountains. Sara received her MFA in creative writing at Washington University in St. Louis. She lives in Oklahoma with her husband and son. *The Possessions* is her first novel.